paper walls

paper walls

A NOVEL

NICOLE FELLER

All quoted song lyrics written by BRIGHT BONES
Used by permission.
www.brightbones.com

Line editing by Tanya Gold
www.tanyagold.com

Cover design by Okay Creations
www.okaycreations.com

ISBN: 0-9903644-4-5
ISBN 13: 978-0-9903644-4-3

Printed in the United States of America

For my children:
Avery, the one I live without
&
Jude, the one who put me back together again

"I know it's hard to see the light
To feel the warmth that makes this feel right
I want you to hold me
I know that you love me
So, for one more night, I'll stand and I'll fight."

— BRIGHT BONES

paper walls

A NOVEL

NICOLE FELLER

one

Leighton hung on every word the psychology professor spoke. She striped her syllabus with highlighter and etched notes in its margins, ready to take on the semester with strict determination.

A sudden loud cough broke Leighton's concentration, and she turned her head toward the sound. That's when she saw him. He stood out in a way no one else ever had. She certainly didn't believe in love at first sight, but a curiosity settled in, prompting stolen glances as her scholastic focus faltered.

Finally, Leighton's wandering eyes connected directly with his—a shock of silver-blue, blank and unnerving. She quickly looked away, slinking low in her seat. She didn't dare lift her gaze again.

When class ended, the other students began filtering out of the room, but Leighton hesitated at her seat. She watched him pass by, his tall frame sagging as if he bore the weight of hell on his broad shoulders.

Leighton hated that she wondered about him.

"How boring was *that*?" Quinn fell into step beside Leighton on the sidewalk.

"What do you expect college to be?" Wesley

asked, hooking his thumbs around the backpack straps at his chest.

Quinn shrugged. "I just don't care about any of this stuff."

Wesley snickered. "Ah, that's right. You're just here for your M-R-S degree."

Leighton furrowed her eyebrows. "A *what* degree?"

"M-R-S. Like *missus*. She's just here to find a husband."

Quinn reached across Leighton to swat at her twin. "Shut up, Wes! I am not."

Leighton tried to chuckle.

Wesley cocked his head and looked at her. "Everything okay?"

Leighton nodded. But she knew it wouldn't convince him. It had always seemed that Wesley shared more of that so-called 'twin-tuition' with Leighton than he did with his actual twin.

Quinn rolled her eyes. "Go make some real friends, Wes, and stop bothering mine." She locked her arm through Leighton's and dragged her toward the women's restroom.

Leighton shot Wesley an apologetic glance over her shoulder as they left him behind.

Leighton lay on her stomach on the top bunk in her dorm room, her algebra homework spread out in front of her. With a sigh, she dropped her pencil onto her notebook, the haze of summer freedom still clouding her brain.

The door to the small room opened and

Quinn barreled in, tossing her bag to the floor. She flopped down on the bottom bunk and let out a groan.

"Lemme guess," Leighton said with a smirk Quinn couldn't see. "You hate your theater class too?"

"No, actually, I like it a lot."

"Then what is it?"

Quinn let out a long breath. "I just...wish my brother wasn't *everywhere* I go."

Leighton bit her lip. "Why are you so mean to Wesley lately?"

"I'm not mean to Wesley."

"Quinn. You have two out of five classes together. He's not everywhere."

Quinn huffed. "I keep running into him around campus even when we're *not* in class together. Ew, and earlier, someone asked me if he was my *boyfriend*. So, yeah. He *is* everywhere."

"Well, he's your brother. He's going to be around you from time to time."

"That's the problem."

Leighton leaned over the side of her bunk and peered into Quinn's. When she saw her friend's humorless demeanor, she maneuvered herself to the floor and sat at the foot of the bed. "What's going on, Quinn?"

"I'm tired of being *the twins*. For once, I wanted to just be Quinn. Literally, since I came into existence, Wes has been *right there*. From the second we were born, we were constantly dressed in coordinating twin colors, and we've had to share birthday parties, toys, and now a *car*. He's always tagging along with us when you're *my* friend—"

"I'm Wesley's friend too, Quinn. I've always liked it being the three of us," Leighton said. "And if you recall, I met him on the playground first, so technically, you stole me from *him*."

Quinn twisted a strand of blonde hair around her finger. "I just don't understand why Wes had to choose the same school we did. It would've been fun to *really* go off on my own to college."

"It's a good school and it's only an hour from home. Why wouldn't he choose it too?" Leighton reasoned. "You're lucky he's such a great brother. I wish *I* had a brother. Or a sibling at all for that matter."

"Great, now you're trying to make me feel bad."

Leighton laughed. "No. I'm just saying. Wesley's a good guy. And if he wasn't here, you know you'd miss him."

Quinn tried to deny it, but they both knew it was true.

In psychology class, Leighton kept a discreet watch for the boy with the long hair. She found herself disappointed when class began without him.

Ten minutes into the lecture, the door opened and he walked in. He embraced his tardiness with a lifeless saunter to the only empty seat—right beside Leighton.

Dr. Gibson stood impatiently at the podium, glancing at his attendance list. "Cole MacHendrick, I assume?"

"Yup." His voice was deeper than Leighton had expected.

"I would advise from now on, Mr. MacHendrick, that you arrive to my class in a timely manner," Dr. Gibson said before continuing.

His name is Cole, Leighton thought, filling in just one of the many blank spaces her mind craved to learn of him. The name didn't quite suit him, she decided. Cole sounded more like the preppy student body president, or the captain of the football team rather than a guy who had apparently given up on haircuts, and whose countenance would suggest he hated the world.

And she struggled yet again to follow along with the lecture, consumed with nothing but the fact that Cole was right beside her, a captivating figure in her peripheral vision. She turned her eyes in his direction, straying as far as they could without straining.

Cole was bent over his desk, strands of hair falling into his face. He brushed them behind his ear, giving Leighton a better view of his lovely profile and chiseled jawline. He stared at his textbook through long, dark lashes beneath his furrowed brow. He looked so troubled, as if his mind was elsewhere.

Leighton forced her thoughts aside, irritated by her lack of self-control. She'd hoped her weakness for him had only been a one-time fluke, a by-product of first-day-of-college jitters. But this boy still piqued her interest in a way she couldn't pinpoint.

After Dr. Gibson dismissed the class at the end of the hour, Leighton turned toward Cole.

"Hi," she stammered. "I, um, wrote down the reading assignment you missed at the beginning of class."

Cole's ice-blue eyes met hers in a blank stare, then wandered to the piece of paper in her outstretched hand. He silently took it and shoved it into his bag along with his book. When he stood to leave, Leighton followed suit.

"I'm Leighton Tucker, by the way," she said, hoping her smile would mask her unease.

Cole stopped suddenly, the color draining from his face. Avoiding her gaze, he cleared his throat. "I'm sure you caught my name already, and if not, oh well."

Then he continued past her, slipping out the door.

Leighton sat across from Quinn in the cafeteria, picking at her lunch as her mind latched onto her recent interaction with Cole. His rejection had stung her. He wasn't what she'd imagined, or dared to hope.

As Quinn gave a detailed report on her latest run-in with her newfound crush, Leighton spotted Cole several tables down. Her stomach dropped. He sat sullen and alone, with his temple pressed against his propped fist, and his untouched tray before him. Despite his unpleasantries, the mystery of him continued to nag at Leighton.

"Um, *hello*, Leighton."

Leighton shook away her thoughts. "Yeah?"

"Were you even listening to me?" Quinn asked, turning to look in the direction Leighton had been staring. Quinn turned back to Leighton and pointed her thumb behind her. "Why were you looking at him?"

Leighton reached across the table to grab Quinn's arm. "Don't point!"

"Then tell me."

"Okay." Leighton sighed. "Has anyone ever just interested you? I mean, in a curious way?"

Quinn shrugged. "Not really. If I'm interested in someone, it's because I *like* him."

"I don't know how to explain it," Leighton said, blushing. "He makes me wonder. I guess I just want to know who he is."

Quinn snickered. "He's intimidating, although hot. But he seems to be in a constant state of serious brooding. Like I bet he hates puppies and babies, and he probably tears the wings off of butterflies. There. Mystery solved."

Leighton chuckled. "Oh, yeah right. And no complaints about his hair? I'm surprised."

"It's prettier than mine," Quinn replied. "He definitely needs to keep that."

A motion to Leighton's right prompted her to look up. Wesley smiled down at her.

"Hey, Leighton." He set his tray down and filled the seat beside her.

His familiar brightness made Leighton instantly feel at ease. "Hey, Wes."

"What's going on?"

Quinn smirked. "Oh, nothing. Leighton here is just obsessing over strange men."

"I am not obsessed with him," Leighton protested.

Wesley turned to her, his expression serious. "Who?"

"Cole." Leighton pointed discreetly. "He's in our psych class."

Subtly peering around his sister, Wesley narrowed his eyes. "Oh, *him*? The guy who was a total douche to you after class today?"

Leighton hadn't realized anyone had noticed their unpleasant interaction. "Well, yeah."

"And you *like* him?" Wesley didn't hide his disgust.

Leighton rolled her eyes. "No. I don't know. I just...Ugh, forget it." She figured her intrigue was too absurd to explain, and she got up from the table to avoid even trying.

She made her way across the cafeteria, heading straight for Cole. Maybe he needed someone to care about him. What if it mattered?

When Leighton reached his table, she placed her hands on the back of the chair across from him to keep them from shaking.

"Is this seat taken?"

Cole raised his eyes to look at her. "Do you see anyone sitting there?"

Leighton chewed her lower lip, wondering if this was a bad idea. This boldness was so unlike her, but something inside her forced her to be brave. She pulled the chair out to sit down.

"So...how are you liking your classes so far?" she asked.

He stared at her incredulously. "Did you lose a bet?"

"What?"

"Someone dare you to talk to me?"

Leighton shook her head. "I'm just trying to make friends. That's what you're supposed to do at college."

Cole sat back in his chair and snickered, revealing a pleasant smile beneath his hostility. "You wanna be friends..."

She shrugged. "Yeah, why not?"

"Trust me," he said, his voice low. "You don't want to be my friend."

Leighton fought against the surge of wonder that fluttered in her stomach. "Can't I be the judge of that?"

Cole stood, his eyes fixed on hers. "Nope."

He turned and walked out, just like Leighton feared he would.

"You're going to that freshman mixer thing on Friday, right?" Quinn asked Leighton as they made their way back to the dorm.

Leighton shrugged. "I guess so."

Quinn laughed like she'd just said something ludicrous. "You guess? Of course you're going. You need to meet some *real* guys. Nice ones this time."

Leighton scowled. "Is that why you're going? To meet guys?"

"Nope. I'm bringing Marcus."

"Doesn't bringing a date kind of defeat the purpose of attending a mixer? Aren't you supposed to go to meet people?"

"Whatever," Quinn said, pulling open the door to their residence hall. "At least I'm not chasing after ax murderers."

She hurried inside before Leighton could think of a comeback.

At the start of Friday's psychology class, Cole slipped into the room at the last second. Once again, the seat beside Leighton was his only choice, and she watched him sigh as he made his way over to it. Leighton chewed at the inside of her cheek, wishing his avoidance didn't bother her so much.

Dr. Gibson began his lecture, but, of course, Leighton was only half-listening. Halfway through class, Dr. Gibson broached the topic of midterms.

"I know it's only the first week of the semester," he said. "But this project may take some time. You'll be pairing up with a partner and drawing a topic at random. You'll work together to deeply explore your topic and answer the questions I'll be supplying."

Quinn peered past Wesley and grinned at Leighton, as if silently claiming her as her partner.

"With that said," Dr. Gibson continued, "Count off in twos from the front right of the class."

Leighton's stomach twisted as she turned to her left and caught Cole's annoyed glance.

"Dammit, Wesley," Leighton heard Quinn whisper to her new partner.

Dr. Gibson made his way around the room holding a large mason jar filled with folded slips of paper. When he got to Leighton, she reached her hand into the dwindling selections and chose one. Cole watched her intently as she unfolded the paper.

Depression and suicide.

Leighton held it out to him and he quickly waved it away, slinking low in his seat.

Dr. Gibson was back at the podium with his empty jar. "Now you've got your partners and your topics. You cannot change either. I will come around and pass out your project sheets, then I'd like you to spend the remainder of the hour with your partner to begin discussing your project."

When Dr. Gibson had passed out the sheets, Leighton looked over her copy. There were some intense questions and activities regarding their sensitive topic. She looked at Cole, who was leaning over his sheet, his hair shielding his face from her view.

"So," Leighton began cautiously, "this seems like a pretty interesting project. What do you think?"

Cole was silent for a moment, then tucked his hair behind his ears. "Interesting? Really?"

Leighton offered a shrug. "Yeah, I guess."

He shook his head. "I take it you've never been depressed or suicidal before."

"Well, I—"

"And I don't mean, like, 'I'm so depressed I didn't make the cheerleading squad' or 'oh, he's taking someone else to prom, I'm gonna kill myself.' It's the serious shit that makes you wish you were dead."

Leighton felt her face getting hot. "Don't treat me like I'm some stupid girl who's never dealt with anything. You don't even know me."

"Okay, so I'm not allowed to make assumptions based on your appearance?" Cole asked.

"Absolutely not."

"Fine. Then *you* can't make assumptions about *me* either."

Leighton narrowed her eyes. "When have I done that?"

"You assume I want to be your friend. Or that you can fix me. I don't. And you can't."

His words should've driven her away. But she foolishly only felt more drawn to him, as if he were presenting her with a challenge rather than a brick wall.

"Fine," she replied, keeping her cool. "So, you think I look like I'm into cheerleading, then?"

Cole looked her over. "Not really. You just...kind of remind me of my ex-girlfriend. She was a cheerleader." He bit his lip and turned away.

"Ah, I guess that explains why you're so bothered by me," Leighton said. "But I was never a cheerleader. Or athletic at all, for that matter, so..."

"Great. I'm so relieved."

"So I'm guessing *you're* the one who got dumped, then?"

The muscles in his cheek flexed as he clenched his jaw, and she almost regretted stooping to his level.

"Let's also agree not to assume you have *any* right to pry into my life. So back the hell off, okay?" Cole gave her one last cold glare before he gathered his things and hurried out the door.

"I'm seriously so screwed. I don't know how I'm going to do this project. I'll probably have to do it myself. You're so lucky you got paired with Wesley."

Quinn turned away from the mirror that hung on the closet door, mascara wand in hand. "Leighton. Can you please stop obsessing over Cole? It's Friday night. We survived our first week of college. Let's just have fun."

Leighton slid off her bed, her feet hitting the floor with a thud. "I am not obsessing over him."

"But you're into him."

"No...okay, *maybe* if he wasn't so difficult. And if I got to know him better."

Quinn snickered. "Please just be careful. I hate to even mention it, but I don't want you getting hurt like last time."

"You don't have to mention it, thank you. I learned my lesson," Leighton said curtly.

"Okay then. Now get ready for the mixer." Quinn eyed Leighton's jeans and tank top. "You're *not* wearing that."

"What's wrong with what I'm wearing?"

Quinn sighed. "You wore it all day. And it's not sexy."

Leighton slumped her shoulders. "I don't care if it's sexy."

"Maybe you should. I think it might be time to get back out there. Who knows who you might meet tonight?"

Leighton turned to her reflection on the back of the closet door. She realized how sloppy her attire looked compared to Quinn's. Maybe it was time to make an effort and put herself out there.

"All right," Leighton said. "Help me get ready."

Leighton followed Quinn and Marcus into the student union, nervously smoothing her sundress. She glanced around the decorated room, complete with a huge *Welcome Freshmen!* banner across the back wall above tables of assorted food and drinks. Music played from large speakers as students began to mingle.

Once she'd scribbled her name across a name tag and found an appropriate spot on her dress to affix it to, Leighton ventured over to the refreshment tables for a drink. She found herself foolishly wondering if Cole would show up when Wesley approached.

"Hey," he said with a wide smile.

"Hey, Wes."

His eyes traveled over her. "You look *really* nice."

Looking down at her feet, Leighton tucked a strand of hair behind her ear. Her bare shoulders suddenly felt too exposed.

"Really? I dunno. I let Quinn do my hair and makeup. I feel like it's too much."

Wesley shook his head. "No, not at all. You're perfect."

She began to relax. "Well, thank you. You don't look too bad yourself."

He grinned, running his hands over his dirty-blond hair. It wasn't until a couple of girls passed by, batting their eyelashes at Wesley, that Leighton considered how attractive he was. She'd never given it much thought before, never allowed herself to see him from *that* perspective.

Shaking away her awkward thoughts, Leighton scanned the room. She was annoyed with herself when she realized which face she was looking for.

Quinn returned, Marcus trailing behind her. "There you are. Why are you with *Wesley*? I thought you were gonna get back out there. You won't meet anyone if you're hiding over here."

Leighton made a face. "I'm not hiding. Chill out."

"If you're waiting for Cole to show up, you're crazy."

"Cole? Yeah right. Why would I be waiting for him?" Leighton asked.

Quinn touched her arm. "I'm just not so sure about him. You've already had your fair share of not-so-nice guys."

"I'm *fine*."

Quinn took the hint and walked away, dragging Marcus with her. Leighton watched her effortlessly melt into the crowd, wishing for even a speck of the same wild confidence Quinn possessed.

"Sorry about that," Wesley said with a sigh.

"You don't have to apologize for her."

"I know. She can be overbearing and obnoxious sometimes—okay, all the time—but she has good intentions."

A thin smile curved Leighton's lips. "I wish she was as good to you as you are to her. If you ever decide you're fed up with her crap, you can come be *my* brother. I hate being an only child."

Wesley's gaze dropped to the floor and he let out an uneasy chuckle. "Yeah, no, that's okay."

Leighton glanced at the time on her phone.

"Don't feel like you have to babysit me. I'm sure there's a girl or two out there you'd rather be spending time with."

"Actually, I—"

Leighton reached up to pat his shoulder. "Thanks for keeping me company, Wes. I'll see you later?"

Wesley nodded and wandered off, quickly disappearing into the crowd.

Leighton looked at the strangers scattered about the student union. Some had already formed cliques, some mingled casually, but few stood alone. She hardly knew where to begin with guys anymore, as if she'd been out of the game for much longer than two years. How had she allowed herself to become this timid person?

Just when she'd finally gotten him out of her head, Leighton spotted Cole across the room. He stepped cautiously across the wood floor as if he were an intruder in a place he didn't belong. Leighton was torn between the instinct to run and her masochistic need for information.

As Cole came closer to the refreshments table, a rush of bravery unglued her feet. She moved toward him, meeting him in front of the drinks.

"What are you doing here?" she asked, crossing her arms over her chest.

Cole's hand stopped mid-air in its reach for a soda and he gingerly turned his head toward her. His countenance instantly hardened.

"Well, I *am* a freshman. That makes we welcome," he scoffed, motioning to the banner above them.

"I'm just shocked that you would come to a function that exists for the sole purpose of making friends," Leighton said. She noticed he wasn't wearing a nametag and it didn't surprise her.

Cole grabbed a soda, popped it open, and took a long swig. "Relax, I'm just here for the free food. They closed the cafeteria early because of this stupid thing so I missed dinner."

She snickered. "Ah, now it makes more sense."

He let out a quick, agitated huff. "Go ahead...keep judging me. I don't care. But *don't* act like you know me. You know *nothing*."

Leighton's eyes stung. "I know you're a jerk."

He laughed, but he looked anything but joyful. "Then why the hell do you keep wasting your time?"

Anger burned in her chest as she clenched her fists at her sides. "I don't know. Maybe I am just some stupid girl, after all."

Cole's eyes darted away from hers, his expression tortured. "You're stupid if you don't back off like I told you to."

Leighton realized that she should've walked away, but her frustration consumed her, pushing her over the edge. "What is *wrong* with you?"

Cole slammed his drink onto the table and came at her, his tall form looming over her. But she didn't cower, didn't fear him. There was no danger in his closeness, just a desperation in his eyes.

"*Please*," he begged through his teeth, "leave me alone."

A hand slipped into Leighton's and gently

pulled her away from Cole. She spun around, her eyes locking with Wesley's.

"Come on, let's go," he said.

His hand was warm and unfamiliar against hers as he led her toward the exit. He guided her out the door and into the dusk, and he still didn't let go of her.

"Are you okay?" Wesley's dark eyes were wide and intense.

She nodded, but her tears contradicted her.

"Leighton..." Wesley cupped her shoulders, his hands like fire on her bare skin. "Tell me what's wrong."

She swiped at her wet cheeks. "He just makes me so angry," she admitted in a small voice.

"Cole?" Wesley put his hands on his hips and breathed a deep, growling sigh. "I knew there was something off about him. You should probably keep your distance. He obviously doesn't deserve your attention."

Leighton rolled her eyes. "Too bad he's my psych partner."

"Yeah, but he doesn't have to be your friend. Doesn't seem like he's interested, which clearly makes him insane, because...who could resist you?"

A smile broke through Leighton's frustration. "Why are you so good to me, Wes?"

"Because that's what you deserve."

She chuckled. "You can go back to the mixer if you want; I'm fine."

"I'm not leaving you."

"I'm okay with going back to the dorm."

Wesley bit his bottom lip. "Listen...they're

showing a movie in a bit out on the green. I was wondering if you wanted to go with me. I know you wanted to possibly meet someone tonight, so it's not quite what you were hoping for, but I think it could be fun."

Leighton blushed, feeling foolish for allowing Quinn to infiltrate her mind and influence her motives. Getting all dressed up to go after random guys? That wasn't her at all.

"Okay, Wes," she agreed.

He grinned cheekily. "It's a date, then."

Two

The green was a sprawling stretch of grass directly behind the science building. The last traces of day had faded into the black sky as friends and couples spread out along the hill. A projector flickered to life, casting a large square of light onto the backside of the white building, and the movie began. It was the 1989 classic, *Say Anything...*, starring John Cusack.

"Oh man, no way," Wesley said, his face animated by his approval. He removed his cardigan and laid it out in the grass.

He motioned for Leighton to sit, and she obliged, smoothing out her dress and carefully tucking her feet beneath her. Wesley sat in the grass beside her.

"This is one of my favorite films of *all* time," he whispered. "Have you seen this one?"

"No, I haven't," Leighton answered.

"What? How have I allowed this for so long? It's so good. You're going to love it." He leaned back onto his hands and crossed his ankles out in front of him.

Leighton shifted her attention to the movie,

but she couldn't silence her mind. "Thank you for rescuing me, by the way. You didn't have to do that."

Wesley smiled at her. "You don't have to thank me."

"Well, you could've brought a real date instead. I'm sure there are a lot of other girls you would've enjoyed being here with."

He cast his eyes to the ground and began picking at a blade of grass. "Who says I'm interested in any of those other girls?"

Leighton shrugged. "I don't know."

"Well, for the record, I enjoy being here with *you*."

"Okay, good." She crossed her arms tightly over her chest as the early September breeze blew between them.

"Are you cold?" Wesley asked.

"Yeah, a little."

"I'd offer you my sweater, but you're sitting on it," he said with a chuckle.

He scooted closer and wrapped his arm around her, pulling her into his warmth. Leighton decided not to resist, and leaned into him. It was a foreign thing to be this close to Wesley in more than a friendly hug, to feel his body against her, to inhale his scent, to feel the rise and fall of his breaths. In all their years as friends, she'd never experienced him this way. But she found it surprisingly...pleasant?

Leighton glanced across the green and caught sight of Quinn, who had apparently joined in on the movie with Marcus.

"What are you doing?" Quinn mouthed to her.

"Quinn is here. And she's looking at us," Leighton said to Wesley, amused.

"Oh, is she?"

"Yup."

"She thinks this is weird?"

"Uh-huh."

"Okay." Wesley slid his arm tighter around Leighton's shoulders and guided her head to his chest. His heart beat rapidly beneath her ear as he stroked her arm with his fingertips. "Then she probably thinks it's *really* weird now."

Leighton let out a nonchalant chuckle, but her thoughts ran wild. It *should* have been really weird to be wrapped in Wesley's arms, so close to him. So why wasn't it? This was the boy she grew up with, the boy who'd always been the brother she never had. Leighton pulled away from him.

"You okay?" Wesley asked.

"Yeah, I think I just need some water."

He stood and helped her to her feet before shaking out his cardigan and draping it around her shoulders. They made their way across the green to the bonfire, Wesley's hand on Leighton's back to guide her over the uneven terrain. He reached into a large metal tub of melting ice and fished out a bottle of water for her.

Leighton stared into the crackling fire as she sipped the cold liquid, a myriad of emotions coursing through her. She'd thought going away to college would help her find herself and discover who she was. But at that moment, she'd never felt more lost.

When the movie was over, Wesley offered to walk Leighton back to her dorm. He'd always been the protective type.

"I hope tonight wasn't too awkward," he said as they sauntered down the sidewalk. "I didn't mean to make you feel uncomfortable; I was just trying to annoy my sister."

"I know. Don't worry, Wes. It's okay."

"It was fun, though. I had fun."

Leighton looked up at him and offered a friendly smile. She realized then how safe she felt beside him.

"I had fun too," she said.

They began to cut through one of the campus parking lots when they caught sight of Cole ahead of them. He was leaning against the side of a black Volkswagen Jetta, his foot propped on the back tire.

"Ah, see? Perfect example of why my accompaniment was absolutely necessary," Wesley muttered to Leighton.

Cole looked up at them, and Leighton braced herself. But Cole didn't run, didn't avoid her in his usual, intense manner. He stepped casually away from the car, exhaling a puff of smoke into the air.

"I think you owe Leighton an apology," Wesley said, frowning at the lingering smoke. Leighton glared at Wesley, stupidly fearing he might scare Cole off.

Cole took a long pull off his cigarette before he tossed it to the pavement and put it out with the heel of his untied boot. "I'm sorry, Leighton." The smoke escaped from his mouth as he spoke, his words sounding almost genuine. How was this the same person she'd encountered earlier?

Leighton fanned the drifting cloud away from her face. "Whatever. Listen, I hate this as much as you do, but can we just exchange numbers and get our psych project over with? Then we'll never have to speak to each other again."

He studied her for a brief moment, then shrugged. "I guess." He reached into his back pocket for his cell phone, then typed in his passcode to unlock it before handing it to her. "Put your number in."

Leighton took the phone. She dialed her number on the touch keypad and waited for her phone to ring in her purse with his number. Then she hung up and saved her number to his oddly short list of contacts, her pesky curiosity festering once more.

"So, I'll text you and we can figure out what day works best for both of us?" she asked, giving his phone back to him.

"Uh-huh," Cole responded.

"Why are you such a dick?" Wesley asked.

"Wesley!" Leighton scolded. Surely, Cole would bolt any second now.

But Cole remained unfazed. "No, he's right. I am a dick."

Wesley let out a chuckle. "You actually admit it? How big of you."

"All right, Wes…" Leighton slipped out of Wesley's cardigan and handed it to him. "Why don't you go ahead to your dorm? I'll just talk to you later."

"But…"

"She'll be fine," Cole said. "I'm a dick, not a serial killer."

Wesley eyed him for a moment. "Fine." He turned to Leighton. "Just be careful. Text me when you get in?"

"Sure."

Wesley reluctantly walked off, leaving her with Cole. It was crazy to stay after the way he'd treated her, but something felt different. She'd wanted to hate him, but she didn't feel that now. Every interaction left her more confused, more curious. Somehow, all she wanted was more of him, whatever that meant.

"How long have you two been dating?" Cole asked, one corner of his mouth turning up in a facetious grin.

"We're *not* dating," Leighton answered quickly.

He raised his eyebrows. "Oh. Could've fooled me."

"Wesley's just...protective. We've known each other since we were kids."

Cole looked at the asphalt and cleared his throat. "How nice."

Leighton sighed. "Why do you do that?"

"Do what?"

"Contradict yourself. Earlier, you wouldn't even let me speak to you. Then here, for a split second, you were a normal person who could carry on a polite conversation. Until suddenly, it's like you remembered you're a jerk and had to say something crappy."

Cole stared at her with the same vacant expression she remembered from the first day she saw him. There was something haunting in the silver shine of his eyes.

"That's just what I do, I guess."

Leighton shook her head. "No. People aren't just *mean* for no reason. Things happen to people to make them that way."

Cole gritted his teeth, his breaths quickening. "I have to go."

She'd struck a chord and she selfishly wanted to probe further. Stepping into his path, she stopped him, boldly placing a hand on his chest.

"Cole. I just want to understand you."

Where was this bravery coming from? Wesley's words rang in Leighton's head—Cole didn't deserve her attention, her concern—but she ignored all logic.

Cole looked down at her, his eyes flickering back and forth between hers. She saw a hopelessness, an aching, before he broke their gaze, stepping past her to walk away.

"Cole!" Leighton called after him in protest.

He stopped and spun around. "What? I'm walking you to your dorm so your un-boyfriend doesn't have a conniption."

She tried to stifle the smile that played on her lips. "Oh."

She caught up to Cole and eagerly fell into step beside him. They didn't speak a single word until they reached the door to her residence hall.

"Well, now that you're here safe, I'm gonna

go." Cole said, a foreign tenderness in his voice. "Unless you need me to walk you to your room?"

"Oh. No, this is fine. Thank you."

He pulled the door open and leaned against it as she stepped inside. "You look nice, by the way," he said.

"What?"

"Well, I prefer your usual look, but this is nice too." Cole added a bashful smile to his statement.

Leighton blushed. "Thanks," she said, avoiding his gaze.

"Yeah, I'm leaving now." Cole chuckled and let go of the door.

Leighton watched him through the narrowing space until the door fell closed and she was alone. She considered she might be dreaming, Cole's words still hanging in the silence that followed her up to her dorm room on the second floor. She went straight to bed to escape the thoughts that were chasing away all traces of hatred.

Leighton had somehow managed to fall asleep before Quinn barged in, flipping the light switch and filling the room with an offensive brightness.

"Quinn! Come on!" Leighton groaned, pulling her blanket over her head.

"Oh, you're here? I'm sorry."

Leighton sat up. "Where else would I be?"

Quinn pressed her lips together. "Well, according to Wes, you're still with Cole, so…"

Leighton smacked her hand to her forehead.

"I forgot to text Wesley. I was supposed to let him know I got in okay."

Quinn crossed her arms. "You have so much explaining to do. I don't even know where to start with my questions."

Leighton flopped back onto her pillow. "No comment. On anything."

"Hey, you knew this was coming. First, you and *my brother*? Ew, Leighton. What was *that*? Please tell me it's nothing."

Leighton propped herself up on her elbow. "We were hanging out. He was just being nice."

"Good. Because that would be the worst thing that could ever happen to me."

Leighton made a face. "Oh, really? The worst? How come?"

Quinn climbed up the ladder to Leighton's bed and sat at the foot, her long legs dangling over the side. "Do you know how awful it would be for me if you and Wes somehow decided you were in love with each other?"

Leighton sat up straight. "Why would it be awful?"

"Think about it. I'd become the pathetic third wheel, you'd phase me out, and you'd tell Wes all your secrets instead of me."

Leighton chuckled. "Wow, you have given this *way* too much thought."

Quinn shrugged. "Have you seen you two together? You're, like, the only person who really gets him. And he has no shortage of girls who would give anything for his attention, and yet, he'd rather hang out with you."

"Oh, I doubt that," Leighton said. "And I don't think of him that way. Really, we're just friends."

"Good to know." Quinn turned to face Leighton. "Okay, so now...what the hell is up with you and Cole?"

Leighton tilted her head back. "Ugh, nothing."

"Well, why did you have Wes leave you alone with him?"

"What, do you have Wesley reporting to you now?"

"No. I called him when you didn't answer your phone and he told me. Chill out."

Leighton leaned against the wall. "I'm sorry. It's just that Cole kind of blew up at me at the mixer. And then when we ran into him after the movie, he was so different—almost *nice*—and I wanted to see if I could get him to crack. I know it's weird. But he's driving me crazy; I just have to figure him out."

"I know this is the first guy you've shown any interest in...since Jared." Quinn chewed her fingernail. "But I think you can do better."

Leighton closed her eyes. "Please don't say his name."

"I'm sorry. But Cole doesn't seem very nice. You deserve a *nice* guy."

"Oh, like Wesley?" Leighton smirked.

"No," Quinn answered adamantly, hopping down from the bunk. "I will kill you; I'm not kidding."

Quinn slipped into her pajamas, turned off the light and crawled into bed.

"Oh, how did it go with Marcus tonight?" Leighton asked to lighten the mood.

"Eh, I'm over that. He's too nice."

"Seriously? After all that?"

Quinn giggled. "Good night, Leighton."

Leighton sat at a table in the campus café, taking bites of a pumpkin muffin in between compulsive glances at her phone. She'd texted Cole nearly an hour ago and he hadn't yet replied. She re-read what she'd said to him, over and over, analyzing her words, foolishly fearing she'd chosen all the wrong ones.

Hey Cole. Just wanted to see if you have time to get together this weekend to work on our project. Let me know. Thanks!

Maybe the *Thanks!* was too much.

She sighed and pushed her phone away, forcing herself to stop caring about something so trivial. Wesley approached then, sitting down across from her.

"Hey," he said, sipping from the straw in his cold brew. "How's it going? I see you survived the night."

"Look, Wes, I'm sorry I forgot to text you."

A playful smile curved his lips. "Leighton, it's fine. I mean, I like knowing you're safe and not canoodling with brooding guys who say unkind things to you, but you don't have to answer to me."

Leighton laughed. "Did you just say canoodling?"

"I've always wanted to use it in a sentence. It finally happened."

Leighton laughed harder. "Well, too bad you apparently don't know what it means, because that in no way describes what went on last night."

Wesley took another sip of his coffee. "Well, that's a relief. Since they say kissing a smoker is like licking an ashtray, right?"

Leighton's phone lit up between them, buzzing loudly against the wood table. They both looked at the screen to see Cole's name. Wesley let out a snort as Leighton snatched up her phone and opened the text message.

Tomorrow at noon?

She shouldn't have been surprised by his lack of friendliness.

Okay. Noon sounds good. Where should we meet? she texted back.

The courtyard by the library?

Okay. See you then.

Cole sent nothing else in reply.

Much later that night, Leighton stumbled into the campus laundromat, dragging her large canvas laundry bag behind her. She'd put it off all day, but then fell asleep while studying, not waking until nearly midnight. Knowing the laundromat was only open for another hour, she'd jumped out of bed, grabbed her bag, and rushed out the door.

In her scurry, Leighton had failed to consider her outfit, which was, unfortunately, comprised of a ratty old school T-shirt that still fit her from junior high, and a pair of too-short black cotton shorts. Hopefully, it was late enough that no one else would be there to witness her attire.

Leighton nearly tripped over her own flip-flop when her eyes met Cole's across the room. He was seated on the counter in the folding area, an open book in his hands. Leighton quickly composed herself and continued on to a machine as far from him as possible.

She shoveled her garments into the machine and turned the knobs to her preferred settings, then stopped. She'd forgotten her detergent. Before Leighton could utter an expletive, Cole appeared beside her, silently setting his bottle of detergent on the machine next to her, his eyes still fixed on the book in his other hand.

"Uh, thanks," Leighton said, watching him return to the counter. He didn't acknowledge her.

She grabbed the bottle and poured the proper amount into the cap before dumping it into the machine and closing the lid. Commending herself for remembering her wallet, she unzipped the change compartment and fished out five quarters. As Leighton placed the coins into the slots, one slipped from her fingers and rolled far beneath the row of dryers against the wall behind her. She dug through her wallet but found no more quarters. Groaning, Leighton pulled out a dollar and reluctantly crossed the room to use the change machine near Cole. As luck would have it, the 'out of order' light was lit. She let out a long sigh and returned to the washing machine, digging through her coins once more.

Just as she was about to get down on all fours

to search for her lost quarter, Cole appeared beside her once again, dropping six quarters into her hand—enough to replace her lost coin and pay for drying.

Leighton gawked at him but he just turned away, still consumed by his book.

"Why are you being nice to me?" she asked, slipping a coin into the last slot and starting the machine.

Cole closed the book on his thumb and finally looked at her. "You seem to be a having a rough night."

Her defensive tension instantly dissipated. "Well...thank you."

The machine next to hers fell silent and Cole set his book aside. In all her flustered distraction, Leighton hadn't even noticed the machine had been running. Of course she'd chosen the one right beside it.

As Cole approached again, Leighton moved to the old faded couch and sat down. He'd been surprisingly civil, somehow kind, since she'd run into him in the parking lot the night before. Keeping some distance was the best way to continue the odd trend. She couldn't endure any more wounding words from him, and she still didn't get why it even mattered.

After Cole had moved his wet clothes to a dryer, he brought his book to the couch and sat at the opposite end.

Leighton held her breath. Hadn't he practically begged her to leave him alone only yesterday?

Maybe she was still asleep in her dorm room, dreaming this entire thing. She discreetly pinched her leg to debunk the theory.

"So, what brings you here so late at night? Couldn't wait till tomorrow?" Cole asked casually.

"I spilled coffee on my favorite shirt this afternoon, so I needed to wash it before the stain set in...and also I'm kinda out of certain unmentionables, so it really couldn't wait another day." Leighton pressed her lips together, wishing she'd stopped at the coffee part.

She didn't know how to talk to Cole. She knew how to argue with him or press his buttons—it went both ways. But simply talking, sharing in each other's company? It was uncharted territory. Leighton was afraid to enjoy it, afraid to want it, especially if Cole could just flip a switch and obliterate any bit of peace they'd established together.

"Ah, that makes sense," Cole said, opening his book and resting it on the arm of the couch beside him.

"What about you?" Leighton asked. "Why are *you* here so late?"

"I don't like coming here when it's busy. I'm not very good with people." He smiled at her and she forced a nonchalant laugh, praying he couldn't tell that he'd just sparked a swarm of butterflies in her stomach.

She cleared her throat. "Uh, so what are you reading?"

Cole closed his book to reveal the cover. "C.S. Lewis."

"*A Grief Observed,*" Leighton noted.

He scratched his head. "Yeah, my mom sent it to me. Came in a care package this morning."

"Your mom is already sending you packages? That's pretty lucky."

He shrugged. "Yeah, she's pretty awesome."

As their silence headed into inevitable awkwardness, Leighton said the first thing that popped into her head. "You don't by any chance have a really moody identical twin brother around here, do you? Because I'm really confused right now."

Cole flipped his book open, his eyes dimming. "Nope. It's all me."

Leighton waited, but he read silently, like she wasn't sitting there beside him.

"I'm sorry," she said, her voice barely carrying over the humming machines. "I didn't mean to say the wrong thing."

He didn't look at her. "No, you make a good point—I'm not being myself."

"Cole, please don't."

"I'm just going to read, if you don't mind." He stood and crossed the room, returning to his original spot on the counter.

"Cole."

He lifted his head to look at her. "I'll see you tomorrow, Leighton."

"You won't forget, will you?" she asked.

"I'll be there," he said.

Leighton sank into the couch, settling into the lonely quiet. She bided her time with stolen glances and heavy pondering until Cole was gone.

When noon rolled around the following day, Leighton was in the courtyard sitting at a picnic table beneath the clouded blue northern sky. The late summer heat was still in full force, but a touch of impending fall played subtly on each breeze.

Leighton took out her psychology textbook and her laptop, preparing for Cole's arrival. She checked her email, sent a little "just checking in" text to her mother, and began some research on their project topic.

It never occurred to her that Cole may not show up. But when she looked at her watch and saw that he was over thirty minutes late, she realized it was a possibility. After a full hour, three ignored texts, and an unanswered phone call, Leighton knew Cole had stood her up.

First thing Monday morning, Leighton sprinted to Dr. Gibson's office, hoping to meet with him before he left for class. She caught him outside his door, about to lock up.

"Dr. Gibson? I'm Leighton Tucker, one of your psych students. Can I talk to you for a minute?"

He paused and turned to face her, checking his watch. "Sure, I have a moment to spare."

Dr. Gibson pushed the door open and led her inside, setting his bag on the floor beside his desk before he sat down. He motioned for Leighton to have a seat across from him.

"What can I do for you?"

"I just have a question about the midterm

project. I know you said we couldn't change our partners, but sir, I really need you to make an exception."

Dr. Gibson sat back in his chair, stroking his slightly graying beard. "Oh? And why is that?"

"My partner is impossible to work with. I can't get him to cooperate or care about our assignment. It's a lot of work and I just know I'm going to end up doing all of it by myself."

Dr. Gibson leaned forward, folding his hands on his desk. "Did you ever stop to think that maybe the partner pairings are psychological projects in themselves? Did you read the last item on the topic sheet?"

Leighton thought for a moment. "You asked us to share what we learned from the project, what we learned about each other, and what we learned about ourselves."

"Exactly. I not only want you to learn about your topic, and better understand those who face it on a regular basis, I want you to learn about the workings of another person you may or may not know. And I want you to discover new things about yourself as you work together to figure it all out."

"I understand that, sir, but can't I experience all of that with anyone else but Cole?"

Dr. Gibson nodded as if finally realizing her predicament. "Ah, Cole MacHendrick."

"Yes," she said with relief.

"Leighton, I'm sorry Cole is making things difficult, but you know, life is difficult, and it's full of obstacles that we can't just trade in for lesser obstacles. Have you considered why Cole might be exhibiting this behavior?"

She sighed. "I don't know, because he's a jerk? There's this wall he keeps putting up. It's like it's his goal in life to push everyone out and end up alone."

Dr. Gibson looked at her. "No one really wants to be alone. Maybe he's waiting for someone to care enough to break the wall down and help him."

Leighton scrunched up her face. "I've tried. He doesn't seem to want any help. Especially not from me."

Dr. Gibson stood and picked up his bag. "Leighton, I appreciate your concern for your assignment, but we are out of time. I will see you in class." He walked past her toward the door.

She jumped up and followed him out. "So that's it? I'm stuck with Cole?"

"That negative outlook won't help the situation," Dr. Gibson said, locking his office door. "Just remember, persistence is key."

Then he walked off, leaving Leighton in her frustration.

When Cole sat down beside her in class, Leighton didn't acknowledge him. She ignored his very existence, avoiding even a glance in his direction. When class was over, she ignored him still, gathering her things and standing to leave.

"Wow, so you're really not gonna yell at me?"

Leighton finally spun around, irritated by his blasé attitude. "And would that do me any good, or would you still be a complete ass?"

Cole shrugged. "Probably."

"Probably what? I asked you two questions."

"I'd probably still be an ass."

Leighton rolled her eyes. "Of course."

"Do I get any points for honesty?"

"Honesty? How about you tell me why you blew me off yesterday, why you ignored my texts and my call."

"Ah, there it is," Cole said.

"I'm serious! What is your problem? You can't just screw with people, Cole!"

His demeanor changed suddenly. "Oh, you can't? Tell me what you know about being screwed with. Do you know what it's like? Have you ever *actually* been screwed with? *Have* you?"

Leighton stared at him. "Cole...did something happen to you?"

He looked away as if regretting his outburst. "No. Forget it."

Leighton sighed with defeat, all of her fury deflating. "Can you please cooperate just long enough to get our project done? And then I swear you're done with me."

He nodded slightly. "What are you doing now?"

Cole shielded his cigarette from the breeze with his cupped hand while he lit it. A puff of smoke escaped his mouth as he slipped his lighter back into his pocket. They sat at a picnic table in a remote area of campus—Cole atop, his feet resting on the bench, Leighton farther down from him on the bench, trying to avoid the secondhand partaking of his bad habit.

"I don't know how you do that," she said with a grimace as she took out her laptop.

"It takes some getting used to," he replied, taking another drag and blowing the smoke upward.

"Then why bother?"

Cole tipped the ashes to the ground with a flimsy smirk. "I like punishing myself." He seemed to intend it as a joke, but Leighton got the feeling there was some truth to it.

She changed the subject. "The first thing we had to do was properly define both depression and suicide, find certain statistics, and address some nature versus nurture arguments. I did that while I was waiting for you yesterday."

Cole stumped out his cigarette on the edge of the table, then flicked it into a nearby trash can. "Yeah, that was stupid."

"What?" Leighton was growing tired of his insults and how easily they affected her.

"No, I meant *me*," he said, sliding off the table to sit on the bench beside her. He left a few feet between them. "It was stupid to do that to you yesterday."

"Oh. Is that your way of offering me an apology?"

Cole shook his head, a lock of dark hair falling into his face. "No. I *can* actually apologize." He turned to look at her and pushed his hair back, exposing his entire beautiful face. "I'm sorry. And I meant it the other night too."

Leighton didn't tear her eyes away from his. There was a tender aura to them that she'd never seen before.

"Um, apology accepted," she replied awkwardly, turning back to the table.

Cole reached into his bag for his own psychology materials and spread them out in front of him. He glanced over their project sheet with a frown as he scratched his head.

"What's the matter?" Leighton asked.

"For the next part, we have to write a first-person narrative of a day in the life of someone who is suffering from depression."

She shrugged. "After all my research yesterday, it shouldn't be too difficult to come up with something."

Cole chewed at the top of his pen. "Okay."

"Don't worry, creative writing isn't one of my strong suits either," Leighton said, offering him a smile.

They began their narrative, their subject a teenage boy navigating a day of high school. Leighton typed out their words as they chose them together.

"No, wait, you can't put that," Cole stopped her as their character's day approached lunch time.

"Put what?"

"He wouldn't sit in the cafeteria with his friends like nothing is wrong," Cole said. "He'd go sit outside by himself or hide out in the bathroom. Probably."

"Why would he do that?" Leighton asked.

Cole hesitated. "Um, well, he would avoid

friends and social encounters. He's probably tired of pretending he's okay all the time. And he's sick of making excuses for why he's not eating lunch *again*, so it's easier to be alone."

Leighton's eyebrows knit together. "Okay, so no cafeteria then." She continued on, typing out the character's lonely lunchtime.

Then they wrote through his last classes of the day. "Does he participate in any after school activities?" Leighton asked.

Cole shook his head. "No. He stopped caring about that stuff. He'll probably get in his car, or blow off last period and leave early, and just drive around for a while. He'll get home and his parents will be concerned that he's late but he won't care. He'll skip dinner, which will bother them, and he'll go up to his room and lie on his bed, staring at the ceiling till he can force his mind to be quiet long enough for him to fall asleep."

Leighton moved her hands from the keyboard and placed them in her lap. Cocking her head slightly, she looked at Cole. She studied his face, truly seeing him for the first time. His pleasant features were fraught with traces of darkness and pain. Leighton knew he'd been speaking from a secret place deep within himself, a place he'd buried beneath hostility and sarcasm. She imagined him as the broken, hurting boy they were bringing to life in their fiction, and despite any tension between them, it made her chest ache.

It was evident in Cole's fearful expression that he knew he'd given himself away, and he let out a sheepish chuckle that sounded forced.

"Cole…" Leighton breathed. "What happened to you?"

He clenched his jaw, as if one word might tear him open and expose whatever hideous, festering blackness that may be eating away at him beneath his deceptive exterior. He offered a feeble shrug, but his tortured countenance spoke for him.

Leighton wasn't sure what to say, but she could feel the undeniable tug of sympathy, and the sudden strange desire to console him and take his pain away. She'd insisted that her interest in Cole was merely an innocent curiosity, but she'd failed to admit that it ran so much deeper.

It was more than attraction that drew Leighton to him. Something—instincts, a gut feeling—told her that Cole was much more than he seemed. Maybe his rough facade was only a mask he wore. Maybe he had reasons for the walls he built to keep her out. But the glimpses he'd let slip filled her with more wonder and more compassion than ever.

Leighton couldn't stop herself from acting on the notions she'd denied from the start. She took Cole's face in her hands and she kissed him.

Leighton pulled away first to see his brilliant eyes wide with shock, and she braced herself for his disgusted reaction. Instead, Cole drew her toward him and kissed her right back.

Three

L eighton's lips were tingling. The faint taste of cigarettes lingered in her mouth and she tried not to think of Wesley's recent words. She felt lightheaded, a million thoughts and emotions pulsing through her.

"I think I should go," Cole said, running a hand through his hair. He got up from the picnic table and hastily shoved his things into his bag.

"Cole, wait," Leighton said, her voice cracking.

He slung his bag over his shoulder and looked at her almost longingly. "I can't," he barely whispered.

And then he was gone.

Leighton breezed into her dorm room, her heart still dancing wildly in her chest.

"Hey, did you get my texts?" Quinn asked, nearly startling her.

Leighton fumbled with her phone and frowned at the list of unopened messages on her lock screen. "I'm sorry. I was with Cole."

Quinn raised her eyebrows. "Oh, really?"

"We were just working on our psych project," Leighton said quickly, crossing the room to throw her bag onto her bunk.

"Wow, so the douche finally cooperated?"

Leighton couldn't help glaring at her. "Hey, you don't know him."

Quinn snickered. "What do you care? I thought you were pissed at him for flaking on you yesterday."

"I was. It doesn't matter. There are things you don't know. Things *I* don't know."

"Whatever," Quinn said with a sigh. "But I don't trust him. Just like I didn't trust Jared."

Leighton gritted her teeth. "I can assure you that Cole is *not* Jared." Saying his name out loud made her stomach hurt.

"I'm only trying to look out for you, Leighton. I don't get why you suddenly care so much about Cole. He *obviously* doesn't care about you."

"Then why did he kiss me?" Leighton blurted out, crossing her arms over her chest.

Quinn's jaw dropped. "What? You barely know him."

Leighton rolled her eyes. "So, I know Wesley *too* well and I don't know Cole well *enough*? What do I have to do to please you?"

Quinn pressed her lips together, and Leighton knew she was trying to hide her hurt. "So, um, I was texting you because Wes and I are gonna go off campus for lunch. I was seeing if you wanted to come with us, but..."

Whether it was justified or not, Leighton felt

guilty for lashing out at Quinn. "Uh, yeah. Sure."

Quinn walked to the door. "Wesley is waiting downstairs, so we better go."

At the mall, the three of them sat at a small table, their conversation scarce. Leighton had texted a casual invitation to Cole when they'd first arrived, and as she picked at her waffle fries, her phone finally chimed. She felt Wesley look up at her from across the table as she read Cole's delayed reply.

I told you I can't.

Then he added, *I'm sorry.*

Leighton deflated and shoved her phone back into her purse. The knot in her stomach tightened with the sting of his rejection once again. She regretted kissing him. How could she have been so foolish?

"Hey, I'm gonna go get a refill," Quinn said, shaking the ice in her empty paper cup.

Once Quinn had left them, Wesley crossed his arms on the table and leaned forward, lessening the space between them.

"So, I obviously missed something. Maybe a few somethings. Are you okay?"

The concern in his eyes comforted her a little. "Yeah, I'm fine."

Wesley squinted at her. "Come on, I know you better than that."

Leighton sighed. "I'm just an idiot when it comes to guys, that's all."

"Is this about Cole? Did he do something?"

"It's more like *I* did something...I kissed

him." Leighton bit her bottom lip, waiting for Wesley to scold her. But he didn't.

"Oh," he said, his eyes wide. "So, he didn't kiss you back?"

"Well, no, he did."

Wesley cleared his throat. "I thought he was, like, your arch nemesis. How did *this* happen?"

"I don't know. I guess I was in denial? I told you I'm an idiot."

"Don't say that. You're *not*."

"Well, he already seems to think it was a big mistake," Leighton said. "So, as always, the joke is on me."

Wesley shook his head. "No, Leighton, the joke is on *him*. If he can't see what an amazing and beautiful person you are, then he's even worse than I thought."

She couldn't help but smile. "You're so sweet, Wesley. Why can't Cole be more like you?"

Wesley looked away. "I don't know, Leighton. Some guys are just luckier than others, I guess."

Leighton didn't see Cole again until Wednesday morning's class. Her heart leaped when he sauntered in with all his mystery and allure. Her face went hot when his eyes met hers, but he looked at her as if he barely knew her. As if they hadn't shared a kiss—*twice*—just two days before.

Leighton quickly found that Cole's resistance only made her want him more. She hated how easily she'd given in to her attraction, and she refused to admit how often he invaded her thoughts.

And even now, she didn't hear a single word of Dr. Gibson's lecture. Cole was so close to her, yet so out of reach. All she could do between her stolen glances, was carefully construct in her head exactly what she would say to him as soon as she got the chance.

When the time came, Cole got up from his desk and dashed out of the room before a single word could escape her. Leighton nearly had to sprint to catch up to him outside.

"Cole!"

He kept walking, taking long, quick strides down the sidewalk, and she struggled to get to him.

"Cole, stop!" Leighton yanked at his arm and he spun around to face her, letting out a heavy sigh.

"What do you want from me?" he asked in a defeated tone.

"I just want you to talk to me."

"What do you want me to say?" Cole lifted his hands slightly, then let them drop back to his sides.

"I want to understand what's going on, why you keep pushing me away."

He frowned. "Can't you see that I'm bad for you?"

"Why would you say that?" She reached her hand out to touch him but he stepped back.

"This whole time, you've just stood by and let me treat you like shit when you've done nothing to deserve it. You're too naïve, Leighton. Some people aren't worthy of your kindness."

Leighton looked at the ground. Cole was right. And the situation sounded all too familiar. "I know you've been a bit difficult, but...I care about you."

"Leighton. You know nothing about me."

"That isn't true."

"Yes, it is," he said. "Because if you *did* know me, you wouldn't care at all. Trust me."

"No, Cole. I don't believe that."

He seemed to lose his patience. "I haven't even been myself with you, Leighton! How could you care about this horrible person I've been? And I promise you, the real me isn't any better."

He started to leave but Leighton grabbed his wrist. She didn't let him pull away. "I've seen the real you more than you realize. And I know that things have happened to you. But if you keep shutting me out, I can't help you."

Cole snickered. "I'm not some project for you to work on."

"I know you're not. Can't I just be your friend?" Leighton asked.

He didn't hesitate. "No."

"Why not?"

Cole pulled away from her, a tormented look in his eyes. "Because if you get too close, I'll have to tell you what I did." He froze, as if the words had tumbled out against his will.

Before Leighton could question him, he gave her one last conflicted glance, then turned and hurried away.

four

"Have you heard from him?"

Leighton glanced up at Wesley. The look in his eyes didn't match the concern in his voice.

She shook her head. "No. He avoids me in class and he hasn't answered my texts."

"I'm sorry," Wesley said, returning his attention to Leighton's algebra homework.

It had been nine whole days since Leighton had spoken to Cole. At first, she preoccupied herself with what he'd last said, wondering with fierce suspense what he could've possibly done that he couldn't tell her. But as each day turned into the next, she felt herself withdrawing. She'd been much too quick with her affection, and Cole was obviously hell bent on keeping her away. Maybe it was best to heed his warnings and walk away before she got too invested.

"Hey, you only missed three this time." Wesley handed her homework back to her.

"Really? Wow, you *are* a good tutor. Thanks, Wes."

He took a careful sip of his steaming coffee. "I'm glad it's helping."

"Me too. I *hate* math," Leighton said. "I used to be really good at it until I had teacher who made everything so complicated. Ever since then, I haven't been able to grasp it as easily."

"Oh, Mr. Madsen? Eighth grade advanced algebra?" he asked.

Leighton nodded emphatically. "Yes!"

Wesley groaned. "I had him too! He was *so* intimidating. If you asked for help, he'd embarrass you in front of the entire class. I *hated* that."

"Good, so I wasn't the only one. But at least your brain wasn't damaged for the rest of your academic career," Leighton said.

Wesley chuckled. "I hardly think you have brain damage, Leighton."

"Oh, you know what I mean."

He grinned. "But you know, you needing help with algebra isn't such a bad thing. It gives us the perfect excuse to hang out and drink copious amounts of coffee in the name of education."

Leighton beamed. "Ah, yes. Two of my favorite things."

Wesley raised an eyebrow. "Coffee and education are two of your favorite things?"

Leighton laughed. "No."

"Coffee and algebra, then."

She sighed, reaching across the table to give his shoulder a playful shove. "Coffee and *you*, Wesley, okay?"

He shot her a sly smile. "I know. I just wanted to hear you say it."

Leighton propped her chin in her hand. "You're too much."

Wesley looked at her sideways. "So, how many of these other so-called favorite things am I competing with? I don't want to succumb to empty flattery if you're the kind of girl who is excessive with her favoriting."

She blushed. "Well, right now, I'd say you're top five with the potential to advance."

His eyes brightened. "Challenge accepted."

Wesley tapped Leighton's name in his phone to call her as he made his way to the community bathroom down the hall from his dorm room.

"Hey, you," she answered.

"I'm just calling to say good night, as per your request," he said.

"Aww, you remembered."

Wesley could tell she was smiling. "Of course I remembered. What are you up to?"

"Just studying a bit before I go to bed. You?"

He snickered. "Funny you should ask. Guess what happened. *Again.*"

"Ugh. Connor has his girlfriend over?"

"Yes! Seriously, how was I lucky enough to be assigned to the most inconsiderate roommate on the entire campus?"

Leighton laughed. "Aw, I'm sorry, Wes. What are you gonna do?"

Wesley walked into the large bathroom and saw Cole standing at one of the many sinks brushing his teeth. Wesley gave him an acknowledging nod.

"I don't know," Wesley replied into the phone. "I'll probably hang out downstairs in the common area for a while, maybe doze off on the couch for a bit. Then later, I guess I'll go back to my room and hope that either she's gone, or they're asleep."

Leighton sighed. "That's not fair. Can't you complain or something?"

"No way. Tattling stopped being cool forever ago."

She laughed again, then lowered her voice. "I would tell you to just come here, but you know how Quinn's already being weird about us spending so much time together...Where are you now?"

"I'm in the bathroom."

"Ew, Wes."

"No, I'm not *going* to the bathroom, Leighton, I'm *in* the bathroom. There's a significant difference." He glanced sheepishly at Cole.

Leighton groaned. "Quinn wants me to tell you I have to go because my giggling is keeping her awake."

Wesley smiled against the phone. "All right. I'll let you go, then. Are we still on for breakfast tomorrow?"

"Of course we are. Good night, Wes."

"Night." Trying to contain his grin, he pocketed his phone and took a few items out of his bag, setting them on the counter.

"That was Leighton?" Cole asked, rinsing his toothbrush under the faucet a few sinks down.

Wesley didn't look at him. "Yeah."

"How's she doing?"

"Suddenly you care?" Wesley leaned toward the mirror and eased his bottom eyelid down to remove the contact lens from his right eye, and placed it gently in its case. He then repeated the quick motion on his left eye.

"I know I haven't done much to prove it, but I do care," Cole said.

Wesley uncapped a small bottle and drowned the lenses in cleansing solution. He carefully screwed the lids onto both small compartments and tossed the case into his bag. Cole started for the door when Wesley began rummaging through his bag again.

"She's good," Wesley finally said, stopping Cole from leaving. "To answer your question...Leighton is good."

Cole nodded. "I'm happy to hear that."

Wesley snickered. "Are you? You don't look very happy."

Cole let out a long sigh, shifting his gaze to the tile floor. "In general? No. I'm not very happy."

"I appreciate your honesty," Wesley said, locating his eyeglass case. He took out his glasses and put them on.

Cole looked at him like he was waiting for something. "You're not gonna get all nosy and ask me why?"

Wesley chuckled. "You mean like Leighton?"

"Well, no..."

"It's okay," Wesley said. "Her heart's in the right place, I promise. It's just that she's been cursed with this insatiable need to help people. Sometimes against their will."

Cole cracked a smile. "Yeah. I see that."

"Plus, she has highly warranted trust issues, so she doesn't tolerate ambiguity very well." Wesley turned back to the sink to brush his teeth.

"Good to know," Cole said, then paused for a few moments. "Hey, so...I overheard your phone conversation before. My roommate goes home on the weekends, so I've got extra space If you need a place to crash."

"Oh. Yeah. Okay, sure," Wesley accepted, surprised by Cole's kindness.

After Wesley had finished up, Cole led him to his dorm room. The immaculate space was surprising to Wesley, because everything about the way Cole acted and carried himself suggested disarray rather than order.

Cole opened the door to the small closet and reached up to the top shelf. "Here," he said, handing Wesley a folded blanket and pointing to the bed on the right side of the room. "My roommate's pretty clean, but it's still kinda weird since you don't know him."

"Thanks." Wesley climbed onto the made bed and spread the blanket over himself. He removed his glasses and set them on the desk beside him.

Cole turned off the light before making his way to his own bed.

Wesley lay there, staring into the darkness, thinking about the odd turn the night had taken. He never imagined he'd find himself sharing a dorm room with Cole MacHendrick of all people. Up until a few moments ago, Wesley thought Cole was nothing but a heartless, angry person with no regard for other people. Wesley hated the way Cole had hurt Leighton and took her interest for granted. But Wesley didn't see that spiteful person now.

"Hey, Cole?"

"Yeah?"

"Thanks for helping me out."

"It's no big deal."

"I think I may have judged you too quickly," Wesley added.

Cole breathed a slight chuckle. "Most people do."

"But can you blame them?" Wesley asked lightheartedly.

"That's kind of the point."

"What do you mean?"

"I like to keep people at a certain distance," Cole said.

"God, no wonder you drive Leighton crazy." Wesley snickered. "You offer all these vague one-liners that you expect no one to question."

Cole was silent for a short while. "Leighton hates me, doesn't she?"

"No. But I think she's trying to move on, to be honest," Wesley said.

"Oh."

"What did you expect her to do, though?"

Cole sighed. "I don't know. I didn't expect *any* of it."

"I know how that is," Wesley replied.

"And *I'm* the one who's vague."

"What, I didn't say anything."

"You don't have to," Cole said. "It's so obvious."

"I don't know what you're talking about."

"Oh, come on. We like the same girl and you know it."

"And just when I thought we were becoming friends," Wesley joked.

Cole laughed. "Yeah, but you don't have to worry about me."

"But you just said you like her."

"I know. But that doesn't mean I can pursue her. When I told her I was bad for her, I meant it," Cole said.

"And I don't suppose you will explain why that is?"

Cole paused for just a moment. "Good night, Wesley."

Leighton sat down across from Wesley at their usual spot in the café, instantly noticing his tense expression. "Hey. Everything okay?"

He let out a nervous laugh. "Yeah, it's fine. I hope."

"Is this about last night? You didn't get into a fight with your roommate, did you?" she asked.

"Oh, no, I haven't seen him. I ended up staying in someone else's room," Wesley said.

"Oh, good. I was actually kinda worried about you, so I'm glad someone was kind enough to help you out."

Wesley scratched his head. "Yeah...it was Cole."

Leighton's eyes went wide. "*Cole?*"

"Yes," he said, glancing behind her. "He overheard my conversation with you and he offered. But long story short, he came here with me, and now he's coming back from the restroom and he's right behind you, so I'm sorry, I hope you're not mad."

Leighton went rigid when the chair next to her was pulled out, and a tall figure sat down beside her. Even without Wesley's warning, and without turning to look, she knew it was Cole just inches away from her. She knew by the way his familiar woodsy scent and the faint hint of cigarettes graced her and made her heart race.

"I hope I'm not imposing on your date," Cole said, scooting his chair closer to the table. His deep voice played like a song her ears had been craving.

"Uh, no. You're not. It's not. Not a date, I mean," she stammered, well aware that her face had turned every shade of red.

Still, she couldn't bring herself to look at him, to see those silver-blue eyes staring back. His presence was stirring up everything inside her like a savage tornado. Or maybe a vicious whirlpool, threatening to suck her back in and drown her beneath the weight of all Cole was and would never show her.

"So," Wesley chimed in as he stood up. "Now that we're all here, let's go get in line before it gets really busy." He led the way across the café to the short line at the counter.

Cole stood close behind Leighton, his mouth near her ear. "I wanted to tell you I'm sorry," he said quietly.

His breath on her neck sent chills through her whole body. "What, now you're suddenly having a change of heart?" she asked. She finally turned to look at him, feeling everything inside her come alive.

Cole stepped back. "Not exactly. I still stand behind everything I said. I'm just apologizing for the way I said it."

Leighton sighed heavily and shook her head. "Of course. And since you insist you're so bad for me, I guess *I'll* apologize for being too good for you."

Cole frowned. "Please don't. You have nothing to apologize for."

"Give me one solid reason why you're so bad for me, then."

"Because it's the truth," he said with conviction. "You just have to trust me on that."

She huffed with annoyance. "Why do you get to decide that for me? Actually, never mind. It's pointless to ask you questions."

Cole's eyes burned into hers. "This isn't easy for me, you know."

Leighton turned away from him to move up in the line.

Cole moved up behind her, drawing close once again to whisper into her ear. "You have no idea how much I hate this." He brushed his fingertips down her arm.

She leaned back until her shoulders barely touched his chest. "Then don't do it," she said, tempting his resolve and shattering her own.

Cole sighed and rested his cheek against her head for a short moment. "Just forget about me," he said before he backed away from her.

Then it was Leighton's turn to order. She could hardly breathe as she mumbled the first items she spotted on the menu boards overhead.

When Leighton got back to the table, she sat down beside Wesley instead of across from him. Her expression must have mirrored her inner discord, because Wesley was peering attentively at her as he leaned his shoulder against hers.

"Are you okay?" he asked, his tone tender.

She nodded. "I'll live."

He slid his arm around her and gently rubbed her shoulder. "I'm so sorry I invited him. I should've known it would be a mistake."

Leighton managed a smile. "No, it's not your fault, Wes. You were just being your normal sweet self. And as always, Cole is being his usual infuriating self."

She lifted her eyes to meet Cole's across the café as he waited for his order. The tornado-whirlpool mess inside her only raged harder.

"I wish you wouldn't waste so much thought on someone who fails to see your worth. He takes you for granted, Leighton. I would *never* do that to you," Wesley said, looking intently at her.

His heartfelt words evoked a fluttering in her stomach, calming the storm ever so slightly, but Leighton kept her eyes locked on Cole's. She was gripped by the sudden urge to make Cole feel as rejected as he'd made her feel.

As he made his way to their table, an idea flitted across Leighton's mind, and before she allowed herself to realize how truly terrible it was, she acted on it. Tearing her eyes away from Cole, she turned to Wesley, grabbed his face in her hands, and kissed him as passionately as she could.

five

"Should I go?" Cole asked, standing at his chair, coffee in hand.

Wesley opened his mouth to speak, but Leighton piped up first. "Oh, of course not. That would be rude of us."

Cole furrowed his brow. "Are you sure?"

"Absolutely."

Cole shrugged and slid the chair out to sit down across from them. He eyed Leighton's arm as she hooked it through Wesley's.

"I'm sorry you had to see that," she said. "To be honest, Wesley and I have been spending a lot of time together, and...you know how things just happen."

Cole looked at Wesley, searching his face for even a shred of skepticism, but for all Cole could tell, Wesley was completely oblivious. "You know what? I *am* gonna go, actually," Cole said, getting up from his seat. "Wesley, thank you for the invite. And Leighton...be careful." His eyes shifted to Wesley and then back to her before he turned away.

Leighton's rampant thoughts nagged at her conscience as she walked beside Wesley across campus. Laced through the guilt for what she'd done was an unquestionable confusion over what it had ignited in her. But how could that happen? She'd only wanted to make Cole jealous. And she'd used her best friend to carry out the childish act.

"Hey. What are you thinking about?" Wesley asked, his arm bumping hers.

Leighton's guilt burrowed deeper and she sighed. "Nothing really. What are *you* thinking about?"

He threaded his fingers through hers. "You...us."

She swallowed. "Wesley, I—"

He stopped and pulled her to him, gathering her securely in his arms. His smile magnified his boyish good looks.

"I've waited so long for this," he whispered, lifting a hand to caress her cheek.

Wesley slipped his fingers into her hair at the nape of her neck and cradled her head as he drew closer. He kissed her eagerly and Leighton kissed him back. She allowed herself to get lost in him, to explore these foreign feelings, and her mind didn't wander anywhere beyond him and the comfort of his arms. The past week and a half—or maybe their entire friendship—had slowly escalated to this moment, but still she was surprised. How had she never seen Wesley this way before?

He pulled away first, his eyes glinting with euphoria. "There are so many things I wish I could say to you right now."

"Why can't you?"

"Too much too soon," he said sheepishly.

"Then just tell me one thing."

Wesley tipped his forehead to rest against hers, and Leighton could see the flecks of gold in his eyes that she hadn't noticed from their usual distance.

"I like you *so* much," he told her. "I always have."

She offered a bashful smile. "That's technically *two* things, Wes."

He chuckled. "And you said you were bad at math."

Leighton laughed, folding against his chest to see how it felt to be so close. As his arms closed around her, she breathed him in—the familiar soothing scent of childhood mixed with grown up Wesley.

"Pinch me," he said.

Leighton leaned back to look at him. "Do you really want me to? Because I can."

"No, wait, don't. If this isn't real, I'd rather not wake up," Wesley said, grinning.

She shot him a playful smirk, but she couldn't deny the butterflies in her stomach. Maybe she didn't have to feel guilty. Maybe there really was something behind that kiss in the café. Maybe Leighton hadn't done it to make Cole jealous, but to show him she'd chosen Wesley.

Later that evening, Leighton pulled her door open and Wesley's signature smile greeted her. She felt herself blushing as she stepped aside to let him into her dorm room. It was still so strange to have these feelings, to question her future with the boy she'd known half her life.

"So you're sure Quinn won't be back anytime soon?" Wesley asked.

Leighton nodded. "She went to see a movie with her study group, so we're safe for at least two hours."

He groaned. "I can't believe we have to hide from my sister."

"I know, it's stupid. But I don't want to risk upsetting Quinn before we figure out what this is."

Wesley took both of her hands in his. "You don't already know? I do."

She chewed her lip, choosing her words carefully. "I'd like to think I *might* know, but it's all kind of sudden. For me, anyway."

He shot her a sideways, narrowed glance. "Is it, though? Leighton, you can't tell me you haven't been feeling this between us. I mean, you and I have had chemistry for quite some time now."

"Have we, though?" she asked, playfully mimicking him.

"Yes," Wesley said, amused. "You don't have to deny it anymore. I'm not just Quinn's brother. And I'm sure as hell not *your* brother; I don't care how long we've known each other."

"You're right," Leighton said. "Maybe I have denied it, or maybe I never let myself realize it before. I never would've thought you even saw me that way."

He raised his eyebrows. "Seriously? I've always worried I was too obvious."

"Nope. I guess not."

Wesley touched her cheek. "You are endearingly oblivious."

She blushed again, looking down at the floor. Placing his hand beneath her chin, he gently lifted her face, then ducked to level his eyes with hers.

"I know you're concerned about Quinn. And I know you're still dealing with what happened with Cole, and I respect that. So I'm willing to go along with whatever makes you comfortable. I've waited this long; I'll wait as long as I have to."

Moved by his impossible thoughtfulness, Leighton leaned forward a little too eagerly and their mouths collided roughly. He smiled against her lips, inadvertently causing her to kiss his teeth. She laughed, her teeth clinking against his.

"Okay, that was embarrassing," Leighton said, pulling away.

Wesley placed his hands on her waist and drew her toward him, planting a soft kiss on her temple. "Okay, so we lack a little grace, but we make up for it in other ways."

"Yeah? Like what?"

He shrugged. "Your beauty...I don't know, my pretentiousness?"

Turning toward the ladder to her bunk, Leighton let out a giggle. "You're calling yourself pretentious?" She climbed up and sat on her bed, leaning against the wall.

Wesley sighed. "Well, it's what I've been told."

Leighton patted the space beside her when Wesley reached for the desk chair. He quickly abandoned it and hoisted himself up to sit with her.

"I don't think you're pretentious," she said. "I think you're visibly intelligent and it makes some people jealous."

"I'm just being myself. What is there to be jealous about?"

"Looks *and* brains? Some would call that unfair, Wes."

"Looks? No, I dubbed *you* the beauty, remember?"

"Does that make you the beast, then?"

Wesley stifled a laugh. "Yes. It absolutely does. What is it with girls and Disney films?"

"Do you really think that? That I'm...beautiful?" Leighton asked.

"Of course I do."

Her gaze flitted bashfully to her hands in her lap. "No one's ever told me that before."

His eyes widened. "No one? Really. No one at all?"

"Well, aside from my parents, no. Jared always said I was *cute*."

Wesley growled a deep groan of disgust. "Yeah, well, Jared is an asshole."

A silence settled between them. They hadn't spoken of Jared in over a year.

"Hey, so, are you missing home at all?" Leighton asked to change the subject.

"I miss my mom's cooking, and watching Jeopardy with my dad every night after dinner. And I miss Atlas, although I do *not* miss walking him. But no, I don't really miss home. It's kind of exciting to be on my own, starting a new chapter in life," Wesley answered. "How about you?"

"I don't know. I guess it helps to know we're not very far from home. But it feels good to get away, leave things behind."

Wesley nodded, taking her hand. Leighton knew he understood exactly what she meant and she liked that.

It wasn't long before they had shifted their positions, lying side by side. They talked endlessly as the evening light faded, the room gradually growing dark, and the two of them gradually moving closer.

Leighton had never before shared such comfortable closeness with a boy. But she'd never expected that when she finally did, it would be with Wesley.

Wesley Alexander Brooks: the boy she knew *so* well but had never really *seen*.

Until now.

"If you could be any animal, what would you be?" Leighton asked when their conversation had transitioned into a random question and answer game.

"A bird. So I could fly," Wesley answered. "What about you?"

"Hmm…maybe a cheetah, so I could run really fast, and I wouldn't have to worry about anything eating me," she said.

"Good point. Favorite song of *all* time?" he asked.

"Oh, I can't."

"Yeah, me neither."

Leighton laughed. "What's your favorite smell?"

"Bookstores. Or coffee shops," Wesley replied without much thought. "Yours?"

"My mom's freshly baked pumpkin bread."

"I *love* your mom's pumpkin bread," he said. "What's your favorite word? And don't say 'onomatopoeia.' Everyone says that."

"My favorite *word*?"

"Yeah, like a word you think is fun to say."

"Oh, Chechnya," Leighton answered immediately.

Wesley grinned. "Well, that's a place, not a word, but okay."

She pressed her elbow into his side. "Fine, Mr. Technical. I'll go with serendipitous. What's yours?"

"Juxtaposition. Or effervescence."

"Oh? I thought it was canoodling," Leighton teased.

"I think I more prefer its definition," he said facetiously.

The butterflies had returned to Leighton's stomach. "Wow, it's gotten really dark in here. We should probably turn on the light."

Wesley chuckled, looking to the light switch across the room. "It's so far away, though."

"Oh, I thought of a good one," Leighton said, diverting the attention back to their game. "What's your earliest memory?"

"That *is* a good one," he replied, pausing to think. "All right. You know that game where you jump from couch to couch, pretending that the carpet is lava? Well, this one specific time was at the apartment my family used to live in when Quinn and I were really little, so I know we weren't any older than three. But my mom was vacuuming and we were pretending the vacuum was a dragon as we jumped on the couches. I remember my mom playing along, roaring at us, and we were all laughing so hard. It was awesome."

Leighton smiled and snuggled closer to him, easily picturing a younger Mrs. Brooks and tiny Wesley and tiny Quinn. "That's really sweet. Mine is kind of embarrassing–slash–funny. My family and I were at some wedding when I was maybe four. I was dancing on the dance floor, having a great time, when I realized I didn't know where my parents were. I panicked and ran to my dad, throwing my arms around his legs. But then I looked down and he was wearing these weird loafers I didn't recognize, and that's when I figured out that he wasn't my dad. I was hugging a complete stranger. Everyone laughed and thought it was so cute, but I was mortified."

Wesley chuckled. "Aw, that's sad! If I had been there, I assure you I wouldn't have laughed."

"Yeah, but you're laughing right now."

"I'm not laughing," he insisted. "I'm just amused by your sweetness."

"Fine," Leighton said with a snicker. "But if you *had* been there, you probably would've been too busy wooing all the other little girls on the dance floor."

"Is that what you think I do?"

She shrugged against him. "Intentional or

not, that's how it is, Wes. Girls notice you *a lot*."

Wesley cleared his throat. "Well, if that really *is* the case, it's only a matter of time before they all come to their senses."

Leighton cracked up. "I hate to break it to you, but I'm pretty sure that's not true."

He sighed. "But does it really matter how many girls I attract if none of them are the one I want?"

Leighton hesitated, peering at him through the darkness. "Wesley...how long have you liked me?"

He breathed an uneasy chuckle. "I can't tell you that."

"Why not?"

"Because it's much longer than I'm willing to admit to you."

In the quiet, they could hear the jingling of keys outside the door as Quinn let herself in. Leighton threw her hand over Wesley's mouth, praying Quinn wouldn't turn on the light.

"Leighton?" Quinn said softly.

Leighton made a rustling sound as if stirring. "Yeah?" she muttered, forcing a groggy voice.

"Wow, you're asleep early for a Saturday night," Quinn said. "This better not be because you're depressed about Cole."

Leighton felt Wesley's body tense with the threat of laughter, and she sighed loudly to drown out any potential sound. "I'm not depressed about Cole. I'm just *really* tired."

"Okay, just making sure." Quinn fiddled with some things in the dark before heading back to the door. "Actually, sleep does sound really good. I'm just gonna run to the bathroom. I'll be right back."

After Quinn had gone, Wesley burst into a fit of laughter. "Oh my gosh. That was so close," he said.

Leighton sat up. "I can't believe we lost track of time. We need to be more careful. And *you* need to get out of here."

"Can I ask for a good night kiss?"

She didn't need to see him to know he was grinning. She leaned into the darkness, searching for him. His hands gently found her face, and she felt the warmth of his lips cover hers. As he let go, the door flew open, and Leighton immediately shot into a horizontal position, pulling Wesley down beside her. She tried to slow her heated breaths, hoping Quinn didn't suspect a thing.

"Good night, Leighton," she said, climbing into her bed.

Leighton didn't answer. Instead, she brought her mouth to Wesley's ear. "We'll wait until she falls asleep and then you can sneak out," she barely whispered.

She felt him nod as she settled against him to wait.

"Leighton! What the hell!"

Leighton opened her eyes to see Quinn standing on the bunk bed ladder, her face scrunched with sheer disgust. When Leighton felt Wesley's arm tighten around her, she realized what was happening.

"Oh, God…Wesley, wake up," Leighton said, nudging him.

He quickly became aware of their faux pas and untangled himself from her.

"What is going on?" Quinn demanded. "Have you been sneaking around behind my back?"

"Sort of, I guess? But only since yesterday morning," Leighton said.

Quinn stepped down from the ladder and crossed her arms over her chest. "Wesley, can you please get out of her bed? It really freaks me out to see you two this way."

He huffed as he slid himself off the top bunk. "Come on, Quinn, you're being a little ridiculous, don't you think?"

She gawked at him. "No. I don't think so. You two probably thought you were so clever last night, fooling me. But what would you have done if I'd turned on the light, huh?"

Leighton pressed her lips together. "I'm sorry, Quinn. That was wrong of us."

"You *knew* this would bother me, Leighton. You *told me* you didn't see him like that," Quinn said.

Wesley looked at Leighton. "You said that about me?"

"That was before—"

"Before you found out you couldn't have Cole?" he asked.

Leighton gave him a pained look. "Wes…"

He turned to his sister. "I don't know why this is such a big deal to you, but you're being selfish."

"Leighton is *my* best friend. If she's *your* girlfriend, then everything changes," Quinn said, her voice shaking.

"We're not little kids anymore, Quinn," Wesley said. "Everything is already changing."

"Yeah, my best friend and my brother are backstabbing liars. That's definitely a change," Quinn scoffed.

Leighton climbed down to the floor. "I'm sorry we didn't go about it the right way, but to be honest, it kind of snuck up on us. We're just trying to figure it out ourselves."

"I don't like being left out." Quinn kicked at the rug with her toe. "I'm not in favor of whatever this is, but please don't lie to me anymore."

"I promise, I won't," Leighton said with a thin smile.

Wesley grumbled. "Fine, Quinn, whatever. I've gotta go. I'll see you later, Leighton."

As he stepped into the hallway, Leighton wanted to stop him, but it would be catastrophic if, in this moment, she chose Wesley over Quinn.

"Are you going to the Fall Festival later?" Leighton asked, hoping to lift the heaviness in the air between them.

"Will you be there with my brother?" Quinn asked.

"As far as I know, yes."

"Then no," Quinn replied, darting her eyes away.

"Come on, Quinn. Are you really gonna be like this?"

Quinn rolled her eyes. "Ya know, it's one

thing to disregard everything I admitted to you and completely go against my wishes. But to lie about it and sneak around literally right in front of me? You made me feel so stupid."

"I know. I'm *so* sorry," Leighton said.

"And I really was concerned about you last night," Quinn added. "About you and Cole. How dumb of me."

Leighton reached out to touch her friend's shoulder. "No, it was sweet of you. You're a good friend, Quinn. I'm sorry I wasn't."

"Does this mean you'll stay away from my brother?"

Leighton grimaced. "I really think I might like him."

"Oh, God. Wait...have you *kissed* him?" Quinn asked reluctantly.

"Yes?"

"Ew, Leighton, that's gross."

Leighton chuckled. "Of course you think it's gross; you're his sister."

Quinn pondered for a moment. "Ugh...so you and *Wesley*? Are you sure?"

"Honestly, no. I'm not sure. But he and I need to figure that out."

Quinn sighed. "Fine, you win. But if he breaks your heart, I'll kill him."

The peak of golden hour painted the campus with a warm glow as they made their way to the Fall Festival out on the green. Wesley took Leighton's hand.

"Oh, barf," Quinn said with a groan and an eye roll.

Wesley snickered. "I don't know why you're complaining. If this all goes well, it has the potential to turn your best friend into your sister."

Quinn patted him on the shoulder. "Slow down there, Wes. You don't want to freak the poor girl out."

Wesley turned to Leighton. "I'm sorry. I'm not trying to rush anything, I swear."

Leighton smiled. "No, I know. Don't worry about it." She tried to imagine marrying Wesley someday, but she wasn't sure if she could see it. The uncertainty gave her an uneasy feeling.

The bonfire was alive and crackling when they reached the green. A DJ was playing an upbeat Walk the Moon track as people mingled among decorative scarecrows and refreshment tables. The changing colors of the surrounding trees added an appropriate backdrop to the event.

"I'm sorry about this morning," Wesley said, once Quinn had left them alone by the fire.

Leighton stabbed a metal skewer through a marshmallow and held it close to the flames. "What are you sorry for?"

"For what I said about you only liking me because things didn't work out with Cole. It was rude and insecure of me." He set a square of chocolate on a graham cracker and held it out to her in his palm.

The pang of guilt had returned. "It's okay, Wes. I understand."

She added the roasted marshmallow, and Wesley pressed the remaining graham cracker into the melted mush, holding it together while Leighton removed the skewer.

"Good job." He grinned, offering it to her.

"Wow, I haven't had s'mores in forever," Leighton said, wiping the excess marshmallow from her lip.

Wesley leaned in to take a bite. "For me, it's been since that summer after freshman year when you came camping with my family."

She thought for a moment. "Yup. That would be my last one as well."

"That was a good weekend," he said. "I especially enjoyed being sent out of the tent to check for bears every time you and Quinn thought you heard a noise."

Leighton laughed sheepishly. "Yeah, I remember that. I'm sorry."

Wesley placed his hand on her waist. "I didn't mind. If it made you feel safe, I was happy to oblige."

"Why are you so nice, Wes?" she asked, toying with a button on his open sweater.

"Kindness should always be the rule, not the exception," he replied, like it was the most obvious answer.

On a mischievous whim, Leighton responded by shoving the last bite of s'more into his mouth, smearing chocolatey marshmallow across his bottom lip.

"*Kindness*, Leighton," he said with his mouth full, fighting to suppress his grin.

Swallowing, Wesley grabbed her and kissed her, sharing the wealth of sticky sweetness. Then he lingered, kissing her tenderly. For a fleeting moment, the fluttering in Leighton's stomach returned, nearly drowning out her doubts. But as she watched the flickering of the flames reflecting in his eyes, she saw something in his intense gaze that scared her.

"Hey," she began, leaning back from him. "I'm gonna go grab us some drinks, okay? Be right back."

Leighton turned away from Wesley and headed for the refreshment tables across the green. When she approached them, a hand closed around her forearm, stopping her in her tracks. She spun around, and her eyes went wide when she saw Cole standing before her.

"What are you doing?"

"Hello to you too," Leighton scoffed. "I'm getting a drink."

Cole sighed. "No. I mean...why are you leading Wesley on?"

She raised her eyebrows. "What are you talking about?"

"Tell me you didn't kiss him right in front of me yesterday just to make me jealous."

"Wow, you are so arrogant," she said, shaking her head.

Cole let out a snort. "Am I? Because it wasn't all that long ago that you were kissing *me*. How could you suddenly be so into *him*?"

Leighton's frustration began to boil beneath her skin. "It wasn't sudden! It just took me a while to realize there was something between us."

"Are you really going to pretend that you just *happened* to realize you're in love with your best friend after you *randomly* kissed him the *exact moment* I was approaching you? And right after we had an argument too. Tell me I'm wrong."

She put her hands on her hips. "Fine. Maybe initially it *was* my intention to kiss Wesley just to piss you off. But it made me realize that I have feelings for him. And I never said I was in love with him."

"Then what are you doing?" Cole asked.

"I'm trying to figure that out. Why does it matter to you?"

He hesitated, biting his lip. "Because you will hate yourself if you break his heart."

Leighton rolled her eyes. "Oh, please. Like you care about Wesley."

Cole lifted a shoulder. "Maybe I do. He's a good guy. You forget I'm not the dick you think I am."

"Oh, right. You're just the dick you *pretend* to be, putting up your fake walls to keep me away from you for God only knows why, while torturing me and driving me crazy."

He lowered his voice. "I'm sorry it has to be that way. I wish I could make you understand, but I can't."

Her frustration finally boiled over, sizzling on her every last nerve. "You haven't even *tried* to make me understand. I don't get what could possibly be so bad that you have to deprive and isolate yourself like this. Whatever it is, you shouldn't have to deal with it alone."

"It's not that simple, Leighton. You have no idea."

She snickered. "Of course I don't. Tell me what I have to do to be worthy enough for you to let me in."

Cole stared at her. "Is that what you think this is about? That I don't think you're *worthy* enough? It's the exact opposite. And that's what scares me."

"Then why do you fight so hard to push me away? You make me feel stupid and unwanted, and I hate it."

A pained expression flashed across his face. "That is *not* what I want at all. I'm just trying to protect you."

"From what?"

"*Me.*"

Leighton took a step toward him. "What if I don't want to be protected from you? What if I want to tear through your stupid walls and just let myself in? How can you stop me? I see through your act now, Cole, and you can't scare me away anymore."

"I swear to God, Leighton, you don't want this."

"But I do. I've tried so hard not to care about you. I've even tried to hate you. But I can't," she said, an undeniable certainty rising inside her. She could see the desperation in Cole's brilliant eyes and it made her ache.

"Leighton...please."

She shrugged, drawing even closer. "I'm sorry."

"Should I let you know I'm standing right here?" Wesley's cheerless voice interrupted them. "Or should I wait until *after* you kiss?"

six

"Wesley, wait!" Leighton followed him, Cole trailing cautiously behind her.

Wesley stopped near the hay bale maze and spun around. "I get it, Leighton. I don't need you to explain it to me."

"How much did you hear?" she asked.

"Enough to know what you really want. And it's not me," Wesley said, a sadness in his voice.

Leighton rubbed her temples and closed her eyes, fighting to hold back her tears. "I like you, Wes. I just..."

"You just like *him* more," Wesley finished, motioning to Cole behind her. "And he's practically *begging* you to run. Don't you wish Jared had given you a warning like that? Would've saved you a lot of pain."

Leighton clenched her jaw. "Don't compare them; it's not the same."

"Fine. Do what you want," Wesley surrendered, the heartache evident in his eyes. "But be careful. I can't promise I'll be there to save you this time."

Then he turned away and disappeared into

the crowd of people beyond them, leaving Leighton in her guilt and misery.

"Are you okay?" Cole asked carefully.

She dried her cheeks and took a deep breath, working to compose herself. "You were right. I broke his heart and I hate myself. And it's all for nothing because you don't even want me."

As fresh tears formed, Leighton stalked off, slipping through the entrance of the hay bale maze.

But Cole came after her, catching up quickly. "I never said I didn't want you."

She reached a fork in the maze and made a left. "You didn't have to," she said, rounding the corner to find a dead end.

Leighton leaned against the wall, loose strands of hay poking into her.

"I'm really sorry, Leighton."

She raised her eyes to meet Cole's, surprised by his concerned demeanor. Despite everything, she still felt that same nagging ache to know him.

"Can you tell me *one* secret?" she pleaded. "Just one thing. Anything at all. I think you at least owe me that."

He dropped his gaze, his hair casting a shadow over his face. "Leighton…"

She uttered a harsh snicker as she sat down in the grass, her back against the hay wall. "Of course not. I'm an idiot for even asking."

Cole sighed. "Last year, I lost every friend I've ever had. I've spent the past year alone." He lowered himself to sit beside her "And now you know why my social skills are shit."

Leighton turned to him. "Why did you lose your friends?"

He shook his head. "You can't ask why."

She frowned. "I should've known."

A giggling group of girls rounded the corner, then turned back once they saw the dead end.

"So, who's Jared?" Cole asked, picking at the grass.

"No. You don't get to know *my* secret. How would that be fair?"

"I think I have the right to know why I'm being compared to this supposedly terrible person, don't I?"

Leighton slumped her shoulders. "Fine." She paused for a moment to collect her thoughts, to will herself to dredge up the unpleasant memories. "Jared was my boyfriend for three months of my sophomore year. He was this hot senior on the football team, and for some reason, he was interested in *me*. He was great at first, all attentive and sweet...but as time went on, he stopped being on his best behavior, and the only thing he cared to talk about was himself. When we were together, all he wanted to do was make out, and if I didn't, he'd get mad and take me home."

Cole made a face. "He sounds like an ass. Does that mean *I'm* an ass?"

Leighton managed a chuckle. "Oh, I've barely scratched the surface of why Jared sucks. But, no, you're not an ass. Well, maybe...for other, unrelated reasons."

Cole smirked. "I deserve that. Continue."

"Jared took me to his senior prom, and he

went all out. He and his friends rented a limo, and it was really fun. We danced and laughed all night, and I thought maybe things were getting better between us. Afterwards, we all went to a hotel because he told me there was an after-party there. It turns out, he lied. He'd rented a room for us and he took me there."

Cole looked nervous. "Uh oh. I don't like where this is going."

"Just wait." Leighton half-smiled. "Obviously, Jared wanted me to sleep with him, but I didn't want to. I was only fifteen; I wasn't ready. He got pissed and left the room. I sat there for thirty minutes before I realized he wasn't coming back. He just left me there at midnight, all by myself."

"I hate this guy," Cole said.

"He actually gets worse."

Cole groaned. "Great, then what happened?"

Leighton bit her lip for a brief moment, glancing up at the couple who'd made the wrong turn and had temporarily discovered their little spot. "I called Wesley. He snuck out and drove across town to pick me up and bring me home. He sat in my driveway with me for an hour while I cried and told him everything. He was furious with Jared. He'd never liked him."

"Probably because he was in love with you," Cole chimed in.

"Back then? I doubt that...Anyway, at school the following Monday, Jared dumped me in front of *everyone*. And he spread rumors all over school that he wouldn't sleep with me because I had an STD."

Cole's eyes went wide. "*What*? This guy

needs a punch in the face."

Leighton continued. "I got my very own, real-life teen movie cliché—douche guy goes after the young virgin to take advantage of her naïveté. I guess he couldn't handle that I'd turned him down. It bruised his ego or something. But he sure got most of the school to believe his lies, which haunted me until I graduated. You know, because no one wants to date the girl who *might* have herpes."

Cole looked at her, his jaw tightening. "That's not fair. I am so mad right now."

She laughed despite herself, pleased by his interest. "Yeah, well, one morning, Wesley walked up to Jared in the hallway and punched him right in the face. So that helped."

"Yes!" Cole rejoiced. "That makes me feel so much better. How did Wesley pull that one off?"

"Wes has been six-foot-four since he was fourteen, so no one in Jared's clique was willing to take him. They harassed him pretty badly for the rest of the year, though. And he got suspended for a week." Leighton looked at the ground, the guilt swelling in her chest yet again.

"When Wesley mentioned saving you...*that's* what he meant."

She nodded. "Yup. He went through a lot to protect me. And this is how I repay him."

"I know you didn't want to hurt Wesley, but being dishonest with him would've been worse." Cole gingerly placed his hand on her shoulder, almost like he was afraid to touch her. "And I promise you, I'm not like Jared. You can trust me on that."

Leighton squinted her eyes at him. "Why do

you keep doing that?"

He pulled his hand away. "Doing what?"

"You are constantly contradicting yourself. You insist nothing can happen between us, but then you seek me out to discourage me from being with Wesley. And now you're convincing me to trust you as if I have the option to choose you instead. I don't get you, Cole."

He ran a hand through his hair, a long breath escaping his lips. "What I want and how it has to be are two completely different things. Was I jealous when you kissed Wesley? Yes. Have I enjoyed my horrible attempts to drive you away? Absolutely not. But I haven't figured out how to have what I want without..." He stopped himself and looked away. "I hoped you'd eventually get sick of my attitude and move on. But I also hoped that you wouldn't."

Leighton studied his face, ruminating on his words. He felt so different, so much softer. "This would all make more sense if I knew what you were hiding," she said.

Cole frowned. "I know. I'm sorry."

"But maybe I shouldn't complain *too* much; you've spoken more words to me tonight than you have in the entire time I've known you," she said with a chuckle.

He offered a playful smirk. "I need to start being meaner again."

Leighton should've wanted to run away from the boy who couldn't be honest with her, who kept ugly secrets he couldn't even speak of, but something pushed her to ignore it.

"Can we make a deal?" she asked.

His expression grew inquisitive. "What kind of deal?"

She took a deep breath and let it out. "I'm sorry, but I don't think I'm wrong about you. This might make me look pathetic or too eager, but I don't care anymore. If nothing else, I want to be your friend. I don't want you running from me all the time. So, that's the deal—I'd be willing to stop prying and let you have your secrets, if you would stop pushing me away and just be yourself."

Cole gaped at her, and she was sure she'd gone too far this time. "Really...you would be okay with that?"

"Yes. Just you and me, getting to know each other in the now."

He hesitated for a moment, then cracked a smile and nodded. "Okay. It's a deal."

After making it through the rest of the hay bale maze with Cole, and after calling Wesley several times with no answer, Leighton headed toward her dorm. As she reached her residence hall, she ran into Quinn at the door.

"Are you done now?" Quinn asked, her voice charged with snarky attitude.

"Done what?"

"Breaking my brother's heart. What is wrong with you?" Quinn answered, her hands on her hips.

Leighton's stomach twisted. "I didn't mean to hurt him."

"Yeah, well you did. And to choose that *jerk* over Wesley?"

"I didn't ch—"

Quinn put her hand up. "You really didn't learn anything from Jared, did you?"

Leighton's eyes stung. "How could you say that to me?"

"Oh, it's easy," Quinn said, storming off into their building.

Paralyzed by Quinn's words, Leighton stood there with no place to go. She wasn't about to follow Quinn up to their room after their altercation. With shaking hands, she slipped her phone from her pocket and stared at the screen. Her initial thought was to call Wesley, and it made her feel nauseated. She hadn't realized how often he'd been there for her, and she feared she'd taken him for granted.

Left with no other options, Leighton called the only person she had left.

Cole answered on the second ring, surprise in his deep voice. "Leighton, hey."

"I'm so sorry to bother you," she said quickly. "I just got into a fight with Quinn and I have no one else to call."

"It's okay," he said. "Where are you?"

"Outside my hall. South entrance."

"I'll be right there."

Within minutes, Leighton caught sight of Cole walking briskly toward her down the sidewalk. She couldn't believe she was able to reach out to *Cole* for help, and that he was so willing to come to her rescue. Somehow, this was the same guy who had stood her up in the courtyard, and who had spoken so coldly to her on several occasions. But this was also the same guy who had cared about her deepest secret, and who was rushing to her aid when even her best friends were against her.

"Hey," Cole said, slightly winded. "Are you all right?"

Leighton's eyes welled up, and she fought off the urge to collapse against him. She shook her head instead.

"Let's go for a ride," he said, his gaze soft and attentive, unlike the Cole she'd known before.

Leighton followed close behind him as he led the way to the parking lot. She observed his gait, noting his straighter posture. When her eyes wandered to his broad shoulders, he stopped and turned around, fishing his keys out of his jeans pocket.

"Here we are." Pointing the key fob at his car, he pressed the button with his thumb to unlock it before he opened the driver side door and got in.

Leighton slid in on the passenger side, shocked by the impeccable state of Cole's Jetta. Not a hint of cigarette smoke or a piece of trash to be found. Cole was never what she expected, she decided, closing the door and shrouding them in darkness. Maybe that was the excitement—his unpredictability and his contradictions.

"Where are we going?" Leighton asked as Cole started the car.

He turned down the music that sprang to life with the engine. "There's this place I want to show you that I found a few weeks ago."

Nodding, she turned to the window, watching the campus disappear. She listened to the melodic, instrumental music that still played quietly. It was the perfect soundtrack for a night drive.

"What is this?" Leighton asked, pointing to the CD player in the dash.

Cole grimaced. "Why, do you hate it?"

"No, quite the opposite actually. It's beautiful. Who is it?"

"Explosions in the Sky," he answered, turning it up a little. "I like music without lyrics. It doesn't force me to think about things I'd rather not think about."

She wanted to ask him what those things were, but she knew she couldn't.

"What are you into?" he asked quickly, as if he could sense her curiosity.

"A lot of different stuff. But right now, mostly Jonah Tyler," Leighton answered.

Cole took a quick glance at her. "Jonah Tyler? Really?"

"What, you don't like him?"

He snickered. "No, he's good...if you like that pretty-boy type."

"Is someone jealous?" she teased.

Cole stifled a sheepish smile. "Maybe, okay? It's just...I can't carry a tune to save my life. And I've tried to learn how to play the guitar. But it turns out I'm much better at *listening* to music than making it."

"Well, I'm sure you're good at other things," Leighton said.

"No. Not really."

"Oh, come on. I doubt that."

He shrugged. "I played sports in high school."

It was yet another filled-in blank that surprised Leighton. He didn't seem like the athletic type, although his physique did suggest otherwise.

"Oh yeah? What did you play?"

"Football mostly," Cole said, keeping his eyes on the road ahead.

"What position?"

"QB."

"Wow," Leighton replied. "I'm sure you were good at it if you were the quarterback."

"Maybe."

His sadness was visible in the soft blue and red glow of the dashboard lights, and Leighton felt that same insatiable need to rescue him from whatever it was that he kept hidden inside. But she feared he might rescind his agreement to their newfound, limited friendship and shut her out completely. She had to be careful not to push too hard.

"You know, I hate to break this to you," Leighton began, after her long, stolen gaze.

Cole took another glance at her, a concerned expression on his shadowed face. "What..."

"You're kind of a pretty boy too. If I'm being honest," she said, a twinge of excitement dancing in her stomach.

His solemn countenance faded away as he laughed. "Well, now you're just trying *way* too hard. Are you heading up some jerk outreach program or something?"

"Jerk outreach? No, I told you I was being honest. All this angst you hide behind doesn't hide the fact that you're pretty, okay?" Leighton's heart was racing. Boldness wasn't usually her strong suit, but at this moment, it came easily.

Cole brought the car to a stop and put it in

park. Unbuckling his seatbelt, he turned to face her. "I mean, I don't see what you're talking about, but…can you say I'm ruggedly handsome or *anything* else instead?"

Leighton pressed her lips together and shook her head. "Nope. I'm sorry. You're just too pretty."

He breathed a heavy sigh. "Why? Do I look like a girl?"

She couldn't keep from giggling. "No, you don't look like a girl at all."

"Then why am I *pretty?*"

Leighton studied his face as he shyly avoided eye contact, and she let all her thoughts pour out as they came to her. "Well, for one, you've got long, dark eyelashes. And your eyes—that blue is beautiful. Then you've got these full lips and perfect teeth. And your hair? It's just *pretty.*"

Cole chuckled bashfully. "Are you finished yet?"

"I was gonna mention your cheek bones, but I guess I won't." She was shocked by her own forthrightness. He seemed to stir a bravery within her.

"Well, anyway, we're here." Cole motioned to the windshield and the scenery beyond it. "Come on. Let's go."

They stepped out of the car into the cool night air, closing the doors behind them. A lake shimmered in the moonlight beyond the parking lot, encircled by picturesque landscaping and a wide sidewalk.

"Wow." Leighton let out a long breath. "I didn't even know this was here."

"I didn't either. But I was driving around one

night to clear my head and I sort of ran into it. It's nice, right?"

She nodded, wandering over to the sidewalk, and Cole fell into step beside her, lighting up a cigarette.

"Do you come here often?" she asked.

"Yeah, actually. I come here to run—sometimes in the middle of the night when I can't sleep. And sometimes I just sit and look at the water. I don't know. I really like it here."

Cole led her to a bench and she sat down beside him, careful not to sit too close.

He exhaled a puff of smoke away from her, then cleared his throat. "For the record, I think you're pretty too. I meant to tell you that."

"What?" Leighton felt her cheeks flush. "Oh. Thanks."

"And I also meant to thank you for your overly generous words," he continued nervously. "But I guess I'm not very good at taking compliments."

Cole looked like the kind of guy who received compliments quite often. But then she remembered his claim of having lost all his friends. And she remembered his current knack for being unapproachable, as if she'd once again forgotten he was that same intimidating, antisocial person she'd nearly grown to despise, and then it all made sense.

"So, where are you from?" Leighton asked, tucking a breeze-blown strand of hair behind her ear.

"Lachlan. It's a really small town about three hours north of here," Cole said, bringing the cigarette to his lips.

"I'm from Winchester, an hour east, and I have never heard of Lachlan," Leighton replied.

"I'm telling you, it's *really* small. It's the kind of town you see on TV, where they all obsess over the high school sports teams because they have nothing else to do. And everyone knows everyone else's business." He rolled his eyes.

"You must have been pretty famous then," Leighton said.

Cole swallowed, his body tensing. "Why do you say that?"

"Because you were the quarterback?"

"Oh. Right."

"Do you have any siblings?" she asked, ignoring his on-edge behavior.

He shook his head. "Nope. Only child."

"Me too!" Leighton remarked. "Do you hate it? I do."

Cole paused briefly, tipping the ashes from his cigarette. "I don't know. I guess it hasn't been too bad."

Leighton let out a long breath. "Well, with your town being so close-knit, you probably had a lot of friends growing up, right?"

Cole shifted his gaze to the lake like he was getting lost in his head for a moment. He took one last drag of his cigarette before dropping it to the ground and stomping it out.

"Yeah. Sure," he finally replied, the last bit of smoke escaping his mouth.

She offered a kind smile. "I like learning about you."

His expression changed, suggesting amusement and surprise. "Well, tell me more about you."

"What would you like to know?" she asked.

Cole tilted his head back and squinted his eyes in concentration. "Let's see. I already know you grew up with Wesley and Quinn. You're from Winchester. You have no siblings. You were never a cheerleader. You had a sucky boyfriend in high school. You're *probably* a psych major, given how invested you are in other people. But you have a questionable taste in music and you apparently like pretty boys."

Leighton laughed at his rundown of recollected facts. "You're right, I am a psych major."

"What made you choose that?"

She took a deep breath. "Long story short, my parents separated for nearly a year when I was fifteen, and if they hadn't finally gone to marriage counseling, I *know* they'd be divorced now. The separation was really hard on me, which is probably why I flocked to Jared so easily. But anyway, it's all kind of left me with a gratitude and a passion for marriage and family counseling. I want to help keep families together."

A half-smile appeared on Cole's lips. "That's very noble of you. What else can you tell me?"

"I don't know. I'm not very exciting."

"Sure you are. Tell me what makes you happy," Cole suggested.

Her bravery crept back in. "Right now, *this*."

A grin spread over Cole's face, igniting a light in his eyes Leighton had never seen before. "You're funny," he said.

"I'm sorry, I'm not usually like this. I don't know what it is, but when I'm around you, I feel like I can say anything." Her face was bright with the thrill of confidence, and it made Cole smile all the more.

"Then do it. Say anything. Right now."

Leighton didn't allow herself to think too much before speaking. "I *really* like you...and I know it's silly because I hardly know you, but I just can't help it."

Cole looked at her, his expression unreadable. He didn't reply.

Afraid she'd gone too far this time, Leighton jumped to her feet and reached for his hand, pulling him up off the bench. "Come on, let's walk."

He chuckled, which relieved her worries, and he followed beside her on the sidewalk that ran along the one-mile perimeter of the lake. They lost count after the third lap. Most of the time was spent in a comfortable silence, accompanied only by the sound of their steady breaths and the rhythm of their shoes on the pavement.

When Leighton had gotten too cold, they ended up in Cole's car with the heat on and seats reclined, listening to James Bay while stargazing through the sunroof overhead.

"Wow. I actually forgot about everything with Wesley and Quinn," Leighton marveled.

"Glad I could help distract you," Cole said.

She sighed. "The thought of facing either one of them still makes me feel like I'm gonna throw up though."

Leighton glanced at the clock. It was nearly

two in the morning. They both had class in just six hours.

"What do you wanna do?" Cole asked, turning his head toward her.

She tilted her head in his direction, immediately flustered by their closeness. "I don't know," she managed. "How about we just start driving and never come back?"

He shot her an incredulous smirk. "So out of *everyone* you know, you'd run away from all your problems, *forever*, with *me*?"

Leighton shrugged against the cloth seat. "You *are* the only person I know who isn't against me."

"Yeah, but they're against you *because* of me."

She cast her eyes to the sunroof, shaking her head. "Whatever. I don't care anymore. I'm so tired of always living to please everyone else, and always worrying what everyone thinks of me. I'm done."

"All right. Road trip, then?" Cole asked playfully.

She broke into a smile. "I wish. But for now, let's just listen to this song."

"Good idea," he said, reaching over to turn up the volume.

seven

"Getting accustomed to a world without color. Oh, and I wonder just where you are now."

LAST SUMMER

C ole didn't care about the stiffness of his black suit or how it trapped the summer heat against his skin. All he could think about were the events that brought him to this pew in this church, where he couldn't bear to lift his head.

In his mind, he replayed the frantic phone call from his father, and he remembered the unintentional relief in his father's voice that *his* son was safe. Cole could still picture the petrified expression on Delaney's face, and the way it contorted as he told her the unfathomable truth. Even now, he could practically feel her fists slamming against his chest in protest and devastation, the way they had that night. Her hysterical wailing still rang in his ears, haunting him.

The raw aching in Cole's chest threatened to tear him apart from the inside out. And he was afraid of what would happen when he saw what was at the front of the church sanctuary. He already hurt so badly; he wasn't sure he could handle much more.

The guilt had already begun wreaking havoc, gnawing at every thread of his existence, fraying every bit of who he'd been. He swore he could feel the glares of blame burning into him from all directions.

And of one thing, he was quickly becoming certain...

If it wasn't for me, Tucker would still be alive.

Cole had to hold his breath and clench his jaw to stifle the sob that rose from somewhere deep within him. He tried not to focus on the heart-wrenching eulogy being delivered by Tucker's younger brother, Gavin. Cole tried not to hear the sniffling and whimpers all around him, tried not to picture Mrs. Lindsley's tear-stained cheeks and puffy red eyes in the front row. He couldn't handle this reality. It felt so wrong and impossible.

As Cole struggled to calm himself, his father's hand gently squeezed his shoulder. Somehow, it lent him a small sliver of strength. He knew he had to be brave. He had to experience every miserable part of this tragedy. He owed it to Tucker to accept the full excruciating weight of it all without softening the blow or hiding from it like a coward. It was all he had left of Tucker now. Cole ran his tongue over the split in his lip, and he decided it was time.

He lifted his eyes first. Flowers. *Lots* of flowers. Two larger-than-life, black and white photos displayed on easels. Tucker's familiar, happy smile. Cole slowly lifted his head. The casket. Shiny dark steel. Closed. Cole's chest tightened, and he felt as if he were suffocating. But he didn't look away. He didn't tune out Gavin's words. He didn't fight the tears. He embraced the grief and it became a part of him, filling all his cracks and creases, and blocking out the light.

eight

Cole yanked the classroom door open, letting Leighton in ahead of him. They evoked Dr. Gibson's most scrutinizing glare as they hurried to the two closest desks. Right behind Wesley and Quinn.

When Dr. Gibson continued with his lecture, Leighton leaned forward. "Hey, Wes," she whispered. "Can I borrow some paper? And a pen?"

He sighed and took a quick glance over his shoulder. "Where's your stuff?"

"Please, just help me?"

Wesley reached into his bag and passed her several sheets of notebook paper and a pen. His eyes met hers only briefly, but Leighton saw the pain in them before he faced forward once again.

Leighton handed a few sheets of paper to Cole. She turned back to Wesley, tapping him gingerly on the shoulder. "I'm so sorry, but...do you have another extra pen? For Cole?"

Wesley lifted his eyes to Cole's in a blank stare before he returned to his bag for another pen. Without looking at Cole, he held it out, and Cole took it, exchanging uneasy glances with Leighton.

Leighton tried to focus, taking sloppy, fragmented notes as Dr. Gibson spoke, but all she could focus on was Wesley—his arms that she now knew the comfort of, his lips that had kissed her only hours before, his heart that lay shattered in pieces because of *her*.

And Quinn hadn't once glanced back at her. She was obviously ignoring Leighton, dragging out their argument into a full-on fight. Had Quinn even cared, deep into the late night, when Leighton still hadn't returned to their room?

When class was over, Quinn left immediately, giving Leighton no chance to confront her. But Wesley lingered.

"Can I talk to you outside? Alone?" he asked her, bitterly eyeing Cole.

Leighton folded her notes and stuffed them in her back pocket. She offered her pen back to Wesley, but he spun around and headed for the door.

"I'll talk to you later?" Leighton said to Cole, a nervousness in her voice.

"It'll be okay," he promised, waving her off.

She nodded, reluctantly leaving Cole to follow after Wesley.

"What is going on, Leighton?" Wesley asked once they were outside.

He looked tired and unusually disheveled. Leighton imagined him in the hours since she'd last seen him. Had he spent the night tossing and turning, unable to sleep after how badly she'd hurt him? Had he cried for her? The images made her feel sick.

"Nothing is going on."

"I'm not stupid," he said. "You're both in the

same clothes from last night. You were late for class *together*, and without any of your stuff. Did you spend the night with him?"

"Come on, Wes."

"Did you?"

A door down the corridor behind Wesley opened, catching Leighton's eye. Cole stepped out of Dr. Gibson's classroom, pausing to offer her a slight smile before he headed in the opposite direction. She found herself longing to run after him, the idea of his presence so surprisingly comforting. But he disappeared around the corner. Leighton felt alone, despite having her best friend standing right before her.

"Yes," she finally said, distracted.

Wesley's complexion paled and he clenched his jaw. "You did? I know we had an argument, but…to go and sleep with him?"

"Wait, *what*? I did not sleep with Cole. Okay, I literally slept alongside him, but that was it."

Wesley looked confused. "What?"

"Nothing happened, Wes. We went for a drive, we took a walk, we listened to music, and we fell asleep. We woke up in his car *ten minutes* before class started, and came straight here. That's all."

Wesley took a deep, relieved breath and let it out, placing a hand over his chest. "Oh, thank God. You scared me for a second."

Leighton tried to fight off her agitation. "How could you think I would do that? You know how I feel about it. I wouldn't just throw it all away on some angry impulse."

He put his hands on his hips and looked to

the ground. "I'm sorry, you're right. I know you better than that. I was just afraid."

"Afraid of what?"

"Of losing you to Cole." Wesley raised his eyes to meet hers, a tender vulnerability radiating from their warmth.

Something inside Leighton sank. "Wesley, I'm not sure I was ever yours to lose."

The look in his eyes changed, and she knew she'd said the wrong thing.

"I'm sorry," she continued. "But I told you I was trying to figure things out. We were just hanging out and seeing what happened, right? All of this is still so new and strange to me. I never planned on anything happening between us."

"And do you think I did? I've waited around for you for *years*, Leighton, hoping you'd finally see me. Do you think I wanted that? Do you think it's been easy to watch you choose complete assholes while I was standing right there in front of you? You never considered *me* as an option. I don't know why I expected you to see me as one now."

Leighton had tears in her eyes. "I'm sorry I never realized how you felt. I never considered the possibility."

"Until you kissed me to piss off Cole," Wesley said.

She breathed a heavy sigh, the shame heavy on her chest. "I am so sorry I did that to you. I honestly thought Cole would turn and leave. And I thought you would pull away, and be all grossed out and annoyed with me."

He crossed his arms over his chest. "No. It was only the moment I've fantasized about for the last four years, that's all. Except it wasn't. And I'm just a pawn in your quasi-vendetta against Cole."

"No, Wesley, please understand. When I kissed you, I finally realized that all of the closeness we've been sharing, and all the warm, happy feelings I get when I'm around you are not just because we're friends. I wasn't lying when I told you I liked you. I do, Wes. I really do."

"Then what's the problem?" he questioned.

She lifted her shoulders in an ashamed shrug. "I don't know how to explain it to you. Because I know it sounds really stupid."

"Try me."

"I just have this strong feeling, like I *have* to be around him. It's like a strange pull that makes no sense, but I can't control it. Believe me, I've tried to forget about him. I wanted to. I thought I could be with you and he would go away."

Wesley grimaced. "So now what? You're going to chase after the one who doesn't want you back?"

"I don't know, okay? I hate this. I hate hurting you." Leighton paused, fighting back her emotions as they pooled in her eyes once again. "I can't lose you. I'm so afraid I will…because I deserve to."

As if melting at the sight of her tears, Wesley opened his arms and drew her into his embrace. "And where would I go?" he asked softly, resting his cheek in her hair.

She clung to him, his mercy tearing her open. How had she forgotten how safe Wesley made her feel?

"I need you, okay?" she said quietly, nestling her head against his chest. "I can't promise you anything. I know it's incredibly selfish and I don't deserve you, but I have to have you in my life."

She heard his lungs deflate beneath her ear in a surrendering sigh. "Well, I'm still here. Just...please be easy on me, okay?"

Leighton squeezed him tighter. "I don't ever want to hurt you."

"It kind of scares me how much power you have to obliterate me," Wesley confessed with a nervous chuckle. "But I know you'd never hurt me on purpose. You have every right to choose Cole. So, if he's what makes you happy, and you think he can take care of you better than I can, you should choose him."

Leighton pulled back to look up at Wesley. "Why would you say that?"

He took her face in his hands. "Because I love you. You shouldn't have to worry about hurting me, and I don't want this to ruin our friendship. I just want you to be happy."

She grasped Wesley's wrists as he leaned down to kiss her on the forehead. He tenderly wiped the tears from her cheeks with his thumbs before removing his hands from her face.

Wesley was the first boy to ever tell her he loved her, and for an instant, Leighton wanted to say it back. Because Wesley was incredible. He was a gentleman. He was witty, wise, and sweet, and she wished her adoration was enough. No one knew her like Wesley did. There was a comfort in his familiarity, and a trusting contentment in his presence—the remedy for all she'd been through in the past. Leighton couldn't help but love him for who he was and how he made her feel, but it wasn't in the way he deserved. She had hoped it could be, but it simply wasn't.

Blinded by her overwhelming emotion, Leighton brushed a soft kiss across his lips.

By the look on Wesley's face, she could tell he knew exactly what the kiss was. It was platonic affection and sentimentality. It was goodbye.

As Leighton bent her head in embarrassment, he placed a hand beneath her chin and gently lifted her face. Wesley pressed his lips to hers, kissing her like it would be the very last time. Maybe he knew that it was. Leighton reciprocated for a moment before pulling away.

"I'm sorry," Wesley whispered, tears brimming in his eyes.

Leighton had never seen Wesley cry before, and the guilt nearly gutted her. "It's okay, Wes."

He cleared his throat and composed himself. "If I ask you something, can you tell me the truth?"

"Of course." She returned her head to his chest, wanting so badly to comfort him.

Wesley rubbed her back lovingly as he held her. "If Cole said he wanted to be with you, right now, would you choose him?"

Leighton couldn't respond to his question. Not because she didn't know the answer, but because she couldn't bear to hurt him.

And in her silence, she knew she'd given Wesley the answer he'd known all along.

When Leighton let herself in to her dorm room, she was startled to see Quinn.

"I thought you had class," Leighton said, her heart racing.

Quinn sat in the chair at the desk and crossed her arms over her chest. "I skipped. You're not the only one who can be reckless."

"I'm not being reckless," Leighton said. "I haven't done anything wrong."

Quinn raised her eyebrows. "Seriously? Do you wanna tell that to my brother?"

Leighton sighed, setting her bag down on the floor. "You know, it wasn't all that long ago that you absolutely *hated* the idea of Wesley and me. If I recall, you said it was the worst thing that could ever happen to you, *and* you would kill me. So why do you suddenly care so much?"

Quinn leaned forward in her chair, her eyes studying the rug as if she'd find the right words etched in its fibers.

"You're right," she began quietly. "I was so mad when I found you two yesterday. I really was. But after seeing you together, it just made sense. And I've never seen my brother so happy."

Guilt-ridden yet again, Leighton looked away. "I know. I honestly have no idea how things happened the way they did."

"You have no idea? You ditched Wes at the festival and ran off with Cole."

Leighton made a face. "That is *not* what happened. Wesley left *me* at the festival. And *Cole* was there for me."

"I thought Cole wanted nothing to do with you."

Leighton shrugged. "He didn't. But I know it's only because there are things from his past—"

"Oh, that sounds *great*," Quinn interrupted.

"It's not like that. I think something really horrible happened to him that he doesn't want anyone to know about. That's why he's been so difficult. He's trying to keep people away."

"That's kinda sad," Quinn admitted. "But how did you end up with him…all night?"

Leighton snickered. "Do you remember how angry you were with me? Do you think I wanted to come up here after that?"

"No. I guess not."

"Wesley was angry, you were angry. Cole was the only person I could call. He took me to his favorite spot, this beautiful lake across town. And we just talked and he made me forget how upset I was."

"He actually cared?" Quinn asked.

"He's much different than you think, trust me. I told him all about Jared, and you should've seen how much it infuriated him. He definitely cared."

Quinn chewed at the inside of her cheek the way she always did when she was battling against her pride. "So, you guys are friends now?"

"We kind of made a deal," Leighton said sheepishly, scratching her head. "We can be friends if I don't get all nosy about his past."

"Are you kidding me?" Quinn laughed. "How can you trust someone like that? Why would you even want to be his friend? And you actually have *feelings* for him? Come on, Leighton."

Leighton clenched her teeth to abate her mounting fury. "I don't expect you to understand. But I do expect you to be my friend and trust me. I made *one* mistake falling for Jared and I haven't heard the end of it. How many losers have *you* dated? And how many guys have you toyed with? I've never held any of it against you because you're my best friend. I'm tired of being treated like this fragile little girl you have to protect and control."

Quinn looked at her with a pained expression. "I'm sorry. I don't mean to be like that. I just wanted you to be—"

"More like you?" Leighton finished. "Well, I'm not like you. You're confident and outspoken, and I'm self-conscious and apparently a pushover. But you know what? When I'm with Cole, I'm different. I don't know what it is, but I feel brave and I speak my mind. I've never been able to do that before."

"That's kind of ironic. The guy who can't open up is teaching you how to."

"Yeah, I guess so. And for some reason, I think he needs me."

Quinn thought for a moment. "Fine. As your best friend, I will respect your choices and I will *really* try to stay open-minded."

Leighton released a long, relieved breath. "Good, because I really don't want to fight with you.

Wesley and I are okay now, and I want us to be okay, too."

Quinn stood and approached her. "I'm sorry I come across the wrong way sometimes. I guess when I think I'm helping you, I'm actually just being pushy and annoying."

Leighton smiled. "Well, yeah. Kind of."

Quinn let out a chuckle. "I'm glad we can be honest with each other. We should probably do that more often." She reached out to Leighton. "Truce?"

Leighton accepted her hug. "Truce."

COLE

As the pink clouds faded into dusty evening ash, Cole sauntered down the sidewalk toward the café, and he tried not to wonder where Leighton was.

It had been so long since he'd enjoyed the company of another person, and despite his resistance, he'd enjoyed hers. Leighton was kind when he didn't deserve it, and for some reason, she trusted him and found solace in his presence. As great as that felt, Cole feared it, dreaded it.

When Cole came up on the cafeteria, the door opened and Wesley stepped out, holding it open for Quinn and then Leighton. Cole considered speeding off in the opposite direction, but Leighton caught sight of him before he could act on it.

"Cole, hey!" Her smile was bright and joyful as she waved him down.

"Oh, hey," he breathed, pretending he'd just now noticed the three of them.

Quinn gave him a thin smile. "Study date. Later, guys." And then she was gone.

Wesley stood awkwardly between Cole and Leighton, looking almost pale. And he did what Cole least expected. "Hey, so…I'm sorry about last night. And I wanted to thank you for being there for Leighton."

Cole shook his head. "No. I'm sorry I got in the way."

"It was too good to be true anyway," Wesley said quietly, looking down at the concrete. "Hey, ya know what? I'm gonna go."

"Wes, you don't have to," Leighton said, her voice sad.

Cole hated himself for causing the rift between them.

"No, I do. But it's fine." Wesley took a few steps backward and turned away.

"I'm really sorry about all of that," Cole said, slipping his hands into his pockets.

"It's okay, it's my fault, not yours."

"So, I guess it went all right earlier, taking to Wesley and Quinn?"

Leighton shrugged. "It went much better than I thought. Things are mostly back to normal."

"Good," Cole said warmly. "I told you it would be okay."

She smiled, like all of her doubt had faded. "What are you doing right now?"

"I was just going to grab a coffee. You wanna come with me?" he asked.

Her smile widened. "Sure."

At the café, Cole insisted on paying for Leighton's latte. Then, taking advantage of the beautiful night, they decided to take a walk.

"How big of a heart attack was this morning?" Leighton asked as they strolled aimlessly down the sidewalk.

Cole snickered. "Yeah. That sucked. I can't believe we fell asleep."

"Well, I guess I can add 'sleeping in a car' to my list of college experiences," she said.

"Hanging out with me is real exciting, huh?"

Leighton smiled. "Actually, I had a really good time."

"I did too," Cole said. He opened his mouth to say more, then realized he'd already said too much.

"You know, I hate to be a pain about this," Leighton began timidly, "but we really need to finish our psych project. We only have two more weeks till it's due."

"That's plenty of time."

"But we still have to find someone for our interview. How do we do that? We can't just walk up to random people and ask them if they've ever dealt with depression and suicide. Do *you* know anyone we can interview?" Leighton asked, stress in her voice.

Before Cole could reply, his phone buzzed in his pocket. He retrieved it, gawking at the number on the screen. "Hold on a sec," he said to Leighton, putting the phone to his ear. "Hello?"

He watched Leighton walk to a nearby bench, carefully sipping her drink.

"Cole?"

"Yeah. Who's this?" He wasn't sure why he asked; he already knew.

"Oh, my gosh. It's so good to hear your voice."

Her overplayed sentiments made him feel nauseated. "How did you get this number, Ava?"

"I'm so sorry it's been so long. Are you doing okay?"

He clenched his jaw. "Are you kidding?"

"I know I should've called you months ago, but I didn't know what to say after I heard what happened."

"You haven't spoken to me in *eleven* months. Suddenly you care?"

Ava sighed into the phone. "Of course I do. I've been so worried about you. And I really miss you."

"What happened to Josh?"

"We broke up six months ago. It just wasn't right."

"Ah, you finally realized. Thanks for that one, by the way. It really helped make everything *so* much better," he retorted.

"Cole, please don't be like this."

"What did you expect? You dumped me over a year ago. You helped all my friends betray me. Did you think I was sitting around missing you?"

"I made a mistake. Things were really bad and I was confused," Ava said with a whimper.

Cole lowered the phone and, for a second, he considered hanging up before he returned it to his ear. "No. Don't make excuses for turning your back on me at the worst time in my life. I faced it all without you then. I sure as hell don't need you now."

She sniffled. "I'm sorry."

"It's too late, Ava."

"Please, Cole. Just let me make it up to you."

He snickered. "Why, so you can make yourself feel better? Don't pretend that this is about me. You don't give a shit about me. I bet you never did."

"No, you're wrong," she cried. "I loved you."

"Yeah. *Loved*. Past tense. Goodbye, Ava. Please don't call me again."

Cole ended the call and shoved his phone back into his pocket. His hands were shaking so much that he couldn't hold onto his coffee. It splattered on the pavement.

Leighton was there immediately, placing her hands on his chest. "Cole, are you okay?"

He shut his eyes and sucked in deep breaths, trying to calm down.

The warmth of Leighton's hands radiated through the cotton of his shirt. Cole swallowed as the fear crept back in, and he slowly backed away from her.

nine.

"I was a body in a sea of flowers, still walking in a hole.
Are you gonna ease my buried heart?"

Cole sat on the edge of Ava's bed as she sat at her computer, her back to him. He stared blindly at her shelf crowded with trophies.

"Should I just go home?"

Ava slowly spun her chair to face him. Her expression held no apologies. With a sigh, she crossed the space between them and sat beside him. Cole folded against her like a needy child. He ached for her comfort; he needed her to take the pain away.

When Cole brushed his lips against the space beneath her ear, Ava pulled away.

"What? What's wrong?" he asked, reaching for her hand.

Ava dodged his touch and stood, crossing her arms tightly over her chest.

"Ava, what are you doing?"

"I can't do this anymore, Cole."

His breathing quickened. "You can't do what?"

"I can't be with you after what you did."

Cole felt his lip begin to quiver. "I'm so sorry about Delaney. I don't know what else to tell you. I don't have feelings for her. I love *you*. You *know* that."

Ava ran a hand through her dark hair. "Cole..."

"God, Ava, you don't know how badly I wish that I could take it back."

"Because then Tucker would still be alive," she added, her cold voice breaking what was left of him.

Cole stared at her. "How could you say that to me?" he asked in a cracked whisper.

"I know you think it's your fault, and I'm sorry you have to carry that burden, but I can't pretend that I don't think you deserve it."

He swallowed hard, pressing the heel of his hand to his forehead. "Does everyone blame me?"

Ava shrugged in reply.

Cole chewed his lip, not bothering to hide the tears that soaked his cheeks. "If you, of all people, are against me, then I'm sure I've got no one."

Ava didn't try to assure him otherwise. "I'm sorry, Cole."

"So that's really it?" he said in one more desperate attempt. "You're just gonna leave me when I need you more than ever? I am not okay right now, Ava. And this does *not* help."

Ava wiped at the mascara-stained streams running down her face, and looked away. "I think you should go."

Cole didn't argue. He slipped silently out the door, more dead inside than he was when he'd arrived.

Ten

"**I** know I'm not supposed to pry, but can you at least tell me if you're all right?" Leighton asked.

Cole wanted to tell her all of the ugly thoughts that were plaguing him, but he liked being the person Leighton thought he was. He couldn't bring himself to ruin the way she looked at him. Turning away from her, he began walking toward the green, knowing full well she'd follow, but he didn't know what else to do.

Cole slowed his pace when he reached the green, hearing Leighton's footfalls in the grass behind him. He stopped and clasped his hands on top of his head, tilting it back to gaze into the darkness above them. Leighton rounded Cole and stood before him, hesitating for barely a second before she wrapped her arms tightly around him.

Cole froze, tensing in her embrace. But it didn't take long to feel the comfort it offered him. He unclasped his hands and slowly lowered his arms, closing them gingerly around Leighton. She didn't say a word; she just let him cling to her. Cole couldn't believe how incredible it felt to be held, and by someone who cared about him the way Leighton seemed to. It soothed an aching in him ever so slightly.

"Ava is my ex-girlfriend," Cole said quietly.

"I kind of put that together. It sounds like she really hurt you."

He didn't let go of Leighton. "It really hurt. *All* of it. It hurts so bad; I don't know how to make it stop." He choked back a sob that caught in his throat.

Leighton stepped back from him, her gaze soft and kind. She demanded nothing from him—no answers, no explanations. Her silent support meant more to him than any sentiment ever could, and he wondered what he'd done to deserve her unwavering kindness.

"Why do you care about me?" he asked, a sadness in his eyes.

Leighton shrugged. "I get the feeling you need someone to care. And honestly, I can't help myself."

He managed a thin smile. "Thank you."

Worn out from his emotions, Cole took a few steps and sat down in the grass. Leighton waited until he motioned an invitation to her before she joined him.

After a moment of quiet, Cole finally spoke. "You can interview me for our psych project."

She turned to him with a furrowed brow. "What?"

He kept his eyes fixed on the grass before him. "We need someone who's dealt with depression and suicide, right?"

"Yeah…"

Cole took a deep, quivering breath and forced himself to speak the impossible words. "Seven and a half months ago, I tried to kill myself."

Leighton gaped at him. "Cole…what happened?"

"Um…I broke into my dad's safe and found his gun." He straightened his thumb and first two fingers into the shape of a gun and pointed it at his temple, pulling an imaginary trigger. Because it was easier to show her than to say it. "But it wasn't loaded. And my mom caught me before I could get the bullets in."

Leighton pressed her lips together. "Oh, my God," she whispered, putting her hand over her mouth. "If it *had* been loaded…if your mom hadn't been there…you wouldn't be here."

"You're right, I wouldn't be," Cole said dryly.

Leighton squinted at him like she was trying to read behind the meaning of his words. "You don't still wish you weren't…do you?"

He shrugged, hanging his head in shame. "I don't know. Sometimes. But not when I'm with you."

"Then can I stay with you all the time?" she asked, her quivering lips curving into a flimsy smile.

Cole let out a long sigh. "Leighton, I promise I won't try anything again. But I can't promise I won't want to. I'm sorry."

"Please don't apologize. You have nothing to be sorry for."

"I wish that was true," he muttered. He looked out over the green, drifting into his loud thoughts. And they shared the silence together for what felt like forever.

Leighton tried to imagine how hopeless and profoundly unhappy Cole must have felt when he'd tried to take his own life. She pictured him raising a gun to his beautiful head and choosing death as a better option. What had he been running from? What had made his life no longer worth living? She knew this confession was not Cole's deep, dark secret. Whatever had made him want to die was.

"I'm so sorry you've had to face that," Leighton said, her trembling voice breaking their long quiet. She couldn't ask him anything more. She was lucky he'd given her this much.

Cole sighed. "Please don't be upset. I don't want you to feel bad about *my* issues."

Leighton nodded in reply because she couldn't quite speak. She couldn't explain exactly why it shook her so severely. Maybe she felt more deeply for Cole than she'd ever thought possible.

She leaned into him, burying her face in his chest, and she didn't care if she should, or if he wanted her to. But he wrapped his arms around her, resting his chin on her head.

"I'm so glad you're still here," Leighton barely whispered against his chest, the sound of his beating heart beneath her ear.

Cole held her a little tighter, his breaths shaky. Leighton wasn't entirely sure, but she thought she felt his lips brush against her hair, kissing her ever so softly.

eleven

Leighton sat across from Cole in a quiet, upstairs corner of the library as they studied for their psychology test.

She looked up from her textbook, her eyes meeting his. "What?" she asked self-consciously.

"What's wrong? You seem sad."

She breathed a soft sigh. "I'm sorry. I just…I can't stop thinking about what you told me last night."

"Please don't worry about it. I'm still—" He stopped himself, casting his eyes to the book on the table before him.

"Still what?" Leighton prodded.

"I was *going* to say I'm still the same person. But you don't really know who that is. So there isn't much comfort in that, I guess."

"I do know you, Cole," she countered.

"Barely," he said. "Which is a good thing."

"Stop saying that. It isn't true."

"Leighton. You have no idea what you're talking about."

"Sure I do. What you've done in the past is not who you are. You're the guy who pretended not to care, but walked me to my dorm to make sure I was safe. The guy who gave Wesley a place to stay and looked out for him. The guy who cared about my deepest hurt, who came to my rescue the second I called, who helped me forget all the reasons I was sad. *That's* who you are, Cole. As much as you try to hide from me, I still see you."

He stared at her for a moment, and Leighton could feel him nervously bouncing his knee under the table. "I have to go," he said, standing up.

"Where are you going?"

"Smoke break."

Leighton grabbed his wrist. "Please stay. You promised you wouldn't run away from me anymore."

Cole huffed before he sat back down, letting his hair fall into his face. "Can we just get the interview over with so you can forget about last night?"

"I can't just forget something like that. You underestimate how much I care for you," Leighton said, her Cole-induced bravery returning.

One corner of his mouth curved slightly. "Okay, ask me the questions. Before I change my mind."

And she did. The questions started out simple. Cole's answers didn't differ much from what he'd already told her the previous night, but still, Leighton felt the shock and the horror as if she was hearing it for the first time. He went into slightly greater detail, but he described the event robotically, like he'd relayed it countless times before to therapists or doctors. It was as though he'd found a way to separate himself just enough to avoid the emotions it evoked.

"What happened after that?" Leighton asked.

"After my epic failure, you mean? My parents arranged for me to stay at a mental health facility for a week. I kind of freaked out when they told me I had to go. It probably didn't help my case much, trying to prove I was sane, but at the time, I felt like I was being punished for being in pain." Cole hung his head like he was reverting back to those raw moments.

"What was the facility like?" Leighton asked. She wished she could ask about the pain that had led him there, but she knew he didn't want her to.

"It wasn't fun. I had a roommate who was there for the same reason I was. He was pretty unstable, worse off than me. After lights out, he would tell me all these ideas he had of how he was going to try again when he got out. In the long run, it was probably the best place for me, but it was the longest week of my life."

Leighton tried to imagine such an environment and it made her hurt for Cole and others like him who'd reached such a low point. "What did you do while you were there?"

"Each day, I had group therapy sessions with other kids who were either suicidal or had attempted suicide. I hated having to talk in front of strangers about something so personal. But then again, I hated the private therapy sessions. I didn't mind the activities though. They really do let you paint and watch movies and stuff like they show on TV. I also read a lot. So it wasn't all bad. The food sucked though. And I constantly got in trouble for not eating."

"They cared if you ate?" Leighton asked.

"Well, they kind of equate your desire to eat with your will to live. I was already fifteen pounds underweight at the time, so they were a bit concerned," Cole explained.

"You look healthy now."

He glanced down at himself and shrugged. "I am. It's a struggle, forcing yourself to eat when you've been sick to your stomach for thirteen months straight, but I've gained most of the weight back. And I've been running and working out to rebuild the muscle tone I had before I quit football. But of course, my mom still calls me every day to make sure I'm taking care of myself."

"How did day-to-day life change after the incident?"

Cole's mouth curved into an amused smirk. "The *incident?*"

"That's what it says on the paper. I'm sorry. Is that bad?"

He shook his head. "No, it's fine. But you can say 'suicide attempt.' That's what it was. No point in sugar-coating it," Cole said in a calm and causal tone.

"Fine then. How did day-to-day life change after the suicide attempt?" Leighton asked, trying not to let the words affect her.

"There ya go...I was prescribed an anti-depressant—which is also for anxiety—and I have to see a therapist once a week. That was the only way my parents would let me go away for college."

"So you must be doing better then?" She didn't ask out of curiosity or because it was on the question sheet, but to satiate her own worry.

"Yeah, I think so. Getting away from home

and being somewhere new where I can start over has helped me a lot," Cole said.

"Good. I'm glad." Leighton scribbled down some notes. "How has everything affected your family?"

Cole grimaced. "My parents haven't taken it well. They removed everything from the house they thought I could hurt myself with. We used plastic knives for months. My mom got pretty paranoid. Some nights, after I first came home from treatment, she would sit in my room and watch me sleep because she was scared something would happen to me. My dad hovered a lot, giving me way too much attention. I think he felt guilty that he hadn't known how bad things had gotten for me, that maybe he'd been too busy to notice. I think they both feel that way. I wish they didn't though. It's not their fault."

"Well, it sounds like they really love you," Leighton said.

He nodded. "I know they do. I was angry with them at first, but I know they were only doing what was best for me. I still feel bad for putting them through all of that. I wasn't really thinking about the consequences. I just wanted it all to go away."

"You wanted what to go away?"

Cole pressed his lips together and leaned back in his chair. "That's not one of the questions."

Leighton slid the sheet across the table and pointed with her pen. "Well, what about this one? 'What experiences, if any, led you to your decision?'"

"My decision to have *an incident*?" Cole asked.

Leighton sighed. "Cole, I'm serious."

He crossed his arms over his chest. "That's a

pretty evasive question."

"I'm sure Dr. Gibson intended these questions for someone who actually wanted to share their story," she said.

Cole made a face like he was considering the truth of her statement. "I'm not interested in sharing *my story*. I only wanted to help us finish our project."

"Fine. I respect that."

"But just so you know," he added, leaning forward once again. "I didn't try to kill myself because of Ava. I don't want you to think that."

"I don't."

"Good," Cole said. "She is definitely not worth my life."

Leighton wanted so badly to ask what *had* been worth his life. What happened to him that took away all of his hope? She feared she may never find out.

"I know this isn't fair to you," Cole continued, as if he could read her thoughts. "I wish I could tell you everything. But I'm not ready to lose this." He motioned to the space between them.

"This?" Leighton's heart was pounding. "And what is *this*, exactly?"

Cole looked away again and chuckled sheepishly. "Well, it's not nothing, right? If we're being honest."

She swallowed. "I don't think it's ever been nothing. I can't explain it; it's never made sense to me why I'm so drawn to you. Since we're being honest."

A grin slowly lit up Cole's face, and he inched his hand across the table to brush ever so slightly against hers. "I know there are things I can't tell you, and I'm sorry, but I can tell you this—being with you at the lake the other night was the first time I've felt happy in over a year. I can't explain it either, but...I need to be around you."

Leighton's eyes stung with a strong sense of honor. After all of the unspeakable, horrible things he'd been through, how could he need *her*?

"I'm okay with that," she managed, the butterflies flitting wildly in her stomach.

"Holy crap, I've been waiting forever. Are you sure you were only studying?" Quinn complained, rolling off her bed as Leighton closed their door.

Leighton certainly couldn't tell Quinn she'd been interviewing Cole. "I'm sorry, I didn't know you were waiting on me. What's up?"

Quinn bounced excitedly toward her. "I scored us an invite to Sterling Curtis's party tonight!"

"Sterling Curtis? He sounds important. Who is he?"

Quinn gawked at her. "Seriously? He's a crazy-popular senior who lives off campus. He throws kick-ass parties. And not just anyone gets invited."

"So how did *we* get invited?" Leighton asked.

"Wesley."

"What? How?"

"Wesley's going on a date with Sterling's little sister tonight. You know Kennedy from our psych class," Quinn said.

Leighton curled her upper lip in disapproval. "Wesley and *Kennedy Curtis*?"

Quinn snickered. "What, are you jealous?"

Leighton hesitated, sifting through the barrage of emotions that ambushed her. *Was* she jealous? "No," she decided. "I'm not jealous. I just don't think Kennedy is right for him."

"Oh, I *know* she isn't," Quinn agreed with a chuckle. "She uses fake words like amazeballs and presh. Trust me, Wes will be writhing in agony by the end of the night."

Leighton smiled at the thought of Wesley's endearing intellect, and for a fleeting moment she missed him the way she didn't want to.

"So this party..." Leighton said, forcing Wesley out of her mind. "Can I invite Cole?"

COLE

Cole could already hear the music when he got out of his car down the street from Sterling Curtis's house. He knew it was a bad idea to accept Leighton's invitation, but the truth was, he didn't care. He wanted to go and he wanted to see her. And he hadn't wanted anything in a long time.

As Cole reached Sterling's driveway, a sick feeling came over him. He didn't want to think about it, but the memories flooded his mind, forcing him to relive things he'd prayed to forget. He swallowed, pushing through the anxiety, and trudged up the brick walkway to the front door.

The music inside was so loud, Cole knew

knocking would be pointless and he let himself in. He could feel the bass in his chest, competing with his pounding heart, as he searched through countless unfamiliar faces in the shadows of the dim rooms. When he saw her, he was surprised how it made him smile.

"Cole!" Leighton's voice barely carried over the music.

Suddenly, she was before him, throwing her arms around him.

"I can't believe you came!" she said, nearly shouting into his ear. She had a hazy countenance that indicated she'd been drinking.

"Where's Quinn?" Cole asked.

Leighton shrugged. "Do you want a beer?"

He shook his head. "I don't drink."

"But you smoke?"

"What?"

"Nothing."

Cole took her by the hand and led her through the clusters of people to a quieter room across the house. "You haven't taken drinks from people you don't know, right?" he asked.

Leighton grinned. "Aw, you're looking out for me."

"Well, yeah."

She placed her hands on his chest. "Don't worry, I haven't been roofied or anything. I just did too many shots with Quinn. I don't know why, because I *hate* tequila."

Cole flashed a half-smile. "As long as you're having fun, right?"

Leighton slid her hands to his waist. "Well, I

wasn't really. But I am now."

He bashfully avoided her doe-eyed gaze. He wondered how inebriation would magnify the boldness she developed in his presence, and it both thrilled and terrified him.

"Do you wanna dance?" Leighton asked as the song changed and the tempo slowed.

"Uh, I don't dance."

She withdrew her hands from him and placed them on her hips. "Okay, so you don't drink and you don't dance. Why are you even here?"

Cole was taken aback by her question. He knew full well he wasn't there for the party, but it probably wasn't fair to let her know that his reason was standing right before him in all her adorable frustration.

"Come here," he caved, opening his arms to her.

Leighton eyed him skeptically for a brief moment before she all too eagerly fulfilled his request. Draping her arms around his neck, she drew close, her body flush with his. Cole slipped his arms gingerly around her, holding her against him. They began moving slowly with the music, swaying gently together.

Cole hadn't danced with anyone since he'd taken Ava to their junior prom. Though he was nervous, it felt so natural to dance with Leighton. His steps were thoughtless, his motions effortless, as he held her. He felt so soothed, as if there were some sort of healing power in their contact.

"I thought you said you don't dance," Leighton said.

"It's just been a while, that's all."

"Do I make you nervous?" she asked, looking up at him with a sly grin.

He breathed a small chuckle. "Yes."

Leighton's grin turned sheepish, her bravery faltering for a moment. "You think *you're* the one who's nervous? I'm a wreck whenever I'm near you."

Cole looked into her eyes, finding her confession unbelievable. "You hide it well."

"And you hide *everything* well."

He sighed, hating that he couldn't offer her the honesty she deserved.

"I shouldn't make you nervous. You have nothing to be afraid of," Leighton said, nuzzling his collar bone. She stretched her short frame to reach the space where his neck met his shoulder, and she softly brushed her lips against his skin.

A chill ran through Cole's body as her kisses left a tingling trail on his neck. He bent his head down and nestled his cheek against hers.

"Leighton, please. I can't do this now."

She pulled away. "Then when?" she asked, her eyes pleading. "Are you *ever* going to stop shutting me out? Because I don't know how much longer I can stand waiting for you to let me in."

He studied the desperation on her face. "I don't know how."

Leighton cupped Cole's face in her hands. "All you have to do is trust me."

He closed his eyes and tilted his forehead against hers. "I do."

"Then what's the problem, Cole?" she asked, caressing his cheeks with her thumbs.

Her affectionate touch began to unravel him, and he tried to take a step back but she didn't let him.

"Please, Cole." Leighton tenderly brushed his hair away from his face with her fingertips. "I won't hurt you."

"Yeah, but I'll hurt *you. That's* the problem, Leighton."

She dropped her arms to her sides, her haziness gone as if her buzz had rapidly dissipated. "I don't care what you say, you are not some monster or whatever it is you think you are. I refuse to believe that there's anything you could tell me that could change the way I feel about you."

Cole clenched his jaw as he watched her eyes well up. "I promise you there is."

He turned away from her and headed for the door, knowing she'd follow. He made it to the bottom of Sterling's driveway before he stopped to face her again.

"Don't walk away from me. It kills me when you do that." Her voice was quiet and strained, and she seemed more afraid than brave.

"I'm sorry," Cole said, pained by her honesty. "I don't mean to upset you."

"That's just it, Cole. You insist you're protecting me, but you're not. I guess you really meant it when you said you would hurt me."

All of the strength that had kept him from shutting down was knocked out of him right then. He thought he could save Leighton from the heartache of learning who he was, but sparing her from the truth was breaking her heart just the same.

Leighton took a few cautious steps toward him. "I don't want your past; I only want *you*. Don't you see that? I like you *so* much, Cole. And I know you like me. Please stop punishing yourself. Because you're punishing me too and I can't take it anymore."

The words had barely escaped Leighton's lips before Cole shot forward and kissed her, nearly knocking her off her feet. She threaded her fingers through his hair, her mouth moving eagerly with his. When Cole released her, she stared breathlessly at him, her eyes wide with shock.

"Is this...happening?" she managed to ask.

He gave a slight surrendering shrug. "I still can't promise I won't hurt you. Because when you find out what I've done..." Cole paused when his voice began to shake, then offered a flimsy, embarrassed smile when a tear escaped down his cheek. "Are you sure you want this?"

Leighton threw her arms around him. "Yes," she said with resounding certainty.

"Please be patient with me," he whispered, choking back the gratitude that threatened to undo him.

Cole gently guided her head to his chest. The feel of her against him cast out his unease, replacing it with a deepening awe and affection for Leighton and her faithful persistence. Despite his elaborate efforts, he hadn't been able to keep her away. He smiled to himself.

"You were right, I couldn't stop you," Cole said.

Leighton leaned back and looked at him. "What do you mean?"

"You know those walls you were so insistent on tearing down? Well, lucky for you, it turns out they were made of paper. I never stood a chance."

Twelve

"Hey, Leighton."

Startled, Leighton lifted her head to discover Wesley's bright smile. How long had she been staring at the table, immersed in her daydream, before Wesley had arrived at the café?

"Hey, Wes," she said as he filled the seat across from her. "I wasn't sure you'd come."

A glimmer of surprise crossed over his face. "It's Saturday morning. This is what we do on Saturday mornings."

"Well, yeah, but I don't really deserve to enjoy our weekly tradition anymore. Especially after I desecrated it with the whole kiss debacle," Leighton said, slouching in her chair.

Wesley grinned, and she knew she'd amused him with her word choices. "I know. But we don't need to talk about that anymore. It's behind us, we're friends, it's okay."

Leighton peered quizzically at him. "Does that mean your date with Kennedy went well?"

He let out a laugh. "God, no."

Leighton cocked an eyebrow, mentally scolding her relief. She had no right to oppose any of

Wesley's romantic endeavors.

"So, what happened?" she asked.

"We're just too different." He shut his mouth as if he were holding back a flood of crueler truths.

"How so?"

Wesley sighed. "Well, for starters, she's the cheerleader type and, as you know, I'm more the closet geek. I'm not exaggerating when I say she took a *selfie*—her word, not mine—every five minutes. She texted during the entire date, probably complaining about me to her friends. And she hates to read. *Hates* to read. That there was reason enough until…"

Intrigued, Leighton leaned forward, resting her elbows on the table. "Until what?"

He shook his head in shame. "She called me totes adorbs, like, four times. It was awful."

Leighton burst out laughing, attracting the attention of several people around the café. She composed herself and cleared her throat. "Sorry. It's not funny."

Wesley shrugged. "No, it is. I wish you could've been there to see it all, actually. I spent half the date wondering if you and Quinn had put Kennedy up to it to play a joke on me." He paused and his eyes widened. "Wow, that sounds so mean. I am terrible."

"You're not terrible. You just know what you want. It might take a few bad dates, but you'll find her."

Chewing his bottom lip, he looked away. "But she can't be you, can she?"

Leighton frowned. "Wesley…"

"I know. I'm sorry."

She dropped her gaze to the table. "I feel so bad already. I probably deserve to feel worse."

Wesley grimaced. "It's not your fault that we don't want the same thing."

"Wes...I need to tell you something."

Apprehension immediately creased his forehead. "Okay."

"It's just that...I don't want to keep anything from you. And I think it would be better if you heard it from me. Because I wouldn't want you to think I was hiding it from you or sneaking around behind your back."

Wesley breathed a sharp sigh. "Leighton, just tell me."

"Things are starting to happen...between Cole and me," she said carefully, afraid of how it would hurt him.

There was no indication of shock, but a flash of pain flickered over his handsome face. "Wow, he sure gave in quickly," Wesley said with a snicker.

"What?"

"Nothing. I have to go." He stood and pushed his chair in. It made a sudden, loud screech that turned more heads.

"No, Wes, wait." Leighton jumped up from her seat. "Please talk to me."

Wesley avoided her eyes. "It's stupid."

She placed a hand on his arm. "Nothing you have to say is stupid. Just tell me."

"Cole told me he wouldn't pursue you, that I didn't have to worry about him. And for some reason, I was dumb enough to believe it." He paused, scratching at his head. "You know what? I don't blame him. Who in their right mind could ever deny you?"

Leighton cast her gaze to the floor, feeling like her chest was being pried open. She couldn't bear to look at him.

"I shouldn't say those things to you, and I'm sorry," he continued. "I appreciate your honesty, letting me know about you and Cole. But I don't want you to feel like you have to protect me."

Tears crept into the corners of her eyes. "Wesley, I'm sorry. I am so scared of hurting you. I hate it so much."

He lifted a shoulder. "I know. But, oh well, right?"

"No. Wes...what happens now?"

"I go back to being your best friend's brother, and you can do whatever you'd like."

Leighton let the tears fall. "Please don't do that. Don't act like you don't mean anything to me. Because you know that's not true. You're my—"

"Don't say it. Please don't tell me I'm your best friend." Wesley's golden eyes were pleading. "I know you mean it in the best way possible, but it does not make me feel better."

"Fine, I won't," she said. "But if you *really* don't want me to be with Cole, then just say it."

Wesley's jaw tightened. "I, of all people, know this sucks, Leighton. But listen..." He softly touched her cheek with his fingertips. "I want you to have what *you* want. And if I'm being honest, I always knew that was Cole. I was just the untimely bout of confusion that distracted you. But I can't be selfish and force you to feel something that isn't really there. Please don't let my feelings for you hold you back. I would hate that more than I hate this."

Leighton squeezed her lips closed, trying to abate her emotions. "Okay," she whispered.

With one last stroke of her cheek, Wesley walked away.

How could it hurt this badly to get what she'd been wanting?

While Cole scribbled out every attempt to answer the final questions of their psychology project, Leighton stared blindly past him at a group of guys playing a game of pool across the student lounge.

"Everything okay?" Cole asked.

His voice snapped her out of her daze. "This is still happening, right?"

He looked at her with a concerned expression on his face, and Leighton nervously continued before he could respond, "It's just, after last night and everything...I'm *so* afraid you're going to pretend like it never happened."

Cole reached across the table to cover her hand with his. "I wouldn't do that."

She gave him a shy smile. "Okay, good. And I'm sorry. I don't mean to be crazy."

He chuckled. "It's okay. I don't blame you for not trusting me. But you have nothing to worry about."

Cole pulled his hand back when his phone began to ring in his pocket, and he quickly retrieved it. "It's my mom. I'll be right back, okay?"

Leighton nodded, and Cole got up, answering

the call as he walked out the door.

She let out a content sigh, returning her attention to her notebook and her own set of final questions. Her eyes wandered to Cole's and his scribbled out words. That same dangerous curiosity infected her senses.

Leighton knew better, but she couldn't stop herself. She slid Cole's notebook toward her, rotating it to glimpse his attempted answers. She couldn't make out any of the words he'd scratched out. With her thirst left unquenched, she thumbed through the notebook, flipping through pages of class notes until something caught her eye.

The heading indicated it was an English class assignment—a poem—simply titled *L*. Leighton's heart thumped so loudly in her ears, she didn't hear Cole coming up behind her.

"What are you doing?"

Leighton spun around to see Cole looming over her, his countenance reminding her of his former, colder self.

"I just wanted to see—"

"You promised you wouldn't pry into my life." He rounded the table to his chair, but he didn't sit down. He snatched his notebook up and stuffed it into his bag.

"Cole, I'm really sorry."

"I don't think I can do this." He slung the bag's strap across his chest and hurried off toward the door.

Leighton followed him outside, cursing her whims. "Cole! Can you please stop and talk to me?"

Cole spun around to face her, but he wasn't

angry. He looked afraid, letting his hair fall into his face as he retreated into himself. Frantically, he began to pat all of his pockets like he was looking for something, and then he stopped, groaning.

"What's the matter?" Leighton asked.

He spoke as if he were thinking out loud. "My cigarettes. I forgot I threw them out. I could really use one right now."

"You threw them out?"

Cole stepped past her to plop down on a bench. Hunching over with his elbows on his knees, he held his head in his hands. Leighton cautiously sat down, leaving ample space between them.

"Cole?" He didn't answer.

Leighton slid off the bench to crouch before him. With gentle fingers, she swept his hair out of his face, unveiling the sadness in his eyes as they met hers.

"I'm sorry," she whispered, pining to understand what made him so fragile.

"This is already so difficult for me. You said I could trust you, but this doesn't make me feel like I can."

"I know. It was stupid of me. But you *can* trust me, I promise you."

Cole crumbled beneath the touch of her hands on his face, and he pressed his forehead to hers. "It's about you," he muttered.

"What?"

"That poem." Cole took her hand, guiding her to sit beside him. "I wanted to tell you about it, but I was too embarrassed."

Leighton bit her lip. "I'm sorry I snooped. I

don't know what I was thinking."

"I do. Your emotionally unstable boyfriend is constantly holding back from you, forcing you to grasp for answers anywhere you can get them. I don't blame you, and honestly, I don't know why you put up with me."

She gawked at him, reminding herself to breathe. "What did you call yourself?"

"Emotionally unstable."

"Not that."

Cole cracked a slight smile and blushed. "Your boyfriend? It's too soon, I'm sorry."

Leighton grinned, tilting her head to rest on his shoulder. "No, it's not. I mean, some would probably say so, but I don't mind."

The cool autumn breeze of the fading afternoon filled their silence until Cole reached into his bag beside him.

"Here." He offered her his notebook. "You can read it."

Leighton straightened and took it from him. "Are you sure?"

He shifted his eyes upward, as if reassessing his thoughts. "Actually...I'd rather not be here when you read it."

Cole stood and grabbed his bag. "I'm just gonna take a walk. Find me when you're done, okay?"

"Okay."

He began to turn away, then stopped. "I'm not a poet or anything. So, please keep an open mind?"

Leighton chuckled. "Don't worry, I'm just

happy to read it."

"But please don't be disappointed if it sucks."

"Would you just get out of here already?" She laughed, shooing him away with her hand.

Cole shot her a grin before he finally walked off, leaving her alone.

Leighton eagerly opened the notebook and paged through to the poem. Taking a deep breath, she began to read his words, unprepared for the way they would affect her.

> She appeared out of nowhere, awakening me with her kindness;
> When all her light shines through my jagged cracks, I almost forget the darkness.
> She slaughters my demons with her simple presence, dulling the ache of the past;
> I can't bear to tell her what brought me here, it all came crashing down so fast.
> This pain I carry like a weight on my chest is numbed by the sound of her voice;
> I am undeserving of her grace, but she never gave me the choice.
> I cannot drag her down with me into the horror of all these trials;
> But this life that hurts so badly is so beautiful when she smiles.

Cole may not have been a poet, but his writing evoked emotion. She gently ran her fingertips over the texture of his words on the page, the slight indentation of ballpoint pen against paper.

Leighton had underestimated Cole's feelings

for her, and she'd failed to fathom the depth of her effect on him. How could she take his pain away when she didn't even know what it was? She was amazed that just by being herself, she could make a difference in the life of another person. Maybe she had been meant to find him. Maybe that finally explained why she'd been so drawn to him from the start. Because whether he knew it or not, he needed her to save him.

With an electric urgency drumming in her chest, Leighton tucked the notebook into her bag and jumped up. Her feet carried her swiftly down the sidewalk in pursuit of finding Cole.

When Leighton reached him, she didn't slow down. Cole let out a grunt as she rushed into him, throwing her arms around his neck. He immediately drew her in and held her tightly against him, their heartbeats racing side by side.

"So, you liked it?" Cole asked timidly, without disrupting their embrace.

Leighton nestled her face in his neck and smiled against the warmth of his skin. "I did. So much. How can you feel that way about me?"

Cole pulled away to look at her, then frowned. "Are you crying?" he asked, his voice soft and his gaze tender.

She breathed a bashful laugh. "I guess I'm a little overwhelmed. To get a glimpse of how much you're hurting...and to think *I* somehow have this power to alleviate it? I didn't know..."

He took her face in his hands. "You didn't know what?"

"That you felt this as much as I do."

Cole smiled. "I think we both fought like hell not to."

Leighton nuzzled her cheek against his palm. "That's a fight I'm okay with losing."

"Me too."

He gazed at her with a captivated yearning, his eyes traveling to her lips as he leaned in. Never had Leighton felt so much emotion in a kiss. Surely, it was much too soon to feel so strongly, but she wasn't quite sure they were in control. She didn't want the solace of the moment to end, but they parted only to catch their breath.

"I think I'm falling in love with you," Cole said in a blissful whisper, still intoxicated by their kiss.

Then, as if reality set in and he realized what he'd just confessed, his expression changed. He swallowed nervously, like he was bracing himself for Leighton's reaction. But she only smiled at him before she settled her head against his chest, letting Cole know that she was falling, too.

Thirteen

"The eyes all staring, burning into my skin. Watching the days roll by, making my head spin."

*I*t was the first day of senior year. Cole entertained the idea of feigning sudden illness so he could stay home, but it would only postpone the inevitable, the dread of facing his peers eating at him for one more day. Cole's father, seemingly desperate to help in any way possible, had offered to drive Cole to school on his way to work so Cole wouldn't have to take the bus. Cole had accepted, trying not to envision the condition of his car as he stared at its empty space in the driveway.

"You doing okay, kiddo?" his father broke the stillness.

Cole stared out the passenger window of his father's car, envying every person he saw, imagining how great it must feel to be anyone but himself. "I don't know, am I supposed to be okay?"

His dad sighed heavily, the crease in his brow deepening. "I would say it's normal to grieve for a long time. And hopefully, one day, it starts to get easier somehow."

Cole turned back to the window, his tongue finding the cut in his lip again. He hated that it had begun to heal. It was ridiculous, but to him, it was the very last connection he had to Tucker. It was an injury Cole had deserved full well, and if Tucker's undeserved injuries from that night couldn't heal, then Cole didn't want his to heal either.

He thought of what the first day of his senior year should've been. Cole could vividly picture sitting in the familiar driver's seat of his black 1998 Mustang GT, tapping his thumb against the steering wheel to the beat of whatever song Tucker was playing. Tucker was always discovering new music and making new playlists to share on their car rides. Cole wondered what song they would've been listening to now.

Cole and his father spent the remainder of the drive in silence, and when they pulled into the school parking lot, Cole felt nauseated.

"Listen, if you need anything, you call me or Mom, all right?" his dad said, an urgency in his tone. "I don't care the reason, I'll come get you if you need me to."

Cole nodded before stepping out of the car. He wished he had the energy to express his gratitude but all he could muster was a monotone, "Thanks, Dad."

Then his father was gone, and Cole grew even sicker. He was painfully alone without Tucker by his side like he should've been. Like he'd always been. Dragging his feet along the sidewalk, Cole reluctantly made his way into the once-familiar building that now felt so uninviting.

He drifted down the hallway toward home-room, his stomach twisting with anxiety. He kept his head down, avoiding eye contact with everyone he passed. But he could feel the stares, could see the heads turning in his peripheral vision, and he couldn't breathe.

Cole ducked into the classroom and took a seat in the back corner. Taking deep breaths, he leaned his head against his propped fist and gaped blindly at the desktop's faded ink smears. As the room continued to fill with his classmates, he wanted so desperately to disappear. Cole hated feeling so exposed, so vulnerable, and he found himself wishing he had a jacket with a hood he could pull over his head, or long hair that could fall into his face and shield him. Or maybe a hole could open up beneath his desk and swallow him whole.

Tucker was all anyone talked about. A remembrance assembly was held for him during fourth period, where the athletics department retired his football jersey. Several teachers shared memories of Tucker, tainted with grief-attacking platitudes and too many plastic smiles. At the end, the faculty thought it would be beneficial for students to write messages to Tucker on a large paper banner in the name of closure.

Cole sat numbly in the gymnasium bleachers, praying for it all to end. Though it made him feel guilty, he couldn't stand before the whole school and pen personal sentiments that Tucker would never see. It was useless, and it certainly wouldn't offer

Cole any closure. Truth was, there were a thousand things Cole wanted to say to Tucker. He'd mentally rehearsed—and sometimes wailed into his pillow in the middle of the night—apologies and pleas for forgiveness that Tucker couldn't hear. He sure as hell wasn't going to pretend he could say goodbye on a stupid banner displayed in his school's gym.

When he'd finished inwardly mocking the grief activity, Cole looked up at the crowded banner, now heavily scrawled with various colors of permanent marker. He found himself pleased by how many people wanted to honor Tucker. But his breath caught in his throat and every muscle in his body tensed when he caught sight of what was written in large black letters across the top of the banner: HEY GOD, GIVE US BACK TUCKER LINDSLEY AND WE'LL GIVE YOU COLE MACHENDRICK!

Cole was on the brink of a panic attack. It was true; everyone blamed him. Everyone hated him. He jumped to his feet and immediately ascended the bleachers. A foot darted out into the aisle to trip him, but he was able to side-step it, making it safely to the shiny wood of the gym floor. Glancing back for just a moment, Cole saw Josh Lindsley, Tucker's cousin, glowering at him as he twirled a thick black marker between his fingers. Cole spun around and hurried for the door, dozens of crumpled paper balls beating down on him like hail.

The next day wasn't any better, instantly heading downhill from the moment Cole first approached his locker. Someone had written GO TO HELL, COLE in bright red paint marker across the blue metal door. Though the words cut into him, he ignored the message and quickly spun the combination. When he jerked the door open, countless squares of paper spilled out, fluttering to his feet. Cole gawked at the littered floor, knowing immediately what they were. Photos. Hundreds of print-offs of the grisly scene the local newspaper had posted online.

Nearly hyperventilating, Cole fought to blink away the image of the unrecognizable twisted metal. Intrusive faces gathered in the hall around him, some laughing, some scowling, all watching like he was some joke on display.

fourteen

"How have you been feeling this week?"

Cole stared at the colorful flower arrangement on the glass table between him and the therapist. He wondered what kind of flowers Leighton liked and he pondered the idea of sending her some. He imagined her sweet, surprised smile when she'd receive them and it sparked a half-smile of his own.

"Cole." Dr. Wade's voice interrupted his musings.

He adjusted himself in the oversized leather armchair. "Yes?"

Crossing her legs, Dr. Wade leaned back into her matching chair across from him. "I asked how you've been feeling this week."

Cole ran a hand through his hair, pushing it back from his face. One strand rebelled, spilling down to rest on his cheek. "It's been a decent week."

Dr. Wade cocked her head. "So, the *week* was decent, but how were *you*?"

He slouched lower in the chair, resting both arms on the armrests, his hands lightly gripping the cold, cracked leather. "Better."

"Can you tell me more about that?"

Cole fought off the urge to smile. "Well, I've sort of started dating someone."

Dr. Wade raised her eyebrows, peering at him over her red-framed glasses. "I thought you were avoiding people."

"I was trying to. Remember that girl I told you about?"

"The one who cared too much and wouldn't leave you alone?"

Cole sighed. "Well, yeah. Her name is Leighton."

"So, you've started dating Leighton. Why the sudden change?" Dr. Wade asked, repositioning her notebook in her lap.

Cole mulled over the question, watching Dr. Wade hold her pen between her fingers like a cigarette. For a brief moment, it made him crave one, but he shook it off.

"I'm not sure. I just really like being around her. It's like I *need* it," he finally said.

"You need *her*?"

Cole bit at his bottom lip. "I don't know. I guess? It's weird. She makes me feel better. Almost like I forget what I've done, like maybe I'm myself again when I'm with her."

Dr. Wade wrote something down, then looked back at him. "Remember what we talked about. You can't keep referring to it that way. That it's something you did. The self-blame needs to stop if you want to heal, Cole."

He rolled his eyes. "Okay, let me just turn it off." With a flick of his finger, he pretended to flip a light switch. "Oh, I'm all better now. Why didn't I just *stop* caring before?"

With a heavy breath, Dr. Wade removed her glasses and dropped them to her notebook. "Cole. I'm not trying to belittle your feelings or imply that they can be so easily changed. It's going to take time and intentional thought patterns—the cognitive behavioral therapy we've been working on—to help you let go of the guilt."

"What if I don't *want* to let it go?" Cole's voice cracked as he spoke.

"I don't understand. Why would you want that?"

He shrugged, his eyes darting away from hers. He focused on the flame of the eucalyptus candle flickering on the bookshelf behind her, and he prayed with all his might that he could hold back his emotions.

"Cole?"

"Because I deserve it," he said. "You and my parents and whoever else thinks they know what happened that night can keep telling me it's not my fault, but that doesn't take back how I hurt Tucker. He *died* angry and upset with me and I can never fix that."

"While that may hold some truth, you are not responsible for what he did with his anger," Dr. Wade said carefully.

Cole sat up and hunched forward. "I didn't pull the trigger, but I gave him the gun."

She frowned at his analogy. "Listen, Cole. I can see why you feel the way you do. And it's okay. All I'm trying to do is get you to spend more time focusing on the positive instead of dwelling on and owning these self-deprecating thoughts."

With a sniffle, Cole nodded. "That's what I've been doing. I wasn't planning on coming in here and being like this today. I really have been doing better, I promise."

"I know. Everyone seems to have—pardon the expression—'trigger' words or topics that set them off, and I think I found yours today. So, for that, I apologize."

Cole settled back into his chair, releasing a deep breath to calm himself. He reached behind his back for the happy yellow and white lumbar throw pillow emblazoned with the word *sunshine*, and he hugged it to his stomach.

Dr. Wade slipped her reading glasses back on. "Tell me more about Leighton. Do you talk to her about Tucker?"

He quickly shook his head. "No way. I can't."

"Well, why not? If you're dating her, you must trust her."

"I do trust her."

Dr. Wade tapped the top of her pen against her lip, her eyes searching along the ceiling as she speculated. "Can I take a guess?" she asked. "You're afraid Leighton won't feel the same way about you after she finds out about Tucker. You think she'll see you the way you see yourself, and you'll lose her."

"How could you know that? I never said..."

Dr. Wade offered him a thin, caring smile. "Cole, this is our tenth session. I can sort of read you by now. I know you're afraid, and it's not easy to open up about something so personal and painful.

But if this girl really cares about you, she'll stick with you through it, and you won't have to do it alone anymore."

"Do you really think that's possible?"

"Sure. But you have to be ready to find out for yourself, ready to tell her."

Cole chewed his fingernail. "I want to. I mean, eventually. But I don't know how. This girl is incredible. I don't know why she chose me, but I don't want to screw it up."

"If she really is incredible, I don't see how you could screw it up," Dr. Wade said. "It isn't healthy for you to hide behind this secret and push people away. You should be able to share your feelings and work through them with someone who will listen. Besides your parents and your therapist. If you think that's Leighton, great. But I really think having someone to talk to will help you a lot."

"Okay. Maybe," Cole said, already queasy at the thought.

Dr. Wade looked at her watch. "We are all out of time, but I'd like you to think about telling Leighton. I want you to get used to the idea of breaking out of your shell and sharing this with someone." She closed her notebook and smiled. "All right, Cole. I'll see you next Wednesday. Have a good week."

"Thanks. You too." Cole stood, setting the bright pillow back in its place. As he let himself out of Dr. Wade's office, he didn't feel any more willing to tell Leighton the truth.

Cole wiped his clammy hands on his jeans as he stood at the door. He'd rehearsed what he would say while on his drive back to campus from Dr. Wade's office, but by now, he'd forgotten everything. Ultimately, he decided he didn't have much to lose and knocked. A rustling inside filled him with a slight dread.

When Quinn opened the door, a bewildered expression fell upon her face, accelerating Cole's discomfort. He couldn't tell if she was surprised or appalled to see him.

"Leighton isn't here," Quinn said as if he should know better.

"She's in algebra, I know. I'm here to see you."

Quinn made another bemused face, her eyebrows knitting together. "*Me?* Okay…" She moved aside to let Cole in, then closed the door and turned to him, crossing her arms. "What do you want?"

"I actually need to ask for a favor."

This time, he could tell Quinn was surprised. "A favor?"

Cole ran a hand through his hair. "I want to take Leighton out on a date, but I want to make sure it's special. I need your help."

Quinn perked up. "Oh. Okay. Sure, I can help."

Cole relaxed a little. "Oh, good. Thank you. I just don't want to screw it up. I mean, I think I know her well enough to plan something she won't hate, but I'd rather get some input from her best friend first."

An amused smile flickered across Quinn's

lips before she brushed past him and flopped onto her bed. She lay on her stomach, gathering her pillow in her arms and resting her chin on it.

"You can sit." She motioned to the desk chair with a tilt of her head.

He spun the chair around and sat down, facing her.

"So, what do you wanna know?" Quinn asked.

"Is there anything you know for a fact she wouldn't like?"

Quinn didn't hesitate. "Don't take her to a movie. She likes one-on-one interaction, and you can't talk during a movie."

Cole gave a nod. "Got it. What else?"

"Don't go overboard. Leighton is a simple girl, and she finds joy in the little things. Sweet, personal touches. No grandiose, show-off bullshit."

Cole scratched his head. "Wait, what do you mean exactly?"

Quinn shrugged. "You figure it out. It's *your* first date with Leighton, not mine."

He sighed. "Fine. Anything else I should know?"

"Yes." Quinn sat up, her expression suddenly stern. "Leighton isn't like other girls. She's sweet and she's innocent. She'd rather look at your baby pictures, and hear stories from your childhood than make out with you. She's more about an emotional connection than a physical one, if you get my drift. So, if this little date of yours is in any way a ploy to get lucky, I swear to God, I will rip off your kneecaps."

Cole's eyes went wide. "Wow. No. It's not. I wouldn't do that."

Quinn peered at him through a skeptical squint. "Why should I believe you?"

"Because I'm not like that."

With a swift, incredulous glance, she looked him up and down. "What, are you a virgin too?"

"Well, no, but—wait. Why'd you say it like that? As if there's no possible way I could be?" Cole asked.

Quinn snickered. "I despise stereotypes, but guys who look like you don't generally have bad luck with girls."

Cole rolled his eyes with an irritated huff. "Just because I don't have bad luck with girls, it doesn't automatically mean I would sleep with any of them."

Quinn laughed. "Except that you did, so…your argument is invalid."

"I was speaking hypothetically. And anyway, I've only had *one* serious girlfriend. I've never slept around or anything." Cole dropped his gaze to the floor, not wanting to think of Ava. "I know about Jared, and I promise you I'm not like that. I respect Leighton and I really care about her."

"Well, that's good," Quinn said. "I guess you can keep your kneecaps, then."

He chuckled, unable to maintain his annoyance. "I appreciate that."

She studied him once more and smiled. "I can't believe I'm admitting this, but…you might not be so bad after all."

Leighton scrutinized her reflection in the long mirror, running her hands over the soft, flawless fabric of the strapless mint-green dress. It contoured her figure a little too well for her liking.

"Yes, that's the one," Quinn said, appearing behind her. "But if you spill even one speck of *anything* on it, I will shave your head in your sleep."

Grimacing, Leighton faced her. "Well, that's a little extreme. Maybe I shouldn't borrow it."

"What, it's my favorite dress. If you had a favorite dress, you'd understand."

Leighton snickered. "I'm sorry I don't meet your fashion standards."

Quinn gave Leighton's hair a final once-over, carefully smoothing any unruly strands in the waves she'd carefully styled herself. "You look amazing. Not that you really need to try."

"What does that mean?"

Quinn smiled. "If you went out tonight in sweatpants, Cole wouldn't even notice."

Leighton laughed. "Yeah, right."

"He *really* likes you, Leighton. It's kind of cute, actually."

"Suddenly you like him?"

Quinn lifted a shoulder. "He's all right. Okay, yeah, I kind of like him. I didn't at first, but for some reason, I trust him with you."

Leighton raised her eyebrows. "Wow. That's saying a lot."

"I know I'm usually a pain in the ass. But I think it's different this time. Cole is different."

Leighton breathed a dreamy sigh. "I think he

is too. It's not something I've been able to explain. It's just this feeling."

"Sometimes we just know things," Quinn said.

Leighton studied her best friend's face. "And how do you know things like how Cole feels about me?"

"No reason."

"Spill, Quinn."

Quinn groaned. "Fine. Cole came by for some tips on your date. He wanted to make sure he planned the perfect night. That's all."

Leighton pressed on her temples. "Oh, God. What did you tell him?"

"Nothing bad, I swear. I told him not to go overboard. And I told him to behave himself."

Leighton rolled her eyes. "You told him to behave himself? Why didn't you just warn him about my virginhood while you were at it?"

A knock made Quinn rush too eagerly to open the door. "Cole! Come in and see how hot your date looks."

Cole was blushing as Quinn grabbed his wrist and pulled him into the dorm room. When his eyes fell upon Leighton, they widened.

"Hey," he said with a timid smile. "You look...really nice."

Leighton looked at the floor. "Thanks. So do you."

"Oh, my God. Awkward," Quinn interrupted. "Just get out of here already, I can't stand it."

Leighton pulled on her cardigan and grabbed her purse off the knob of the closet door. "You suck, Quinn."

"I know, I'm sorry. Wes stole all the good genes in utero."

Leighton chuckled. "Obviously. I'll see you later."

Quinn gave her a quick hug. "Text me if you think you'll be late so I don't worry."

"Okay, Mom."

Leighton and Cole stepped out into the hallway.

"And remember what we talked about, Cole," Quinn added, leaning against the doorframe with her arms crossed over her chest. "Kneecaps."

"Got it," Cole said with an uneasy smile.

Leighton took Cole's hand and pulled him away before Quinn could spew out any additional mortifying comments. Or before Cole could somehow come to his senses and call off their date.

COLE

Cole and Leighton sat on the edge of the sidewalk that dropped off into the lake, their feet dangling above the cold, dark water. A soft breeze created a slight current on the lake. Cole watched it shimmer beneath the night sky as it lapped against the cement wall.

"I had a lot of fun tonight," Leighton said, crossing her arms with a shiver.

Cole scooted closer to her to drape his arm

around her shoulders. "So did I."

An easy cheerfulness brightened her face. "And now I can add first ever picnic by sunset to my list. Who would've thought you were such a romantic?"

"More romantic than sleeping in a car at least, right?"

"Of course. Most guys would've just gone for the typical dinner and a movie—which is fine—but this was much more my style. I wish it didn't have to end."

The usual heaviness Cole carried felt a bit lighter. "Well, it doesn't have to be over yet. We can stay here as long as you'd like...or go anywhere you want."

"You do owe me that road trip we talked about."

He chuckled. "If only."

Slowly approaching laughter and loud chatter caught their attention as a group of young guys goofed off on penny boards and bicycles down the sidewalk. Leighton frowned, and Cole could practically see the surreal and magical peacefulness of the night wither away.

"I think I'm ready to go now," she said.

Cole jumped up, brushing off the seat of his jeans, and helped Leighton to her feet. As she stepped away from the ledge, two of the guys sped toward them, racing each other on their boards. One of them attempted to glide through the narrow space between Leighton and Cole, but his shoulder smashed into Leighton, knocking her backward off the edge of the sidewalk. She let out a shriek as she fell, hitting the water with a splash.

For a fraction of a second, Cole was torn between chasing after the heedless teenager and flocking to Leighton's rescue. But he bolted to the ledge and dropped to his knees to reach for Leighton, who was treading water while frantically trying to cling to the wall. She grabbed for Cole's hand, latching her fingers tightly around his wrist. With all his might, Cole hoisted her up out of the water.

When Leighton was safe on dry ground, she collapsed against Cole, trembling in his arms. He brushed her wet hair away from her face and held her close, hoping his body heat would warm her.

"Are you okay?"

She nodded. "It was just a little scary, that's all."

The two guys had finished their race and were doubling back toward them, boards in hand. Cole's jaw tightened as they approached, and his blood began to boil when they passed by without a single glance.

"Are you *kidding* me?"

The guys stopped and turned around.

"Ya know, maybe an apology would be nice," Cole added.

The one who had knocked Leighton into the water took a step toward him. "Oh, right. My bad."

Cole snickered. "Look at her. I think you owe her an *actual* apology."

The guy looked her up and down and shrugged, scratching his shaved head. "She shoulda moved out of the way."

Cole seethed, gritting his teeth. "Are you really that much of an asshole?"

The guy stepped closer as if to challenge Cole, expressing no concern for Cole's size advantage. "Just take your bitch and get outta here."

Cole laughed incredulously. "Wow. You are *so* cool." He shook his head, forcing himself to walk away before he acted on his rage.

As Cole turned his back, the guy shoved him and he stumbled forward but caught himself. Cole spun around and shoved him back.

"Watch yourself," Cole warned.

The guy laughed, dropping his shoulder back as if he were about to turn away, then threw a quick punch to Cole's face. Cole groaned, instantly cocking his arm and retaliating, knocking the guy to the ground.

"Apologize next time, asshole," Cole said, shaking his throbbing hand.

As other guys from the group began to close in, Cole locked his fingers with Leighton's, hastily leading her away from the scene. Vulgar threats were hurled at them as they fled, but thankfully, no one followed.

Cole leaned against his car in the parking lot, his fading adrenaline rush leaving him exhausted and in pain. "Are you okay?" he asked Leighton, reaching for her.

"Are *you* okay?" she replied. "You're bleeding."

Her concern made him nervous, and he realized where the pain was radiating from as he tasted the blood on his lips. He gently swiped the back of his hand beneath his nose and saw the dark red smeared on his skin.

"It's okay," he said, unlocking the car and opening the back door.

He bent into the backseat and came out with a hoodie, offering it to Leighton. After helping her peel off her soaked cardigan, he guided her into the oversized jacket and zipped it for her.

Once they were both safely inside his car, Cole started the engine.

"I'm so sorry that happened," Cole said, securing his seatbelt. He glanced over to be sure Leighton had fastened hers.

"It's not your fault. That guy was a total jerk," she said.

Cole pulled out of the parking lot and onto the main road. "I know, but I probably shouldn't have hit him."

"Well, he hit you first. He basically asked for it," Leighton said.

"But I shouldn't have stooped to his level. I don't want you to think I go around hitting people when they piss me off. I just hate what he did to you."

She ran the backs of her fingers gently over his cheek. "You didn't do anything wrong. *He* did. Okay?"

"Okay." Cole stole a glance at her. "And tonight was still a good night. Let's not let this ruin that. Okay?"

Leighton nodded with a thin smile. "It was a good night. And you're a good guy. Whether you like it or not."

Cole unlocked the door to his dorm room and let Leighton in ahead of him. When he turned on the light, she gasped, gaping at her reflection in the closet door mirror.

"What's wrong?" he asked. "Oh. Never mind."

In the bright light of the dorm room, they could both see an undeniable yellow-brown tinge to the wetness of Leighton's dress that peaked out from the bottom of the jacket she was wearing.

She ripped off the hoodie and dropped it to the floor, twisting her body to get a look from every angle. The entire dress was blotched with lake water.

"No, no, no...Quinn's gonna kill me."

"I doubt that."

"No, she said she'd shave my head in my sleep if anything happened to it," Leighton said.

Cole grimaced. "Sounds like Quinn. Come here, let me see." He gently turned Leighton around and located the tag of the dress, letting his fingers brush across her upper back. "It's machine washable. Why don't we just go to the laundromat and wash it? Then she'll never have to know."

"Okay, I need to change before this dries," Leighton said, bending to remove her shoes. "Is it all right if I borrow something to wear?"

"Oh, of course."

Cole rummaged through the closet and a dresser drawer before handing her a soft, heather-gray sweatshirt and a pair of black skinny sweat-pants. He turned his back to give her privacy while she changed.

After a short moment, he heard a frustrated

sigh. "Cole, can you help me with this?"

He peered gingerly over his shoulder to see Leighton reaching for the back of her dress, struggling with the zipper. She turned her back to him and lifted her wet hair out of the way. With shaky fingers, Cole slowly unzipped her dress. He darted his eyes away when he saw the clasp of her bra.

"Thanks," Leighton said as Cole spun around to conceal his blushing face. "Oh, man. You might not be getting this sweatshirt back. Just a friendly warning...Okay, coast is clear."

He faced her once more, smiling at the sight of her small frame lost in his clothing. "You ready?"

"Not quite." She opened the mini fridge and took out a bottle of water, then grabbed a tissue from the box on the dresser. Pressing her hand to Cole's chest, she guided him backward to sit in the desk chair, and she stood between his knees. "We wouldn't want to alarm anyone," she said, opening the water to dampen the tissue.

He had completely forgotten about his injury, and was touched by Leighton's desire to take care of him. She cupped his face with one hand, and carefully cleaned the dried blood from his upper lip with the other. As she gently dabbed at his sore nose, Cole's heart raced, and he instinctively placed his hand over hers on his cheek.

Leighton's brow creased with worry. "Am I hurting you?"

"No," he lied.

When she'd finished tending to his face, she slipped her hands through his hair, sliding her fingers over his scalp and stopping at the nape of his neck. She stared into his eyes, a flicker of awe in hers.

"Why do I feel so comfortable with you?" she asked. "It's like I've known you my whole life or something."

Cole thought guiltily of his failed, despicable efforts to achieve the exact opposite effect on her. "I guess some things aren't up to us."

She continued to gaze at him.

"What are you thinking?" he wondered.

Leighton breathed a bashful chuckle. "I don't know if I can say. I don't want to upset you."

He smirked. "What happened to the no-filter-around-Cole Leighton?"

"Okay. I was thinking...how it's so strange that you're the same guy I met a couple months ago. That you were so easily sarcastic and snide. But now you're kind and chivalrous and timid, even."

Cole lifted his eyebrows. "You think that was easy for me—to be so awful to you?"

Leighton shrugged, resting her hands on his shoulders. "I sure believed it."

"I hated every second of it. It literally nauseated me. The more I got to know you, the harder it became. That's why I tried to avoid you. Because I couldn't live with myself treating you that way, and I could not, for the life of me, get you to stop caring about me."

"Yeah, sorry about that."

"No, *I'm* sorry. It was the worst possible defense mechanism ever." He hung his head in shame. "I'm still trying to forgive myself for everything I put you through."

Leighton put her hands on his face, lifting it

gently. "It was painful, sure, and it was confusing and frustrating, but *I* forgive you. So it's okay to forgive yourself and move on."

Overwhelmed by her unwavering mercy, Cole let out a long breath. "You are so good. I don't deserve someone like you."

She rolled her green eyes. "Well, maybe I think I don't deserve *you*."

"You're right. You deserve someone much better."

Leighton's face broke into a sweet smile. "Thank you."

"For what? Helping you finally see the truth?"

"No. For finally letting me in. It's even better than I imagined." She leaned in and planted a soft, lingering kiss on his forehead.

"Even with bloody noses, near-drownings, and neurotic roommates?" he asked with a half-smile.

Leighton laughed. "Yes. Hell or, literally, high water couldn't ruin this."

Cole prayed she was right. Because she still knew nothing of the hell he hid inside him.

fifteen

L eighton stared at the washing machine, hypnotized by its swooshing sound, and the sudsy swirl
of water and flashes of mint-green in the small
round window. She was tired, and could think of better ways to enjoy the fading night, but as Cole leaned
his shoulder against hers, she didn't care that the
wash cycle was taking forever.

"I did not picture spending any of the night
in the laundry room," Cole said with a snicker.

"It adds to the adventure. And makes for a
kick-ass first date story," Leighton said.

"True. Another item on your list of college
experiences, right?" He let out a long, deep yawn and
slouched lower on the small couch.

Leighton glanced at the clock on her cell
phone. 10:23. "Tired?"

He nodded, rubbing his eye. It made him look
like a little kid.

"Not much of a night owl?" she asked.

"No, it's not that. I don't sleep much."

"Every night or just last night?"

"Every night, usually...but last night was
worse," Cole admitted, looking away.

"How come?" She leaned forward, trying to see his face. "Were you nervous about tonight?"

"No."

Leighton knew he was lying and she couldn't contain her amused giggle. "Come here." She patted her lap, motioning for him to lie down.

Cole hesitated for a moment, then repositioned himself, lying on his back with his head resting on Leighton's thigh. He clasped his hands over his abdomen.

"Is that better?" she asked.

He closed his eyes and exhaled, his body relaxing against the worn cushions. "Yes."

Marveling over the beautiful, brown locks that spilled across her lap, Leighton didn't bother resisting the urge that overtook her. She gently combed her hand through Cole's hair, letting the soft strands slip slowly through her fingers. His closed eyes gave her the freedom to gaze at his perfectly structured face to her heart's content.

"So, how come you don't sleep?" Leighton was afraid to disturb him, afraid to violate his boundaries, but she'd asked anyway.

Cole's eyelids fluttered open, but he didn't look at her. His sleepy eyes roamed along the tile ceiling, his eyebrows knit together in troubled introspect.

"I can't shut my mind off at night. I lie there for hours thinking about the things that bother me, and when I do fall asleep, I dream about them." Cole lifted his gaze to meet Leighton's. "That's all I can tell you, though. I'm sorry."

She nodded. "I know. Don't worry, I'll keep

my promise not to pry. But I want to make sure you know that you can talk to me about anything, whenever you're ready. I can be patient."

Cole drew his bottom lip between his teeth, quiet for a moment. Then, he sat up abruptly, turning sideways on the couch to face her.

"How can you just do that?" he asked.

Leighton froze, fear creeping in. "Do what?"

Pinching the bridge of his nose, he squeezed his eyes shut. "You're so willing to blindly walk into this without knowing exactly what you're getting yourself into."

Her heart hammered against her chest. It was finally happening—he was coming to his senses, changing his mind.

Leighton played it cool. "Well, you obviously care about me, so if it really was *that* bad, I'm sure you wouldn't let me be with you." She realized how naïve she sounded and immediately felt foolish.

"Yeah, and I tried to keep that from happening, remember? It *is* that bad, Leighton…but you're amazing and I'm selfish, so here we are."

She took a hold of his face in her hands and leveled her eyes with his. "Are you dangerous? Would you ever purposely cause me harm?"

Cole's gaze was tender as he stared back at her. "No," he answered with conviction, taking her hands into his for just a moment before releasing them. "But I don't think I can ever give you the deepest parts of myself…"

"It's okay, Cole."

"You're willing to just accept that. How is that fair to you?"

"It's not. But I don't care."

Cole raised his eyebrows. "You should care. Like I said, you deserve better."

"Better how? Someone who would seek the advice of my very difficult best friend just to be sure he planned *my* perfect first date? Or someone who would get punched in the face to stand up for me? Cole, I know what it feels like to go after someone who is not a good person. I've been there; I've ignored the nagging intuition as it ate at my insides, and I *knew* it was wrong. But I don't feel that with you. I trust you."

"Just promise me...when you realize I'm not enough, or I'm not what you thought, you won't be afraid to walk away."

"Cole..."

"No, I'm serious. Please, Leighton, just promise me."

Her throat tightened. "Okay, I promise."

Then Leighton scooted closer to him to settle her head against his chest. As he wrapped an arm around her and let out a defeated sigh, she wondered again what had made him so broken. And she wondered if she had the capability whatsoever to put him back together.

Lulled by the rumbling sounds of the laundry room, and the cadence of Cole's heartbeat beneath her ear, Leighton had nearly drifted off to sleep when the washing machine finally stopped.

Cole untethered himself from her and crossed

the room. Opening the washer door, he carefully re-moved the wet dress and cardigan and held them up. "Looks good to me." He offered Leighton a shrug as he moved toward the dryers. "Uh oh," he said, frowning at the dress tag.

"What's wrong?" Leighton asked, standing up.

"It says 'line dry only.' I didn't see that be-fore."

Leighton scrambled across the speckled gray linoleum and took the dress from him to see for her-self. "It'll take all night to air dry. I can't bring it back to Quinn like *this*. She'll kill me. What am I supposed to do?"

Cole smiled at her, as if her flustered out-burst amused him. "It'll be okay. You're sure you can't just explain what happened?"

Leighton let her shoulders slump. "I'd really rather not. That's my only option, isn't it?"

"Not unless you wanna stay with me to-night."

She didn't hesitate. "Okay."

Cole let out a nervous chuckle. "Oh. I was kind of kidding. But you're more than welcome."

WESLEY

Wesley was furious. Not that he was ever in the mood to deal with his roommate's idiocy, but to-night of all nights was certainly not the time for it. Leighton was on a date with Cole. As he breezed down the hall in his building, Wesley tried not to imagine them together, tried not to wonder what they were doing.

Quickly rounding the corner, Wesley crashed into someone with a grunting smack, and a few items fell to the floor.

He immediately knelt to pick them up—a damp towel, a bottle of shampoo, and a bottle of body wash. "I am so sorry," he said.

"Oh. Wesley."

Wesley's head shot up. His name in her voice was something he knew full well. "Leighton...Didn't expect to see you here," he said, glancing at his watch.

He got to his feet, his eyes traveling over her apparel. Her oversized, worn sweatshirt was emblazoned with a large logo that read LACHLAN FOOTBALL, encircling an open-mouthed lion.

"It's kind of a long story," Leighton said, taking her things from Wesley.

"You're not still on your date, are you?"

"Uh, yeah. What are *you* up to?"

Wesley sighed. "Freaking Connor locked me out of my room. I told him I'd be *right* back, and I was literally gone for three minutes. But in that short time, he left and locked the door. So I called him and he's God-knows-where and isn't worried about coming back anytime soon to help me out."

Leighton grimaced. "Can't your RA help you?"

He rolled his eyes. "My RA hates me. He's Kennedy's ex-boyfriend. I'm not even dating her, but whatever."

"That's really not fair," Leighton said. "I wish

you'd report your roommate or file a room change request. *Something.*"

"Oh, trust me, I filed last week after I caught him and his girlfriend making out in my bed."

Leighton's jaw dropped. "What? Ew!"

Wesley smirked. "Yeah, but apparently, there aren't any openings. That, or my RA made sure my request was denied."

"So, what are you doing now?" Leighton asked.

"I was going to take a walk and hopefully Connor shows up by the time I get back."

Wesley finally allowed himself to focus on the elephant in the room—Leighton's freshly show-ered state, clothing that obviously did not belong to her, the lateness of her presence in Cole's dorm—and he chewed anxiously at the inside of his cheek. He wanted so badly to question her, but feared knowing more than he could handle.

He knew Leighton was following his eyes, watching him speculate as his mind reeled with con-clusions that scared him. The shampoo bottle slipped out of her hand.

As she bent to pick it up, Wesley saw MACHENDRICK printed across the upper back of her gray hoodie, and his heart skipped a beat. "Leigh-ton..."

"Wes, it's not what it looks like. I promise you."

He swallowed. "What are you talking about?"

"I know what you're thinking. You don't have to pretend. Because I know how this looks. But I'm telling you, nothing happened."

Wesley slid his hands into his pockets. "Well, it's none of my business, so you don't owe me an explanation."

She frowned. "Well, when I see you falling apart as you stand here and make untrue assumptions, I kind of have to say something."

He shook his head with a slight huff. "Falling apart? Don't flatter yourself."

She seemed stung by his coldness. "Wesley."

"No. I've been way too passive this entire time. Ya know, it wasn't okay to string me along as you experimented with your feelings, just so you could gut me the second Cole came back around. I'm still trying to figure out how you could possibly choose *him*, the guy who made you feel like shit, over me...I have *always* been there for you. I don't understand how, after all this time, after everything we've shared together, I am just nothing to you. How do you not feel the same thing I feel?"

Leighton stared at Wesley with wide, brimming eyes. "Wes, you're not nothing." Her voice came out in a shaky whisper. "You know I never meant to hurt you."

He put his hands on his hips and cast his gaze to the white tile beneath their feet. "But you did. God, Leighton, you have no idea how much it hurts. It's like thinking your wildest dreams have *finally* come true, and then, suddenly, the carpet gets ripped out from under your feet."

The tears trickled down her face. "I'm so sorry. I hate that I hurt you. I was selfish and I should've been more careful. I really don't know what else to say."

Wesley shrugged. "I guess it's my fault for falling for you. Because I was supposed to just laugh off that prank kiss, right? And then everything would still be normal. And you could ride off into the sunset with another jerk without poor, tag-along-Wesley making you feel guilty."

Leighton let out a short, frazzled breath. "Another jerk? I cannot *wait* till you and your sister stop throwing my biggest hurt in my face. Jared was a huge mistake; I get it. But Cole is not a mistake, and I will have you know that he is *not* a jerk. You don't know him like I do, and you don't know what he's been through."

Wesley clenched his jaw. "Please don't defend him to me. And don't act like you share some deep, cosmic connection with him that I could never comprehend. Because I can. Because that's what you and I have shared since we were *nine*. So don't make me feel like *I'm* the one on the outside and he's your most prized and protected possession."

Leighton crossed her arms. "What *do* you want from me?"

Wesley locked his eyes on hers. "I just want you to know how I really feel for once. I'm tired of being *nice*, being 'the brother you never had' that you can take for granted…And you say Jared is your biggest hurt? Well, *this*…" He pointed back and forth between Leighton and himself. "This is mine."

"Are you sure you don't mind if I stay?" Leighton asked Cole.

"Not at all." Cole closed his laptop and got up from his desk to approach her.

He'd changed his clothes while she was gone. His faded gray T-shirt, thin from wear, bore the same football team logo as the sweatshirt Leighton was wearing. His blue gym shorts hung low on his hips, and Leighton realized it was the first time she'd him in something other than jeans.

"Okay, good," she said. She looked away so he wouldn't notice her eyes that she knew were still red and puffy from crying.

"You can sleep in my bed. I'll just sleep in Jay's." He motioned to his roommate's bed behind him.

"So he really goes home *every* weekend?" She asked, sweeping her damp hair up into a messy knot.

Cole sat down on Jay's bed. "Yeah, but now he's actually dropping out of school. He told me this afternoon before he left that he'll only be back to move his stuff out sometime next week. I guess he couldn't take being away from home."

"That's a shame." Leighton pulled down the navy blue comforter and climbed into Cole's bed, pondering the likeliness of Wesley refusing to be Cole's new roommate.

She slid beneath the covers and yanked them tightly around her, instantly engulfed in Cole's calming scent. The butterflies rioted in her stomach as she snuggled against his pillow. It was surreal to be nestled in the very place he slept—or tried to—where he dreamed about the things he couldn't tell her. There was something intimate and sacred about it, making her feel tethered to him, and for just a moment, it was enough to quiet the screaming ache inside her that Wesley had left behind.

"So, I guess this is good night?" Cole's voice brought Leighton out of her head.

"Yeah. Sure." She tried to use as few words as possible so he wouldn't detect the brokenness in her voice.

Cole turned off the overhead light, shrouding the room in complete darkness before he made his way back to his roommate's bed. Leighton listened to the rustling of sheets and the creaking of mattress springs as Cole situated himself. The audible proof of his presence was oddly soothing. Part of her wanted to jump out of her bed and into his, to lose herself in his arms and drown in him.

The realization of how desperately she needed his comfort was enough to undo her. The tears came pouring out, and she held her breath to silence her sorrow. But it wasn't enough to keep her breakdown a secret.

"Leighton?" Cole's concern carried tenderly through the darkness. "Are you okay?"

His question made what was left of her composure crumble into nothing. She threw her hands over her face to muffle her uncontrollable sobs. Instantly, Cole was beside her in the small bed, gathering her in his arms exactly the way she'd longed for. She burrowed into him as he softly shushed her pain.

Cole didn't speak another word until she'd

calmed down a bit. "Leighton, what's wrong?" he asked, gently stroking her arm.

She took a deep breath, feeling her ribcage press against his, and she struggled to maintain her train of thought. "I ran into Wesley in the hall..." She paused to keep from losing control of her emotions again. "I really think he hates me."

"No, Wesley couldn't hate you."

"But I hurt him *so* badly," she whimpered. "I've never seen him like that before. It was horrible."

"I thought everything was okay between you two," Cole said.

Leighton sighed. "So did I, but he wasn't being completely honest with me. The thing about Wes is, he may seem all nonchalant and quick-witted, but you could walk right up to him and punch him in the face, and *he* would apologize for bleeding on you. He would do anything for anybody, like bite his tongue to protect my feelings even when he's dying inside."

"Sounds like a good person. The kind of person who will get past all this and forgive you. Don't you think?" Cole said.

"I hope so. I just want all of us to be friends, but I'm afraid I'm losing him."

Cole held her tighter as she grew upset once again. "Hey, hey. Don't get so ahead of yourself. Everything will be all right. You just have to give it some time."

Leighton nuzzled her face against Cole's collarbone that peeked out from the cotton neckline of his shirt. The sensation of his skin on her lips made the butterflies return with an even stronger force.

She felt Cole tilt his face downward, and she knew if she looked up at him, he would kiss her. The thought filled her with a nervousness that caught her by surprise. They hadn't kissed in nearly a week, but it had been long enough to feel like the first time all over again.

Reaching toward the window directly above them, Cole opened the blinds just enough to let the moonlight spill across the bed. When Leighton finally looked up at him, she could see the shine of his eyes and the hard lines of his face, illuminated by the silvery lunar glow. Though it was weary from the adventures of the night, Leighton decided then that she'd never seen a more beautiful face.

Cole traced his thumb over her cheekbone, then leaned in closer, gently taking her bottom lip between his. Leighton could taste the saltiness of her own lingering tears as he kissed her more passionately, every thread of her existence catching fire.

After a few moments of entangled affection, Leighton reluctantly pulled away from him. "Wait," she said, breathing heavily. "I can't..."

"You can't what...kiss me?"

She bit her lip as she toyed with a strand of his hair. "No, it's not that."

"Then what?" he asked, tracing her jawline with his fingertips.

Leighton breathed a quick, nervous laugh. "It's kind of embarrassing."

Adjusting his position, Cole lay flat on his back. "Come here," he said, lifting his arm to invite her to the space against his side.

She obliged, resting her head on his chest,

and she gingerly slid her arm around him.

"Being a virgin is nothing to be embarrassed about," he said.

Leighton's head shot back up to gawk at him. "What? How did you know that I'm…?"

Cole smiled. "It's okay."

She groaned. "Quinn told you, didn't she?"

"You're not surprised, are you?"

Leighton huffed. "I guess not. But she had *no* right to do that."

"Not to defend her, but I think she thought she was protecting you."

"Protecting me? More like humiliating me and making me look pathetic."

"Leighton. You're not pathetic. Why would you think that's something to be ashamed of? Did you think it would matter to me?"

She darted her eyes away from his. "I honestly don't know."

"Hey," Cole said tenderly, prodding her to meet his gaze. "When I promised you I'm nothing like Jared, I meant it."

Leighton let out a long breath and returned her head to Cole's chest. The topic made her too nervous to look at him. "I know. It's just easy to feel like certain things are expected."

He ran his fingers softly across her arm that stretched over his abdomen. "*Nothing* is expected of you, Leighton. And especially not on our first date. I *never* want you to feel that way with me."

She nodded against him. "I'm sorry I have such a screwed up perception of how guys function."

"It's understandable. Just try not to apply

your bad experience with *one* guy to *all* guys. There are definitely a lot of assholes out there, but some of us know how to be gentlemen. Also, just because I'm not a virgin, it doesn't mean my world revolves around sex."

A sudden burst of Leighton's boldness prompted a question she knew better than to ask. "Was Ava your first?"

His body immediately tensed against her. "Yeah. And the last."

He paused, and Leighton was afraid to say anything else, afraid she'd already said enough to upset him.

"We waited a whole year," Cole proceeded, much to her surprise, speaking like he was thinking out loud. "I thought that was enough time to be sure it wouldn't be a mistake. I'd always thought it was unrealistic or a little old-fashioned to wait until marriage, but I was never one of those guys who couldn't wait to throw it away and sleep with as many girls as possible. I wanted it to mean something. I thought I'd be with Ava forever…"

Leighton was soaking in every single word he offered her, delighted to catch yet another glimpse of who he was.

"Maybe now, I see that waiting isn't so unrealistic," he continued. "I'm sure it's much likelier for someone to regret doing it than to regret *not* doing it. To be honest, I envy you so much."

Leighton raised her head again to look at him. "You envy *me*?"

"Yeah, I do. No one else has ever hurt me the way Ava did. She abandoned me when I needed her the most. She made the *worst* even worse. And now she has a part of me that I can't get back. She will always hold that one sacred place in my history and she does *not* deserve it. But you—you have a clean slate. You still get to decide who that person is. And for the record, it shouldn't be me."

Leighton lifted her hand to touch Cole's shadowed face. She reveled in the fact that he was letting her in, even if only a little, but his nearly incessant self-deprecation was a form of torment she could no longer endure.

"Cole," she started, a sensitive melody in her voice. "I think we should renegotiate the terms of our previous deal."

"I'm listening."

She placed her hand on his chest and rested her chin against it. "I still respect your need for privacy, but if I'm not allowed to know about any of these things, then you're not allowed to insist that they dictate how I should feel about you. So *you* have a clean slate, too—with me. If you want me to leave your past in the past, then you have to leave it in the past, too. Otherwise, spill it all right now and let *me* decide for myself if it changes things. Because I can't take listening to you beat yourself up anymore."

Cole looked at her for a brief moment. "All right, that's fair. I guess I've made my warnings clear, then. This is your last chance to heed them."

Leighton leaned forward to press her lips to his, then smiled at him. "Nope," she said before snuggling her cheek into his chest once more. She wrapped her arm around him and closed her eyes, emitting a tranquil sigh. "You're in a lot of trouble, you know."

He breathed a soft chuckle. "Why's that?"

She turned her eyes up at him. "Because now I like you even more than I already did."

A wide, sleepy grin curved Cole's lips as he held Leighton securely. "Does that mean it's okay if I stay right here with you tonight?"

"Yes. I'm definitely okay with that."

sixteen

C ole stirred when the swelling light of dawn began to stream through the open blinds, bathing the room in a soft, glowing warmth. He lay on his side, his body contouring Leighton's as she faced away from him, curled delicately in his arms.

Cole didn't move. Instead, he basked in the long-awaited relief he'd grown so desperate to obtain. He couldn't remember when he'd last felt this rested, and it was so satisfying, he thought he might cry.

When he'd finished savoring the miracle of a full night's sleep, Cole shifted his focus to marvel at the girl beside him. He listened to her peaceful breathing, and he wondered what she was dreaming about. A corner of his mouth curved upward when he realized he missed her.

"Leighton," Cole whispered, running his hand up and down her arm.

She slowly awoke and turned toward him. "Good morning," she greeted him in a dulcet, sleepy voice. A grin lit up her pretty face.

"What?" Cole asked, unable to resist smiling back.

"I didn't know it would feel this nice to wake up to you."

He blushed. "Yeah. It is nice."

Leighton sat up and stretched. A few dark, wispy tendrils spilled onto her face, having escaped from her loose knot of hair, messy from sleep. She brushed the strands back as she took a glance at the alarm clock on the desk. "It's not even eight yet?"

"Nope. What do you wanna do today?" Cole asked, sitting up beside her.

Leighton gasped suddenly, throwing her hands over her mouth. "Oh my God. I never told Quinn I wasn't coming home last night. She is probably *freaking* out."

Diving out of the bed, Leighton lunged for her purse.

As Leighton's phone powered up, they expected to hear a daunting slew of notification chimes, but it remained silent.

"How is that possible?" Cole asked.

Leighton tapped the screen. "There's nothing here. She didn't call, text, anything."

He ran a hand through his tousled hair. "That's bad, isn't it?"

"I don't know. I think it might be okay," she said with a hopeful chuckle as she stood to her feet. "Hey, get dressed and meet me in the bathroom with some toothpaste."

Then she slipped out the door, and the room suddenly felt cold, like she'd never been there at all.

Leighton quietly unlocked and opened the door to her room, Quinn's dress draped carefully over her arm. She tip-toed inside, Cole following behind her. The shades were still drawn, the room dark, but upon closer inspection, Leighton saw that Quinn's bed was perfectly made.

Cole went to the window and opened the curtain, allowing the morning light to fill the room. "Where is she?"

"I don't know." Leighton reached into the closet to hang up Quinn's dress, thoroughly delighted to be rid of it. She quickly changed into her own clothes, stashing Cole's in her laundry bag.

The door opened and Quinn breezed in with an apologetic smirk on her makeup-smudged face. She wore a black dress that looked a lot like the one she'd lent to Leighton, and she carried a pair of strappy black shoes.

"Leighton, I am *so* sorry if you've been worried. I should've called, but it got late, and then my phone died," Quinn said, tossing her shoes into the closet.

"Where were you?" Leighton asked.

"Sterling Curtis's. I went with my friend, Joanna. But she met up with her boyfriend, and I ended up hanging out with Kennedy. And like I said, it got super late, super fast, and I'd lost my ride home, so Kennedy invited me to stay over."

Leighton exchanged relieved glances with Cole. "Well, it sounds like you made the responsible choice by staying over with Kennedy," Leighton said.

"We're totes besties now, in case you were

wondering," Quinn added. She rolled her eyes, easily resembling her twin brother. "But anyway! How was your date? I guess it was pretty awesome if Cole couldn't wait any later than the crack of dawn to see you again...unless he's actually been with you all night."

Leighton froze, wide-eyed, until Quinn let out a playful laugh. "I'm just teasing," Quinn said, and Leighton joined in with some uneasy laughter of her own.

"Our date *was* awesome, actually," Cole said, shooting Leighton a shy smile. She blushed in return.

"Well, good. I hate both of you," Quinn said, turning to the dresser to rifle through her drawer for a change of clothes. "Oh, have either of you spoken to Wesley? He ignored my texts all night. And even when I texted him from Kennedy's phone to ask for a ride, he still didn't answer."

"Yeah, I saw him late last night...in quick passing," Cole covered for Leighton.

"Nice to know he's not dead somewhere. But now I can kill him the next time I see him." Quinn made her way to the door. "I'll be back. You two be good."

As soon as Quinn disappeared into the hallway, and the metal door had closed behind her, Leighton let out a heavy breath. "Holy crap. That was crazy."

Cole rubbed his forehead with a chuckle. "Yeah. Dumb luck, for sure."

Her smile faded, worry marring her relief. "Cole...do you think Wes is okay? I mean, he wouldn't even talk to Quinn."

"He's just hurt. And maybe a little pissed. I think it'll be okay," Cole assured her.

Leighton chewed at the inside of her cheek. "I wish there was something we could do. Some way we could show him we care about him and not just ourselves."

Cole nodded in agreement. "Hey," he said, placing a hand on Leighton's shoulder. "There's something I have to do. I'll catch up with you later." Cole kissed her on the cheek before breezing out of the room.

Cole knocked in the rhythm of *Shave and a Haircut* on the door, then slipped his hands casually into his pockets while he waited. When the door opened, he painted on a friendly grin and extended his hand to the guy who stood before him.

"Hi there, I'm Cole," he said with forced enthusiasm. "Sorry to bother you so early. You must be Wesley's roommate."

"Yeah. Connor," he replied, his voice a lazy monotone.

"Ah, yes. Hey listen, Connor, is Wesley here?"

"Yup." Connor pointed behind him and moved back to let Cole into the room.

Cole stepped inside, placing his hands on his hips as he surveyed the atrocious state of the small space. Wesley sat on his neatly made bed, his back against the wall, with his computer in his lap. His miniscule area was the only spotless part of the room, Connor's mess infiltrating the majority of it. There were empty pizza boxes stacked in the corner, soda cans strewn haphazardly about, and dirty clothes draped over everything.

Wesley looked up at Cole, first confused, then annoyed.

"Oh, wow, Connor," Cole started, shaking his head. "I sure hope my friend Wesley here isn't responsible for this hideous mess. If he's been any trouble, you let me know, all right? Because horrible roommates are the *worst*. Mine sexiles me, like, every day. Probably uses my bed too, but I just haven't been able to prove it, ya know? Oh well." He shrugged with his hands still on his hips, then turned to Wesley. "Hey, buddy. Can I have a word with you outside?"

Staring at Cole in bewilderment, Wesley put his laptop aside and stepped around various landmines of mess to get to him.

"Oh. Connor. It was *great* meeting you," Cole said before exiting the room.

Cole led Wesley down the stairwell and outside where they sat at opposite ends of a bench by the sidewalk.

"I do appreciate you making Connor feel like a complete ass, but what do you want?" Wesley asked, slouching against the bench back and crossing his arms over his chest.

Cole leaned forward, resting his elbows on his knees. "Well, first, I wanted to tell you I'm sorry."

A look of surprise flickered across Wesley's face. "What are you sorry about?" His question held a hint of sarcasm.

"I know I told you I wasn't going to pursue Leighton. I never meant for things to go the way they did. It just kind of happened no matter how hard I tried to stop it."

Wesley snickered. "That's supposed to make me feel better? If winning Leighton is such a burden to you, I'd be glad to help relieve you of that."

Cole cast his eyes to the pavement. "That's not what I meant. I just need you to know that I didn't tell you one thing, and then purposely go behind your back and do another."

"Well, it was a dick move either way," Wesley retorted.

Cole pushed his hair back from his face. "I know. And you can hate me for it, I don't mind, but please don't be mad at Leighton. She's really broken up about the fight you guys had last night."

Wesley's eyebrows knit together with worry. "She is?"

Cole nodded. "She's afraid you hate her, that you'll never forgive her."

"No. I mean, I'm upset with her. But I could never hate her. That would be impossible."

"It's also really important to her that we get along," Cole said.

Wesley huffed. "Fine. Are we done now?"

Cole leaned back against the bench. "Actually, no. The other reason I'm here is because my roommate is moving out in a few days and I wanted to see if you'd like to be my new roommate."

Wesley stared at him blankly for a moment, then dropped his gaze with a slight snicker. "I am just not allowed to be upset with *anybody*, am I?"

Cole held up his hands. "Hey, you can feel however you want. You can simultaneously hate me *and* be my roommate. It's fine."

Wesley breathed a long sigh. "I don't hate you."

"Well, whatever. I'm not offering out of pity. Or to bribe you to accept Leighton and me. I just want to make that clear," Cole said.

Wesley looked at him. "I know."

A few girls passed by on the sidewalk before them, flashing flirtatious smiles and a singsong unison of "hey, Wesley."

He robotically returned a half-hearted wave, as if too distracted by Cole's unexpected proposal to extend his usual friendliness.

"So, then what do ya say? The shithole, or peace and cleanliness?" Cole held out both hands, palms up, to represent each choice, then moved them up and down as if their weight was teetering on a scale.

Wesley tried to stifle his chuckle, but failed. "Fine. I'll room with you. But only if you promise not to—"

"To sexile you?" Cole jokingly interrupted.

"Well, I wasn't going to say *that*, but yeah."

Cole laughed. "Okay, seriously, I would never do that. I promise."

"Good," Wesley said, drumming his fingertips on his knee. He looked off into the distance like he was imagining his near future without Connor.

"Dude. You have no idea how much you're saving me."

Cole lay on his back, staring into the darkness that surrounded him. He let out a soft hum as he exhaled to cease the lonely silence.

He longed for the peaceful, dreamless sleep he'd experienced the night before. Why had it been so easy then and so impossible now? Cole wasn't sure why he was bothering to speculate at all; Leighton was the missing variable. Maybe it was easier to deny it. Because he didn't want to need her, or miss her, or love her. But he knew full well that nothing in life was ever really up to him.

Rolling to his side, facing the vacant space that Leighton had filled that morning, Cole reflected on the day. Being with Leighton was becoming effortless, but it was all a sham as long as he was keeping her in the dark about his true self. The omission of the truth was the same as lying, and several times that day, it had overwhelmed him with a guilt that had nearly forced him to come undone and spill it in all its ugliness before her. But when he'd played out the confession in his mind, the fear of her reaction overshadowed his desire to do the right thing.

If Cole could at least figure out a way to alleviate the guilt that had been suffocating him for the past fourteen months, maybe he'd be able to sleep at night.

"Cole, can I talk to you for a moment?"

Cole stopped in front of Dr. Gibson's desk after class, letting go of Leighton's hand. "Yes, sir."

Dr. Gibson looked at Leighton with a silent request for privacy. She offered Cole a thin smile before continuing on to the classroom door, leaving him behind.

Leighton stepped outside, graced by the fall breeze and Wesley's face.

"Oh. Hey, Wes." She shifted her bag and avoided eye contact.

"Where's Cole?" he asked.

Leighton glanced over her shoulder at the classroom door. "Dr. Gibson wanted to see him. Maybe because he was late again this morning, I don't know."

Wesley scratched his head. "Look, Leighton, I...I know I said some really harsh things the other night—"

"No, it's okay. You have every right to be upset with me."

"No, it's not okay," Wesley said. "Sure, I can be upset, but you don't deserve to be treated that way. I hate when Quinn throws Jared in your face, and I did the same exact thing. That was so wrong, and I'm sorry."

Leighton looked at the ground and nodded. "Well, it *would* be nice if we could finally erase all remembrance of Jared. Like he never existed. And then maybe Cole could have the clean slate he deserves."

"*Does* he deserve it?" Wesley put a hand up

to halt the aggravation his question had provoked in her. "Wait, I'm not trying to be a dick; I'm genuinely asking you if he really deserves it—does he deserve *you?*"

Leighton crossed her arms over her chest. "You think I would be with him if he didn't?"

Wesley took a step toward her. "Really think about it for a minute, Leighton. Is he good to you? Does he make you feel like you're the greatest thing that's ever happened to him? Do you feel like the entire sky would come crashing down if he walked away? If the answer is yes, just tell me right now and I'll move on. And I'll give Cole his clean slate."

Leighton watched the gold flecks in Wesley's eyes glint in the morning sunlight as he waited for his fate. "Yes, Wesley. To all of it."

He pressed his lips together as her words solidified the space between them. "Okay then. So you have my word—I'll let you go and I won't bring us up again. Cole's your boyfriend, I'm...your best friend. Life goes on." He forced an unconvincing, closed-lipped smile.

Leighton lurched toward him, standing on tiptoe to throw her arms around his neck. His frame bent to accommodate her lack of height, but he didn't return her embrace. He stood there, as if stunned by her affection and afraid to succumb to it.

"Wesley," Leighton whispered, his resistance searing her. "If this is you letting me go, I can't take it."

He let out a long, defeated breath, his body relaxing against her. Slowly, he wrapped his arms around Leighton and held her tightly.

"We'll be okay," Wesley said quietly.

She pressed her head into his chest. "You have to know that I meant it when I told you I needed you. I'm so sorry it's not in the way you want, but I still need you. I always will. Okay, Wes?"

He gave her a gentle squeeze. "And *I* told *you* I'm not going anywhere. I meant that, too."

Wesley was long gone by the time Cole emerged from Dr. Gibson's classroom. Leighton nearly leaped off the nearby bench when she saw him.

"Hey, what did Dr. Gibson want?" She stopped suddenly on her way to him, put off by the sullen cast of his face.

Cole barely lifted his eyes. "He asked me about our project."

Leighton inched closer to him on the cracked pavement as if he'd scurry off if she moved too quickly. "What about it?"

Exhaling a sharp breath, he raked a hand through his hair. "He was concerned for my well-being, said he had to address what I disclosed in the project to be sure I'm not at risk."

"At risk? You're not at risk; you're fine." She wasn't sure if she was trying to convince Cole or herself.

"Yeah. I'm fine. Of course. But it was really embarrassing. It made me feel like some kind of mental case. Like the way it felt when I was hospitalized, surrounded by a bunch of white coats with God-complexes who think they know you better than *you* do." Cole shook his head, a distance dulling his eyes.

Leighton softly touched his arm. "Maybe Dr. Gibson was just doing his job."

Cole snickered. "His job is to *teach*. I knew this was a mistake. I never should've let you interview me."

He turned to escape down the corridor, but Leighton rushed after him, cutting in front of his path. "I really thought we were past this. You know I *hate* when you walk away from me."

"I know. I'm sorry." Cole averted his gaze. "I just want to feel like me again. But if people are going to treat me like this—like some fragile, broken shell, or a bomb that's about to go off at any second—I think I'll lose myself completely."

The proper words eluded Leighton as she studied Cole's distressed features. His eyebrows were furrowed, and his jaw was clenched, but it wasn't anger. It was a raw pain, branded deep into the blue of his eyes. Leighton pined to know his deepest thoughts, to find what it was that nearly killed him and kept him up at night.

"You're not broken, Cole."

He looked at her, the glistening silver-blue like melting ice. "I'm more *and* less than you think I am. All at the same time." He reached behind her and slipped his fingers into her hair, cradling her head in his hands. He gently guided her closer to press a firm kiss to her forehead before he breezed down the corridor and disappeared.

Wesley barreled through the door carrying a large cardboard box.

"Are you sure you don't need any help?" Cole asked from his desk, tapping the eraser of his mechanical pencil against his open algebra book.

"It's all right. I've only got one more. Thanks though."

Cole returned to his homework as Wesley exited the room. Just a short moment later, the door opened once again.

"That was fast." Cole turned around. "Oh, Leighton. Hey."

"Is this a bad time?" Leighton asked.

Cole stood and approached her. "Not at all. Wesley's just moving his stuff in."

A giddy smile brightened her face. "I'm so happy this is happening. I can't wait for you and Wes to get to know each other better."

Cole sighed. "Maybe. If he stops hating me."

She took his hand, breathing a soft chuckle. "He doesn't hate you. Everything is good now, you'll see."

Wesley returned just then with the last bit of his belongings. "I just locked Connor out of his room," he announced with a wide grin.

"Nice," Cole remarked.

Wesley flopped onto his bed next to the boxes, emitting a long sigh. "I can't believe I never have to deal with his bullshit *ever again*. Happy Halloween *indeed*."

"We should all go out and celebrate," Leighton said, excitement bubbling in her voice.

"And do what? Go trick-or-treating?" Wesley scoffed and shot Leighton a facetious smirk.

She rolled her eyes. "Shut up, Wes. We were *not* too old, and you know you liked it."

Wesley looked to Cole, who was lost on the outside of their dispute. "Cole, please tell Leighton that sixteen is too old to go trick-or-treating."

Cole shrugged. "I don't know. Is it?"

"If you're old enough to *drive,* then you're too old to dress up and beg strangers for candy alongside small children. In my humble opinion, of course," Wesley said.

"Anyway!" Leighton interrupted. "I still think we should celebrate tonight. Because there's a lot to celebrate and life is too short not to make a big deal out of it."

Cole smiled at her fervency. "I agree. We absolutely should celebrate."

"Okay," Wesley agreed. "Carpe noctem."

seventeen

"I'm surprised you wanted to come with us," Leighton said as she followed Quinn down the stairwell to the first floor of their residence hall.

Her eyes nervously scoured the dress Quinn was wearing—the infamous mint-green dress. Leighton prayed she wouldn't find any unsightly staining that she and Cole had somehow missed before they'd safely returned it to Quinn's closet. Whether it was ridiculous or not, Leighton worried that Quinn would find out about the stunt she'd pulled with Cole. She'd already hurt her best friend by seeing Wesley behind her back. It could be catastrophic if Quinn discovered that Leighton had been less than truthful yet again.

Quinn stared at her phone in one hand while pushing the door open with the other, and they stepped outside into the bustling evening campus life. "I think I'm a little overdue to spend some time with my best friend," Quinn finally replied. "And I'd also like to get to know her new boyfriend better."

"And what about Wes?" Leighton asked.

"He's still on my shit list for ignoring me last

night." Quinn glanced again at the cellular device in her hand.

"Are you expecting a call?"

Quinn sighed. "I was really hoping to get an invite to a cool party tonight, ya know, since it's Halloween and everything. But so far, nothing."

"What about your new bestie?" Leighton asked sarcastically. "Can't you ask her if *Sterling Curtis* is throwing something?" She put a mocking emphasis on Sterling's name.

"Oh, he definitely is. But I don't wanna bug Kennedy about it. I don't want her to think I'm using her."

Leighton made a face. "Aren't you, though?"

Quinn shrugged. "Kind of. Plus, I'd rather my presence be requested than to invite myself like a loser."

How had Quinn gotten so caught up in popularity? In just the past couple of years, she'd changed so much from the way they were as kids, becoming so concerned with fitting in and impressing people. What made Quinn think she had to try so hard? Quinn, just as she was, had always been good enough.

COLE

As soon as Cole caught sight of Leighton, he felt a huge smile instantly break out across his face. It sparked an equally smitten grin from Leighton.

Quinn groaned. "You guys are gross. Just stop."

"Someone's jealous," Wesley said, smirking.

"You mean *you*, right?" Quinn retorted.

Wesley's face went blank and his jaw tightened. With a huff, he yanked the driver side door open and got in. The SUV shook when he slammed the door closed.

"Quinn, that wasn't funny," Leighton said, glaring at her.

"I was just teasing, geez. You guys need to grow a pair."

Cole opened the back door and motioned Leighton in ahead of him. "Is that *the* dress?" he whispered, leaning in close to her.

"Yup," Leighton answered, sliding across the backseat.

As Cole lifted his foot into the car, Quinn grabbed his arm and pulled him back.

"Would you mind riding shotgun with my grumpy brother?" she asked, peppering in just enough charm.

Cole bit his lip and eyed Leighton with reluctance. "Sure."

She smiled and patted his chest. "Thanks, Cole."

He rounded the car to the passenger side and got in, dropping in on a serious conversation that had somehow taken off in the brief time it took him to get there.

"Okay, I'm sorry, Wes. Seriously, I was just joking around. I didn't know you'd *freak out*," Quinn said.

"I didn't freak out," Wesley countered. "And *humiliating* me isn't an appropriate way to *joke*. You're just acting like a bitch and you know it. Because that wasn't even a real apology."

Quinn gasped. "Did you just call me a bitch?"

"No. I said you were *acting* like one. There's a significant difference." Wesley turned the ignition and put the car in reverse.

"Well, Wes, you *are* a bitch, okay?"

Wesley threw the car back into park and twisted in his seat to face her. "What the hell, Quinn? Are you mad at me or something?"

Cole glanced back, watching her cross her arms tightly over her chest. He just wanted a fun night out with his new friends; he didn't want it to be spoiled by Quinn's dramatics.

"I needed your help last night and you completely ignored me," she said.

Concern replaced Wesley's anger. "Did something happen? Are you all right?"

Quinn uncrossed her arms and slapped her hands to her legs. "Yeah, I'm fine, Wes. But what if something really *had* happened, huh? You would've been too busy licking your wounds to save me."

Cole saw Wesley's eyes flicker to Leighton. "I'm sorry I ignored you. But you really need to watch what you say. I'm not sure why I seem to be a joke to you, or why you suddenly have no respect for me, but don't you forget that I am your brother...I've been *with you* since your heart first started beating. But you are not the only one who has feelings, and this world does not revolve around you."

Wesley maintained lingering eye contact with his sister as if to further drive the gravity of his words. Then he faced forward and calmly backed out of the parking space.

When they came to a stop at the campus exit, Quinn's long arms reached around the seat and wrapped around Wesley's chest. He placed one hand on her forearm, neither of them speaking a word during their brief, sacred exchange of forgiveness.

As soon as Quinn slipped back into her seat, Wesley made a left onto the main road toward the restaurant they'd all struggled to agree upon earlier.

After a few moments of quiet, Cole heard a strange crunching sound coming from the backseat. He turned around to see Quinn reaching into the pockets of her dress.

"What the heck?" she muttered. "Leaves? My God, Leighton, what were you *doing*, rolling around in the grass? Geez, you guys."

Cole exchanged mortified glances with Leighton, and she let out a nervous laugh.

"I have no idea how that happened," Leighton said.

Quinn put the window down to let the wind sweep the withered foliage from her hand, then grinned at Leighton. "I told you that you guys were gross."

"So, Cole." Quinn toyed with the straw in her virgin strawberry daiquiri, gazing at Cole with a bubbly anticipation. "What's your story?"

Cole swallowed a mouthful of food. It went down slowly, as if his throat were closing around it. He grabbed his glass and sucked down some soda to stave off a choking fit. "My story?" he asked, hoping to sound nonchalant.

Quinn stole a french fry from Wesley's plate, but she didn't eat it. She waved it around in her hand as she spoke, like she was conducting a small orchestra in the booth.

"I'm just trying to get to know you better. You *are* dating my very best friend, after all. I'd kinda like to know who you are."

Cole looked down at his plate, his appetite quickly dissipating. "Okay. What do you wanna know?"

Quinn took a bite of the french fry. "Hmm, when's your birthday?"

"February seventeenth."

"Aw, you're exactly four months older than Leighton. How cute. My birthday is April fifth." She turned to her brother beside her. "Hey, Wesley, when's *your* birthday? Ha, just kidding."

Wesley shook his head. "You *do* know there's no alcohol in your drink, right?"

Quinn laughed and returned her attention to Cole. "I only know that you're from Lachlan and you're an only child, so, let's see...what's your middle name?"

"Damian."

"Oh, like in *The Omen*?" Quinn remarked.

Cole grimaced slightly. "Yeah. I guess so."

Quinn reached for another of Wesley's fries, but he shooed her hand away as if it were a pesky fly. "What do you like to do for fun, Cole Damian MacHendrick?" she continued with a cheeky grin.

"I don't really do much," Cole answered.

"Okay, what are you into?"

Cole shrugged. "I don't know. I like music, just like everyone else does. I watch movies, I read. I recently took up running."

"That's cool. What's your major?" Quinn asked.

"I don't know yet," he answered sheepishly, pushing his hair back from his face.

"Well, that's okay. You have plenty of time to figure it out." Quinn smiled, taking a sip of her drink. "Tell me about your parents."

That one surprised him. "My dad's an insurance broker, and my mom's a homemaker. They've been together since high school."

"Aw, I didn't know that," Leighton said. "That's really sweet."

"It's actually pretty amazing that all of our parents are still married," Wesley commented.

"Yeah, that's kind of rare these days, unfortunately," Cole said.

Quinn leaned her elbow on the table and rested her chin in her hand. "Man. It really is a shame that you don't have a brother."

Leighton sighed. "Quinn."

"Fine. Sorry." Quinn squinted her eyes, studying Cole. "Would you rather be a billionaire and be alone forever...or have one epic love for the rest of your life but always be poor?"

Cole raised his eyebrows at Quinn's strangely deep question.

"Wow," Wesley exhaled. "That's actually a good one."

"I know." Quinn grinned. "So, what do ya say, Cole?"

Cole stole a swift glimpse at Leighton beside him. He could think of logical reasons to pick either choice. Being alone sounded much safer, but that answer would probably hurt Leighton.

"The latter," Cole finally said, though it came out more like a question.

"That's what I'd choose," Wesley chimed in. "Being poor would be tough, but being alone would be so much worse."

"Aren't you both just so cute," Quinn said playfully.

When Quinn locked glances with Leighton, Quinn motioned to Cole with a tilt of her head, then gave an approving nod. Cole pretended not to notice the exchange.

Before Quinn could concoct another random question in a feeble attempt to decode Cole, her cell phone chimed beside her plate on the tiled tabletop. Her eyes widened as she snatched it up.

"Finally!" she said, typing fiercely on the touch screen.

"Is it Kennedy?" Leighton asked.

Beaming, Quinn set her phone down. "Yup. She just invited me to Sterling's Halloween party."

Wesley sighed in disapproval. "So, let me guess, you're leaving us now?"

"Nope. We're all going."

"Why, because you need a ride?" Wesley asked.

Quinn gave him a light slap on the shoulder. "Knock it off, Wes. We're *all* going 'cause it'll be fun."

eighteen

"I miss the tender years before all the blood. Pressure is whirling, getting dragged through the mud."

As Cole made his way to the painfully familiar locker room, he tried not to think of when he shared the field with Tucker, and he wondered how it would even be possible to play without him. But to regain some semblance of his old life, Cole had decided he would remain a part of the team he'd loved alongside his best friend all these years.

Cole was met with wide-eyed stares when he entered the locker room to change. Guys who were his friends just eleven days before glared at him, trading hissing whispers and mocking chuckles. Cole prayed he wasn't making a huge mistake. But he'd already lost Tucker; he couldn't lose any more of the fragments of life with Tucker that were still within his grasp.

Out on the field, Coach Carson made no effort to mask his surprise when Cole walked out with the others.

After several drills and exercises, Coach Carson called for a scrimmage. Cole removed his helmet as he jogged to the sidelines for a quick drink of water, and he noticed the cheerleading squad congregating several yards beyond him. He easily spotted Ava at the center of the bubbly group of girls, and he marveled at the way the late afternoon sun illuminated shades of red in her dark hair.

Ava turned and looked at Cole, and for a fraction of a second, he'd nearly forgotten his new broken life and almost lifted his hand to wave. But when Ava's icy expression didn't soften, and Cole heard Coach Carson yell "MacHendrick!" behind him, he was instantly slammed with reality.

Cole took his usual place as quarterback, and the rest of the players fell into formation. Immediately after the snap, Josh charged at Cole in a full-on blitz. He threw Cole hard to the ground, knocking the wind right out of him. Coach Carson blew his whistle as Cole lay gasping for air.

"Lindsley! What are you doing?" Coach Carson shouted. "This is just a scrimmage. I don't need you injuring my starting quarterback."

Josh put his hand over his heart in mock concern. "I'm sorry. I'm just trying to put forth my very best effort, Coach."

"Well, save it for the game," Coach Carson ordered. "MacHendrick, go sit this one out. Porter can fill in for you."

Cole sat up, still coughing and sputtering a bit as he rotated his sore shoulder beneath his pads. "No," he said breathlessly. "I'll be fine." He forced himself up, pretending he wasn't in pain.

The scrimmage continued without incident until Cole was running full speed for the end zone.

Cradling the ball close, he ignored the pain in his back, and he pushed himself to the limit. Aaron was quickly gaining on him. Cole reached the end zone, proudly scoring the touchdown. But his moment of victory was cut short as he felt two strong hands slam into his back. The collision sent Cole sprawling into the turf, his body skidding from the momentum. The whistle blew again.

"Slater!" Coach Carson bellowed. "A little too late, and a little too much. Knock off the crap."

"I just did, Coach," Aaron remarked with a snicker as he pointed to Cole on the ground behind him.

Coach Carson sighed. "I see how this is going," he muttered to himself. "Okay, ladies, we're done for today."

Cole watched the team make their way off the field, his entire body aching. No one paused to help him up or make sure he was all right. He struggled to his feet, feeling lower than ever. He was alone now; he had no team.

Coach Carson sauntered into the locker room after everyone had finished changing and preparing to go home. "Before you go, I wanted to say that I'm pleased with the effort I'm seeing out there. That's the kind of drive I want to see this season."

Cole scratched his head, wondering if his teammates' blatant abuse was part of the applauded efforts, and the coach continued.

"Now, the rest of this week's practices will determine the starters for next Friday's game. And one more thing...I know this is tough, but I'd like you to think about who you want to elect as your new team captain, all right? Now get outta here. I'll see ya's tomorrow."

Cole kept his head down, but he'd still seen a few heads turn his way at the mention of the open captain position. The one that had belonged to Tucker. Cole busied himself with the zipper on his backpack, stalling to let the rest of the team file out of the locker room ahead of him.

As he positioned the straps of his bag on his shoulders, Coach Carson approached him, a look of discomfort spreading over his sunburned face.

"Listen, Cole…this isn't easy for me, but I'm not so sure it's a good idea to keep you on the team."

It took a few seconds for the words to register in Cole's mind. "But I thought you said no one from last season was getting cut…"

Coach Carson let out a sigh that sounded more like a groan. "I'm not cutting you; I'm just *suggesting*…maybe you should reconsider your interest in playing for our team."

Cole felt his heartbeat accelerating. "Why? I've been a part of this team for the past three years. I've been quarterback for two years. I made varsity as a sophomore. This is my *team*."

Coach Carson removed his hat and scratched his head. "Honestly? After the way your own teammates treated you today, I don't think it is. I'm sorry, Cole. Our team needs unity. Our community needs a team they can be proud of. I'm afraid that's been compromised…after what happened."

Cole gritted his teeth, angry that his eyes stung with the threat of tears. He hated how weak he'd become—how easily people could affect him and the way he felt about himself. Before Coach Carson could see how deeply hurt he was, he began to turn away.

"It'd be nice if just *one* person cared how *I've* been compromised after what happened," Cole said, surprised by his own candidness. "But don't worry, Coach. The town pariah will no longer be damaging your team's precious reputation."

The rest of that first week dragged on, the tension remaining thick and suffocating. The stares, glares, and whispers didn't stop.

Cole was profoundly relieved to make it to the end of Friday. As he leaned against the building by the parking lot, waiting for his mother to pick him up, his phone vibrated in the front pocket of his jeans. He slid it out to see that he'd received a text message. From Josh. The anxiety engulfed Cole immediately as he began to read it.

Hey Cole. The team and I have been talking and we decided that things have gotten a bit out of hand. We'd like to try getting past this.

Shocked and confused, Cole stared at the screen. Before he could think of how to respond, Josh sent another text.

I'm sure things are hard enough for you right now without all the shit everyone's been giving you. I just wanted to say I'm sorry.

Cole couldn't believe his eyes. *Yeah, it's been pretty awful. Thanks,* he typed back.

His phone buzzed again. *Hey, if you're not doing anything tonight, a few of us are hanging out at my place.*

Mostly just the guys and some of the cheerleaders. You should come.

How could this be? How could his "friends" who'd been so cruel suddenly have a change of heart? Cole wanted so badly for it to be genuine. He was exhausted and miserable, and he needed it all to be over. But he wasn't sure he could stand to face them again.

He typed out a response on the screen with his thumbs. *Okay cool. I'll try to stop by.*

As Cole's mom pulled up, he received another text, from Ava this time. *Hey Cole, did you hear about Josh's little get-together? I really hope you can make it. I was hoping we could talk.*

With the slightest glimmer of hope, Cole pocketed his phone and got in the car.

Cole pulled up in front of Josh's house in his mom's Jeep around seven o'clock, his heart pounding in his ears. He turned off the engine and took a deep breath. There were more cars than he'd expected, but he was too nervous about going inside to give it too much thought. All he had to do was get through the initial awkwardness, and then everything would be fine again. Maybe he could get his friends back. Then, maybe he'd no longer have to go through all of this alone.

Josh opened the front door, a wide smile on his face. "Hey, man, you made it!"

Cole found himself smiling for the first time since Tucker died, but it was more out of courtesy than actual happiness. "Yeah, thanks for the invite."

"Can I get you something to drink? Aaron scored a bunch of PBR from his brother." Josh chuckled, closing the door behind Cole.

Cole bit his lower lip. "Oh, I don't drink anymore."

"Hey, that's cool. I've got soda, too," Josh offered.

"Sounds good, thanks."

Cole's stomach was in knots as he stepped into the living room. There was music playing, like a full-on party. It was definitely more than the "few" hanging out as Josh had mentioned, but Cole was grateful that the lights were low so he could blend in if he needed to. As he caught sight of Ava across the room, Josh approached him with a red plastic cup of cola.

"Hey, have fun, okay? You could use it." Josh patted him on the shoulder before migrating to the sofa.

Cole stood off to the side, sipping his soda, wondering whether he should go talk to Ava or wait for her to come to him. What would he say? What did she hope to talk about?

While he waited to come up with a good opening line or for Ava to make the first move, he felt that familiar uneasy feeling creep back in, clinging to his insides like jagged rust. The same quick glances. The same feeling that he was being talked about. With his pulse racing, Cole pushed through the crowded room to get to Ava.

"Hey," he said, forcing a smile.

"Oh. Cole. So you did make it. Cool," she remarked.

He watched her take a sip of her beer, knowing how much she hated the taste. But she still drank it every time.

"So, you said you wanted to talk…" He hoped he sounded less nervous than he felt.

Ava looked at him for a moment, as if she didn't know how to respond. She glanced around several times, an urgency in her green eyes. Suddenly, Josh approached, a sly smile playing on his lips.

"Hey, are you having a good time?" he asked Cole.

Cole raised an eyebrow. "Yeah, it's fine, I guess."

Josh nodded, eyeing Cole's drink. "Oh, and I spit in that. Just so you know."

With a swift motion, Josh threw an underhanded swat at the bottom of Cole's cup. The contents splashed in Cole's face and the empty cup clattered to the floor.

"Are you having a good time *now*?" Josh asked, his smile turning manic.

Everything was wrong. He had to leave. When had the music stopped? He looked around. Everyone seemed to be gathering like they were waiting for something to happen.

Cole took a step toward the front door but Josh's hand on his chest stopped him.

"You're not leaving yet," Josh said, shoving him.

Cole stumbled backward. "Yeah, I think I am," Cole tried again.

This time, Josh grabbed Cole by the shirt and

flung him into the waiting hands of a few of his other former teammates. Aaron threw a punch to Cole's stomach, and when Cole doubled over, grunting and gasping, he felt the shock and impact of a fist as it collided with his face. Before he could fall over, someone grabbed his wrists from behind, yanking and twisting his arms against his back. He felt the burn and the ache of muscles and joints as his shoulders were hyperextended. Josh delivered a punch that connected with Cole's jaw, and Cole felt and heard the jarring grind of his teeth as they scraped together.

Cole looked Josh in the eye, spitting a mouthful of blood to the floor.

"Don't look at me like that," Josh growled through clenched teeth. He came in close and grabbed Cole's face in one hand, his nails digging into Cole's cheeks. "You deserve this. You know you do."

When Josh let go, Gavin approached with tears in his eyes, and slammed his fist into Cole's nose. Cole's head shot back and he felt the blood pour down as intense pain ravaged deep in his face.

The room was spinning and spotted black. Cole's head throbbed fiercely as the taste and smell of blood filled his senses. After a few more blows to the face and stomach, they let him go, pushing him forward. Cole felt like a rag doll as he collapsed with a sickening thud.

He looked up at the faces that watched him suffer. When he found Ava, he locked his eyes on hers. She let them do this. She *helped* them do this. She didn't stop them.

Gavin stepped in front of Cole's line of vision and crouched down, bringing his mouth close to Cole's ear. He sniffled.

"He was my brother, Cole," he said, his voice shaking. "I'm sorry." As Gavin got up, Cole felt a couple of Gavin's tears drop to his cheek.

Somehow, Cole drove himself home that night. Sometime after blacking out and waking back up, he'd peeled himself off of Josh's living room floor, and staggered out the front door. No one had spoken a word to him. No one had even looked at him. Not even Ava.

Cole gritted his teeth, struggling through swelling eyelids to see the road before him. How could Ava do that to him? Cole couldn't believe anything that had happened that night. He was disgusted with himself for being gullible enough to fall for their sadistic prank. The texts, the apologies, all a farce. A ploy to trap him and get their revenge.

Cole replayed it in his aching head. Every word. Every sound. Every blow. He never tried to fight back, never tried to break free. Maybe Josh had been right; maybe Cole knew he deserved to be punished. Maybe it felt good to hurt for Tucker, to pay for everything that had led Tucker to his death.

When he got home, his parents panicked at the sight of him.

"Oh, my God! What happened to you?" His mother ran to his side.

Cole wasn't sure where to start.

"Who did this?" his father asked, anger laced

in his features.

"I would say my friends, but they're not my friends anymore," Cole said dryly.

His father took Cole's face gently in his hands. "We should take you to the hospital. Make sure you don't need stitches or anything."

Cole pulled away, shaking his throbbing head. "No. I'm not going to the hospital."

His mother wrung her hands. "Honey, you look like you've taken a serious beating. What if you have a concussion or something?"

"I'll be fine. And if not? Even better." Cole began to turn away but his father gently grabbed his arm.

"Cole...do you need to talk about anything? We know things are impossibly difficult right now, but if you think something might be wrong—mentally or physically—it's okay to ask for help."

"Got it," Cole replied.

He went upstairs to his room with the ice pack his parents insisted he take for his eyes. And his jaw. And his nose. And everything else that had already begun to bruise.

Cole lay in his bed, scrolling through his phone. He deleted the text messages he'd gotten from Josh and Ava. Then he deleted their numbers from his contacts. He scrolled to Gavin's number and, for some reason, he didn't have the heart to write him off.

Cole spent the entire weekend in his bedroom, leaving only to use the restroom, and to join his parents at the dining room table for dinner, forcing down some of his food to appease them.

When Monday morning rolled around, and the effects of his injuries were still at their peak, he begged his mother to let him take the week off from school.

She let out a sigh. "A whole *week*? I don't know, Cole."

"*Please*, Mom. They can't see me like this. It'll make everything so much worse."

"I know, sweetheart." She looked at him for a moment, in a helpless way he'd never seen before. "I think starting school so soon after losing Tucker did much more harm than good...I'll call the school later and let them know to excuse your absence."

"You're really gonna let me stay home for the whole week?"

His mom held his face gently in her hands and kissed him on the forehead. "Of course. I know you're almost eighteen, but you are still my sweet little boy, and I can see that things haven't been going well. I know you need a break."

Tears flooded Cole's eyes at her words. He'd gotten so used to the incessant cruelty of the past week, he'd forgotten what it was like to feel valuable. His parents were all he had left.

A few days later, he overheard his mother telling his father how fed up she was of all the scrutinizing stares and awkward avoidance she kept encountering around their small town. Cole's father shared that he was experiencing similar, uncomfortable behavior from colleagues at work. Cole couldn't see the expressions that accompanied his parents' complaints as he perched on the top step of the staircase, but there was something in their tone that made him feel completely alone.

When Cole returned to school, everything was different. No one stared at him. No one defaced his locker. No one whispered about him or said cruel things. No one did anything. It was as if Cole were invisible. At first, he thought he preferred this treatment. But after a few weeks, he was convinced that if he were to run through the halls screaming, no one would even look up.

After a couple of months, Cole couldn't remember the last time he'd spoken to someone other than his parents. And he barely spoke to them anymore. His teachers stopped calling on him in class, letting him slowly disappear, as if he were some faded stain they stopped trying to treat and no longer noticed.

Cole wondered if all the ignoring was intentional, or if everyone had gotten so used to the habit of avoiding him, they'd forgotten him altogether.

nineteen

Sterling Curtis's house was alive with the sights of Halloween and the sounds of unhindered revelry. Leighton's hand slipped into Cole's as they stepped inside, overwhelmed by the rush of blaring music and the hordes of costume-clad people congesting each room.

They weaved through the sea of disguises, still clutching hands. Wesley and Quinn were somewhere behind them, lost in the spaces lit only by the purple and orange lights strung along the perimeter of the room.

Cole stopped in a small clearing at the back of the large living room, and Wesley caught up soon after.

"Where's Quinn?" Cole asked over the music.

"She *was* behind me." Wesley gave a shrug. "Oh, wait. I see her." He pointed across the room. "She's with some guy."

"Oh well," Leighton said.

"So much for hanging out with us tonight, right?" Wesley looked to the distressed wood floor.

Leighton touched his arm. "You okay, Wes?"

He hesitated, chewing his lip, his features

fraught with hurt. "Actually, can I talk to you outside for a minute?" He turned to Cole. "If you don't mind."

Cole shook his head.

Leighton stood on tiptoe to give Cole a quick peck on the cheek. "I'll be back in a few minutes."

"Okay."

She offered him an apologetic smile before she followed Wesley into the riptide of dancing silhouettes and disappeared.

LEIGHTON

Wesley led Leighton to the quieter backyard where they found a wooden bench swing and sat down. He rocked them gently back and forth, the muffled sounds of the party blurring into the background.

"What did I do to make Quinn hate me so much?" he finally asked.

"She doesn't hate you."

"It's not fair to put you in the middle. But you're her best friend and I know she tells you things."

"Wesley…"

"It's okay, you can tell me."

Leighton sighed, gripping the chain of the swing. "Okay, fine. I know she was upset that you chose the same college."

"What? Why?"

"She was tired of being *the twins*. I guess she didn't feel like she was really going off on her own if you were there too."

Wesley chewed at the inside of his cheek. "I

asked her if she was okay with it. I applied to a lot of schools but this one was the best fit for me. It wasn't intentional."

Leighton shrugged. "I don't know. That's just what she told me. And when classes first started, there were a few instances where people thought you were her boyfriend. And that made her mad."

Wesley snickered. "That is so stupid. Who cares? People could think I'm *your* boyfriend right now. Are *you* mad?"

"Eh, just a little."

He shot her a playfully scolding look. "I'm serious."

She laughed. "I know, I'm sorry. No, I wouldn't be mad. But you're not my brother, and Quinn is a lot different than I am."

"Yeah, what is with that? She can be so...irritating. She wasn't always like that, right? Or am I just crazy?"

Leighton shook her head. "No, you're not crazy. She has become sort of shallow and superficial. It's worse than ever lately."

Wesley looked out over the yard. "I was thinking earlier about when the three of us used to stay up really late together on the weekends. How we'd sneak downstairs to steal a bunch of snacks, and we'd try to get them to my room without my parents knowing. But we'd be busting out laughing the entire way up the stairs, practically begging to get caught."

Leighton chuckled. "Yeah, and we'd pig out and watch movies we weren't allowed to see until the sun came up."

"Quinn would always fall asleep first and we'd tease her in the morning. But it was always the three of us. Like we were a team." Wesley smiled, lost in his reminiscing.

"Yeah, we were. Those were definitely some good times."

"The best times," he agreed. "Oh, and how about that one time I was riding my bike and I accidentally scraped the handle bar down the side of my dad's brand new truck? I still can't believe Quinn took the fall for me. I didn't even ask her to; she just did it. She got grounded for a month for that one. And she never complained."

"I remember that," Leighton said.

Wesley frowned. "What happened to *that* Quinn? *That* is my sister—that goofy, selfless girl who acted all tough, but would ask me to camp out on her bedroom floor in the middle of the night when she was scared. And I always did it. Because I didn't want her to be afraid." He looked at Leighton with a sadness in his eyes. "When did she stop needing me?"

Leighton's heart hurt for him. "I don't know, Wes."

He was silent for a moment. "Those late nights after Quinn would fall asleep...when it was just you and me...*that's* when I fell in love with you."

Leighton gawked at him, instantly nervous. "Wesley..."

He looked away with a sheepish smirk. "I know. I'm breaking my promise. But I just needed you to know that."

She fidgeted on the bench. "Okay."

Wesley pressed his feet to the ground to stop the swing and turned to face her, a vulnerable cast to his warm eyes. "I got you a locket for your sixteenth birthday. On a scrap of paper, I wrote, real tiny, how I felt about you, and I tucked it inside. But I was too afraid to give it to you, and I hid it in a box under my bed."

His candidness knotted Leighton's stomach. She didn't know what to say; she just sat there and stared at him.

"When I left home, I almost brought it with me. In case things were different here and something actually happened between us." Wesley looked at his hands and snickered. "I have never wanted to admit this to myself, but I think I came here for you. I didn't follow Quinn; I followed you. I had to know what would happen. Because I'd always been too scared to say something and find out that you'd never felt what I felt. I guess that's why I couldn't give you the locket on your birthday. Hope was always better than an unfortunate truth."

"I'm sorry, Wes."

He waved off her apology. "No, I shouldn't have been so afraid. If I had just given you that locket two years ago, maybe things would be different now. Maybe you'd be with me instead."

Leighton cursed the faint rustle of butterflies inside her. "I don't know what would've happened, but it's just not how things went. It's probably better not to dwell on the what-ifs and should-haves."

Wesley nodded. "Trust me, I know. It's all I do lately. But I don't want to be like that. Cole's my roommate, and he's kind of my friend now, and I promised you I would let you go."

Leighton studied Wesley's winsome features. They were lined with a brave and raw transparency, and she couldn't help but admire him and his unfailing honesty. She wished Cole could be that honest.

"Why are you telling me all this, Wes?"

"Because I can't move on if I don't."

Leighton stepped into Sterling's house through the back slider, and Wesley closed it behind them. They pushed through the packed kitchen, past the counter covered in bottles of liquor. She felt Wesley's hand find the small of her back as he helped guide her through the dense, rambunctious crowds of people to the living room.

But Cole was not where they'd left him. In his place was Lexi, a girl Leighton—and most of their school—knew of, leaning against the wall, sipping from a red plastic cup. She was dressed like an angel, if angels dressed provocatively and wore pounds of heavy makeup. She nearly stumbled when they approached her.

"Lexi?"

She shot Leighton a curled-lip look of annoyance. "Do I know you?"

"No. But maybe you know my boyfriend, Cole? He was just right here. Have you seen him?"

Lexi looked Leighton up and down, her face still scrunched with a judging sourness. "Yeah, I know who Cole is. He left."

"What? What do you mean, he left?"

Lexi rolled her eyes. "He was here, and now

he's not here."

Wesley moved in front of Leighton. "Did something happen? Do you know why he left?" he asked.

Lexi took a few steps toward Wesley, her sparkly halo bobbing. "No, but I know why *you* should stay."

He bent to level his intent eyes with hers. "Listen, Lexi, I need your help. Can you tell me where Cole went? It's very important."

As if hypnotized by his charm, Lexi switched gears. "Yeah, we were talking and I got him a drink. And the next thing I knew, he freaked and bolted out the door."

"How long ago?" Wesley asked.

She shrugged. "I dunno, maybe fifteen minutes?"

Wesley and Leighton exchanged concerned glances before they hurried for the door.

"Do you think he saw us out back and got upset?" Leighton asked, frantically scanning the unfamiliar faces on the front porch.

Wesley shook his head. "No, there was nothing to see. Lexi probably just pissed him off." He stepped off the porch and surveyed the driveway and yard. "I don't see him."

Leighton brushed past Wesley to the bottom of the driveway and looked both ways down the street. "Something must've happened. He wouldn't just leave." She took out her phone to call him and pressed it eagerly to her ear as it rang.

When it went to voicemail, she left a message. "Cole, it's me. I don't know where you are, or what happened, but I'm worried about you. Please call me back so I know you're okay. Or just come back to the party. We're outside looking for you."

After twenty minutes had passed, and they still hadn't found Cole or heard from him, Leighton was growing more upset. "I can't just sit here and wait, Wes. I need to go look for him."

Wesley grabbed a hold of her, gently gripping her shoulders. "Why are you so worried?"

Her eyes pooled as she pressed her lips together. "I can't tell you," she whispered.

Wesley let go and gave her a concerned sideways glance. "What do you mean, you can't tell me? Leighton, what's going on?"

She cast her guilty eyes to the cement. "Can you promise me you won't say a word? Cole will hate me forever if he knows I told you."

Wesley placed his hand over his heart. "I swear I won't. You know you can trust me."

Leighton took a deep breath. "Something happened to Cole last year. Something so bad, he refuses to tell me. It's the reason he pushed me away for so long and acted the way he did. And eight months ago...he tried to kill himself because of it."

Wesley's eyes went wide. *"Seriously?* Wow...that's...awful."

"Yeah. So now you can see why I might be a bit concerned for him."

Wesley reached into the front pocket of his jeans and pulled out his keys. "Take my car and go find him." He took her hand and set the keys in her palm, letting his touch linger for just a moment. "I'll find Quinn and we'll meet you both right here...Hey, look at me." Wesley touched her cheek, his eyes exuding the sincerest compassion and reassurance. "Everything is going to be okay. Cole is fine, you'll see."

Leighton hugged Wesley, grateful for the unwavering security she always felt in his presence.

Leighton had sped the whole five blocks to the lake. She'd barely put the Explorer into park before she flung the door open and hopped out. The instant her feet hit the pavement, she was dashing across the parking lot, breaking into a sprint as she reached the grass. Cole had to be here.

When the lake came into view, a silhouetted figure on a nearby park bench caught Leighton's eye. The closer she got, the faster her heart hammered in her chest.

"Cole?" There was gravel in her voice from breathing in the cool air.

A cloud of smoke swirled upward, vivid under the golden light of the lamppost as it spiraled into the surrounding darkness. Leighton rounded the bench and cautiously sat down, leaving space between them.

Cole didn't acknowledge her presence; he just sat there with a vacant stare, bouncing his knee in an anxious tremor. Shaking, Cole brought the cigarette to his mouth. He took a long, deep pull as if he were desperately sucking in air after holding his breath for too long. Tilting his head back, he released the smoke with trembling lips before he dropped his gaze to the ground. His windswept hair fell over his face, looking as chaotic as he did.

"Cole," Leighton tried once more. "What happened?"

He dug his palm into his forehead, wincing with emotional anguish. "I promised I wouldn't...I *promised* him," he muttered absent-mindedly.

"Who?" Leighton questioned.

Cole turned to look at her, his eyes dull and lightless, but brimming with fear and pain.

"No one," he said in a low, nasal voice. He took another frantic draw of nicotine.

Leighton slid closer to him. "If you don't talk to me, I can't help you."

Cole let out an incredulous, smoky huff. "What makes you think you can?"

Leighton chewed her lip, trying not to let his words hurt her. "Can't you at least let me try?"

"You can't help me. You can't change what I did. You can't bring him back—"

Cole stopped. He sucked in quivering breaths, his chest rising and falling, quicker and quicker as he began to hyperventilate. Leighton's eyes flooded as she watched him fall apart right before her.

"Bring who back? Please, Cole." She reached out to touch his face but he recoiled.

He leaned forward, picking at the loose threads that surrounded the hole in the knee of his black jeans. Blankly, as if it were a thoughtless habit, he brought the cigarette to the gape in the fabric, and pressed the red, burning tip into the exposed flesh of his knee. He barely flinched as the cigarette burned his skin.

Horrified, Leighton yanked his hand away from his leg. "Cole! Stop!"

The cigarette fell to the ground and she quickly stomped on it like it was a repulsive insect. Cole remained facing forward, grinding his teeth with his eyes closed. His hands gripped his outer thighs, his fingernails digging into his jeans.

Leighton gawked at him, suddenly seeing a stranger in his tortured facade. This was so much deeper, so much darker than she'd ever imagined. A wave of fear surged through her, churning her insides to a panic. Who *was* this boy she'd given her heart to?

Leighton could feel the desperation tightening her chest. "Can you *please* just tell me what happened to you?"

Cole squeezed his eyes closed even tighter, spilling tears down his face. "Please don't ask me that," he barely whispered, dropping his head in shame. "I can't. I just can't. I'm sorry..." He folded over, and clenched fistfuls of his hair in his hands as his emotions escalated once again.

With welling affection forcing her fear into the background, Leighton placed a hand between his shoulder blades and gently caressed him. "It's okay," she said, every bit of her aching for him.

She closed her arms around Cole, clinging to him as if his life depended on it. Because maybe in some way, it did.

Cole leaned into her, emitting a defeated sigh. "I'm so tired," he spoke quietly, his voice cracking. "I'm so done; I just want it all to end. I *need* it to stop."

A swelling nausea clawed at Leighton's stomach. "Cole, you're scaring me."

He remained silent.

Leighton couldn't contain her stifled, petrified whimpers as she clutched him. Cole straightened his back, his eyes meeting hers.

"I'm so sorry," he said, traces of alcohol and cigarettes on his breath. "I never wanted to hurt you. I *knew* I would." He brushed his thumb across her wet cheek. "Please don't cry."

His request made Leighton cry harder. "That's not possible. I am so worried about you, Cole. Do you get that?"

He pressed his forehead to hers and closed his eyes again. "I told you that you didn't want this. It's okay if you want to change your mind."

"No. I don't," she answered without missing a beat.

His demeanor softened slightly as his eyes sprang open, locking intensely on hers. "You still want to be with me?"

"Of course I do."

Cole pulled away. "Yeah. For now," he said under his breath.

Leighton struggled to muster up a sufficient rebuttal, but opted to let it go. "What happened tonight? Can you at least tell me that?" She rested her hand on the side of his neck. His pulse drummed wildly against her palm.

Cole looked out at the lake beyond them. He looked lost inside the depths of his thoughts, and Leighton held her breath, praying he would speak.

"There was a girl at the party," he began, his

deep voice hushing Leighton's loud mind. "She's in my English class—"

"Lexi?" Leighton chimed in.

"Yeah. How did you know that?"

"We found her where we left you," Leighton said.

Cole nodded like it made sense. "After you went outside with Wesley, I kind of started having an anxiety attack. It's not your fault; I just have this weird history with parties turning into traumatic events, so..." He swallowed. "Anyway...sometimes when I get anxious, my throat kind of tightens up and my mouth gets really dry. Of course, as that started happening, Lexi came up to me."

"Did she bother you?" Leighton asked.

Cole shrugged. "I just wanted her to go away; it was making everything worse. And then it got really bad, like a coughing fit. Lexi offered to get me a drink so I told her no alcohol because, as you know, I don't drink." His eyes were glistening again. "Well, she brought me what *looked* like Coke, so I just chugged it to make the coughing stop. By the time I realized what she'd given me, it was too late."

"Okay, so you don't drink. But you only had *one* and it wasn't even intentional. Why is that so bad?" Leighton asked.

Cole let out a long, shaky breath and ran a hand through his messy hair. "I made a promise to someone. Something *really* horrible happened last year...because I was drunk. And I *swore* I'd never drink ever again." He looked at the ground and shook his head. "*God*, I hate myself."

"Don't say that."

"But I do. You don't understand how important that promise was."

"It's not your fault, Cole."

He snickered. "I'm so sick of hearing that. If it's not my fault, then why do so many people blame me?"

"Blame you? For what?"

Cole fell back against the bench and tilted his face upwards, letting out a groan. "If I knew you wouldn't leave, I would tell you."

She touched his shoulder. "I won't leave."

Raising his eyebrows, he smirked at her. "You can't promise that."

"Yes, I can."

"How can you be so sure?"

Leighton opened her mouth to speak the truth, but quickly stopped herself. It had been difficult to admit it even to herself, but she knew why his touch set her skin on fire, and why she craved his scent and the sound of his voice. She knew why her heart danced in his presence, and ached in his absence. She'd nearly memorized every crease and line of his hands, and she could easily lose herself in the shadows of his face. And Leighton knew exactly why. But surely, it was much too soon to confess such a thing. Even if it was the reason that made her so certain she couldn't leave him.

Twenty

"So, tell me again why I have to sit here and do nothing when I could be inside having fun?"

Wesley let out a long breath and turned to his sister. He hopped up next to her on the open tailgate of a random truck. "Well, Quinn, sometimes it's nice to follow through on promises we make to people."

"*You* promised Leighton. I didn't," Quinn said, swinging her dangling feet. The shadow of her legs moved on the cracked pavement, bathed in an orange glow from an overhead streetlight.

"Have you really become that self-centered? Do you even care how upset she is?"

Quinn curled her lip. "Um, of course I care. She's *my* best friend, remember?"

"Then you shouldn't mind waiting here for her," Wesley said, checking his phone for the tenth time in three minutes.

"I would mind less if I knew *why* it was such a big deal. Cole took off, so what? Maybe he's more Jared than we thought."

Wesley snickered. "Okay. It's time to let that go and stop throwing it in Leighton's face every chance you get. That was *three* years ago, and I know she would love to forget about it."

"I just don't want her to go through that again," Quinn said, leaning back on her hands.

"Neither do I, but Leighton doesn't need us to protect her. She's not some fragile, clueless child. She's actually quite strong and brave...especially since she met Cole." Wesley hadn't realized it until he said it. Leighton had grown monumentally since Cole had crossed her path.

"Lucky her," Quinn muttered, turning her head away from him.

"What, are you not happy for her? She's finally moving on and trusting someone again. This is huge for her," Wesley said, hoping to feel happier about it himself.

Quinn leaned forward and bent her head, still hiding her face from him. When she wouldn't respond, Wesley scooted closer.

"I know things have been kind of strained between us lately, but you can talk to me," he said.

Quinn lifted her head ever so slightly. "I don't think I can admit it out loud."

"Sure you can. I won't judge you."

She took a deep breath. "I don't know. Maybe...maybe I'm a little...jealous."

Wesley placed a hand on his sister's shoulder as she hunched over in shame. Her hair spilled like a golden curtain between them.

"Jealous of Leighton? Why?"

Quinn tucked her hair behind her ear and peered at him with a timid vulnerability, and for just a moment, Wesley caught a flash of her younger self.

"She doesn't even try and everyone always loves her. Out of nowhere, she gets this gorgeous, cool guy. *And* she's got you. I've got no one."

Wesley shook his head with exaggerated movement. "That isn't true. You have me, you have Leighton—"

"No, you have each other." Quinn grimaced. "I put myself out there, and I try so hard, but I have nothing to show for it."

"Maybe that's it," Wesley said. "Maybe you try too hard."

Quinn shrugged. "I thought that's what people wanted. The wild, fun party girl, not the tame little wallflower."

He shook his head again, subtler this time. "It doesn't matter what other people want. Sure, if you're the life-of-the-party type, then be that. But if you're not, don't force it. You just have to be *you*— no matter what—not some version you *think* you should be."

"Easy for you to say, Wes. Everyone likes you too."

"I doubt that, but I don't care what people think of me."

Quinn shot him an incredulous smirk. "How can you not care? Everyone wants to be liked."

"Well, of course I'd prefer for people to like me, but I won't lose sleep over it if they don't. I'd much rather be myself and know who truly cares for me, than win over a bunch of fake admirers by pretending."

"So you think I'm pretending?"

He rested his palms on his knees, locking his

elbows. "Honestly, Quinn, I don't know. You've changed so much in the past couple years, I'm not sure who you are."

Quinn pushed her hair off of her shoulder in an annoyed flick. "I guess that's why you and Leighton are so tight, right? Because you're both so nice and perfect without effort?"

"I am not perfect." He considered it possible that Leighton was, but knew better than to say so. "Quinn, I don't know why you seem to think you have to compensate so much. You've always been amazing. And I would know; I've known you my *whole* life."

Quinn crossed her arms over her chest. "So, then why is Leighton more important to you than I am?"

"What?"

She rolled her eyes. "I know you're in love with her or whatever, so obviously, it's different, but you're *my* brother. We've always been a team; we've faced everything together since the beginning. But now, it's like you took my best friend from me and then replaced me with her. You two have that bond that you and I should have. And now it feels like it's you and Leighton against me."

Wesley hopped off the tailgate, the rubber soles of his boots making a crunching sound against the pavement, and he stood before her. "We're not against you, Quinn. And I'm sorry if you feel like I stole Leighton from you, but she and I have always been friends—the three of us have been for a long time—but I have never replaced you."

Quinn's eyes pooled. "Then why do I feel like

you don't care?" Her voice was a cracking whimper. "I used to feel like I could always depend on you, and now I'm not so sure."

Wesley flinched. "Why would you think that?"

"Okay, here's a good, hypothetical clichéd question for you: if both Leighton and I were drowning, who would you save?" Her tone was raw and honest, devoid of her typical sarcasm.

"Come on, Quinn..."

She slid carefully off of the tailgate, keeping her eyes locked with his. "No, it's okay. See, I picture you rushing for Leighton and saving *her*."

"Why does it have to be one or the other?" Wesley's shoulders slumped with sadness. "I'd rather drown saving you both."

Quinn pressed her lips together as her tears spilled down. She struggled to reply, but couldn't seem to get a word out. Instead, she threw her arms around her brother, nearly knocking him over, and cried against his chest.

Wesley held onto her, surprised by her behavior. "It's okay," he said quietly, rubbing her back.

She didn't let go of him. "No, Wes. I've been so mean to you. It's *my* fault we've been drifting apart. But I blamed it all on you instead of admitting I was jealous."

He pulled back, keeping his hands on her shoulders. "You have nothing to be jealous of. Sister trumps crush any day."

Quinn managed a smile. "Crush? Yeah right, Wes. You would marry Leighton tomorrow if you could."

He sighed. "Yeah, probably. But I have to let that go now."

Quinn looked at him like she was seeing straight through his projected nonchalance. "God, I'm so selfish," she groaned, hugging him once more. "I've been giving you grief about being there for me, but I haven't been there for you at all. I'm so sorry."

"It's okay," he said again.

Quinn jerked away. "Wesley, no. It's *not okay*. This whole Leighton and Cole thing must be so hard for you. And you just sat here and let me whine about how it makes *me* feel...You really are a good brother, you know that?"

Wesley scratched his head and breathed a soft chuckle. "See? You don't have nothing, right?"

She laughed. "Just the best brother in the whole world, that's all."

A grin spread over his face. "So we're good?"

"Of course. And you're right, ya know."

"About what?"

"I have been pretending. But I'm not going to do that anymore."

"Good," Wesley said. "I've missed you."

LEIGHTON

Leighton sat in the backseat with Cole as Wesley drove toward campus, but no one spoke a word. When they passed beneath the occasional street light, the golden glow would swell and fade, briefly illuminating Cole as he leaned his head against the window. His arms were wrapped tightly around his body as if he were trying to console himself.

Leighton watched him from the opposite end of the bench seat, worrying over what kind of storm was thundering inside of him as he sat there so silent and still.

Wesley pulled into the parking lot in front of the girls' residence hall and turned off the engine. The four of them simultaneously stepped out of the vehicle, and the doors slammed closed like a string of rapid fire.

Quinn offered Leighton a thin, sympathetic smile as they rounded the back of the car to where the boys were standing.

"It's been real, guys," Quinn said, patting Wesley's shoulder before she made her way to the door of the building. "Leighton, you coming?"

Leighton looked to Cole, who stared helplessly back at her. He opened his mouth to speak, but nothing came out.

"Uh, I think I'm going to stay with Cole a bit longer," she told Quinn.

Quinn nodded, pulling the door open. "All right, take your time."

Once Quinn had slipped inside, the three of them stood awkwardly on the sidewalk.

"Okay, I'm gonna go," Wesley said, heading away from them.

"Wes, wait." Leighton caught up to him and stood on tiptoe to slip her arms around his shoulders. "Thank you so much for your help tonight."

He gave her an affectionate squeeze. "Is everything okay?" he whispered.

She tried to keep her voice from shaking. "I'm

not really sure…but I guess so."

Wesley stepped back from her. "It'll be all right. Let me know if you need *anything*."

"I will. Thank you." She returned his warm smile as he turned away, his long strides quickly separating them.

Cole slowly approached Leighton, and in their struggle to find the words to speak, they ended up just watching Wesley disappear.

"Are you finally realizing you picked the wrong guy?" Cole asked.

His voice nearly startled her. "What?"

"It's okay if you've made a mistake. You can tell me."

"Cole…" Leighton pursed her lips. "Please don't talk like that."

He slipped his hands into his pockets and raised his shoulders in a slight shrug. "I just want to make sure you're happy."

She hooked her arm through his and laid her head against his bicep. "I *am*. Being with you makes me very happy."

"Well, that's good," he replied, relief in his tone. "Can I walk you to your room?"

Leighton lifted her head. "Actually, do you think we could take a walk? I'm not ready to say goodnight just yet."

"Okay." Cole pulled his hand from his pocket to entwine his fingers in hers.

They were silent for a moment as they ambled along the deserted sidewalk.

"I think I owe you an apology," Cole said, piercing the quiet.

"For what?"

"The terms of our agreement...I've violated them miserably."

Leighton breathed a slight chuckle and gave his hand a squeeze. "Oh, it's all right."

He frowned. "I promised you I would stop putting myself down and telling you how to feel toward me. I don't wanna be that guy—the guy who breaks his promises. Or the guy who throws a pity party any chance he can get."

She looked up at him, his face half shadow, half light. "Well, tonight—it wasn't the best of circumstances, so violation forgiven. But I think I owe *you* an apology. I shouldn't have left you alone at the party."

"You didn't know what would happen. Neither did I. It's okay."

Leighton pondered for a moment. "Can I ask you something?"

"Yeah...?"

"Shouldn't your medication keep you from having an anxiety attack?"

With a snicker, Cole looked away. "I said I was *prescribed* it. That doesn't mean I *take* it."

Leighton stopped. "Cole. There's a reason you were prescribed it. You can't just not take it."

He let out a long breath. "There are some pains we deserve to go through. I don't want to numb anything; I want to feel *all* of it."

"But you shouldn't have to suffer. Everyone deserves to be happy."

He shrugged. "Maybe. But I still have a lot to pay for."

Cole continued down the sidewalk, and Leighton knew she wouldn't get any more out of him.

"It was a good night up until the party though, right?" she asked, following alongside him.

Cole nodded. "It was, actually."

Leighton raised her eyebrows. "Even twenty questions with Quinn at dinner?"

He smiled. "Yeah. Tonight was the first time in a *really* long time I felt like I had friends."

A warmth swelled in her chest as joy rushed through her. She let go of his hand and slid her arm around his waist, leaning into his side. He draped his arm around her shoulders, curling his fingers over the bare skin of her upper arm.

"Oh, you're covered in goosebumps," he noted, stopping.

Leighton wasn't sure if it was the cool air or Cole's closeness that gave her chills. He removed his jean jacket and helped her into it.

"Thank you," she said, letting the unbuttoned sleeves fall over her hands. She loved the feeling of his heat surrounding her, the incredible scent of him magnified. Her goose bumps didn't go away.

Cole smiled and reached out his hand to tuck a stray lock of hair behind her ear. "I like taking care of you." He fixed the collar of the jacket, his fingers brushing across her neck. "I know you can take care of yourself, but...it's nice."

"Don't worry, I do not mind being taken care of. But I also wouldn't mind taking care of *you* a bit more." Leighton placed her hands on his chest, his skin still warm through his white T-shirt.

Cole covered her hands with his. "You do take care of me. More than you even know."

Suddenly, she could feel the weight of the full pack of cigarettes against her, in the left chest pocket of Cole's jacket. "So, you're okay...after tonight, I mean?" she asked cautiously.

His jaw tightened, his cheeks flexing, and he averted his eyes. "Not really. But I don't wanna talk about it anymore."

Leighton drew her hands away and nodded. "I'm sorry."

Cole gently lifted her chin. "I know I said some things tonight that might make you think— that might make you worry that I..." His chest rose before he let out a heavy sigh, and he locked his captivating eyes on hers. "But you don't have to worry. I promise."

Leighton tried to keep herself composed, but her bottom lip trembled. The truth was, she had been terrified since the moment Cole went missing at the party. Every morbid, gut-wrenching possibility had instantly invaded her mind. Even now, the horrid images still lingered, their residue staining her thoughts.

Cole stepped closer and took her face in his hands. "Leighton, I'm so sorry," he whispered.

"If anything ever happened to you..." Her breath caught in her throat, halting a statement she knew she couldn't finish anyway.

Cole wrapped her in his arms and pulled her into him. "I'm not going anywhere," he said, running his hands over her back.

Leighton nestled her ear against the firm but soft plane of his chest. She closed her eyes and cherished the sound of his heartbeat, and the rhythm of his steady breaths. She matched her breathing with his, his rib cage inflating against hers. He clung to her, melting against her like they were one person.

"Please stay with me tonight?" His quiet voice carried fragments of fear, like a child asking his mother to leave the light on as she tucked him in at night.

Relief enveloped Leighton, and she immediately nodded her head against his chest before looking up at him. "Okay."

Leighton felt herself slipping, her entire body tingling with static. Her mind was shrouded in a thick fog as Cole's mouth pressed against hers, his warm hands anchored at the small of her back. They lay face to face in Cole's twin bed, so close they shared one pillow. It only took a matter of minutes for them to fold into one another, despite their agreement to refrain from any contact for Wesley's sake.

Cole kissed her almost desperately, like it was what he needed to survive, like the escalating heat between them was welding the shards of his broken heart back together.

Just as Leighton began to feel the temptation that could quell all inhibition, Cole pulled back, resting his head just inches from hers. They were both breathless, staring at each other in the moonlit space. Cole's wide, glazed eyes flickered over her face like he was memorizing every minute detail. He swallowed, moving a hand to gently cup her cheek.

"What?" she asked, her heart still fluttering.

The slightest hint of a smile played on his lips. "I love you," he said slowly.

His confession caught Leighton by surprise. "I love you too," she barely managed, her mouth forming a delighted grin.

Cole gazed at her. "You do?"

She nodded eagerly, sliding his hand from her cheek to plant a kiss in his palm. Then she guided it to her chest to place it over her racing heart. Cole breathed a soft, relieved chuckle, his eyes crinkling. Leighton had never seen him look so utterly happy, so full of life.

"I've been wanting to tell you," he whispered, pressing his forehead to hers. "But I was afraid it was too soon...or that you didn't feel the same way."

She twirled a strand of his dark hair between her fingers. "No. That's what I wanted to tell *you* to-night—when you asked me how I could promise I wouldn't leave. I wanted to say it's because I love you."

"You're incredible, do you know that?" His smile was so broad, so genuine, he was nearly unrec-ognizable.

Leighton savored his joy, and this monumen-tal moment as she slowly came down from the clouds. The fog in her head began to clear. "Oh, no. *Wesley*," she murmured, twisting her body to peer be-hind her.

Across the narrow room, Wesley lay in his bed, his back to them.

"It's okay, he sleeps with headphones," Cole

said. He turned onto his back and guided her head to his chest.

Leighton settled against Cole. "Oh, he still does that? He's done that since we were little."

"He said he can't sleep in silence," Cole added.

"Because his ears ring when it's too quiet," she finished.

"That's exactly what he told me." Cole chuckled. "Ya know...Wesley's a good guy."

Leighton wrapped her arm tighter around Cole's abdomen. "I'm so glad you think so."

"How did you meet?"

"How did I meet Wesley?" His question surprised her.

"Yeah."

Leighton lifted her head to glance over her shoulder once more at Wesley. He'd rolled to his back, his white earbud headphones visible in the blue-green glow of his nearby alarm clock.

"I met Wesley in fourth grade. We were nine," she said after returning to Cole's side.

"Okay. But how did you *meet*?"

"Oh, you want the actual story?"

"Sure," Cole said. "He's your best friend. I should know about these things."

She smiled against his T-shirt. "All right, then...so, Wesley was in my class, but he missed the first four days of school because he was recovering from the chickenpox. So, when he showed up on day five, most of the other kids in our class teased him, calling him 'new kid,' and they made fun of him because he still had some healing scabs on his face and his arms."

"That's so mean," Cole commented.

"I know. Fourth graders can be surprisingly brutal. But Wesley ignored them, like it didn't even bother him. I was amazed by that, because if it had been me, I would've been bawling my face off and hiding under my desk. So, at recess that day, Wesley had climbed on top of the monkey bars and he was just sitting up there all alone. He seemed so cool— he was obviously super brave and immune to bullies, and he was the only kid *I* knew who could so easily get on top of those monkey bars. So I climbed up the ladder and I remember I said, 'Hi, my name is Leighton. I'd like to be friends with you.'"

Leighton could feel the rumbling bass in Cole's chest beneath her cheek as he chuckled. "That's what you said to him?"

"I know, it's lame."

"No, no, it's sweet. What did he say back?"

"He said, 'I'm Wesley. I'm really good at being a friend.'"

Cole chuckled again. "Well, he wasn't wrong."

"That sure is true. At the time, I thought he said that because he was trying to be cool. But really, he was just being a typical, honest nine-year-old, and he truly believed he was a good friend. It was like he wanted to assure me that I was making a smart friending decision."

"It's funny because it doesn't seem like he's changed much," Cole said.

"No, he really hasn't," Leighton agreed. "After our incredible introduction, I wanted to be cool like he was, so I climbed up onto the monkey bars to sit beside him. I was so afraid I would fall, so Wesley held onto me until I wasn't scared anymore."

"Like he does now."

"What do you mean?"

Cole shrugged against the pillow. "From what I know, it seems like Wesley has always kind of guarded you and protected you—well, until now. Because you're not scared anymore. So he's let go of you."

Leighton lay silent, realizing the correlation between the two circumstances. "Wow, I guess I didn't notice a lot of things with Wes. Like how he felt about me. How did I miss that for so long?"

"I don't know," Cole replied. "Maybe sometimes we don't notice the things we're not looking for. If that makes sense."

"It does. Probably how you felt about me at first, huh?"

He snickered. "Yeah. I guess you're right."

Smiling, Leighton lifted her head to press a quick kiss to his lips, then returned to his chest.

"So, what happened next on those monkey bars?" Cole asked.

"Oh, nothing much. We just talked about all the pressing things nine-year-olds talk about—siblings, pets, cartoons, that kinda stuff."

"So, when did Quinn happen?" Cole asked facetiously.

Leighton slowly strummed her fingers over his ribs through the soft cotton, thrilled by his interest. "I actually didn't meet Quinn until a few weeks later. Her class's recess time got changed one day and it overlapped with our recess time. Wes and I were hanging out at our usual spot—the monkey bars—and Quinn came running up and she yelled, 'Hey, Wes, who's your girlfriend?'"

Cole playfully rolled his eyes. "Why am I not surprised?"

"That is so Quinn, I know," Leighton said, laughing. "And Wesley goes, 'this is my best friend, Leighton. She can be your friend too if you promise to be nice to her.'"

"Seriously?"

"Yes, and they pinky swore!"

"And then she stole you from him," Cole added jokingly.

"Yeah, I guess that's kind of what happened. I mean, the three of us were together *a lot*. I practically lived at their house on the weekends and every summer. And I even got transferred to their bus so I could go home with them every day after school— my parents both worked and didn't want me to be home alone."

"That's cool," Cole said.

"Yeah, but not the most thrilling of stories. Are you sorry you asked?"

He tilted his head against hers. "No. Not at all. I like learning about you, and all the things I missed before I knew you."

Leighton straightened up to level their eyes. "I love you," she said, then giggled. "I love being able to tell you that; it makes me so happy."

Grinning back, Cole reached out his hand and stroked her face. "You're so beautiful," he told her, his voice an awestruck whisper.

Leighton bit her bottom lip and averted her eyes, her bashful smile widening. "Shh, go to sleep," she said, burying her blushing face in his neck.

Twenty-one

Traces of the rising sun had just begun to lighten the room when Leighton awoke, wrapped in Cole's arms. He was still asleep, a look of serenity gracing his beautiful face. Leighton smiled as she softly brushed a loose lock of hair from his cheek. When he stirred, she pressed a gentle kiss to his lips, and his eyes met hers like a shock of color in a grayscale landscape.

"I'm gonna go before Wesley wakes up," Leighton whispered as Cole's long eyelashes fluttered with drowsiness.

A sleepy grin curved a corner of his mouth. "Okay."

Leighton slipped quietly out of the warmth of Cole's embrace, pulled on her shoes, and disappeared out the door.

When she let herself into her own dorm room, Quinn awoke, sitting up in her bunk. Leighton braced herself for the lecture or the teasing she was sure would ensue. But it never came.

"Good morning," Quinn said in a groggy, cheerful voice. "Is Cole doing better?"

Leighton was speechless for a moment,

caught off guard by Quinn's pleasant behavior. "Uh, yeah, he's much better."

"Oh, good. I'm glad to hear that. I bet it helped to have you there, so he wasn't alone all night."

Leighton kicked off her shoes. "Yeah, I hope it did."

Quinn lay back on her pillow and yawned. "He's lucky to have you."

"Thanks, Quinn."

Leighton climbed up the creaky ladder to her bunk and curled up on her side, feeling cold and lonely without Cole beside her.

Leighton stopped at the edge of the sidewalk to let Cole catch up. "Everything okay?" she asked.

"My mom called me, like, four times. She knew I had class." He tapped his phone screen, then raised the phone to his ear.

He sauntered over to a nearby picnic table and stepped onto the bench to perch on its weathered tabletop. Leighton was glad when he didn't object to her settling within earshot on the bench below him, a mere two feet between them.

"Mom, what's wrong?" Cole said when the call connected. His tense shoulders quickly dropped as he sighed. "Seriously? Then why did you call me so many times? You knew I was in class. I thought something happened...No, it's okay. What did you wanna talk about?...Mom. I already told you. I don't *want* to come home for Thanksgiving...Because. I'm not ready to go back there...Yeah, maybe Christmas...Uh, yeah. She's right here. Why?" He slowly glanced at Leighton. "Mom, no...Ugh, fine. Just *please* don't embarrass me."

Cole nervously held his phone out to Leighton. "My mom wants to talk to you."

Surprised, Leighton eagerly accepted the phone and raised it to her ear. "Hello?"

"Leighton, hi," came a friendly, young voice. "I'm Ivy, Cole's mom. How are you?"

"I'm good, Mrs. MacHendrick. How are you?"

"Oh, I'm fine, thank you. Listen, Leighton, I know this is probably weird, but I wanted to ask for your help, if you don't mind."

"Sure, what do you need?" Leighton asked, ignoring Cole's mortified expression.

"I know you spend a lot of time with my son, so I figured you would know how he's doing. I've been a little worried about him lately, and I thought it might help to hear someone else's point of view. Because I never know if he means it when he tells me he's okay." There was a hint of desperation in his mother's voice.

"I know what you mean," Leighton said, choosing her words carefully in Cole's presence. "The semester started out a bit rocky, but things are getting better. I was worried about my classes for a bit there, but now I know it's going to be okay."

Cole's mom breathed a soft chuckle into the phone. "Thank you for being discreet; I know he's right there. He doesn't talk to me like he used to, and I don't think he understands how easy it is for a mom to worry…So, I shouldn't worry then?"

"No, I don't think so."

"Okay. Thank you so much, Leighton. One more thing…do you think you could subtly try to persuade Cole to come home for Thanksgiving? He's been dead set against it so far, but his father and I would really love to see him."

"Sure, I'll see what I can do," Leighton said.

"Thank you so much," his mom repeated. "I appreciate it more than you know. Oh, and I'm sure Cole will want to know what we talked about—just tell him I'm Christmas shopping and wanted to pick your brain for gift ideas."

Leighton laughed. "Okay, I'll do that."

"All right. Well, I hope to actually meet you sometime soon. Give my boy a big hug for me."

"Yes, hopefully soon. And I will."

After they'd hung up, Leighton returned the phone to Cole, then stood to wrap her arms around him. "This is from your mom," she said with a giggle.

He hopped down from the table. "Oh, no. What did she say?"

She shrugged casually. "Eh, not much. She was out Christmas shopping for you and just wanted my input."

Cole rolled his eyes. "That was all?"

"Yup."

"I'm surprised she didn't bug *you* about Thanksgiving. She's been hounding me for weeks already."

"Well, maybe she just misses you. I'm sure any parent would want their child home for a special holiday."

He turned his eyes to the cement between their feet. "I know. And I feel bad about that. But I can't go back there. Not yet."

Leighton pressed her lips together, suppressing the urge to push harder.

"Well, you still have a couple weeks to change your mind. And I think you should." Painting on a smile, she pulled away to pick up her bag. "And if you want, I could come with you. Your mom *would* like to meet me, after all."

An amused grin transformed Cole's face. "Oh, is that right?"

She nodded. "Uh-huh."

He reached around her, splaying his fingers across the small of her back, and pulling her into him. He pressed a firm kiss to her lips, then lingered close, slyly cocking an eyebrow.

"Nice try," Cole said. "But not even *you* could change my mind."

Quinn barged into Cole and Wesley's dorm room, heaving her large bag onto the foot of Wesley's bed.

"Okay, I'm ready to go," she announced. "Where's Wes?"

Leighton lifted her head from Cole's shoulder. "He got a phone call so he stepped out."

"Am I interrupting you two, then?"

"Nope. We're just saying our goodbyes before you all head out," Cole said.

Quinn plopped onto Wesley's bed across from them. "Seriously, Leighton? You *still* haven't convinced him to come home with us?"

Leighton shot him a cheeky smile. "I've tried, but he's just so stubborn, ya know?"

"I thought he loved you. I guess not," Quinn added, tapping her chin.

Cole rolled his eyes. "I love that you're talking about me like I'm not right here."

"Do you love that we really want you to come home with us for Thanksgiving? Because you should," Quinn said, enthusiasm in her grin.

Cole snickered. "Only if saying otherwise somehow translates into me not loving Leighton."

The door opened and Wesley breezed in, slipping his phone into his pocket. He looked at Quinn with a sigh. "That was Mom. It turns out, Dad forgot the turkey in the trunk yesterday, and apparently, all the stores are sold out. So they're canceling Thanksgiving dinner and will be ordering Chinese tonight."

Quinn grimaced. "Ew, sick. Why is Dad such an airhead?"

Wesley turned to Leighton. "I don't know what your parents are doing, but my mom said they decided to make other plans."

"Oh, my mom is texting me now," Leighton said, removing herself from Cole's embrace to look at her phone. "Ugh, my parents are going to my Aunt Valerie's. I hate going there. She still treats me like I'm twelve. And her sons always pick on me like *they're* twelve."

"Great, now what? I am not eating Chinese take-out for Thanksgiving, and I am not going to some creepy aunt's house," Quinn said adamantly.

All eyes darted to Cole.

"What?" He glanced nervously at each of them.

"What is *your* family doing tonight, Cole?" Quinn asked.

"No. I'm not going home. I told you guys. A million times."

"Come on, how bad can it be? It can't be worse than staying at *school. Alone,*" Wesley said.

Leighton placed her hand over Cole's, wishing she could will him with her touch. "You know your parents would really love to see you."

Cole exhaled, puffing his cheeks out. "I don't know..."

Quinn clasped her hands together. "Please, Cole. The fate of this very important holiday lies in *your* hands."

"How cool would that be?" Wesley chimed in. "The four of us on a fun little road trip to surprise your parents who think you're not coming home? How can you say no to that?"

"Yeah, and you'd be our hero, saving the day." Quinn batted her eyelashes with a playful pout.

"It would be really great," Leighton said, putting on the slightest pout in case it would help. "But only if you're comfortable with it."

"We'll pay for gas," Wesley offered. "Please, just say yes."

Twenty-Two

Cole's fingers tightened around the steering wheel as he turned onto his street. His stomach was already in knots.

"Aw, your house is so nice, Cole," Leighton said when they arrived and got out of the car.

"Thanks." Cole pressed the button on his key fob to open the trunk.

Quinn leaned in and grabbed her mammoth bag, dragging it toward her.

"Do you need some help?" Wesley asked.

"No, I got it." She let out a strained groaning sound as she hoisted it over the bumper.

"You sure do," Wesley said with a smirk, taking his much smaller duffel bag and slinging it over his shoulder.

Cole grabbed his bag and Leighton's and slammed the trunk closed. Taking a deep breath, he headed toward the house.

Cole unlocked the front door and eased it open, allowing the girls and then Wesley in ahead of him. The glorious aroma of Thanksgiving greeted them as they set down their bags and removed their coats in the foyer. Cole led them into the large kitchen where his mother was tending to a pot of boiling potatoes as Bing Crosby crooned a Christmas song on the radio. When his mom turned around, her jaw dropped and she drew in a gasp.

"Cole! Oh my gosh! You said you weren't coming." She pulled him close and hugged him tightly.

"Yeah. Change of plans," Cole said. "These ones talked me into it."

His mom released him and eagerly turned to his guests, her face bright and smiling.

"This is Wesley, my roommate, and his twin sister, Quinn," Cole said, pointing. "And this...is Leighton."

"So *you're* Leighton..."

"Hi, Mrs. MacHendrick. It's so nice to meet you." Leighton offered her hand, but his mom gathered her into a friendly embrace.

"Oh, sweetie, it's nice to meet you too," she gushed, before pulling away to give welcoming hugs to Quinn and Wesley.

Then her sunny countenance dimmed and she looked at Cole. "There's something I need to tell you."

Cole was instantly nervous. "What..."

"When you told me you weren't coming home, I went ahead and invited the Lindsleys to join us for dinner."

He felt the blood drain from his face. "They're coming?"

She bit her lip and nodded. "Should I call them and cancel?"

Cole quickly shook his head. "No. Don't do

that. Wait…do they think I won't be here?"

"They didn't ask, and I didn't say. Please don't worry, honey. I'm sure it'll be fine."

Cole sucked in a deep breath. He could feel his friends' eyes on him, but he couldn't meet their gazes.

The sound of the closing front door demanded their attention, and seconds later, Cole's father entered the kitchen, carrying two bottles of wine in his arms. His face was bright and cheery as he set the bottles down on the counter.

"What a surprise!" he said, pulling Cole in for a manly hug. "I'm so glad you changed your mind. Now tell me, which of these pretty ladies is yours?"

Both Leighton and Quinn blushed.

"*That* one is Leighton," his mother chimed in, pointing.

"*Mom,*" Cole scolded her through his teeth.

Leighton extended her hand and his dad shook it gently. "It's a pleasure to have you with us, Leighton," he said. "And who are your friends?"

"They're my best friends from back home— Quinn and Wesley—and they're our roommates at school," Leighton answered.

"They're twins," Cole's mom added.

"Yup. Still twins," Quinn said with an amused smirk.

Cole sighed. "Please don't mind my mother. She doesn't get out much."

"Oh, Cole. Your mom is just excited. Cut her a break," his dad said with a chuckle, then bent to kiss her on the cheek.

"Oh, wait. That's four more people for dinner," his mom said. She turned her eyes upward like
she was taking some sort of mental inventory. "Oh,
crap. I don't have enough cranberry. Or drinks. And
probably not enough rolls either."

"We can go to the store," Wesley offered.

"I like this kid," Cole's dad said, clapping
Wesley on the shoulder. "Cole, do you mind?"

"Not at all. I'm just gonna take my stuff upstairs and then we'll go."

His dad reached into his back pocket for his
wallet and slipped out a few bills for Cole. "Thanks,
guys."

"Hey, Cole, can you show the girls to the
guest room?" his mom asked. "And Wesley,
hmmm...we have a pullout couch here in the living
room. Is that okay with you?"

"Absolutely," Wesley said, grinning.

She smiled. "Oh, good. Well, I hope you will
all make yourselves at home. We're really glad to
have you."

"Thanks, Mrs. MacHendrick," Quinn said.

"We'll be back down to give you a hand,"
Leighton added.

"Aw, thank you, Leighton," Cole's mom said
warmly. "That would be great."

Cole led them up the staircase and down the
hallway, away from his parents' room.

"Here's the bathroom," Cole said, pointing to
the left.

"Cole, seriously, your house is beautiful,"
Quinn said. "And PS. Your dad is *hot*."

"Oh, God," Wesley groaned.

Cole ignored her, preoccupied with the heaviness that was crushing him. "And here is the guest bedroom." He opened the door to the quaint space, most of it taken up by a king bed. He looked at the long shelf filled with all of his trophies ever so briefly before he turned away, moving along to his room at the end of the hall.

Leighton plopped her bag on the floor in the guest room and followed Cole. She leaned gingerly in his doorway as he tossed his bag onto his bed. He sat down beside it and motioned for her to come inside.

She stepped in and looked around. Cole's room was rather plain. Nothing adorned the gray walls—just remaining tacks still pinned into the drywall, suggesting where things *used to* be. It felt lonely.

Leighton had hoped to feel closer to him here, to see his most personal space and how it reflected him. But it reflected nothing at all.

"Yeah, I'm not much for decorating," Cole said, as if he could sense the direction of her thoughts.

"Oh, no, it's nice."

He crossed the room and slipped his arms around her, drawing her into him. "It's so weird to see you standing in my bedroom."

"Good weird?" she asked.

He shrugged. "I don't know. It's just strange. Like a mixing of two *completely* separate worlds."

Leighton bit her lip, wishing Cole didn't have

such a hard time equating her with *home*.

"So, are your parents always that nice?" she asked, changing the subject before he said something else to make her feel even more disconnected from him.

"Yes. They are, actually," he answered with a smirk.

"That's cool. They sure seemed happy to meet me."

Cole sighed bashfully. "They may know a bit about you."

"Oh, really?"

"Yeah, I was like, 'there's this girl who's stalking me, but she's kinda cute, so it *might* be okay.'"

A facetious grin curved his pretty lips, and she couldn't help but smile back at him.

"Well, I better get going before the Lindsleys get here," he said, all traces of his happiness vanishing. He pressed a quick kiss to her forehead.

Then he left, calling out to Wesley in the hall, and Leighton was all alone, surrounded by four walls she wished could talk. She was certain they'd know all the things she didn't. All the things Cole couldn't tell her.

COLE

Cole rounded the corner, Wesley close behind him, and breezed down the aisle, scanning the shelves for the items his mother had requested.

"Cole?"

He stopped, the sweet, familiar voice nearly taking his breath away. He knew before he even turned around that he would see her standing there.

"Delaney, hi."

Delaney shifted the basket of groceries she was clutching and offered him a nervous but endearing smile. Her blonde hair was swept up into a messy knot on the top of her head, and despite her faded, oversized sweatshirt and no makeup, she was still beautiful.

"Wow, it's been a long time," she said. "You're home for Thanksgiving?"

"Uh, yeah. It was kind of a last minute decision. So now I'm picking up some things for my mom because she wasn't expecting the extra company."

"Well, I'm glad you decided to come home. It's good to see you." Delaney eyed Wesley curiously and Cole followed her gaze.

"Oh, I'm sorry. This is a friend of mine from school."

Wesley grinned and extended his hand to her. "Hi, I'm Wesley. Delaney, is it?"

Her face brightened as he shook her free hand. "Yes. I'm an old friend of Cole's from high school."

"It's a pleasure to meet you, Delaney." Wesley reached for the basket she was carrying. "Here, let me help you with that."

"Oh, thanks."

Cole glanced over at the contents of the basket. "What's all this?"

Delaney made a face as she shrugged, the sleeves of her sweatshirt falling past her hands. She didn't push them back up. "Dinner?"

Cole looked at the microwavable meal, package of Oreos, and half gallon of milk in her basket.

"You're not celebrating with family?" Wesley asked.

"It's just my dad and me. He's a truck driver, and unfortunately, he's away for the rest of the week, so I'm on my own."

Cole could sense her sadness. He could see it in her face. It was built into her structure. It may have been more than a year since they'd last spoken, but she hadn't changed at all. Cole could still easily read the emotions she thought she hid so well.

"Hey, Delaney," he began carefully. "Why don't you come to my house and have dinner with us tonight?"

Her eyebrows lifted with a sense of relief. "Really? That would be okay?"

Cole chuckled. "Of course. But I have to let you know, the Lindsleys will be there. My mom invited them."

Delaney pressed her lips together. "Oh. Okay. It's actually been several weeks, so it'll be nice to see them." She hesitated for a brief moment. "I'm gonna go home and get cleaned up first." She glanced down at her ensemble with a bashful laugh.

Wesley shot her a playful smirk. "I'll go put all this nonsense back for you, then."

After Wesley had disappeared from the aisle, Delaney turned to Cole and sighed. "Thank you so much. Today has been really hard. I thought holidays would be so much easier the second year, but they haven't been. Not really, anyway. I'm so glad I don't have to be alone tonight." Without waiting for Cole's reply, Delaney threw her arms around him, squeezing him tightly. "You don't have to be so kind to me. I was such an awful friend to you, and I'm so sorry."

He held on to her small frame. "You could never be an awful friend, Delaney."

"I should've been there for you. If anything had happened to you..." She sniffled. "I came to visit you when you were in treatment, but they wouldn't let me see you because I wasn't family."

Cole pulled away to look at her. "You came to see me?"

She nodded. "I tried calling too, but I guess you changed your number. And I drove by your house so many times, but I was afraid."

"Why?"

"Because if I found out that you hated me, I couldn't handle that," she said quietly, her gaze falling to the speckled terrazzo beneath their feet.

"I could never hate you, Delaney. You did what you had to do, and I deserved it."

Her lip trembled. "You don't still blame yourself for what happened..."

He shrugged. "Do I have another option?"

"Hey, I found the cranberry," Wesley's voice interrupted them. He approached with a jovial grin, holding up a can.

"I'll let you get back to your shopping," Delaney said. "I'll see you guys a little later." With a quick wave, she turned away. Cole swallowed hard when he saw LINDSLEY, faded but loud, printed across the back of her sweatshirt.

Cole parked next to the Lindsley's familiar SUV in his driveway. The little stick-figure family of four that was still displayed on its back window made Cole feel sick. He turned off the engine, hoping Wesley wouldn't notice that his hands were shaking.

"And who are the Lindsleys?" Wesley asked. "Friends of the family?"

"Yup." Cole grabbed the grocery bags from the backseat and led Wesley up the front walk.

Cole struggled to unlock the front door with a steady hand. He dreaded stepping inside. But there was nothing to be done now. He had to face them.

Cole gingerly pushed the door open, motioning Wesley in first. Friendly chatter resonated from the living room where Cole's parents were entertaining their guests. Cole couldn't wait to find Leighton, hoping to draw from her steadfastness. He needed to keep calm enough to endure whatever the evening might bring.

Following behind Wesley, Cole passed through the foyer and the family room before reaching the kitchen.

Cole instantly caught sight of Tucker's parents in the living room, donning pleasant smiles and sipping from glasses of white wine. Gavin slouched on the leather sofa, staring at his cell phone. He looked bored, but not angry or upset.

Leighton nearly startled Cole when she appeared beside him, taking the groceries and setting them on the counter.

"What took you so long?" she asked light-heartedly, planting a soft kiss on his cheek.

"We ran into an old friend of Cole's," Wesley

chimed in, picking up a bottle of wine. He removed the cork and breathed in its scent.

"Nuh-uh," Cole's mom said with a laugh as she took the bottle from Wesley's hand and replaced it with a can of soda. She turned to Cole. "What friend did you see, honey?"

"Delaney," Cole said. "I hope it's okay, but I invited her to come to dinner. She was going to be all alone tonight."

His mother smiled. "Of course it's okay."

"Good, because she should be here any minute."

"Perfect, dinner is just about ready. And Leighton and Quinn have been such a huge help, no matter how many times I've told them to sit and relax." She shot both girls a grateful grin as she got back to work.

Cole looked up at the living room beyond the long counter, making perfect eye contact with Mrs. Lindsley. Her thin, polite smile made him feel nauseated, but he gave her a nod.

"Oh, hey, Cole. Would you mind bringing us more wine?" His father asked, waving him over.

Taking a deep breath, Cole picked up the bottle of Moscato. It felt much heavier in his hands than it actually was. He carried it across the living room to his father, who stood with Tucker's parents.

After he'd handed his father the bottle, Cole's hands started shaking again and he hid them in his pockets. It was odd to feel disturbed by the presence of the Lindsleys. They'd been a second set of parents to him. But now, he didn't even know how to look them in the eye.

"Cole surprised us this afternoon, showing up with some friends from school," his dad said, tousling Cole's hair like he was a little boy. "It's good to see the Lindsleys again, isn't it, son?"

Cole nodded, painting on an awkward smile. "Yes, it is." He finally turned to face them. "Hi."

"Hi, Cole," Mr. Lindsley greeted him, extending his hand.

Cole shook it, his heart racing. "Hello, sir."

"How's college?" Mrs. Lindsley asked, sipping from her newly topped off glass.

"It's going fine," Cole answered. "I, um…"

The only thought infiltrating his brain was that Tucker never made it to college. Surely, that had to be exactly what the Lindsleys were thinking too, and Cole could hardly breathe, let alone speak.

Cole wasn't sure when Delaney had arrived, but suddenly she was right beside him, offering her tender-voiced hellos, saving him from his agonizing speechlessness.

"Oh, sweetie, it's so good to see you," Mrs. Lindsley gushed, wrapping Delaney in a secure hug that somehow didn't spill her wine.

Mr. Lindsley leaned in to give her a fatherly kiss on the cheek. "How are classes going at the community college?"

"Oh, they're going okay. I'm trying really hard to keep my grades up so I don't lose my scholarship," Delaney said, a subtle stress interwoven with her tone.

"Listen, if you ever need anything, you let me know. I don't want you and your dad worrying about your education," Mr. Lindsley offered.

Delaney's mouth hung open for just a moment. "Thank you so much. That really means a lot to me."

"It's our pleasure, sweetie," Mrs. Lindsley said, rubbing her arm.

Cole felt useless standing there, like he was eavesdropping on a conversation he had no right to be a part of. He thought about the college fund they must've been building all Tucker's life, and how they could probably afford to help Delaney because Tucker never got to use it.

Just when Cole's nausea was nearly prompting him to make a mad dash for the restroom, he felt Leighton's soft hand slip into his. The faintest thread of relief stitched him back together.

"Oh, now that this lovely girl has finished giving my wife a hand, I can properly introduce you," Cole's dad said. "Tim, Maggie, this is Cole's girlfriend."

"Hello, Mr. and Mrs. Lindsley. I'm Leighton Tucker." She grinned warmly, shaking their hands.

Instantly, Cole noticed the frozen looks on their faces when they heard her name. He knew they were experiencing the same brutal punch in the gut he'd experienced when she'd first introduced herself to him in psychology class. It had been such a cruel coincidence, and he'd reacted with such coldness that now filled him with guilt.

"It's nice to meet you, Leighton," Mrs. Lindsley said, taking a gulp of her wine.

Cole released the breath he'd been holding when he heard his mother announce that dinner was ready.

"So, twins, huh?" Mr. Lindsley said to Quinn.

She sighed and nodded. "Yes, sir."

"Who's older?" he asked.

Wesley raised his hand slightly from the opposite end of the large farm table. "I am. But only by two minutes."

"Oh, I always wanted twins," Cole's mom said with a wistful smile.

"Do you share that special twin thing I've heard about? Like you know each other's thoughts, or you can sense if something is wrong with the other?" Mr. Lindsley asked.

Quinn shook her head. "Not at all. Actually, Wes and *Leighton* have that more than Wes and *I* do."

Cole watched Wesley and Leighton exchange sheepish glances. "Well, I don't know about *that*," Wesley muttered, shifting in his chair.

"So, Mrs. Lindsley, how has your practice been going?" Delaney asked. "I've been meaning to come in and see you again. Things have just been so busy with work and school."

"Oh, that's all right, sweetheart. It's been going well. Thank you for asking. I feel like I'm really making a difference." Mrs. Lindsley gave her husband a slight smile when he reached over to squeeze her hand.

"What is your practice?" Wesley asked.

"Grief counseling."

"And I am so proud of her," Mr. Lindsley chimed in. "She worked so hard for that degree when we first got married, but kids kind of derailed the whole thing."

Cole saw Leighton eye Gavin at Mr.

Lindsley's plural usage of *kids*. He feared the curiosities that he knew were already blooming in her mind.

"Oh, we know how that is," Cole's mom said warmly. "My college plans went out the window completely when Cole came along."

"Yeah, you got a marriage license instead of a degree," his dad joked. "Let's just say Cole's high school graduation wasn't the *first* high school graduation he took part in."

Cole's mom blushed. "Michael, I think you've had enough wine."

"Oh, we're all adults here. I'm sure Cole has done the math. He knows he was born eight months after we graduated. And only five months after we got married."

Cole actually hadn't done the math. And he hadn't given much thought to the timeline of his parents' early years. But as he imagined them finishing out their senior year with a presumably horrifying pregnancy bombshell, and abandoning their dreams just for the wretched disappointment he'd turn out to be, he knew he was the biggest mistake they'd ever made.

"Anyway," his mom said, shooting his dad a stern look. "Maggie, I'm proud of you, too, for what you're doing. I'm sure you're able to use what you're going through to help comfort so many hurting people."

Cole hung his head, letting his hair fall like a shield over his face.

Cole hadn't been thrilled in the slightest when his father suggested he and Gavin go to the garage to find his old football.

He hadn't touched a football since his final practice at the beginning of senior year. He wasn't sure where his parents had stashed his old ball—one of his many visual triggers in earlier, weaker days— but he was sure he didn't want to be looking for it with Gavin.

"I know about what your parents said at dinner," Gavin said, opening a cabinet and closing it again.

"What are you talking about?" Cole asked, rummaging through a storage chest.

"Josh and Ava were talking about it once a while ago. Josh said your mom was friends with his mom—my Aunt Vanessa—in high school. He said she went to a clinic with your mom after she found out she was pregnant with you, but your mom chickened out."

Cole stopped looking for the ball and froze. "What?"

Gavin wet his lips, hesitating to continue. "Josh said your mom made a mistake. That she should've gotten rid of you when she had the chance."

Cole glared at Gavin. "Why the hell are you telling me this?"

Gavin struggled to mask his nervousness. "Because I wanted to tell you it's not true. After what you…tried to do on Tuck's birthday, and when I saw the look on your face at the table earlier, I felt like I had to tell you."

Cole let out a long breath. "Tell me what, exactly?"

"That you're *not* a mistake. You're not a bad person, Cole."

Cole's throat tightened, and he returned to the storage chest to continue his search. "Can you just help me find the damn ball?"

Gavin pulled a crate down from the shelf and looked inside. "I'm just saying...if anything happened to you, it'd be like losing another brother."

A deep ache radiated in Cole's chest. When he finally turned to Gavin, Gavin tossed him the football.

"Found it," Gavin said with a casual smile. "Come on, QB. Let's see if you've still got it."

Cole was speechless as Gavin stepped out the side door to the yard where their fathers waited for them.

WESLEY

Wesley stepped out onto the back porch. Delaney was sitting on the railing watching the game of catch.

"Hey," Wesley said, pulling himself up to sit beside her.

"How come you're not out there?" Delaney asked, pointing to the yard.

"I'm not really the athletic type."

She timidly looked him up and down. "No? What type are you?"

He chuckled. "Raging nerd?"

Delaney let out a joyful laugh. "Really? You

look like one of the cool kids to me."

"I don't know. I'm really just a big geek."

"You don't try to hide this magnificent geek-ery, do you?" Delaney asked playfully. "I know how pathetic the demands of social acceptance can be."

"I don't hide, but I suppose I don't necessarily advertise it. So not many people know me as the brainy bookworm and film buff who thoroughly enjoys *Jeopardy* and Bob Ross."

"I *love* Jeopardy," Delaney said, her face serious. "And Bob Ross is my spirit animal."

Wesley nodded approvingly. "I knew I liked you."

She turned her shy gaze to the yard to watch Cole spiral the football flawlessly through the air. A cold gust of wind made her shiver, and Wesley removed his coat to drape it around her.

A content smile graced her lips. "Thanks."

"You're welcome."

"I am so glad I didn't have to work today," Delaney said, making herself comfortable in his jacket.

"Where do you work?" Wesley asked.

She made a face. "This sketchy convenience store on the edge of town."

"If it's so bad, why do you work there?"

"This is a pretty small town, so the choices are limited when it comes to employment. I need a job so I can help my dad out and put myself through college, and this was all I could find."

"But at least you're off today," Wesley said.

"Yes. And that gave me the chance to run into you guys."

He flashed a wide grin. "I'm glad you did. No one should have to spend Thanksgiving alone."

She snickered. "Yeah, I was in for a long, lonely night of junk food and binge-watching *Friday Night Lights* on Netflix."

"That actually doesn't sound *too* terrible, minus the lonely part."

Delaney breathed a tender sigh. "That's definitely the terrible part."

Wesley watched her expression dim with a sadness that her face seemed to know by heart. "I would think a girl like you would be...you know, spoken for."

"A girl like me?"

He blushed. "Well, I mean, I only met you a few hours ago, but...you certainly have *my* attention."

Delaney dropped her gaze to her hands in her lap, brushing her fingertips delicately over the tarnished silver bracelet on her wrist. "I used to be...spoken for." Her voice was quiet and filled with longing. "My boyfriend...he passed away last summer."

Wesley felt every trace of cheerfulness drain away, replaced by an all-consuming shock. "Oh my God. I am *so* sorry." He hesitated for a moment. "Can I ask what happened?"

Delaney gave a slight nod. "It was a car accident."

"Wow...I can only imagine how awful that must be."

Her eyes shot to his like something had clicked, resonating with her. "Thank you."

"For what?"

"For saying you can imagine it." Delaney paused, snickering at herself. "This probably sounds stupid, but every time someone says 'I can't imagine,' my heart just skips a beat. Because I think if they were willing to picture what it would feel like, they *can* imagine it. When they say they can't, it makes me feel like they don't want to be bothered to feel something. They just want to block it out because it's inconvenient to face something sad. And when they say they can't imagine, it makes me feel so alone. Like their life is so perfect and painless, they couldn't possibly relate to how broken *mine* is. That's probably distorted thinking, and I know people mean well, but that's how I feel."

Wesley wanted to touch her hand, but he didn't. "I don't think it's distorted; I think it makes sense. If my imagining the loss of the person I love can bring you a fraction of comfort for even a second, then I can do that. If you're forced to live this reality for the rest of your life, people can sure as hell stand to feel uncomfortable for a measly minute to give you the proper condolences."

Delaney studied his face. "Have you ever lost someone close to you?"

He rubbed the back of his neck. "Well, my great-grandfather died when I was four, but no. I haven't lost anyone I was *really* close to. Why do you ask?"

A thin smile curved her mouth ever so slightly. "It's just that no one's ever made me feel so understood...besides Tucker."

"Is that his name? Tucker?" Wesley asked,

the name already so familiar to him.

Delaney's eyes were welling up again. "Everyone always says *was* when they talk about Tucker. But it's nice to not speak of him in past tense for once."

"Well, his name *is* still Tucker. Even if he's not here," Wesley said.

Delaney stared off past the yard, like her mind was somewhere far away. "Do you think we keep our names in Heaven?"

Wesley's eyes followed hers toward the horizon as if he would somehow catch a glimpse of her thoughts. "Sure, why not? I'd say God had enough creatures to name; I doubt He'd want to rename all of us, too."

Delaney turned back to him, a sudden chuckle escaping her lips. "How is it that you seem to know all the right things to say?"

He shrugged. "I'm just talking. You're easy to talk to."

"So you're just so magically intuitive all on your own?"

Wesley laughed. "If you say so, then I guess I am."

"Well, whatever it is, it really helps to be able to talk like this," Delaney said.

"Don't you have anyone you can talk to that you actually *know*?"

"Honestly, I feel like I know you just fine," she replied with a smile.

He couldn't help smiling back. "What about Cole? Did he not know Tucker?"

Delaney stared blankly at Wesley. "Tucker

was Cole's best friend. He's never said *anything* to you about him?"

Wesley chewed his bottom lip and shook his head. "No. Cole's mostly been a huge mystery. Probably the most closed-off person I've ever met. Leighton has been hell bent on decoding him since the second she met him."

Delaney frowned. "He wasn't always like that, ya know. He was fun, and silly, and happy…"

"Until the accident," Wesley finished. "But why such a drastic change?"

Delaney sighed. "Because Cole and this entire town believe *he* killed Tucker."

Twenty-Three

"Those cigarette burns and blackouts, just a symptom of the breakdown. I know you don't get it, but it's more than I can handle right now."

At lunchtime, Cole went outside and sat in the courtyard by himself. Avoiding the crowded cafeteria was probably in his best interest, considering the outcome of yesterday's assembly. Not that he felt like eating anyway. He hadn't been able to fight off the incessant sick feeling in his stomach long enough to muster up any appetite.

Cole's attention shifted to a motion out of the corner of his eye when Delaney came traipsing toward him across the courtyard, her face devoid of her usual cheer. Cole hadn't spoken to her since that night—when he'd been the one to tell her that her boyfriend was dead.

Delaney sat at the opposite end of the bench and, immediately, Cole could feel the rift between them.

"How are you doing?" she asked.

Her question surprised him at first. But of course, Delaney of all people could never lose her compassion for people. Not even him.

"I'm not sure, actually. It's been pretty bad," Cole finally answered. "Are you doing okay? I mean, considering…"

She shrugged, her eyes glistening. "I'm not. I don't know how I'm going to do this every day for the rest of my life. I keep finding myself forgetting that this is never going to end. Missing Tucker will *never* be over. I guess I can't wrap my head around that. He's just never coming back."

Cole nodded, casting his eyes to the ground. "I know exactly what you mean. Between that and the guilt, I'd say I'm a mess."

Delaney snickered despite her tears. "Oh, yes. The guilt. I've got that too." She stopped for a moment, struggling to calm her emotions, then whispered, "Cole…why'd you have to kiss me?"

His stomach dropped as he turned to look at her.

Please, not Delaney too.

She wiped her red eyes. "I can't blame you like the others do, because I had a hand in what happened that night."

"It's not your fault that I kissed you," Cole countered.

"I didn't stop you…" She sighed. "But no one knows that. No one is blaming me for what happened."

Cole narrowed his eyes. "What are you trying to say?"

"I don't think I can be seen with you," Delaney admitted in a quiet voice. "I know it's awful to say this, but I can't handle anyone blaming me. If they see us together, they'll think something is going on between us. I still love Tucker and it would kill me if anyone thought I'd do that to him, that I could so easily move on. I know I really need your friendship right now, but I just can't do it."

"Delaney…"

"I'm so sorry, Cole. You're strong; you'll make it through this. But I don't think *I* could survive their judgment. I'd like to avoid it if I can. I really hope you understand."

Cole couldn't look at her. He clenched his jaw, trying to abate the urge to fall apart as she hurried off. Delaney had always been so selfless and kind. Of all the times to finally be selfish, this was the absolute worst.

But he understood.

Twenty-four

When it came time for Delaney to head home, Wesley and Cole walked her out to her car.

"Thanks again for having me over, Cole. I had a good time," Delaney said, smiling.

"Thanks for coming," Cole replied. "It was really nice to see you again."

"I promise it won't be as long till next time." Delaney moved in close and hugged Cole tightly, giving his back a caring rub. "Wherever Tucker is, I know he loves you," she whispered before letting go.

Cole gaped at her, holding his breath to restrain the sob that was rising in his throat. He couldn't fall apart now, not with Wesley right beside him and Leighton just inside.

Delaney moved on to Wesley with a secure, lingering embrace, then pulled away. "I'm so glad I met you," she said. "Thank you for tonight. I needed it more than you know."

Pulling away, she slipped a folded piece of paper into his hand. "Call me, okay?"

Wesley smiled. "I will."

Delaney gave a reluctant wave before getting into her car and driving off. Once she'd disappeared around the corner, Wesley unfolded the slip of paper, grinning.

Cole peered over at Delaney's familiar, pretty handwriting. "She gave you her number?"

"She did." Wesley slid his phone out of his front pocket to add her to his contacts.

"So I guess you two hit it off tonight?" Cole asked, a brick settling in his stomach.

"Yeah. She's pretty amazing."

With his hands on his hips, Cole looked at the ground and took a deep breath. "I don't know, Wesley. Delaney's not a good idea."

Wesley furrowed his brow. "Why is that?"

"You can't just—you have to be careful with her," Cole stammered.

"I know."

"No. You don't know."

Wesley sighed. "I know about Tucker."

Cole felt his face flush at the sound of Tucker's name. "What? What do you know about...Tucker?" Cole asked, his voice shaking.

"I know what happened."

Cole pushed a hand through his hair, gripping a handful on top of his head. "Delaney told you...everything?"

Cole was beginning to unravel. And as he saw Leighton step out of the front door behind Wesley, he thought his heart just might implode.

"She told me he was her boyfriend and that he died in a car accident," Wesley said.

Relief began pulling Cole back together. "That's all she said?"

Wesley nodded.

"Hey, Cole," Leighton said cheerfully as she approached. "Your mom is making hot chocolate and I'm supposed to find out if you want any."

"Oh. No thanks."

She turned to Wesley. "How about you, Wes?"

"Yeah, I was actually about to head inside. I'll see you guys in there," Wesley replied, walking off like he was purposely leaving them alone.

Leighton studied Cole's face. "What's wrong? You've been quiet and closed off all day. Did something happen?"

"Nothing new."

She took his hand in hers. "Please talk to me. I can't stand seeing you like this."

He didn't look at her. "I can't."

Leighton let out a frustrated huff. "You know, I was hoping I'd feel closer to you here, but you're more distant than ever. Will you ever let me in, or is this it?" A tear slipped down her cheek.

Cole bent his head, avoiding her desperate gaze. "Please don't make me do this."

"Do what, tell the truth? Or break up with me because you can't? Which one am I *making* you do, Cole?"

His head snapped up to look at her. "Break up? No. I'm not asking for ultimatums."

"Neither am I, but can you just imagine for a second how this makes me feel? You *know* it's hard for me to trust people, and you expect me to be okay with so many secrets."

"Why does it have to matter?" Cole asked,

growing weary. "You didn't want my past, remember?"

"It matters because these secrets aren't in the past. They affect us every single day. You drift off into these quiet, dark moments that I'm not allowed to ask you about or help you out of. How is that okay?"

Cole crossed his arms over his chest and shrugged. "I'm sorry."

She took a hold of his face, forcing him to look her in the eye. "How about the fact that I have *no* idea why my boyfriend tried to kill himself only *months* ago? Without any explanation, I'm expected to not live in fear that he might try again?"

Cole fixed his eyes intently on hers, his resistance
waning. "Is that really how you feel?"

Leighton dropped her hands and her gaze, hiding herself from him.

"You think I still want to kill myself?" he asked.

Placing his hand beneath her chin, he gently lifted her head.

"Well, when you know absolutely nothing, your imagination fills in the blanks pretty morbidly," she said.

Cole brought his face close to hers, bending to level their eyes. "I don't want you to worry about me."

Leighton slid her arms around his shoulders. "Something happened to you that was so bad, you wanted to *die*, and I'm just supposed to look the other way? How can you ask me to do that?"

"I don't know," he said, drawing her into him. "I wish I could give you more than that, but I love you too much."

"I love you too," she whimpered. "More than you can imagine."

Cole threaded his fingers through her hair, cradling her head tenderly against his chest. "That's what's saving me."

Squeezing his eyes closed, Cole let the warm water pour over his face for a long while, wishing he could wash away the strange tension that had seemed to settle between him and Leighton.

As he tried forcing his focus to less stressful things, he thought he heard the bathroom door creak open ever so softly, and he froze.

"Hey, Cole, can I talk to you for a minute?"

It was Quinn. Her voice was hushed but completely casual. As if she'd simply happened upon him in the kitchen or living room—not barged in on him while he was completely exposed with just a mere sheet of fabric to separate them.

"Holy shit, Quinn! Are you serious?"

She put the toilet seat cover down and sat, right outside the shower. "How come there's no lock on the door?"

After his suicide attempt, Cole's parents had removed the locks from all the doors for his safety, but he wasn't about to tell her that. "Because people usually knock?" he retorted instead, half expecting her to yank the shower curtain open at any second.

"Okay, Cole, relax. I'm not gonna peek or anything. Although…"

She flicked the curtain, and Cole's hands shot down instinctively to cover himself. "Quinn!"

She laughed. "Okay, I'm sorry. Seriously. I'm here for Leighton."

"Leighton sent you in here?" Cole asked incredulously.

"Yes, Leighton sent me in to see her naked boyfriend," Quinn said sarcastically. "No, she thinks I went to use the restroom. But I'm here because I'm concerned about her."

He sighed. "Why?"

"I don't know what's going on with you two, but she seems sad lately."

"Let *me* worry about that," Cole said.

"I know you think I'm nuts right now, but I just want to help her. Imagine if *your* best friend was hurting…you'd do anything, wouldn't you?"

Cole pressed his forehead against the tile wall, Quinn's words twisting like a rusted knife in his heart.

He heard her stand up, and he knew she'd made her way to the door when her voice sounded farther away. "Okay, I'm sorry. I'm gonna go now. It just seems like Leighton needs something more from you, and I thought you should know…Because I like you. And I don't want you to lose her."

Cole's annoyance melted away. "Thanks, Quinn. I like you too. Just not right now."

She laughed. "Hey, nice abs, by the way."

"*What?*"

"Ha, gotcha!"

Cole heard the door open and close and he was alone again. Alone with an unsettling thought. His fear was coming true. He was losing Leighton.

Wesley couldn't sleep. As he stretched out on the pullout couch in the MacHendricks' living room, staring at the shadowed ceiling, all he could think about was Delaney.

He thought about the heartache she'd been suffering since losing Tucker, and he hated that someone that lovely had to endure such a tragedy. How had it changed her? What had she been like before she knew such pain? Wesley considered it possible that she hadn't allowed it to change her much. Because he couldn't fathom how she could possibly be any more pleasant.

But that wasn't the only thing keeping him awake.

Wesley had lied to Cole. Delaney *had* told him everything—all the horror of Cole's past. Wesley thought about the burden Cole carried, the agony he lived with every single day, hidden deep within the corners of himself. All this while, Cole had been bearing it alone, and Wesley knew it was crushing him.

A creak on the staircase interrupted Wesley's thoughts and he sat up, reaching over to the end table for his glasses. In the dim light, he could easily make out Leighton's frame as she tip-toed into the kitchen. She quietly took a glass from the cabinet and filled it with water from the refrigerator door. She gulped half of it and stood there, staring at the stainless steel appliance.

Wesley remembered seeing Cole's senior portrait in a wallet-sized magnetic frame on the refrigerator door, and he guessed it was what Leighton was fixating on now. Cole had looked so different in the photo, smiling like Wesley had never seen Cole smile before. Now that Wesley knew what had happened, he knew it was the old Cole in the photo, taken before loss had reconfigured him. Was Leighton noticing how much Cole had changed?

Wesley frowned as he heard her sad sigh. How had he managed to think about anyone but her? Despite her unavailability and his unrequited affection for her, he felt a slight pang of guilt.

"Hey," he whispered.

Leighton jumped. With her hand over her heart, she set the glass in the sink and rounded the counter into the living room.

"Did I wake you?" she asked.

Her concern sparked a slight smile. "No, I was already awake. I can't sleep. Sorry I scared you."

"It's okay. I can't sleep either."

Wesley patted the spot beside him, and she hesitated for a fraction of a second before she settled in at his side.

"Why can't you sleep?" he asked. "Is it Quinn's horrendous bed-hoggery?"

Leighton blew out a frustrated breath, picking at the fringe on the fleece blanket before her. "No. Well, she is pretty bad, but...I'm worried about Cole."

A knot formed in Wesley's stomach, but he tried to remain objective. "Did something happen?"

"Well, no, not really. It's just the same thing it's always been. The same secrets and the same distant moments. I thought I could handle it and respect his privacy, but it's so much harder than I imagined. And coming home has made him even worse."

"Have you tried talking to him about it?"

Leighton nodded. "I have. Way too much. That's why I'm so afraid."

"What are you afraid of?"

She paused, and Wesley could tell she was trying not to get upset. "I promised I wouldn't push, but I just need to be closer to him. I'm afraid I'm going to push him too hard, and he's going to leave me."

Wesley put his arm around her. "He won't leave. Don't think like that."

Wesley recalled a time when Leighton feared *he* would leave her, and it filled him with a reluctant aching. But as she rested her head against him, he realized she still needed him, even if it wasn't in the way he wished she did.

"I don't know what to do anymore," Leighton continued. "It's like we've hit this wall. I hate that he's hurting, and I can't even comfort him because he won't let me get close enough."

"I'm sure he'll tell you when he's ready. He just needs more time," Wesley said.

He saw that their mutual intuition didn't always work in his favor when Leighton sat up straight, gawking at him. "Wait, do you know something? Did Cole say something? Did Delaney?"

Wesley placed a hand on her shoulder while a conflict stirred inside him. As much as he loved her and wanted to alleviate her pain, he couldn't betray Cole that way. It wasn't his secret to tell.

"I don't know any more than you do," he lied, guiding her head back to his chest so she couldn't see the guilt in his eyes.

Leighton's body relaxed against him. "Delaney is nice, huh?" she said after a moment.

Wesley uttered a sheepish chuckle. "Yes. She is. Why?"

Leighton shrugged against him. "I just couldn't help noticing how you two kind of fit together."

"We just met."

"I know. But I saw the chemistry between you, and I just wanted you to know it's okay if you like her."

"Like I said, we just met," Wesley insisted.

"Like I said, it's okay," Leighton mimicked him in a deep voice.

"That is *not* what I sound like."

"Hey, don't change the subject." She pulled away to look at him. "You forget how well I know you, and that you can't lie to me."

The guilt returned and Wesley forced a smile. "Okay, yeah, you got me. Delaney is definitely a cool girl."

"I thought so." Leighton grinned proudly. "And I'm serious. If you want to move on—possibly with Delaney—I think that's great. You never have to worry about me."

Wesley forced another smile, hopeful at the thought of Delaney, but saddened by Leighton's enthusiasm for him to pursue someone else. She never seemed to notice how painfully honest her words were, but it was her endearing innocence and humility that kept her from realizing the effect she had on him.

"I think I'm finally tired," Leighton said with a yawn as she stood to her feet. "Night, Wes. Thanks for listening to me." She bent and gave him a quick hug before she breezed silently up the stairs to bed.

And still, Wesley didn't sleep.

COLE

Cole awoke early the next morning after a restless night of sleep. The second his eyes opened, he felt a sense of dread, like something was wrong. But that was how he woke up every day. Every day since Tucker died.

Then a slight glimmer of joy swept over him when he remembered that Leighton was just across the hall. He was excited to spend a simple day with her without the hindrances of school or awkward holiday gatherings.

Cole got out of bed and crept down the hall to the bathroom. As he brushed his teeth, he read the scribbled note his mother had taped to the mirror informing him that she and his father had left early for Black Friday shopping. Cole took a quick glance at his reflection, raking his fingers through his disheveled hair before he eagerly made his way to the guest room.

The door was slightly ajar, and Cole carefully and quietly eased it open to peek inside. The soft light of early morning was just enough for him to see that Quinn was alone, still fast asleep. Closing the door, Cole headed downstairs to find Leighton.

When he got there, he found only Wesley sitting at the kitchen table, staring blindly into his mug of steaming coffee.

"Oh, hey, Wes."

Wesley seemed startled, suddenly alert. "What?"

Cole noted Wesley's tired eyes behind his glasses. "Have you seen Leighton?"

Wesley shook his head. "Not since last night. But your parents left like two hours ago."

"What time did you get up?" Cole asked.

"I didn't," Wesley muttered. "I never went to sleep."

"Why not?"

Wesley looked up at him. "It's hard keeping your secrets."

Cole's heart skipped a beat in his constricting chest. "What?"

"I lied to you last night. I'm sorry."

Cole looked around fearfully. "Shh...I can't talk about this now. I need to find Leighton."

"Yeah you do," Wesley said, sipping his coffee.

"What is that supposed to mean?"

Wesley's weary gaze didn't falter. "You may think your secrecy is saving *you*, but it's killing *her*."

Cole stood frozen for a moment, mortified, before he turned away. He moved feverishly through the silent rooms, searching urgently for Leighton.

As her whereabouts continued to elude him, Cole grew more anxious. He tore up the stairs, two at a time, and checked his room, the guest room, and the bathroom. He still didn't find her. Pausing at the top of the staircase, he eyed the open door of his parents' room at the end of the hall. It was the only place he hadn't looked.

Swallowing the trepidation that tightened his throat, Cole drifted down the carpeted hallway toward his least favorite room in the house.

He hadn't set foot beyond that doorway since the day he'd snapped.

Twenty-five

*"I'm not living for today 'cause tomorrow never comes, and
I just don't know that I can stay."*

Cole had been dreading February tenth. After dragging himself through a half-hearted version of his morning routine, he got into the new Jetta his parents had recently surprised him with, but instead of going to school, he went to King's. It took him several moments, sitting in the cold car, watching his breath form puffs of vapor in the air, before he could find the courage to go into the arcade.

When the familiar, musty scent of King's greeted Cole at the door, his stomach knotted and his throat tightened. He'd never been here without Tucker.

After purchasing a handful of tokens, Cole headed to the back where he knew their favorite game would be waiting for him—just like it had at Tucker's eighth birthday party, when their friendship truly began. Except, when Cole got there, he found a newfangled, high-tech piece of equipment in its place, complete with flashing lights and electronic music. Cole stood gawking at it for several seconds, then wandered all over the arcade searching for the game they had played together on Tucker's last ten birthdays. But he didn't find it.

By the time Cole was back in the car, his eyes stung with tears that were equal parts angry and sad. As time continued on, he was losing more and more remnants of Tucker. But on this day that should've been Tucker's eighteenth birthday, Cole couldn't handle losing any more.

He and Tucker were always the same age, except for the one week between their birthdays each year when Tucker was the older one. But that wouldn't be the case *this* year. In just seven days, Cole would be eighteen. And Tucker would be seventeen forever.

Several minutes later, Cole found himself at the cemetery where he laid a few King's Arcade tokens on Tucker's gravestone. Cole stared at the granite slab, his eyes tracing the familiar name etched so majestically—TUCKER MADDOX LINDSLEY.

It looked so wrong in such a place; it belonged labeled on school supplies by his mother, or printed in flawless calligraphy across a high school diploma or a wedding invitation. Instead, it was an immortal engraving on the earth, yet such measly proof of a unique and beautiful life and soul, blurring into the oblivion of those lost before and after him. The inadequate monuments spanned forever in every direction, as far as Cole could see. Were these countless souls together, somewhere beyond the sky? Were all these strangers with his best friend at this very moment and for all eternity? Cole felt jealous of the faceless, lifeless names that surrounded Tucker, and he cried and apologized until he thought the tears had run out.

Cole drove toward home, pulling over when he reached the crash site. He hadn't planned to go, but somehow he'd ended up there. For the past six months, he'd gone out of his way to avoid this spot, but today he needed to see it.

Cole got out of the car and inched toward the telephone pole, the sight tearing his chest open. When he got close enough, he placed his hand on the flawless wood. It must've been so damaged that they'd had to replace it, and its perfection bothered Cole. He'd wanted to see proof that Tucker had been here. And no matter how ridiculous the notion was, he thought it would make him feel closer to Tucker. Something he couldn't feel anymore.

The fierce, nauseating guilt gripped Cole the way it had in the early days as he drove home. He'd allowed himself to grow too numb in the past couple of months. But he didn't deserve a reprieve. His best friend was dead because of him.

His body convulsing with sobs, Cole entered the house and dragged himself up the stairs. He paced his room, nearly hysterical, clenching fistfuls of his hair. He drew in deep breaths, but he couldn't breathe. He couldn't stop dwelling on, couldn't stop hearing, his last words to Tucker, damning and deafening inside his pounding head.

Get the hell out of here.

And Tucker did…in a way Cole never imagined he would.

Cole wanted it to stop. He *needed* it to stop—the grief and the guilt and the missing. The wound was so raw, it would never heal, never stop bleeding. Cole's life had ended the night Tucker's did. There was nothing left.

Without hesitating, Cole left his room and bolted down the hall to his parents' room as if something else propelled his legs.

He went straight into their closet, sliding his father's hanging shirts to one side to expose the small safe on the shelf. Cole tried his parents' wedding anniversary as the combination, but it didn't open it. He tried his mother's birthday. Still locked. He tried his own birthday. The safe opened and a faint whimper escaped him.

Cole reached his shaking hand into the safe, closing it around the cold metal object inside. Carefully, he pulled it out, watching the light reflect off the barrel. Choking back his sobs, Cole tightened his fingers around the handle and lifted the revolver to his temple, pressing it hard against his skull. Before his fear could deter him, he squeezed his eyes shut and pulled the trigger.

Click.

Nothing.

Click click click.

It wasn't loaded.

Torrential tears blurred Cole's vision as he ripped through the safe looking for the bullets. He heard horrible howls and moans that he hadn't realized were coming from his own mouth. When he found the box of ammunition, he tore it open, then released the cylinder on the revolver. He struggled to

load the bullets into the chamber, but they kept slipping from his trembling fingers. He let out an
exasperated cry as his mother appeared in the doorway of the closet, horror twisting her face.

"Cole! No!" she screamed.

She lunged at him, pinning him against the
wall. Cole surrendered the gun to her immediately,
crumbling against her with guttural wails. She held
his head against her chest, weeping uncontrollably
with him.

"Oh, my sweet boy...don't you dare leave us.
Please," she begged. "Cole, I love you. We love you *so*
much. You know that, don't you?"

Cole couldn't respond. He held onto his
mother, until he could no longer feel the lingering
sensation of the gun barrel pressing into his head.

Twenty-six

C ole stepped inside his parents' bedroom, reluctantly approaching the closet. The light was on and he could hear movement. Placing his hand on the doorframe, he peered inside. Leighton's small form huddled against the wall, her knees pulled tightly in to her chest. Anger immediately replaced Cole's worry.

"Leighton? What are you doing in here?"

Leighton's head shot up at his sudden outburst. Her cheeks were wet with tears, her eyes red and desperate as she looked up at him.

Cole's gaze shifted frantically, the sight of the closet triggering a panic. "Why are you in here?" he tried again, reaching down to grab her hand.

She pulled away from him and crossed her arms, her fists clenching.

"Leighton, this isn't funny. Please. Get up."

"No," she said in a grating protest.

Cole took a few deep breaths, finally taking in his surroundings. His father's shirts were pushed to the side, the safe exposed. Cole's composure instantly shattered, his crippling anxiety stirring a riot within him. He dropped to his knees beside Leighton, the dread of impending defeat heavy on his shoulders. He wanted to run away but he couldn't move.

"What are you doing?" he asked, calmly this time. "Leighton…"

"I thought coming here would help me feel close to you," she cried.

He gaped at her, trying to understand. "How would *this* make you feel close to me?"

"What else do I have, Cole?"

"Me. You have *me*."

Leighton shook her head and closed her eyes. "Barely."

"How can you say that?"

"Because, Cole! I know we agreed that the past doesn't matter, but it just isn't true. I can't do this anymore. Say *something*, tell me *anything*, because I don't know who you are."

Leighton's words stung Cole like a slap in the face. This was it. He'd finally hit that inevitable wall. As it crumbled down around him, he knew he could no longer hide. Wesley was right—Cole was hurting Leighton to protect himself.

Trembling, Cole raised his eyes to meet Leighton's. His words were like sandpaper as they rose to his quivering lips. "I killed my best friend…"

"What?" she barely whispered. She stared at Cole like he was a stranger and it terrified him.

His shame like a crushing weight on his chest, he let himself fall back against the closet wall. He buried his face in his hands.

"Cole…" Leighton whimpered after a moment. "What does that mean? Tell me that's not it."

He slowly lifted his head. He looked directly at Leighton, silently begging for grace.

"I don't understand," she said. "How…how can that be true?"

Cole's face contorted with renewed pain. "I'll tell you everything, I promise. Just please…not *here*."

Leighton eyed Cole from the passenger seat as he stared intently ahead, his long fingers wrapped tightly around the steering wheel. The muscles in his jaw flexed as he ground his teeth. She wondered what was going on in his mind but she was afraid to ask. Even after months of speculating about the nature of Cole's secret, none of the scenarios she'd naïvely imagined came close to the truth.

Leighton didn't know where Cole was taking her, but she knew, in just moments, she would finally know the full story—the darkness that shattered Cole and made him give up. His vague but terrifying confession played over and over in her mind, twisting her stomach.

She stole another glance at Cole, still seeing in him the beautiful broken boy she loved and longed to heal. How could this tender and timid boy beside her ever be capable of intentionally hurting someone? No matter what Leighton told herself, no amount of internal reasoning could quell her anticipation.

Cole pulled over after a curve in the road and killed the engine. Leaning back in his seat, he remained still and silent for a moment.

After sucking in a deep breath, Cole opened the door and stepped out, and Leighton followed. She trailed behind him as he slowly approached a telephone pole, and she watched, confused, as he stood there staring at it.

"Tucker Lindsley has been my best friend since we were eight..." Cole hung his head, his brown locks spilling around his face. "Had been. He *had* been my best friend..." Then he looked up, sliding both hands through his hair and locking his fingers behind his head at the base of his skull.

"Tucker..." Leighton repeated. "When we first met...*that's* why—"

"Yeah. I know," Cole interrupted her, dropping his arms to his sides. "When you told me your last name—when I heard *his* name—the coincidence felt like a cruel joke. Like God or the universe was punishing me for what I'd done. But I acted like such an asshole, and I am so sorry. You never deserved that."

"And that was Tucker's family yesterday..." Leighton realized. "That's why you acted so weird all day."

Cole nodded. "But they sure were graceful, like always, despite spending the holiday with the person who killed their son."

Leighton nervously shifted her weight, searching for the correct reply. "But, Cole...I find it hard to believe that you could do something like that."

He turned to face her, those same old vacant eyes looking back at her. "Well, I did. You might think I'm exaggerating or being dramatic, but that's what happened. I promised I'd tell you everything. And when I do, if you decide you don't love me any-more...I'll understand." His lip quivered ever so slightly.

Leighton was fearful for the first time. Sud-denly, she was questioning everything she felt for him, everything she knew about him. "Okay."

Cole walked back to his car and leaned against the front fender, facing the telephone pole. Leighton followed him, crossing her arms as she leaned against the back door. She'd purposely put a few feet between them, but Cole didn't seem to no-tice.

"It was the second to last Saturday of summer break before senior year," he began, staring at the woods beyond the pole like he could see the scene in his mind playing out before him. "There was this crazy end of summer party, and I drove Tuck and me in my car. We didn't want to worry about a ride home, and I had plans with my dad the next morning that I didn't want to be hungover for, so I'd promised to stay sober and be the designated driver."

Cole paused for a moment, chewing his bot-tom lip. "But I drank anyway, and I got so drunk, I kissed Delaney—Tucker's *girlfriend*—and like a fuck-ing movie, Tucker walked in at that exact moment and caught me."

Leighton's eyes went wide. "Oh, wow. Delaney was Tucker's girlfriend...You had feelings for her?"

He breathed a heavy breath. "No. I didn't. That was the thing. I have no idea, to this day, why I did it. I was in love with Ava. And yeah, Delaney and I were always good friends, but I'd *never* considered crossing that line."

"So, then what happened?"

Cole swallowed. "Tucker ran outside and I went after him. He was *so* angry with me. And he was pissed that I was too drunk to drive him home like I'd promised, so he asked for my keys. But he was more drunk than I was, so I wouldn't give them to him, which only made him angrier. I just kept apologizing, and finally, Tucker got so fed up, he punched me."

Cole stopped and touched the corner of his mouth. "When he punched me, I stopped feeling bad about what I'd done. We'd never fought before, nothing more than silly disagreements. But I was mad that he believed I'd hurt him on purpose, and I was mad that he hurt *me* on purpose. Everyone was watching and I was embarrassed. That's when I took out my keys and threw them at him. And I told him...I told him..."

"It's okay. Take your time," Leighton said softly.

He closed his eyes as if mustering the strength to continue. "I told him to get the hell out of here...and he looked at me with this betrayed look that I will never forget, and he got in my car, and he left. And that was the last time we saw each other...the last things we said to each other."

Stepping away from the car, Cole returned to the telephone pole. He carefully brushed his hand over the smooth wood.

"Tucker hit this pole and died instantly," Cole said, his voice trembling as he cried. "Well, not *this* pole. The impact damaged the old one so badly, they replaced it with this one."

"Oh my God," Leighton breathed, her hand on her chest as it quickly rose and fell.

Cole hung his head. "I know everything I did that night led Tucker here. I made so many selfish mistakes and he is *dead* because of that."

Leighton stepped through the brush to get closer to him, but she couldn't speak.

"So this is me," Cole said shakily, lifting his arms like he was presenting the scene to her. "Do you blame me too? Everyone else does."

She didn't know how to answer his question. "How do you know they do?"

Cole snickered sadly. "Well…Ava broke up with me specifically because of it. I was humiliated on more than one occasion in front of the entire school. I was kicked off the football team. I got the shit beat out of me. Then I was ignored like I didn't exist. They made me disappear because that's what I deserved. Trust me, everyone in this town hates me for what I did. And they should."

Leighton slipped her hands into her back pockets, casting her eyes to the brown withered grass and dirt at her feet. She tried to picture Cole as that different version of himself, the one who'd made terrible choices that unfolded in the worst way possible.

"What are you thinking?" Cole asked, his voice low and anxious.

Leighton struggled to look him in the eye, afraid to see his exposed darkness, afraid to see someone she didn't recognize. After a moment, she gathered enough courage to meet his gaze, and when she did, her chest tightened with pain and guilt—pain because part of her still wanted to heal him, and guilt because another part of her wasn't sure at all how to feel.

When Leighton could offer no reply, she realized that her usual brave boldness—the quality she proudly possessed in Cole's presence—was no more.

"So that's it? You've wanted to know what I've been keeping from you. Telling you has been the second hardest thing I've ever been through, and you can't even tell me what you're thinking?" Cole's eyebrows were furrowed with something between frustration and sadness.

"I'm sorry, Cole. It's…a lot to take in. I'm just not sure what to think or say right now."

"No, don't be sorry. *I'm* the one who's sorry. You have *no* idea how sorry I am." He rubbed his forehead and pressed his lips together to keep them from trembling.

"Can I ask you a question?"

"You can ask me anything," Cole said.

"So, it was six months after Tucker died, then…when you tried to kill yourself. Was it guilt that made you do it, or did something else happen?" Leighton asked. Maybe her boldness hadn't left her after all.

Cole sighed heavily. "It was Tucker's birthday, so it was an especially rough day, and yeah, guilt was a big part of it. I was so done missing him and hating myself. I just didn't want to feel anything anymore. I guess I wanted what I deserved."

Leighton just stared at him, trying to process his answer.

"Is there anything else you wanna know?" he asked, stuffing his hands into the pockets of his jean jacket.

"I don't know, I wish you'd just told me from the beginning."

"Why? So you could run away then instead of now?"

"No. I don't know," Leighton said. "This was such a huge thing to keep from me. You just decided I couldn't handle it, like you didn't trust me at all. And I was with you, falling in love with you, without really knowing you."

"Don't do that, Leighton. I told you countless times to stay away from me but you didn't listen. You ignored every single warning."

"It's just...more than I imagined," she said, shuddering at her own insensitivity.

"What did you imagine?"

Leighton shrugged. "I don't know, Cole. But I thought when you finally told me the truth, it wouldn't affect me. I didn't think it would make me feel like this."

"Are you afraid of me?" He took a step back, looking stunned like he'd been hit. "Don't worry, you couldn't possibly hate me any more than I already hate myself."

Leighton started crying. "I don't hate you, Cole."

"Then *what*?" he asked, defeated.

A sudden chill engulfed Leighton as a gust of autumn wind blew by, whistling through the trees surrounding them. Was it the wind or the unsettling feeling inside her that made her feel so cold? She wrapped her arms tightly around her body, shielding herself from the breeze. Or maybe from *Cole*. She wasn't quite sure.

"I wanna go now," Leighton said, unable to look at his devastated silver-blue eyes. "Can we please go?"

She didn't glance up as Cole brushed past her on his way to the car. She couldn't bear to see the pain in his beautiful face. The entire ride back to Cole's house, Leighton kept her eyes fixed on the windshield. And neither of them spoke a single word.

Twenty-seven

"But who can I be now, now that you're gone?"

When Cole and Tucker arrived at Aaron Slater's, the party was in full force.

"There you are. What took you so long?" Ava grabbed Cole's hands and tugged him toward her, planting a kiss on his lips.

He smiled against her cheek, wrapping his arms around her waist. "I know. I missed you too," he said.

Tucker had immediately flocked to Delaney. "Hey, Cole, I'm gonna grab a drink. Want anything?" Tucker asked, his arm draped around Delaney's shoulders.

Cole bit his lower lip, already regretting his vow to remain sober. "Sure. I'll take a soda," he answered with a reluctant frown.

"In a kid's cup. With a bendy straw," Ava added, jabbing Cole in the ribs. Teasing him was one of her favorite hobbies, and she was good at it.

The night carried on in a typical fashion, complete with loud music, beer pong, and several other creative ways to consume alcohol. And it didn't take long for Cole to surrender his self-control and join in.

It had been a couple hours since Cole lost count of how many times he'd refilled that red plastic cup at the keg. He mentally congratulated himself for being so skilled at beer pong, sparing himself the extra consumption. It didn't matter much though, considering how many shots he threw back after that. He knew he'd regret it all come morning, but right now, all he cared about was letting go and embracing the night.

Cole staggered down the hall toward the bathroom, running his hand along the wall to keep himself steady. When he reached the bathroom, it was occupied, and a line of three people waited outside the door. With a sigh, Cole turned away too quickly and a sudden dizziness came over him. Holding his head, he dragged himself toward Aaron's bedroom, hoping he'd feel better if he lay down for a moment.

He opened Aaron's door and stumbled into the dim room, finding Delaney sitting on the bed.

"Oh, I'm sorry. I didn't know anyone was in here," Cole said, taking a step backward.

Delaney let out a sheepish chuckle. "It's okay. You don't have to leave. I was just hiding out for a minute. Taking a break from all the craziness." She patted the space beside her.

Cole flopped onto the bed, immediately soothed by the softness of the pillows beneath his foggy head. "Ugh, I drank waaaaaaay too much," he groaned, rubbing his hands over his numb face.

"Me too," Delaney said. "It doesn't take much for me, though. I never do this." She sighed, lying down next to him. Her hair brushed his cheek.

"I know you don't. You're usually so responsible. Delaney Mae, *what* is happening to you?" Cole asked with playful disappointment.

She laughed, tapping him lightly in the side with her elbow. "Hey, I'm finally succumbing to peer pressure, okay? What's *your* excuse?"

He dropped his jaw, pretending to be offended. "Ohhh...you got me. Yeah, I don't have an excuse. I'm just your average reckless and stupid teenager."

"No, you're not. You're a kind, mature, and intelligent guy...who's going to wake up with a really bad hangover tomorrow, unfortunately."

She laughed again. Her laugh was almost as pretty as she was.

Cole turned his head toward her, looking at her through heavy eyelids. "You're really nice, you know that?"

Delaney shrugged against the pillows, tilting her face toward him. They held each other's gaze as Cole reached over and brushed a stray lock of hair off her cheek. His fingers lingered for a moment, running softly across her jawline toward her chin. With all inhibition gone, Cole drew closer and pressed his mouth against hers. Losing himself in his inebriated haze, he kissed her more intensely, sliding his fingers into her hair.

Before Cole could grasp the reality of his actions, the door to Aaron's room flew open. Cole pulled away from Delaney so quickly, he nearly fell off the bed. Breathless, he looked to the open doorway and saw Tucker staring at him, his mouth hanging open in wounded bewilderment.

"Oh, shit...Tuck..."

Tucker stormed out of the room, and Cole scrambled off the bed to follow after him. He finally caught up with him outside on the front lawn.

"Tucker, I'm so sorry. Just *please* don't be mad at Delaney. It wasn't her fault," Cole said in a desperate tone. "I don't know what happened."

Tucker ran his shaking hands over his hair. "You don't know? You *kissed* my girlfriend!"

By this time, there was quite an audience scattered around the yard, tuning in to the spectacle heating up before them.

"You kissed Delaney?" The small, cracking voice came from behind Cole.

He turned to see Ava, her eyes welling with hurt, and he didn't know what to say. He just gaped at her, watching the tears finally spill down her cheeks when his silence gave her the answer she dreaded. Cole hated that he'd betrayed her. And Tucker. And Delaney. How did he let that happen?

"I can't believe you would do this to me," Tucker said.

"I didn't mean it. It meant nothing."

Tucker clenched his jaw. "It sure means something to me. What the hell, Cole!"

Cole inhaled deeply and let out a trembling breath. "I'm so sorry. You have to believe me."

"Take me home. I wanna go home," Tucker said coldly.

"I, um...I'm not okay to drive."

"Dammit, Cole! You couldn't do *one* thing right tonight?"

"I'm sorry, Tuck! How many times do you want me to apologize?"

"I'll drive myself, then. Give me the keys," Tucker demanded, his hand outstretched.

Cole shook his head. He may have been far from sober, but he could easily tell Tucker was just as drunk, if not more so. "I'm not letting you drive like this."

"I'm fine. Just give them to me."

"No."

Tucker grew uncharacteristically angry. "Give me your fucking keys!"

"C'mon, Tuck, let's just talk about this, please? I'm sorry. I swear I don't know why I kissed her...I don't know what else to say. I'm *so* sorry."

With each bumbling apology, Tucker seemed to grow more agitated. As if he couldn't keep his infuriation at bay any longer, Tucker threw a punch at Cole, connecting with the corner of his mouth. Cole's head jerked to the side and he stumbled, struggling to stay on his feet.

Cole could hear the snickering and whispering around him, and humiliation sank in. Cole couldn't believe Tucker would actually hit him. Couldn't Tucker see how sorry he was? Did Tucker really believe Cole would hurt him on purpose? Cole's remorse quickly turned to anger as he wiped the blood from his throbbing, swelling lip.

"You wanna leave? *Fine.*" Cole dug his keys out of his pocket. "Then get the hell out of here." He flung his keys at Tucker, who flinched and grunted when they hit him in the chest.

Tucker bent to pick them up, and gave Cole

one last wounded glare before he turned toward Cole's Mustang. Cole took a step forward to follow after him, but stopped, deciding Tucker had had enough of his groveling. Seconds later, Tucker peeled out and sped off, screeching out of the neighborhood.

In the sudden silence, Cole finally dropped to the ground, forcing away the lump in this throat. And what felt like only moments later, he heard the faint wail of sirens in the distance. Someone joked that they were coming for Tucker. But by the sickening knot in his stomach and the tormenting dread in his heart, Cole feared it was the truth.

Tucker Lindsley was a good guy and an even better friend. He was kind and well-mannered but still knew how to have fun. He adored his girlfriend. He loved his family and his friends, and there was nothing he wouldn't do for any of them. He was handsome but humble, and never took himself too seriously. He loved sports and muscle cars, and had been restoring a 1970 Pontiac GTO with his dad on the weekends. He was excited to graduate and go off to get a degree in fire science and become a third generation firefighter. He wanted to marry Delaney one day and give her the life she always dreamed of.

But when Tucker wrapped Cole's car around a telephone pole just two miles from the party, all these things that made Tucker who he was, became all the things he used to be.

Twenty-eight

Wesley set aside his tattered paperback copy of F. Scott Fitzgerald's *Tender is the Night*, letting it close without caring that he'd lost his place. He'd just read the same page four times, distracted by his phone that was like a hot coal in his pocket, begging for him to give in to the urge that plagued him. And finally, he did.

But he got her voicemail.

"Hey, Delaney, it's Wesley...I was probably supposed to wait a few days or whatever to call you, but I don't have a few days, so here I am...I just wanted to see if maybe you wanted to hang out today. If you're not working or don't already have plans...Yeah, so...give me a call back if you want to, and I'll talk to you then. Or I won't. Whichever is fine. Okay, bye."

With a groan, Wesley ended the call, already regretting the clumsy nature of his message. Articulation had always been one of his strong suits, but suddenly, he was more of a bumbling idiot than anything else. Not even Leighton could render him speechless. But *this* girl—someone he'd just met but felt like he'd known forever—made him feel something that, for once, he could not put into words.

As Wesley began to fear that he hadn't had even the slightest bit of a similar effect on Delaney, his phone rang with her name across the screen.

His stomach was in knots as he answered it. "Hey."

"Hi, Wesley. It's Delaney."

"I know." He rolled his eyes at himself.

"I'm sorry I missed your call. I'm at work, but I snuck away to the restroom so I could call you back really quick."

Wesley smiled. "When do you get off?"

"Not till nine," she said, emitting a reluctant sigh.

"Well...if you're not too tired by then, I'd still love to see you...if that's okay."

Delaney chuckled. "It's definitely okay. And I'd love that, too."

Just two minutes past nine o'clock, Delaney texted Wesley, *I just left work. I'm heading to Cole's now.*

Wesley fought the urge to wait by the front window for her arrival, and instead, parked himself on a barstool in the MacHendricks' kitchen. He busied himself by studying the flecks of gold in the granite countertop.

"What are you doing?"

Wesley looked up at Cole's puzzled face. "Huh?"

"You look like something's wrong," Cole said.

Wesley felt like he could say the same to Cole, but breathed a sheepish laugh instead. "No, I'm fine. Delaney is on her way over. I guess I'm just a little nervous."

"Delaney's coming over?"

"Yeah. She's picking me up."

Cole bit into his bottom lip, his expression even more troubled. "Oh."

Wesley stood and approached him. "You don't want me to see her..."

Cole lowered his head, his hair falling into his face. "I don't know. It's just—"

"It's Tucker, isn't it?" Wesley asked cautiously.

Cole flinched ever so slightly, his eyebrows furrowed like he was experiencing a deep, physical pain. He nodded.

"Because Delaney is *Tucker's?* And I would be replacing him?" Wesley asked.

Cole nodded again. "I know. I shouldn't feel that way."

"It's okay. I know this has to be really difficult for you. But I don't want to make things worse. If it would hurt you too much for me to pursue Delaney, then tell me right now, and I won't."

Cole stared at Wesley. "You would do that?"

Wesley shrugged. "Well, I wouldn't be thrilled, but...yeah. I would."

Cole let out a long sigh. "No. I can't do that to you. If Delaney is finally ready to move on, then I'm glad it's with you."

"Thanks, but I haven't gotten the girl yet,"

Wesley said, smiling. "I want you to know that I understand how big of a deal this is, and I don't take it lightly. I know Delaney is not just some girl."

"You're right. She's not."

"And I will treat her like—"

"Like you'd treat Leighton?" Cole finished.

Wesley took a deep breath. "Like I *would've* treated Leighton had I *really* gotten the chance? Yes. And I know that sounds crazy, because I only just met Delaney, but…something about her finally gives me hope that Leighton isn't the only *one*."

"It's not crazy. I get it, trust me," Cole said with a smirk.

Wesley placed his hand on Cole's shoulder. "And just so you know, no one is ever going to replace Tucker."

Cole swallowed like he was fighting back a rush of emotions. A knock on the front door interrupted them before he could reply.

"That's probably Delaney." Wesley grinned, giving Cole's shoulder a pat before turning away.

His long legs carried him out of the kitchen and through the living room to the foyer. He glanced nervously at his reflection in the mirror by the door before he pulled it open. When his eyes met Delaney's, his grin returned, bigger than ever, and hers quickly matched it.

"Hi," Wesley said, admiring the golden glow of her blonde hair under the porch light. "Do you want to come in, or…?"

Delaney looked down at her disheveled work uniform. "Ugh, actually, the fewer people who see me like this, the better."

"I think you look fine."

Delaney chuckled as she blushed, smoothing some flyaway hairs back from her face. "Oh yes, an oversized used-to-be-white-but-is-now-basically-baby-yellow polo with a huge Pepsi stain on the front, and these nasty, pleated khakis *are* really nice." She pulled her coat closed and crossed her arms.

"All right, fine. Give me a second," Wesley said, grabbing his jacket. "Cole says hi."

"Hi, Cole!" Delaney called into the house as Wesley pulled the door closed behind him.

He followed her to the end of the driveway where her older model Maxima was parked and they got in.

"So, how was your day?" Wesley asked once they were heading down Cole's street.

Delaney didn't take her eyes off the road. "Long. And that was *without* grumpy customers and exploding soda fountain machines. Hence aforementioned hideous polo." She added a lighthearted laugh to her complaint.

"I'm sorry," Wesley said.

"Oh, it's okay. I am so used to it by now. How was *your* day?"

"A hell of a lot better than yours."

"Hey," Delaney scolded, removing one hand from the steering wheel to playfully shove him. "Okay, I don't doubt it, though."

"I'm sorry, I'm usually much nicer than that." He flashed a facetious smile when she glanced at him.

"You wouldn't be here right now if I didn't already know that." She'd tried to sound stern but cracked. "Anyway, tell me about this day that was *so* much better than mine."

Wesley rested his arm on the door against the foggy window. "Oh, it actually wasn't that great."

Delaney rolled her eyes. "Ugh, Wesley! Seriously?"

He hesitated. "Well, no. I just spent most of it thinking about you and I wasn't sure if it was appropriate to admit that."

She pressed her lips together to stave off a grin. "I guess our days weren't that different after all."

Delaney let Wesley into her house, locking the door behind them and tossing her keys into a bowl on a nearby table. She took Wesley's jacket and hung it up beside hers on the hooks in the foyer.

"Make yourself at home," Delaney said, kicking off her shoes.

Wesley followed suit, untying and pulling off his boots.

"I'm gonna take a quick shower, if you don't mind. You can just hang out in my room."

"Is your dad home?" Wesley asked.

"He won't be home for another three days."

"So you're just alone here for days at a time, all by yourself?"

She smiled. "Yeah, it's okay. I'm used to it. And we have a security system, so I'm safe."

Delaney grabbed Wesley's hand and led him across the cozy living room and down the hallway to her room, turning on lights along the way. She rummaged through a couple dresser drawers and vanished into her closet for a moment, reappearing with a change of clothes tucked in the crook of her arm.

"I'll be as quick as I can," she said, stopping in her doorway. "And you can sit, you know. My bed won't bite you."

Once she'd gone, Wesley sat at the foot of her queen bed, letting his eyes wander about the rectangular room. It was very tidy, but there was so much to look at.

On Delaney's desk, was a worn paperback collection of poetry by Edgar Allan Poe, its curled pages an aged golden yellow. An old Royal typewriter sat on the far corner of the desk and Wesley wondered if it appealed to Delaney because she liked to write or if she simply enjoyed vintage things. Next to the desk was a tall bookshelf, stuffed to capacity with rows and rows of novels, many of which Wesley recognized.

In a frame on Delaney's nightstand, was a photo of a blond, good-looking guy he assumed was Tucker, his blue eyes gleaming. Wesley wondered what Tucker had been like. And he wondered how Tucker would feel if he could know that Wesley was in his girlfriend's bedroom, sitting on her bed as she showered just across the hall. How much of Tucker's brief life had he spent in this very room with Delaney?

For a brief moment, Wesley felt guilty. It was awful what had happened to Tucker, and how it devastated everyone who knew him. But then Wesley decided that, in some small way, Delaney might need him, just as Leighton felt that Cole needed her. Wesley wasn't sure what could happen between them, but if he could offer Delaney even the slightest bit of joy, he wanted to do that for her.

"I hope that wasn't too long." Delaney's voice sounded behind him like a soft strum in an empty sanctuary.

Wesley twisted to glance at her. "No, it was surprisingly quick. You forget I have a somewhat vain twin sister, so anything under an hour is impressive to me."

"Okay, good." Delaney crossed the room to toss her work clothes into the hamper in her closet.

When she turned around, Wesley got a better look at her. She wore a black sweater, its wide neck hanging off her bare shoulder. Her wet hair was pulled up into a tight knot on top of her head.

"What?" Delaney asked, blushing.

Wesley dropped his gaze. "I'm sorry. You're just...really pretty."

She dismissed his comment with an incredulous '*pfft*' as she flopped onto her bed behind him. Leaning against the headboard, she crossed her ankles.

"Netflix?" she asked, loudly patting the empty space at her left.

Wesley stood and rounded the bed to sit beside her, catching the faint, sweet scent of honeysuckle. "Sure. That sounds perfect."

Delaney reached over to her nightstand for the remote near Tucker's picture and turned on her TV and streaming device. As Netflix was loading, she said, "Thank you...for saying I'm pretty. I have a terrible habit of not accepting compliments."

"Well, *I* have a terrible habit of being too honest sometimes."

"Well, I like it," she said with a shy smile.

Wesley tried to wrangle in the curving corners of his too-wide grin. "What are we watching?" he asked.

Delaney shrugged, tapping the small black remote against her chin. "I don't know. What do you wanna watch?"

"Whatever you want. Anything," he answered, chuckling.

She clicked the remote at the TV to access her favorites list and selected a title.

"Wait. What did you just choose?" Wesley's face was blank with disbelief.

"*Say Anything...*" Delaney replied casually. "Why?"

His wide grin returned, spreading slowly across his face. "It's my favorite film. Of *all* time."

She looked at him through a skeptical squint. "Nuh-uh."

"Yuh-huh. I have a penchant for '80s films."

Delaney raised her flawless eyebrows, her face serious. "So do I. *Pretty in Pink* is my all-time favorite. But this one is tied for second with *Can't Buy Me Love.*"

"My second is *Better Off Dead.* I guess I'm a bit of a Cusack fan," Wesley said. "What's your third?"

"*The Breakfast Club*, of course. It barely beats out *One Crazy Summer*. Another Cusack."

Wesley shook his head in astonishment.

"You are unbelievable."

"I have good taste, huh?"

He chuckled. "Yes. Absolutely. We both do, apparently."

In unison, they both reached a hand over their own shoulder to pat themselves on the back. Then they gasped and laughed at the perfect coincidence of their synchronized action. How had Wesley only known this girl for one day?

Delaney fell silent, her ocean eyes studying Wesley's face.

"What?" he asked, growing self-conscious.

"How did I meet you just *yesterday*? I feel like I've known you my whole life. Like you're *me* manifested in male form."

Wesley smiled. "I was just thinking the same thing."

"Really? It's so weird, isn't it? Just when you think you've lost the *only* person you'll ever *really* connect with..." Delaney averted her gaze, casting her eyes to the TV mounted on the wall ahead of them.

"It is not at *all* the same situation, I know, but...I understand that feeling," Wesley said, tilting his head to peer at her. He thought he saw tears in her eyes.

Keeping her attention fixed on the screen, Delaney scooted closer and settled against him, leaning her shoulder into his. They didn't speak for the remainder of the movie.

By the end credits, Delaney's head was resting on Wesley's shoulder.

"I just love that ending," Wesley said. "How

she's so afraid of flying, but he tells her she'll know everything is okay when she hears the 'ding' as the 'fasten seat belts' light turns off. How he just holds her as they wait. Then you hear the 'ding' and it goes black and it's just over. I *love* that."

Delaney breathed a soft chuckle, keeping her head in place. "I love your enthusiasm."

"I'm sorry. I'm such a dork."

"No, I really mean it. Tucker was more into sports movies, and he loved *The Fast and the Furious* franchise because he was so into cars. He didn't get my '80s movie obsession." She finally lifted her face to look at Wesley. "Maybe it's actually possible for someone to understand me even better than Tucker did."

Before Wesley could reply, Delaney leaned in, pressing her lips to his. The kiss was timid at first, but it evolved quickly, growing more impassioned as he followed her lead.

Then she pulled away, shooting a hand over her mouth. Her wide eyes were locked on Wesley's as they brimmed with tears.

"Oh my God," she whispered.

"What's wrong?" he asked.

The tears flowed down Delaney's cheeks as she glanced at Tucker's photo on the dresser behind Wesley. "Tucker wasn't the last person who kissed me—*Cole* was—and that has made me feel so guilty for the past fifteen months. But Tucker was the last person *I* kissed, and I held onto that. Somehow, it made me feel better. But now...that's gone too."

Wesley exhaled like he'd been holding his breath. "Delaney...I am so sorry."

She shook her head, placing her hand on his knee. "No, it's not your fault. It's just...*so* much harder to move on than I thought it would be."

"That's okay." His voice was tender, matching the affection he knew was visible in his eyes. "It's a big step, and it takes time."

Delaney blotted her cheeks with her sleeve. "But how long am I going to put my life on hold? I'm so tired...I'm tired of hurting so badly. I'm tired of being the girl whose boyfriend died. I'm tired of feeling guilty if I notice another guy...But I'm so scared to let Tucker go. Then he *really* won't be mine anymore, and what's left of him will disappear. I'm so afraid I'll forget him."

Wesley put his arm around her when a sob shook her small frame. "You'll never forget Tucker, I promise. Don't think of it as *moving* on, but as *living* on. Because you're still here, and you deserve to live your life. I didn't know Tucker, but he sounds like he was a really great guy, and I'm sure he would want you to be happy." Wesley stroked her damp cheek with his free hand. "And I'm not saying that just because I really want to kiss you again. I'm saying it because, for some unknown reason, in a ridiculously short amount of time, I've come to care about you. I want you to be happy whether that includes me or not."

Delaney looked at him, her watery gaze tracing his features. A slight smile flitted across her lips as she slipped her hand into his. "I can't explain it...but *this* makes me happy. I think it's the first time I've felt happy since Tucker was here."

She cupped Wesley's face with her hand,

guiding it closer to hers, and she kissed him again. It was more delicate this time, but still charged with the same inexplicable magic. They kissed until Wesley's phone went off in his pocket, emitting a single *"ding!"*

"Everything is okay," Delaney whispered, smiling against his lips.

Twenty-nine

"So, things seem to be going well," Cole said, backing his car out of Delaney's driveway.

Wesley dropped his head back against the headrest, his exhaustion lending him a slightly drunken feeling. "Oh, *that's* for sure."

"Oh yeah? And why do you say that?"

Wesley tilted his head toward Cole, grinning. "She kissed me."

"Oh. Wow. That was quick."

Wesley clicked his tongue. "It is too quick, isn't it? Is this bad?"

"No," Cole said, glancing at him for a brief moment. "It's okay, I'm just surprised. Delaney is very likable, but I didn't think you'd fall for her so fast."

Rubbing his face, Wesley groaned. "Shit, what is wrong with me?"

"Nothing. You're finally getting over Leighton."

Wesley stared straight ahead out the windshield. "Is it really possible to get over *Leighton*?"

"I hope so."

Wesley twisted sideways in his seat, instantly wide awake. "Wait...what?"

Cole stopped at a red light and looked over at him. "I told Leighton the truth."

"Whoa, Cole, that's huge. Why didn't you tell me earlier?"

"You were excited about Delaney. It wasn't the right time."

"Okay, so tell me now. How did it go?"

The light turned green and Cole accelerated. "Just as horribly as I imagined."

"Are you serious?"

Cole nodded.

Wesley sighed heavily, facing forward and slouching in his seat. "What did she say?"

"Nothing," Cole said. "She could barely look at me."

Wesley scratched his head. "I never would've expected that from her."

"How come you didn't turn on me when you find out?" Cole asked, stealing a glance at him.

"Because I'm not in love with you," Wesley answered.

Cole snickered. "Yeah, but I'm your friend. That's enough."

Wesley shrugged against the seat. "I don't know if it was how Delaney presented it to me, or if I just have an easier time focusing on the *good* in people..."

"I don't know what I'm gonna do. I can't believe this is happening. I never should've told her," Cole said, like he was thinking out loud.

"I don't think you would've gotten away with

it for much longer, though."

"So I would've lost her either way…"

Wesley straightened in his seat. "Don't say that. You don't know that you've lost her. She could still come around."

Cole shook his head. "I don't think so. I never should've given in. I should've just let her keep thinking I was an asshole and walked away."

"No," Wesley adamantly disagreed. "I've seen the way you've changed her, how you've brought her back in a way none of us have been able to. And without you, I never would've met Delaney. Now, I know that's very selfish of me to say, and definitely premature, but still—I'm glad you didn't walk away."

Cole pulled into his neighborhood, the dread heavy on his features. "Well, at least someone wins."

Wesley had just drifted off when something tugged him back to consciousness.

"Wesley," he heard again, an urgent whisper in the shadows.

He sat up, squinting into the darkness. "Leighton?"

Just as he made out her face, she rushed at him, throwing her arms around his neck. The force knocked him backward, pulling her down into the bed with him.

"Leighton…" Wesley tried to sit up but she clung to him, burying her face in his shoulder. It took him less than a second to realize she was crying and he gave in to her embrace.

"Hey," he breathed, rubbing her back. "Talk to me."

Leighton sniffled, lifting her head, her face just barely visible. "Wesley…" She struggled to choke back her emotions. "He told me."

"Well, that's good, isn't it? That's what you wanted."

"But I didn't know it would be so…horrible."

Wesley slid out from beneath her and sat up. "Isn't that a bit harsh?"

She pushed up from her stomach and sat on her heels facing him. "How would you know?"

"Leighton, I know everything."

Even in the dark he could see her mouth fall open. "You *knew* and you didn't tell me?"

Before he could respond, she hurried off the bed, but Wesley grabbed her wrist. "C'mon, Leighton, don't go. Just sit down and listen to me for a second."

She flopped down at the edge of the bed with her back to him.

"Delaney told me about Cole last night," Wesley said.

Leighton crossed her arms. "So you lied to me when you said you didn't know anything. How could you do that, Wes?"

"Oh, I wanted to tell you. You know I would do anything for you, Leighton. But it was *not* my place. It needed to come from Cole. Not me."

Leighton uncrossed her arms and dropped her face into her hands. Her trembling frame made the bed shake.

"Leighton, I'm sorry." Wesley scooted closer,

placing a hand on her shoulder.

"It's okay. You're right. You're always right."

"Well, I wouldn't say *that*."

"That's why I always need you," she said. "I somehow managed to avoid Cole all evening, and once his bedroom light was off, I figured it was safe to come down. I've been waiting all day to talk to you."

"So talk to me."

Leighton took a deep breath and forced it out. "I'm scared."

"You're scared of Cole?" Wesley asked.

"No. I don't know. This is all just...*so big*. It's like I've been falling in love with someone I didn't actually know."

"You know him, Leighton. He's still Cole."

"I'm so afraid to believe that," she whispered, her voice shaking. "There's so much darkness, so much pain inside of him...it scares me."

Wesley moved to the edge of the bed to sit beside her, and he slid his arm around her shoulders. "It must've been hard to hear the truth. But it was probably much harder for Cole to tell it."

"I know," Leighton said, nodding.

When her tears returned, she folded against Wesley, resting her head on his chest. Her closeness didn't set him ablaze, didn't send his pulse into hysterics. For the first time in a long time, she was just Leighton.

Cole was still awake when the first flurries of the season began to fall. He sat by his window with the shades drawn, watching the white flakes flutter to the ground, illuminated by the street light at the edge of his yard. He let his mind wander, drifting aimlessly like the snowflakes, because he couldn't sleep, and he preferred his own dark thoughts over whatever horror his dreams would most likely force upon him.

And Cole was still awake, still sitting by his window, when the snow stopped falling, ample coats of white left on every visible surface. The sun had begun to rise, igniting the white canvas before him. The newly dusted landscape was so fresh, so pure, he wished he could feel the way the scene looked before him, and he wanted more of it.

Unlatching his window, Cole pushed it open, inviting the heavy, sharp air into his bedroom. He gripped the window sill and leaned his head out, closing his eyes as the frigid wind brushed his face like prickling bristles. Somehow, Cole felt invigorated by the chill that ran through his body, and the smell of snow that sparked warm images of childhood.

Cole looked longingly at the large front yard, imagining his younger self playing in the snow with his best friend. They'd built dozens of snowmen and had countless snowball fights together in that yard through the years. He didn't have an inkling then of how terribly he'd miss it now.

Cole stood and grabbed his shoes, pulling them on before he climbed out the window and hoisted himself onto the roof above it. He crawled to the peak and sat down, his breath like disappearing ghosts in the morning air. Folding his bare arms tightly over his white T-shirt, he shivered. He didn't care how cold he was. He was where he wanted to be.

Cole loved how he could see most of the neighborhood from that height, a sea of powdered-white roofs stretching out before him. Then he remembered he was always able to see Tucker's house from there, a warm splash of yellow in the distance. But now it was lost among all the glowing white, and he silently berated himself for caring, as if it mattered or would bring him closer to Tucker.

LEIGHTON

Leighton flung the door open and breezed outside, stopping at the edge of the front walk before the vast, perfect landscape. She'd always loved the untouched nature of freshly fallen snow, so smooth and uncharted, practically begging to be disturbed.

Forgetting all of her troubles for a moment, Leighton stepped out into the yard, grinning at the familiar soft crunch beneath her feet as she made her way to the center. She turned, looking back at the shoe prints that marred the flawless surface.

A motion above caught her eye and she spotted Cole on the second-story roof of the house, getting on his feet. Leighton's breath caught in her throat as she watched him take a few steps forward, looking straight ahead with a seemingly determined expression.

"No," Leighton whispered to herself. "Oh my God..." She took off toward the house, waving her arms. "Cole!"

Her sudden shout startled him and he lost his footing, his shoes slipping against the frosty shingles. Leighton let out a scream as he fell to his backside, sliding down the roof. He planted his feet and dug his hands into the steep incline, halting himself just before the edge.

Without hesitation, Leighton tore through the snow and back into the house, hurrying up the staircase as quickly as her legs would carry her. She burst into Cole's bedroom just as he climbed back through the window, both of them breathing heavily.

Leighton closed the gap between them, collapsing against Cole in a hysterical mess. He stood rigidly at first, his arms limp at his sides before he slowly closed them around her.

Then she pushed him away, her entire mood shifting. "How could you do that, Cole?" she asked, scraping the tears from her face. "You said I didn't have to worry about you."

Confusion wrinkled Cole's forehead as he gawked at her. "What are you talking about?"

Leighton tried to speak, but her tough facade had cracked, allowing her fear and her distress to resurface. She gripped her chest over her heart with one hand, and covered her mouth with the other to stifle her sobs.

"Wait," Cole said, glancing back at the window. "Did you think I was gonna *jump*?"

Before she could respond, Cole's parents barreled into the room, charged with worry.

"Cole? What's going on?" his father asked.

Cole tilted his head back, emitting a frustrated sigh. "Nothing is going on."

His mother crossed the room and frantically closed the window, double-checking the lock. "Cole, honey..." Her voice trembled as she wrung her hands. "You would tell us if something was wrong...wouldn't you?"

Cole pushed a hand through his messy hair, then placed his hands on his hips, letting his tall frame sag with mental exhaustion. "Something is always wrong. Don't you get it? But having you both constantly breathing down my neck and walking on egg shells does not help. Just stop smothering me; I can't take it anymore."

His parents exchanged glances, both looking like they'd been slapped in the face.

"Cole, we love you," his dad finally said. "I'm sorry if we've made things any more difficult for you, but you have to understand how difficult this has been for us, as your parents, *because* we love you. We don't want anything to happen to you."

"Who said anything was gonna happen to me?" Cole asked.

Cole's father motioned to the window. "Well, what just happened? Delaney said Leighton ran up here freaking out because you were—"

"I wasn't going to jump off the roof," Cole interrupted his father.

"You weren't?" Leighton asked, confused.

Cole shot her a sideways glance. "Thanks to

you scaring the shit out of me, I almost *fell* off the roof...but no. Why the *hell* would I jump? Is that really what you all expect from me?"

Leighton cast her eyes to the carpeted floor.

"What were you doing up there, then?" Cole's mother asked. "You know you're not supposed to do things like that."

Cole tightened his jaw. "Oh my God, this is getting ridiculous. Can everyone please just leave? I can't do this right now."

Cole's parents moved to the door, his father stopping in the doorway. "But you're okay?"

"Yes! Please go!" Cole stormed over to his bed, plopping down at the edge with his back to the door. He buried his face in his hands.

Leighton lingered in the room, nervously chewing her fingernail. "Cole?"

He lifted his head to look at her, his cheeks streaked with tears. But Leighton couldn't tell if he was angry or sad. She saw nothing but emptiness.

"Why are you still here? What, suddenly you can stand to look at me now?"

Her eyes stung. "I'm sorry. I probably didn't react in the best way yesterday—"

"Don't worry; you reacted just like I thought you would," he huffed, standing to his feet. He began pacing the room. "I knew this was a mistake. I *knew* this would happen."

Cole stopped in front of his dresser, glaring at the mirror. With a sudden, swift motion, he smashed his fist into the glass, shattering it to pieces.

"Cole!" Leighton cried out.

He swiped both arms over the dresser top, shoving his few belongings and all the glass shards to the floor with a crash.

Leighton was shaking as Cole went for the door in response to the sound of his parents coming down the hallway. He slammed the door shut with open palms, the walls of his room rattling from the resounding force. He pressed his back against it, fumbling with the knob for a lock that wasn't there. Then he slid to the floor, finally coming undone.

"Leighton? Is everything okay in there?" Cole's father asked through the door.

"Yes," she answered, praying it was the truth.

Leighton gaped at the bright red blood Cole had smeared on the white door with his hands. Without hesitation, she was on her knees before him, reaching for his face as he resisted her.

"I'm so sorry I hurt you," she whispered, pressing her forehead against his. "You finally confided in me and I let you down."

Cole's breathing slowed down and he calmed as if willed by her touch. "I don't blame you," he barely whispered back.

He gripped her wrist as she held his face, and his desperate eyes stared into hers. "Please don't leave me."

Leighton brushed his hair out of his face, her heart cracking. "I won't. I promise."

Cole swallowed hard, his lip quivering, and he lifted her into his lap to hold her against him. They remained still with nothing but the rhythm of breaths and heartbeats.

After a short while, Leighton removed herself

from Cole's grasp and tended to his hands, checking for glass shards.

Carefully gripping his hand, she led him to his bed and guided him to lie down on his back. Leighton lay down on her stomach beside him, half of her body overlapping his. She rested her head peacefully on his chest, and Cole relaxed beneath her, softly stroking her arm with one hand, and cradling her against him with the other.

"I was looking for Tucker's house," Cole said suddenly, after several quiet moments.

"What?"

"That's what I was doing on the roof. I used to sit up there a lot when I was younger, and I could always see Tucker's house from there. But I guess the trees have grown or something, because I can't see it anymore...I don't know why I cared."

Leighton tilted her head to see his face. "It's okay to care."

Cole grimaced. "Not if it makes everyone think you're suicidal. Again."

"I'm so sorry that was my first instinct," she said.

"It's okay. I guess I deserve it."

Leighton nestled her cheek back into his chest, and they fell into a tense silence.

"I haven't meant to avoid you," she said.

Cole said nothing.

"I guess I needed time to think it through so I could respond the right way," she added.

"And what did you come up with?" he asked, pulling himself away from her. He sat up and put some distance between them as if bracing himself for more rejection.

Leighton sat cross-legged facing him. "I don't think it's a black and white situation, what happened with you and Tucker. You *both* made bad decisions that night."

"Yeah, but mine *killed* him." Cole dropped his gaze, studying the smudged, dried blood on his knuckles. "I can't believe I lost it like that earlier. I'm sorry, I'm just so tired of the way people see me."

"How do they see you?"

"As the suicidal kid...the reason Tucker's dead..." Cole picked at his knuckle until it started bleeding again, and Leighton grabbed his wrist to stop him.

"Can I ask you a question?" She didn't wait for his reply. "If it had been *you* who drove off and hit that pole, wouldn't Tucker be the one to blame for punching you and then letting you drive drunk? Because it has to work both ways, right?"

"But that's not what happened."

"That's not the point. You both did things that put the other in danger. Tucker just happened to make the worst choice of all...and you weren't the only one at that party who didn't stop him from driving."

Cole stared at her, frozen.

"Maybe *everyone* is to blame...even Tucker," Leighton continued, her mind ironing out the messy creases as revelations unfolded before her. "Or maybe no one is to blame because bad things just happen sometimes. People like to point fingers because they need answers so badly; they want an explanation. But you know that saying, *everything happens for a reason*? It's bullshit. Most of the time there is no reason and shit just *happens*."

Cole turned away from her and put his feet on the floor, gripping the edge of the mattress on either side of him. "I'm the reason. It happened because of *me*."

Coming up beside him, Leighton placed a steady hand on his back. She knew it would be a grueling feat to convince him. It was what he'd believed for too long, what he'd nearly given up his life for.

"I think you're wrong, Cole. I think this is something that happened *to* you. Not something that you did."

He faced her, his tired eyes red and his cheeks stained. "How can you believe that?"

She took his hand into her lap and carefully threaded her fingers through his. "Because you've been wrong before. You said once I knew the truth, I wouldn't love you anymore. But I still do."

Cole's face contorted with a burst of raw emotion and he collapsed against her. "Thank you," he managed, clinging to her.

Wishing his hurt away, Leighton held him for what felt like forever, but still not quite long enough.

Thirty

After they'd found parking, Cole walked with his friends the three blocks to the center of downtown. The five of them had arrived at the Lachlan Christmas kick-off. Twilight fell upon them as the sun dipped behind the quaint surrounding buildings and slipped past the horizon, taking a few degrees of warmth with it.

The light posts along the street were decorated with large wreaths and strings of white lights, and peaceful, instrumental versions of classic Christmas songs played over the sound system.

"I'm really glad we came," Leighton said, turning to smile up at Cole behind her. "I'm glad you let us talk you into it."

Her childlike excitement made him grin. "Me too."

Cole moved in closer behind Leighton, his body flush against hers as the crowd thickened and space became more scarce at the edge of the street. Draping his arms around her shoulders, he rested his cheek against her head.

She gripped his arm with her hands. "This is

one of those moments where life just feels completely perfect," she said.

Cole leaned in to kiss her on the cheek, shocked to nearly catch a glimpse of the same feeling.

The parade was in full swing, float after float passing by, each one more elaborate than the last. The crowd clapped and cheered all the way through to the last float, which, of course, carried as Santa.

When the parade was over and the crowd had started thinning to gather around the large Christmas tree in front of the old courthouse, Cole's knee buckled from the force of something knocking into it from behind.

He spun around, instantly horrified. His jaw tightened as every shred of newfound happiness drained out of him. Anxiety replaced it, tunneling through his veins like a plague.

"Ah, so it *is* you." She smiled like she'd been reunited with a dear friend and it made Cole's stomach turn. "I almost didn't recognize you with all that hair. Wow, it's gotten long. Anyway, how are you?"

She stepped forward, reaching out to touch Cole's hair, but he backed away.

"Ava."

He spoke her name like a warning, and her lips turned in a pained frown. "What?" Ava asked.

"Don't play dumb. You *know* what."

She laughed, putting her hands on her hips. "Oh, c'mon, Cole. Grudges rot your insides."

"It's not a grudge. I'm just done with you."

The playfulness faded from her face. "Just like that? After all the history we have together?"

"It's not 'just like that.' Have you completely forgotten the past year?" Cole asked.

Ava huffed with an exaggerated rise and fall of her shoulders. "*No one* could forget the past year. *You* know that."

Cole felt his heart palpitate. How could she do this to him? Was she really that cruel? He watched her cross her arms over her chest, her face ugly with spite, and he knew she *was* that cruel. Had she always been this way? Maybe he'd been too naïve or blinded by his affection to notice. Or maybe it took meeting someone as pure and kind as Leighton for him to realize all the things Ava had never been.

"What do you want from me, Ava?" he finally asked.

His question seemed to surprise her. "I don't know, Cole. Maybe I think *you* should be the one asking for *my* forgiveness. Not the other way around."

Cole couldn't breathe. How had he ever loved her? As he looked at her now, clenching his jaw so tightly he thought his teeth might shatter, he couldn't see one favorable thing. "I do not owe you an apology," he said.

Ava raised an eyebrow. "Really. Not even for kissing another girl?"

"I already apologized for that! A hundred times at *least*."

"Okay. Then how about for making all of us lose Tucker?" The coldness ebbed from her features, replaced by a look that could only be described as broken. "And I had to lose you because of it."

Cole stood frozen, sure that his heart had stopped beating. He wanted to run, to yell, to cry, to disappear. But by some divine providence, Leighton appeared at his side, her simple touch jumpstarting his heart.

Leighton's smile was bright and sweet as she looked up at him. "Hey, the light show is starting in five minutes. You ready to head over?"

"Excuse me. We're talking," Ava said, her tone and stance reeking of hostility.

Leighton turned her attention to Ava, her eyes wide. "And you are?"

"I'm Ava," she said proudly, as if assuming her reputation preceded her.

Leighton's face went blank. "Oh."

"Yeah. I dated Cole for *two years*, honey. Who are *you*?" Ava's hands were back on her hips.

Cole reached his arm around Leighton, pulling her into his side. "This is Leighton. My girlfriend."

Ava gave Leighton a quick once-over with scathing eyes. "Your girlfriend?" She snickered, flipping her hair over her shoulder. "So, tell me, Cole...does *she* know what you did?"

A chill shot through his body, igniting anger, pain, and grief. His mouth went dry and his throat closed, and even if he could have articulated a reply, he wouldn't have been able to deliver it.

"He didn't *do* anything," Leighton said, stepping between him and Ava.

Ava looked at her with pity. "Is that what he told you? You must not know the whole story."

"Oh, no, I do. Cole told me everything."

"So you know it was all his fault, then. Because if he hadn't gone after Tucker's girlfriend, and if he hadn't *given* Tucker his keys, Tucker would be alive."

Leighton took a step closer to her. "Were you drunk at that party?"

Ava rolled her eyes. "*Maybe* slightly buzzed. But if you're questioning my knowledge of what went down, you don't have to. I was right there, and of sound mind. I know exactly what happened."

Leighton raised an eyebrow. "Then why didn't *you* stop Tucker?"

Ava's face went blank. "What?"

"Cole was really drunk. He wasn't of sound mind and his judgment was off. But yours wasn't. So if we're gonna stand here and point fingers, shouldn't *you* be to blame for knowing exactly what was going on and not doing anything to stop it?"

Ava tried to laugh it off but her nervousness seeped through. "Who are *you* anyway? You weren't even there. You don't have any right to throw such a horrible accusation at someone."

Leighton crossed her arms over her chest. "Oh, like you do to Cole?"

Ava's gaze flickered to Cole. "It's different..."

"It's not different, Ava," Leighton said. "You all feel better letting Cole take the blame so you don't have to admit that you just *stood* there and let it happen. If you were of such sound mind, why did *you* drive Tucker home?"

Ava's face went white and she swallowed. "No. That's not it," she said, her voice small.

"Then what is it?"

Ava fidgeted for a second before she pushed past them, barreling ahead through Wesley and Delaney to break apart their entwined hands. The force nearly knocked Delaney over.

"Watch it, bitch!" Quinn called after Ava as she vanished in the crowd.

Cole hadn't been to Smitty's since he'd been on the football team. With Tucker. It was strange to be there again now, walking in beside Leighton, who he hadn't the slightest clue even existed the last time he'd entered through those same doors. Cole tried to focus on his gratitude for having found her instead of the uneasy feeling in his stomach.

"I can't believe you guys are leaving in the morning. I know it's only been three days, but I've kinda grown fond of having you around," Delaney said with a sheepish smile.

Wesley slipped his arm around her shoulders, pulling her closer to him in the booth. "Let's please not talk about that right now." He laughed, though it was obvious to Cole that it bothered him.

"Ya know, Wes," Quinn began from her chair at the end of the table, "I was totally gonna harass you for falling victim to a pathetic case of instalove, but it's so much more than that..." She looked to Delaney. "After spending all day with you, I don't blame Wesley one bit."

Delaney grinned. "Aw, thank you."

"And thanks to Cole for inviting you to Thanksgiving," Wesley added, pressing his cheek against Delaney's head.

Quinn reached over to Cole, who sat catty-corner from her at the end of the booth, and patted him on the shoulder. "Good job, Cole."

Cole half-smiled.

"I'm so sorry for the wait," the waitress said as she appeared at the table, looming over Cole. "The Christmas kick-off has got us so busy tonight."

Cole looked up at her. "Oh, it's okay."

"Wait a second...you're Cole MacHendrick," she said, her face alight with wonder as if she'd just happened upon an endangered species.

"Yeah..." he answered slowly. He held his breath, awaiting her reaction.

"You probably don't know me—well, I sat behind you in AP English, junior year, but we never really spoke."

"Megan. I know who you are," Cole said.

Her eyebrows shot up and her mouth fell open like he'd surprised her. "Anyway," she went on, "it seemed like you dropped off the face of the earth. One second, you were everywhere, then you were just nowhere."

Cole didn't know how to respond, so he just shrugged.

"I mean, I've heard a lot of things, but you never know what's actually true," Megan added, flicking her hair off her shoulder with her ballpoint pen.

Cole raised his eyes to look at her. "What have you heard?"

Megan brought her pen to her mouth and bit nervously at its cap. "Well, you know, all that Tucker Lindsley stuff with the accident and all—everyone knows about that."

"What does everyone *know* about it?" Cole pushed Leighton's hand away when she tried to get his attention.

"Well, the story I heard was that you and Tucker got in a fight at Aaron's party because he found out you were sleeping with his girlfriend—"

"Whoa, that is *not* what happened," Delaney cut in. Her face was red with embarrassment and anger. "*I* was Tucker's girlfriend. I did *not* sleep with Cole."

"I'm so sorry. That's just what I've heard," Megan said.

"Yeah, well, for the record, I *kissed* Delaney when I was drunk and without her permission. Not that anyone cares about the actual truth." Cole turned to Delaney, his gaze speaking silent apologies.

"I care about the truth," Megan said. "So...did you hit Tucker and then make him leave the party? Or is that just more rumors?"

Cole hung his head, pinching the bridge of his nose as he tried not to hyperventilate. "No...that's not what happened either," he finally answered in a quiet voice. "He hit *me*—which I deserved—and then *he* insisted on leaving. I didn't want him to."

"Oh." Megan shifted her weight from one foot to the other. "It's crazy how people gossip and stories get so twisted."

"At least *one* more person in this town knows what really happened," Cole scoffed.

"Guess that explains why you disappeared

then," Megan said. "And why you did what you did…" She made a face like she knew she'd said too much.

"Do I even wanna know?" Cole asked, staring down at the faux woodgrain of the brown laminate tabletop.

"Probably not. It's most likely another lie. And it's pretty bad."

Cole ran a shaky hand through his hair and let out a heavy breath. "So's the truth."

Megan cast her eyes to the floor and shook her head. "I don't want to talk about this anymore. Can I just take your drink order?"

Cole stood up and came in close to her, gently gripping her by the forearm. "Please just tell me. I have to know what people are saying."

Swallowing, Megan nodded. "I heard that you…tried to kill yourself."

"That's true." He smirked. "So what did I do? Did I hang myself? Take a bunch of pills? Slit my wrists?"

Megan frowned, bringing her mouth to his ear. "You shot yourself in the head, but you survived. That's why you act so different now. And that's why you grew your hair out—to cover the scar."

Cole took a couple steps back from her, rubbing his temples as her words made his head ache. "I have to go…"

He spun around and hurried off, weaving through the full tables to get to the door. He shoved it open with both hands and stormed outside, the cold air like ice picks in his throat.

Making his way to the empty picnic tables in

front of the restaurant, Cole slipped his cigarettes out of the pocket of his jacket and beat the pack against his palm. He stepped onto the bench and then turned, taking a cigarette from the pack with his front teeth before he sat down on the tabletop facing the parking lot.

Cupping his hand over the cigarette, he lit it with a sparking flick of his lighter and took a long drag. He inhaled the smoke deep into his lungs, all of his muscles relaxing as a slight tingling, light-headed sensation swept over him. He breathed the smoke out and watched it swirl against the dark sky and disappear before he took another pull.

Cole cursed himself for thinking he could slip right back into society completely undetected. For not expecting to run head-on into his past and all the things he'd spent the last year running from.

He'd begun to ponder how long it would take for Leighton to come find him with her usual attempt at damage control when a slamming car door across the parking lot caught his attention. It took him barely a second to see who was heading toward him.

Convinced he was the target of life's most ridiculous torment, Cole threw his head back and let out a rancorous laugh.

Thirty-one

Josh Lindsley's snide smile mocked every thread of Cole's existence as he approached.

"Wow. Cole MacHendrick." Josh swatted at the cigarette smoke that was nowhere near him. "I see you're still trying to kill yourself."

Cole gritted his teeth, bringing the cigarette to his lips. Keeping his eyes locked on Josh's, he took a quick drag, then exhaled in Josh's direction.

With a swift motion, Josh knocked the cigarette from Cole's hand and it fell to the ground. Cole snickered incredulously, scratching the back of his head as he tried to retain his composure.

"Hey, have you seen Ava? She's supposed to meet me here." Josh said it like a jab.

"I heard you broke up," Cole said, resting his elbows on his knees.

Josh shook his head with an arrogant smirk. "Nope. But *I* heard some bitch tried telling her off tonight."

Cole shoved Josh and stood to his feet on the bench, glaring down as Josh stumbled back a few steps.

Josh laughed at him. "If you're thinking of

jumping, you might wanna try the roof instead. Fatal injuries from *that* height are more likely."

Cole stepped off the bench, his boots crunching in the icy remnants of the day's snowfall. "Wow, you really seem to want me dead."

Josh shrugged, coldness in his stare. "Better you than Tucker."

Grabbing Josh by the lapels of his coat, Cole jerked him closer, their faces just inches apart. "Do you think I don't know that?" Cole asked through clenched teeth. "Every day, I wish I could trade places with Tuck." Cole pushed Josh away from him.

"I have never liked you, Cole. Did you know *that*? I always pretended for Tucker's sake, since, for some reason, you were his best friend...Well, *I* used to be Tucker's best friend. We grew up together. But when you came along, I got dropped just like that." Josh snapped his fingers. "Ya know, if he was never friends with you, he'd still be here."

Cole stood there and said nothing. Because he agreed.

"So, all of this because you're *jealous*?"

When Cole heard Leighton's voice, he spun around, wondering how long she'd been standing there beside Wesley.

Josh snorted. "I'm not jealous."

"Yes you are," Wesley said, motioning for Leighton to stay put before he moved from the sidewalk to stand beside Cole.

"Who even are you?" Josh asked, wrinkling his nose in disgust.

"Oh, he's no one," Ava chimed in as she approached. "Just Delaney's rebound."

Josh turned to Ava, his eyebrows raised. "*This guy?*" He turned back to Wesley, scanning him with critical eyes and a mocking sneer. "She's replacing my cousin with this tool?"

Delaney came out of nowhere. She flung herself at Josh, pounding her fists against his broad chest. Wesley grabbed her by the waist and pulled her back, wrapping his arms around her from behind.

"Screw you, Josh!" She glared at him as she gripped Wesley's arm across her heaving chest.

Josh laughed. "You've got a real stand-up crowd here, Cole. Almost gives you something to live for, huh?"

Wesley quickly but gently moved Delaney aside to throw a punch at Josh, striking him in the nose. The impact snapped Josh's head backward, but he was instantly in retaliation mode, his eyes wide with fury as blood poured from his face.

"All right, that's enough. We're just gonna go," Cole said, putting himself between Wesley and Josh.

Josh violently shoved Cole out of his path, lunging at Wesley with a raised fist. The force of Josh's bulky build knocked Wesley to the ground, and Josh straddled him, delivering several rapid punches to his face.

As Cole worked to free himself from the sharp tangle of bare bushes he'd fallen into, Quinn rushed at Josh and jumped onto his back. She gripped tight handfuls of his hair, fighting to tug him away from her brother. Cole snatched up Quinn just as Wesley knocked Josh off of him and scrambled to his feet.

The manager of Smitty's barreled out the front door. "You all need to leave now before I call the police," he gave a thunderous warning.

"Chill out. We're going," Quinn retorted.

The manager went back inside and let the door close behind him, but he stood in the window with his arms crossed over his chest, waiting for them to comply.

"Are you okay?" Delaney asked Wesley, taking his face in her hands.

Wesley winced, flashing his bloodstained teeth, and he pulled away. "I've been much better." He touched the swelling flesh over his cheekbone.

Josh put his arm around Ava and shot Cole one more glare before he turned away.

"Hey, Josh," Delaney stopped him. "I really hope, for your sake, that Tucker isn't watching over us."

"Why's that?"

"Because I think he'd be really disappointed in you." Delaney slipped her hand into Wesley's and led him toward the parking lot.

Before he followed, Cole took one more glance at Josh, who stood frozen in his shame.

LEIGHTON

"Okay. What the hell is going on?" Quinn demanded from the back of Cole's car.

Delaney stopped tending to the cut on Wesley's lip. "Can we pull over or something so I can see what I'm dealing with here?"

Cole silently reached up to the ceiling and

flipped on the light. Leighton turned around to assess the damage. She frowned at the bleeding gash above Wesley's eyebrow.

"Should we go to the hospital?" Delaney asked.

"What? No. I'm fine," Wesley insisted.

"Are you sure? What if you need stitches?" Leighton chimed in.

"I don't." Wesley took the napkins from Delaney and dabbed at the blood that had dripped down to his cheek.

"Can someone *please* tell me what's going on?" Quinn tried again.

Leighton looked at Cole, who kept his eyes on the road, then exchanged glances with Delaney. Wesley let out a sigh.

"Am I the only one who doesn't know?" Quinn asked.

"What do you wanna know?" Cole's voice was low and lifeless.

Leighton put her hand on his shoulder, hoping to offer him comfort or strength or whatever he would allow her to give him. "You don't have to do this now."

He shook his head. "It's okay...Quinn?"

For once, Quinn was speechless. "Um...I don't even know where to start...Did you really try to kill yourself?" She sounded heartbroken.

"Yeah," Cole answered after a long moment.

Then Quinn asked him every question she had, until she, too, knew everything.

As they all made their way up the walk to the Ma-cHendricks' front door, Quinn, who was lagging behind, called out Cole's name. He turned around after motioning the others into the house, and took a few steps toward her.

He put his hands on his hips. "It's okay if you think differently of me—"

Quinn jolted forward, silencing him as she threw her arms around him. Slowly, he returned her embrace.

"I'm so sorry, Cole," she said, clinging to him. "I'm sorry you lost Tucker. And I'm sorry all your friends let you down." She held onto him for a few more moments before she released him. "I'm really glad I called Ava a bitch, though."

A genuine laugh erupted from Cole. "You are really something, Quinn. Thank you."

"I hope you know how much we care about you," she said. "And I hope you know how happy you make Leighton."

He shrugged. "Do I? I feel like I've only been causing her pain lately."

Quinn shook her head. "No. I've never seen her this way before. It's like she's finally who she's supposed to be."

Cole averted his gaze to the brick pavers beneath them. "I really love that girl."

"I know you do," Quinn said, touching his shoulder. "I understand now...why you two *had* to be together. You both needed each other more than anyone ever knew."

When Cole followed Quinn into the living room, he found his father pacing, shaking his head as he passed back and forth in front of the couch where Leighton, Wesley, and Delaney were seated. Cole's mother stood off to the side, wringing her hands like she always did when something was wrong.

The rubber soles of his father's shoes made a slight screech on the wood floor as he came to a halt and dug his phone out of his pocket. "He can't keep getting away with this. I'm calling Pete."

His mother sighed. "Mike…"

"Dad. Please don't," Cole said sternly. "If you call Josh's dad, it'll just make everything worse."

His father pointed at Wesley, who held an icepack over the left side of his face. "Isn't it already worse, Cole? Look at your friend! Josh doesn't even know him! Yet, he obviously had no problem with attacking him."

"Well…I *did* hit him first," Wesley said.

Cole's father spun around to face Wesley. "What? Why?"

Wesley lowered the icepack. "Sir…I promise you, he deserved it."

"He deserved a lot worse," Quinn muttered, then looked at Cole's dad. "Wes was just sticking up for Cole."

Cole's father tossed his phone onto the otto-man and rubbed his hands over his face. "I can't do this anymore," he said under his breath. "That kid is out of control. I am so sick of standing by and watching my son suffer."

"Well, at least you're not Tucker's dad," Cole said.

Then he turned and left the room.

After giving Cole ample time to calm down, Leighton went upstairs to see him. She knocked softly on his partially open door, gingerly peering her head into his room.

"Come in," he said quietly.

Cole was lying on his bed, clad in a pair of black sweatpants and holding a rectangular piece of paper in his hands. As Leighton climbed onto the bed, she realized he was looking at a photograph. It was tattered and bent at the corners, like it had been handled and looked at countless times before.

"That's Tucker?" she asked, lying down beside him.

Cole nodded, still staring at the photo. It was a shot of Tucker and Cole together, wearing football uniforms and huge smiles, holding their helmets triumphantly in the air.

"My mom took this after we won state, junior year," Cole said. "We were tied, with only seven seconds left on the clock, and somehow Tucker got wide open. I made the pass just before I got sacked, and he scored the winning touchdown. It was amazing."

Leighton could practically see the stadium lights reflecting in his eyes. "You both look so happy."

"We were. We always were." Cole didn't hide

his tearing eyes. And he didn't stop looking at the photo. "I hate that Tucker's become this ugly secret. I hate not talking about him. I miss him *so* much."

He closed his eyes, forcing the built up tears over the edge and down his cheeks.

"Tell me about him," Leighton said tenderly.

Cole placed the photo carefully on his bedside table and shifted his eyes to the ceiling. "Tucker was probably the nicest guy you could ever meet," he said. "Nicer than Wesley, even."

Leighton chuckled. "Wow, that is definitely nice."

Cole moved his hand across the space between them to find hers, and he ran his fingers over her open palm. "Everybody liked Tuck. He was popular, but it was like he didn't realize it. He was just him—friends with the jocks and cheerleaders, and friends with the mathletes and chess team. He was funny and smart, and one of those guys who's good at everything, but he never showed off. All the girls liked him, but he was naïve to it—he only noticed Delaney. He was so good to her. And somehow, he always had the time to be the greatest best friend I will ever have."

"Sounds like he was an incredible person," Leighton said.

"It feels so good to talk about him. I've wanted to so many times." Cole turned his head toward her. "I'm so sorry I didn't know how to tell you. I was so afraid you would see it the way everyone else does. The way Ava does...the way I do."

"Well, I'm not Ava. I hate that she left you to

go through this alone. And I hate that you still believe the lie they've created."

"If it's *all* a lie, and they're wrong, then why has it been so easy for people to believe it? Why do I feel this guilt?" Cole asked.

"Because judgment is powerful and grief made you vulnerable. But it's not the truth, Cole. No matter how many people were duped into it."

He stared at her like he was desperate to believe her words and siphon the relief from them. "But *everyone* has turned on me. People I've known my whole life, people who have watched me grow up...And even my *friends*. Why would they do that if I didn't deserve it?"

Leighton sighed. "You heard it yourself tonight that most people don't even know the real story. And I'm willing to bet that Ava and Josh had a lot to do with that. They weren't *really* your friends. *Real* friends do things like tell off your ex-girlfriend or get pummeled by your arch enemy."

Cole rolled to his side, propping himself up on his elbow. His face loomed over hers. "*You* are not my friend."

"I don't think I ever was." She smiled nervously, a mass of wild butterflies taking up residence in her stomach.

The silver in his eyes was alight with awe and affection as he brushed his lips over hers. "Well, you kind of ruined that when you decided to kiss me out of the blue that one day."

Leighton blushed and groaned, placing a hand on her hot cheek. "That was not my finest moment."

Cole chuckled. "Until then, I was so sure you hated me."

"I thought I did…and I thought you hated me too."

His grin widened. "I kissed you back, though, didn't I?"

"Surprisingly, yes."

Cole's gaze traced every contour of her face. "I noticed you the very first day of class."

"Oh, when you caught me checking you out?" she asked, her smile bashful.

"No. When you walked in the door."

Cole's lips found hers once again and he kissed her feverishly, like he'd never kissed her before, his hand running along the curves of her frame.

"I love you so much, Leighton," he whispered, his breath on her cheek making her skin tingle. "Thank you for not giving up on me…even when I begged you to. I don't know where I'd be right now if it wasn't for you."

Leighton ran her hand softly over the bare skin of his ribcage and every nerve ending in her fingertips ignited on contact. "Well, you'll never find out. Hell or high water, remember?"

"Okay, I'm gonna go up to bed," Quinn said, hopping off the couch.

Wesley got up from his spot beside Delaney. "Hey, Quinn…I wanted to thank you for having my back tonight. It means a lot."

Quinn playfully rolled her eyes, then opened her arms to embrace him. "I'm just glad you're okay," Quinn said, pulling away. "I mean...you look like shit, but you're okay."

Wesley chuckled. "There she is."

"I guess I should get going," Delaney said, standing.

"No, don't go," Quinn insisted. "Mr. MacHendrick said you could stay as late as you want."

Delaney set her purse down on the end table, toying with the strap. "I know...I just wasn't sure if I should." Her shy gaze met Wesley's.

"Please stay?" he requested, his voice tender and hopeful.

It was all the convincing she needed. "Okay."

"All right, then. Good night," Quinn said, turning away. "Behave yourself, Wes."

"Good night, Quinn," Wesley said, quickly.

He faced Delaney with a sheepish smile and took her hand, guiding her back to the couch to sit beside him. "You weren't sure if you should stay?" he asked.

"I didn't know if you wanted me to."

His brown eyes went wide. "Of course I want you to. To be honest..." He weaved his fingers through hers. "When I think about saying goodbye to you and going back to school tomorrow, it kind of makes my stomach hurt."

"Really?"

"That's weird, isn't it?"

Delaney smiled. "No. When *I* think about it, I wanna cry."

Wesley looked at her, his eyes falling to her

lips. He'd last kissed her just the night before, but the fluttering in his stomach made it feel like the first time all over again. He leaned closer, pressing his lips softly to hers.

"Is this crazy?" he whispered, brushing Delaney's hair away from her face with his fingertips. "How can we feel this way when we barely know each other?"

One corner of her mouth lifted in a half-smile. "You're the analytical type, aren't you?"

"I guess I am."

"Well, I feel like I know you. I've felt that way since I met you," Delaney said.

"Yeah. *Two* whole days ago."

She turned sideways on the couch cushion and pulled her feet up beneath her. "Tell me what I'd know about you, then, if I'd known you as long as I feel like I have."

"Okay, like what?"

"Like…what's your dream?"

Wesley bit his lip. "Wow, jumping right into the big stuff. Okay…I've always wanted to be a film director."

"That doesn't surprise me at all," Delaney said. "What else you got?"

"I've never been stung by a bee?" he offered.

"Wow, that's pretty lucky."

Wesley grimaced. "My luck, I'm probably allergic."

Delaney snickered. "Oh, gosh. Just don't pull a *My Girl* on me, please."

"I won't, I promise."

"Favorite music?" she asked.

He didn't hesitate. "The Cure, Bowie, and New Order."

Her eyebrows shot up. "I *love* The Cure. Do you listen to anything more current?"

"Sure. Bad Suns, Brandon Flowers, The Pains of Being Pure at Heart...to name a few. How about you?"

Delaney smiled. "I'm a huge Michael Jackson fan."

"Really? Me too."

"To be honest, I listened to *You Are Not Alone* on repeat for weeks after Tucker died."

Wesley gripped her knee. "I wish I knew you then so I could've been there for you."

"Well, you're here now. And I can assure you, my songs are a lot happier these days."

He averted his eyes. "Listen...I don't know if I'm being presumptuous, but I want you to know I won't be seeing anyone else. I'm not asking you to do the same; I just wanted you to know."

Her grin returned, wider this time. "I'm definitely willing to see this craziness through."

He chuckled. "So you *do* think this is crazy."

"Okay, yeah, we met *two days* ago and we're essentially talking about our future. I guess that's pretty crazy. But I don't care."

"I don't care, either," he said with certainty.

Delaney's joyfulness dimmed. "For the record," she began, running her finger over her bracelet. "You're the only guy I've given a second thought since Tucker."

Thirty-Two

Delaney pulled back from Wesley, her face looming over his as she lay on her stomach beside him. They'd long since pulled the couch out into a bed to make more room, but they huddled closely in the center as if the space hadn't multiplied.

Delaney savored Wesley's nearness, absorbing every detail of his face as if committing them to memory—the faint spray of faded freckles across the bridge of his nose left over from childhood that were only visible from this proximity. The single, dark freckle just below the right corner of his perfect mouth. His warm eyes, flecked with gold, somehow so familiar, like she'd gazed into them infinite times before.

"What are you thinking?" Wesley asked, reaching up to touch her face.

Delaney blushed. "I was thinking about how beautiful you are."

He let out a soft laugh, the color of his cheeks mirroring hers. "You're silly."

She traced his bottom lip with her fingertip. "I'm serious. Has no one ever called you that before?"

Wesley shrugged against the thin mattress beneath him. "You mean besides my mother? I don't know…"

"Really? Not a girlfriend or anyone?"

Tilting his head to the side, he looked away. "Uh, no…no girlfriends."

"Wait. None of your girlfriends told you that, or you've had no girlfriends?" Delaney asked.

His silence indicated his answer.

"Wesley…you've never had a girlfriend?"

Still avoiding her gaze, he faintly shook his head. Delaney cupped his face, prodding him to look at her.

"How is that possible?" she asked.

"Well, I spent all of high school waiting for Leighton to see me *that* way. But she never did—minus the twenty-fourish hours a couple months ago when she *thought* she did."

"Ohhh. Leighton…I didn't know." Delaney gently stroked Wesley's puffy cheekbone where he'd caught one of Josh's fists. "You didn't date anyone else while you waited?"

"I've gone on dates," he said. "But I didn't want anyone else."

"And now?"

"I want you," Wesley said without hesitation.

A smile spread out slowly over Delaney's face. "Just like that?"

"Like what?"

She toyed with the collar of his navy button-down, willing her heart to stop racing. "I somehow, so suddenly, can replace the love of your life?"

Wesley's eyes moved back and forth between

hers as if trying to read her inner thoughts. "This is different," he said.

"How so?"

"*You* see me," he answered, smoothing a lock of hair behind her ear. "I would never speak poorly of Leighton. She's my best friend, and she's an incredible person. I will always care about her, but she's not for me. That didn't stop hurting until I met you."

"Two whole days ago," Delaney added facetiously.

"Yeah, we're ridiculous. You're just gonna have to accept that," Wesley said, chuckling. Then he gently pulled her down to kiss him, locking his fingers in her hair.

"Tell me about your family," Delaney requested some time later. Her head laid on Wesley's stomach as she stared up at the high ceiling, their bodies forming a T on the bed.

"Well...Quinn is my only sibling. Mom's a kindergarten teacher and Dad's an attorney. Your turn."

"Dad's still single. I have three half-sisters and a step-brother from my mom's second marriage and her current marriage. But they don't live around here so we're not close."

Wesley frowned. "I'm sorry."

"No, it's okay, really. What are your parents' names?" Delaney asked.

Wesley stroked her hair, twisting strands around his index finger. "Cam and Jodie."

"Aww...that's cute."

"Why's it cute?"

"I don't know. They just sound nice."

"Well, they are. So that's an accurate deduction on your part."

Delaney laughed.

"What?" Wesley asked.

"I just love the way you talk. It's like I'm in constant anticipation of every word that comes out of your mouth."

"Glad I can offer you adequate entertainment." He let out a snicker, his tightening abdomen slightly bouncing her head. "Anyway. I also have a dog. He's an old American bulldog. His name is Atlas."

"Not a cat person?"

"Oh, God no. Quinn has a cat. He's an asshole."

Delaney laughed again. "Oh yeah? And what's his name?"

"Shaq."

"You're not serious."

"Oh, I am."

"Well, it being Quinn's cat, I guess I'm not surprised. Why do you hate him?"

Wesley sighed. "Well, if he's not stealing my shit, he's knocking it on the floor. And he literally hides so he can jump out and attack my feet. I have *scars*."

"Oh, you poor baby," Delaney said with mock pity.

"Okay, seriously? Try coming downstairs at night for water in the dark kitchen of your 1928 Victorian house and have a creature suddenly spring from the shadows and sink its claws into your flesh.

Then you can laugh at me."

At first, Delaney wanted to laugh again, but she found herself filled with a stifling sadness. A sadness that seemed to travel throughout her body, coating every inch of her insides. It made her feel heavy enough to drop through the springs of the mattress beneath her. She could picture herself falling into an endless pit, much like the way she had when Tucker died. As much as it didn't make sense, she knew her dread was a direct effect of Wesley's impending departure. Delaney hadn't felt this alive since Tucker was. But now she could see that dark pit waiting for her return, when the only darkness she wanted to fall into were the shadows of Wesley's face.

"Hey," Wesley breathed, squeezing her shoulder.

Delaney felt too foolish to answer him.

"Are you crying?" he asked, his voice tender with concern.

He sat up, her head sliding to his lap. She turned away from him to hide her face.

"Delaney...what's wrong?" He leaned to the side, trying to peer over her shoulder.

Finally, she sat up and faced Wesley, letting him see her wet cheeks and sad eyes. She didn't need to hide from him. With him, she could be her true self, bare her soul, drop her guard. She trusted him completely.

"Oh, Delaney," he whispered, his eyebrows stitching together. He opened his arms and drew her in, pulling her into his easy comfort.

Somehow his arms felt like home. She could

live there forever.

"I don't want you to go," Delaney whimpered, clutching him tightly.

"I know. I don't want to." He pressed his cheek against her head and rocked her gently.

"I don't understand how I could feel like I *need* you. But I do," she said, letting her tears mark his shirt like bleeding ink on a page.

"I certainly don't mind being needed," Wesley said, caressing her back.

"I just don't want to miss you. I'm so tired of *missing*. That's all my life has been for the last fifteen months."

Wesley pulled away and took her face in his hands, lifting it so her eyes would meet his. "Please don't be sad. This is a good thing. I know in my heart it is. I promise you, you'll be okay. It's just three hours between us, not a lifetime and the universe."

Delaney's throat tightened when she realized he was referring to her distance from Tucker. But Wesley's words were spoken too tenderly and with too much affection to upset her. And he was right. Wesley would be only a car ride away, a weekend plan here and there. Tucker was *gone*. Forever. Her situation was improving, not continuing, and she needed to allow that to comfort her.

A small smile curved Delaney's lips. "Thank you, Wesley. Sometimes I think I've forgotten how to just be happy."

"It's okay," he said. "I'll help you remember."

"Can I just not go home tonight?" she asked, half joking.

He chuckled. "Sure. We'll stay up all night

and talk…I want to know everything there is to know about you."

"There's really nothing too exciting," she said.

"It's exciting to me." A fondness warmed Wesley's gaze. "Forget staying up all night. Let's just drop out of school and run away."

Delaney raised her eyebrows, an amused smirk on her face. "Where would we go?"

"Where do you wanna go?"

"Paris?"

"Okay…Hmm, but what about London?" Wesley asked. "I've always wanted to go to London."

She winced. "Ooh, but *I've* always wanted to go to Paris."

He bit the inside of his cheek and squinted his eyes at her like he was contemplating his next move. He reached into his jeans pocket and pulled out a quarter, holding it up between his thumb and forefinger.

"Okay. We'll flip on it," he resolved. "Heads, we go to London. Tails, we go to Paris. Ready?"

"Ready."

Wesley flipped the coin into the air, the glint of nickel and copper spinning upward then dropping back into his palm. He slapped it onto his other hand, hesitating before revealing the result. His eyes met Delaney's with a giddy grin as he uncovered the quarter.

"Guess we'll be making out under the Eiffel Tower. Surely, no one's done *that* before," Wesley said, his grin broadening.

Her smile was even bigger than his. "I'll pack

my bags right now."

"In all seriousness, I wouldn't mind sharing every cliché with you," he said.

Taking her hand in his, Wesley turned the tarnished bracelet on her wrist. 'TUCKER LOVES DELANEY,' engraved across its surface, caught the light and Wesley's eye. He stared at it for a brief moment before pressing a tender kiss to her hand.

Sitting cross-legged, Wesley slid his hands beneath Delaney and lifted her into his lap. She leaned into him, resting her cheek on his collar bone.

"I wish we were actually going to Paris," she said, after she'd adjusted against him. She couldn't help noticing how perfectly she fit in his arms, how safe and content she felt in his closeness.

"You'd go to Paris with some guy you just met?" he asked playfully.

"No. I'd go to Paris with *you*."

Wesley wrapped his arms tighter around her. With the soothing drum of his heart beating beneath her ear, Delaney knew she wouldn't be going home any time soon.

And she didn't.

WESLEY

They were still together, still awake, fighting fatigue with all their might when the sun crested the horizon, bringing the morning they'd dreaded all through the sacred night.

Wesley pulled their shared blanket tighter around them as he sat beside Delaney on the railing of the back porch. The sky was blooming before them, the rising light transforming the whispery hues, and Wesley thought about the last time they sat here together—three days ago now, but it felt like much longer. He thought about seeing Delaney at the grocery store, and how, even then, his stomach flipped when he saw her, as if she'd been special from the start. As if love at first sight and intuition and destiny and divine providence were all real and true and possible in his lonely world, in Delaney's broken one.

Could he really gather all those shattered pieces of her world? Could he reunite sea and shore and make it whole for her again? Could he stitch the fibers of her gray sky back together, covering the jagged tears and imperfect seams with vivid colors and rainless clouds, much like the sky they sat beneath now? Wesley wasn't sure, but he hoped so. And he would try. Oh, would he try.

LEIGHTON

Leighton was coming down the stairs as Wesley closed the front door behind him. He leaned his back against it, wiping his eyes with the backs of his hands.

"Are you okay?" Leighton asked, breezing across the wood floor to his side.

He straightened his posture and cleared his throat as if embarrassed to be caught in a moment of weakness. "You're up early," he said.

"So are you."

"I was walking Delaney out."

Leighton's eyes widened. "She *just* left?"

"Yeah. She went home to get some sleep before her shift," he said, yawning.

"She stayed up *all night* when she has to work today?"

Wesley pressed his lips together. "She just told me. If I'd known she had to work, I never would've let her stay this long." He moved past Leighton, drifting toward the living room like a ghost grieving its old life.

She followed and watched him flop onto the pullout bed. He buried his face in the pillow, his shoulders rising and falling with deep breaths.

"Wesley...are you okay?" she asked, hoping he'd answer this time.

After a moment, he lifted his head, resting his chin on the white fluff. "Please tell me I'm not insane."

Leighton chuckled, moving to the armchair nearby. "Why would you think you're insane?"

"Leighton...I *really* like this girl. And honestly, even that is an understatement."

She'd never seen Wesley's eyes so intense, or a truth so evident in someone's face. "She's amazing, Wes. I think you'd be insane *not* to like her."

He tapped his thumb against the metal frame of the bed, staring blindly past Leighton like his mind was far away, pondering possibilities and epiphanies. His countenance transformed, as if Leighton's approval had the power to chase away his doubts.

"I have to thank you, Leighton," he said

sleepily, closing his eyes.

"For what?"

"For not giving up on Cole. If you never fought for him, I never would've found Delaney…so, thank you." He'd barely slurred through the words before he drifted off.

His back rose and fell with each breath as he sank deeper into a long-evaded sleep, and Leighton watched him. She fondly noted how his eyelashes curled so perfectly, and how his full lips had a slight pout to them as he slept. But she frowned at the bruising across his brow and cheekbone that had developed through the night, and it made her angry that anyone could bear to hurt someone as kind as Wesley.

Then Leighton reflected on his words, considering the importance of one's decisions and how they have the power to affect others. For so long, she'd feared she'd been too selfish, that she'd inflicted irreparable damage when she let Wesley go, when she chose to fight for Cole. She hated the way she'd broken Wesley, the way she'd ripped the rug out from beneath his feet, cruelly stripping him of a dream fulfilled.

But the story changed. Somehow, Leighton's most hurtful transgression had become Wesley's greatest blessing. And it healed the piece of her heart that ached for him.

Leighton stood, grabbing the blanket at his feet, and carefully pulled it over him. Then she bent to press a soft kiss to his temple. She knew she was no longer Wesley's dream. And that was okay. She felt privileged to have captivated his heart at all.

Cole loomed in the doorway of his parents' bedroom, the tips of his toes stopping right where the hardwood of the hall met the plush carpet of the room. The thought of crossing that line still tightened his chest and made his palms sweat. He took a deep breath as his mother looked up from the pile of laundry she'd been tending to.

"Oh, hey, honey," she said cautiously, putting on a thin smile.

Cole knew he'd made her unsure of how to treat him yet again. Sometimes he wondered if she was afraid of him. Swallowing, Cole stepped into the room and stood at the other side of the bed, facing her.

"I just...wanted to apologize for yesterday. How I treated you and Dad. I said some terrible things, and I'm so sorry."

Her lips trembled. "No, it's okay. I understand. Dad and I have been entrusted with your life. It's our job to keep you safe. But that hasn't been the easiest task in the last year. I hope *you* understand how much we love you...and how hard we're trying to do what's best for you."

Cole's gaze dropped guiltily to the towel she was folding. "I do understand."

"I'm sorry we don't always know what's best," she added, wiping a tear from the corner of her eye. "I know we hover, and I probably call you too much, but Cole...you are my baby. You're my little boy, my heart. I could never live without you. Everything I do is because of that, and I need you to be patient with me as I learn how to tend to these much more complicated boo-boos."

Cole managed a smile as he rounded the bed to gather his mother into his arms. He bent to lay his head on her shoulder. She stroked his hair and cried.

"I love you, Mom. You're amazing, I hope you know that."

She stepped back and held his face in her hands. "I love you too, and I'm so proud of you. I hope *you* know that."

Cole looked away, placing his hands on his hips.

"What is it?" his mother asked, resting her hands on his shoulders.

He lowered himself to sit on the edge of the bed, and leaned forward with his elbows on his knees, his hair shielding his face.

"I need to ask you about something."

His mom sat beside him. "Okay."

"On Thanksgiving…Gavin told me he heard Josh and Ava talking once. Something about you and Vanessa, when you knew each other in high school."

"Okay, what about it?"

Cole tilted his head to look at her. "I guess Josh said that his mom went with you to an abortion clinic after you found out you were pregnant with me. Is that true?"

She let out a heavy breath and shook her head in disbelief. "No. It's a *huge* exaggeration. Vanessa made me an appointment—just for a consultation—because she thought I should be aware of my options. She thought she was being a good friend. But I was not interested. I never showed up to the appointment. I never planned to."

"Really?" Cole's face flushed with relief.

"Of course. I wouldn't lie to you about something like that. Your father and I never questioned keeping you. We loved you the second we knew of you."

His eyes welled up, threatening to spill over. "Josh said you made a mistake...that you should've gotten rid of me when you had the chance."

His mother clenched her jaw. "That kid needs to shut his damn mouth."

"Well, you can thank Wesley for punching him in the face," Cole said with a smirk.

"I think I will, actually."

Cole sat for a moment, running his fingertip over one of the cuts on his hand. "I wasn't going to bring this up, but I'm really glad I did."

"So am I," she said. "It kills me that you could ever think you're a mistake. That couldn't be a bigger lie. You believe me, right?"

He nodded.

"Good...Okay, now there's something I want to talk to *you* about."

"What's that?" he asked.

"I've been pretending not to notice, but I know you've been smoking. I don't need to tell you that it's extremely unhealthy; you know it is. But if you don't want to quit for your own health or to appease your nagging mom, then do it for Leighton."

Cole nodded again. "I know. It was stupid to start."

"Can I ask why you even wanted to?"

He rubbed his forehead. "It seemed like a good punishment," he confessed quietly.

Then he slid the hem of his blue gym shorts a few inches up his thigh to reveal a cluster of circular burn scars above his knee, all in various stages of healing. His mom bit her bottom lip, her eyes quickly brimming, and she placed her hand over his.

"Cole, sweetie..." she whispered, heartbroken. "Why?"

He hung his head. "The first time was an accident. But then I noticed how good it felt to hurt in a different way for once." He paused when shame and emotion made his voice shake. "When I smoke, and when I burn myself...I feel like, in a *very* small way, I'm paying for how I hurt Tucker. I never got to fix it. He never forgave me. I don't know what else I can do."

She brushed his hair out of his eyes. "You can forgive yourself."

"That's not possible. I don't deserve to be forgiven."

"But you do. You've always loved Tucker. And he loved you. I know he still does. He wouldn't want this life for you."

"How can you know that? You don't know for sure."

"Yeah, but I knew Tucker like he was my own, and I know he's not completely gone. I believe he's in Heaven, carrying us with him just like we carry him with us."

Cole stared at the carpet without blinking, letting the tears blur his vision. "I just don't know how to come back from this."

"What would it take for you to feel like you could move on? Not to forget Tucker, of course, but to move past this, to be happy and live your life again?"

Cole shrugged. "A time machine? Tucker's resurrection?"

"No, really think about it. What might help you? You seem to have this insatiable desire for penance. Do you think there will come a point where you'll feel like you've suffered enough? You can't do this to yourself forever, sweetheart."

Cole couldn't imagine bearing it forever, but he didn't think he had a choice. "I don't know," he said. "Since it happened, I've lived every second knowing I've *killed* my best friend. If I can't bring him back, or go back and save him, then I'm not sure how I could ever feel better about it."

Thirty-Three

"Hey, Wes, did you really stay up all night with Delaney?" Quinn asked, leaning across the back seat to poke him in the ribs with her elbow.

"Yes. Why do you care?" He put up his hands, silently telling her to back off.

Quinn mocked him, making the sound of an angry cat meow. "*Someone's* tired and cranky."

"That reminds me..." Wesley leaned forward and gripped Cole's seat in front of him. "I *really* need coffee. Is there anywhere we can stop?"

"You had coffee before we left," Quinn said.

"Yeah. Past tense. That's the problem," Wesley retorted.

Leighton turned back to face them. "Please tell me this isn't going to be our lives for the next three hours."

"Hey, don't look at me," Wesley said, pointing at his sister.

Quinn put on an innocent smile. "Sorry, Mother."

"There's a little coffee shop-bookstore at the edge of town," Cole said. "We'll stop there."

As they drove on silently, the surrounding

scenes of Lachlan began to change, looking more run down the further they got.

"Hey, is that where Delaney works?" Wesley asked suddenly. He practically threw himself against the window to get a better look at the familiar car in a gas station parking lot as they passed by.

Cole chuckled. "Yeah. That's the one. Good eye."

Wesley frowned. "She wasn't kidding. That place looks shady as hell."

Cole stayed outside to smoke while the rest of them headed into the historic brick coffee shop.

Leighton and Quinn went straight to the bookshelves filled with bestsellers. Wesley followed, then held out a five-dollar bill to Leighton.

"Hey, there's something I have to do real quick. Can you get me the biggest coffee this will buy? Oh, and black, please."

Leighton took the money. "I know how you take your coffee, Wes."

"Thanks, Leighton," he called over his shoulder as he disappeared.

"Are you getting anything?" Leighton asked Quinn, who was returning a book to its spot on the shelf.

"That depends if it's *real* coffee and none of that basic sludge," Quinn said.

Leighton chuckled, following Quinn to the back counter.

"Holy shit..." Quinn stopped suddenly and

Leighton nearly bumped into her.

Directly ahead of them, behind the counter, was the last person Leighton had ever expected to see, the very last person she ever wanted to see. She blinked a few times to make sure she wasn't hallucinating.

"What the hell are you doing here, Jared?" Quinn smacked her palms onto the stainless steel countertop.

Jared stood there, his face looking as shocked as Leighton felt. His light, surfer-shag hair was covered by a black cap, and his muscular build, which had only improved in the past few years, was clearly visible beneath his white polo and blue apron. He was still tan, like he spent every day at the beach, and his flawless teeth were as white as the creamer he'd just spilled on the counter.

"I think I could ask you the same thing," Jared said, trying to smile through his nervousness as he grabbed a rag to clean up his mess.

Leighton shuddered at the sound of his voice as it catapulted her into the past, dredging up ugly feelings she'd spent months—years—trying to unfeel.

"None of your damn business," Quinn told him.

Jared bit at his lip as he sighed. "Can I get you anything?" he asked, remaining professional.

For the first time, his blue-green eyes locked with Leighton's and she thought she might vomit. But there was something different in his gaze, not the arrogance or superiority he'd exuded in high school. What did Leighton see now? Was it humility? *Remorse?*

"I'll just have this bottle of water," Quinn said, plucking it from the cooler along the front of the counter. Then she dumped out the tip jar in front of Jared before turning on her heel and storming out of the shop.

Jared surveyed the pile of coins like it had already defeated him. Slowly, he began sliding coins to the side, counting out the price of Quinn's water.

Leighton set her purse down. "I'll pay for her," she offered, digging out her wallet. "I'm sorry."

Jared stopped and lifted his head to look at her. "No, Leighton. *I'm* sorry."

Her stomach dropped. What exactly was he apologizing for? There was no way he was admitting to his despicable deeds from their past. There was no way he was even *here* right now.

"So, what *are* you doing here?" Leighton asked. "You live in Lachlan now?"

He shook his head. "No, I live, like, thirty minutes from here. My parents relocated to help take care of my grandparents. I ended up moving with them because I lost my scholarship and had to drop out of school."

"Oh. That sucks."

Jared shrugged. "Yeah, but I had it coming, so I shouldn't complain. I just partied and acted like an asshole ninety-five percent of the time. I'm sure that doesn't really surprise you, does it?"

Leighton snickered. "Is that rhetorical, or do you really want me to answer?"

"I already know what you'd say. And you'd be

right. I *was* an asshole. Worse than that, even. I mean it—I really am sorry, Leighton."

She cast her eyes to the menus above Jared, busying herself with its choices so she could get out of there as quickly as possible. "Can I get an extra-large black coffee, please?" She slapped Wesley's five-dollar bill onto the counter and slung her purse onto her shoulder.

"Sure thing." Jared grabbed a white paper cup from the stack behind him and began filling it with coffee. "I saw you with Wesley. Are you two finally together?"

Leighton blew out a heavy breath, shoving her hands into her back pockets. "No. We're not. I'm with someone else."

"Oh. Really? I always thought you'd end up with Wesley," Jared said, securing a plastic lid onto the steaming cup. He slipped it into a cardboard sleeve and set it gently in front of her.

"Nope. He's with someone else, too." Leighton pushed the wrinkled bill closer to Jared.

"It's on me," he said.

"You don't have to do that. It's not even mine. It's for Wesley."

Jared smiled. "Fine. Then Wesley's drink is on me—to prove there are no hard feelings for decking me in the face in front of the entire school."

"You deserved that," Leighton said.

"I know I did. Leighton, can you please just listen to me for a second? I'm trying to make things right."

"What the hell for?" she questioned. "It's been *years*. It doesn't even matter anymore."

"It does matter," Jared said, his eyes wide and serious. "I think about you all the time. Would you believe me if I told you I lie awake some nights, wondering how badly I really hurt you, hoping you don't still carry what I did to you? Because I do. I hate who I was back then. I hate that I hurt you."

Leighton stared at his face. She used to imagine this moment in the miserable days following their break-up. She'd craved his regret and his apologies. Now she had them and it didn't matter.

Because she didn't think about Jared anymore.

"You *did* hurt me then. But I'm fine now," Leighton said, feeling the confidence shining from her face.

"I'm glad to hear that." Jared's head bobbed with a nod as a small smile flickered over his lips. "Take care of yourself, Leighton."

"Thanks. You too." She turned away so quickly, she nearly dumped Wesley's coffee on Cole as he approached. "Oh my gosh. Cole, I'm so sorry."

"It's okay." Cole grinned, steadying her with an affectionate hand on the small of her back. "You ready to go?"

With her free arm, Leighton drew herself against Cole with a grateful squeeze that made him chuckle. "I am so ready," she said.

She took Cole's hand and led him to the door, eager to end Jared's chapter in her life.

Delaney hurried to finish her final tasks as closing time drew near. Wesley was all she'd been able to think about as the day dragged on. How had she let herself get so attached to him? Was it even real? He'd come and gone so quickly, like waking up from a sweet dream only to be slammed with horrid reality.

The instant the clock struck ten, Delaney rushed to the door, turning off half of the lights and flipping the open sign before she let herself out and locked the door. Glancing cautiously at her surroundings, she sprinted to her car across the empty lot.

Delaney noticed it immediately—something wedged in the space beneath the door handle. She yanked it free and got in the car, pressing the lock button the instant the door closed. After starting the engine, Delaney turned on the light to inspect the mysterious object wrapped in white tissue. She curiously peeled away the thin paper, revealing a miniature replica of the Eiffel Tower. She laughed warmly and looked it over, finding a small folded note tucked among its four tiny feet.

Rain check? it read in cool, all-caps handwriting.

Wesley.

Delaney's grin widened as she clutched the metal souvenir to her chest. Something inside her changed in that moment. A joy, a peace, a thrilling anticipation for her future. *This* was what it was like to feel happy again.

Placing the trinket safely in her cup holder,

Delaney clicked her seatbelt into place and pulled onto the road toward home. She couldn't call Wesley fast enough.

It was Monday morning. Dr. Gibson was droning on about memory and the incredible intricacies of the human mind. But mentally, Leighton was somewhere else. She'd been living in a different reality for the past four days. So much had happened, it was difficult to return from. The last time she'd sat in this desk, she was someone else. Her days in Lachlan had changed her permanently, laying a new foundation for the woman she would be for the rest of her life.

And Leighton was grateful to have finally solved the mystery that was Cole MacHendrick. Already, it was strange to remember a time when she didn't know him the way the previous days had allowed her to. She didn't doubt that Cole would always be the other half of her.

Out of the corner of her eye, Leighton saw Wesley's head bob beside her. When Dr. Gibson turned his back to write on the dry erase board, she reached over and backhanded Wesley in the arm.

His eyes sprang open and his body jolted.

Leighton shot him a look that asked, "What's going on with you?"

Just past him, Quinn held up her notebook to Leighton, where she'd written DELANEY across the page in big letters.

Wesley rolled his eyes and slouched in his

chair, crossing his arms over his chest. It seemed he was intending to appear annoyed, but he couldn't contain his giddy smirk.

Keeping his eyes on Dr. Gibson, who still faced the board, Cole leaned over to Leighton and whispered, "Wes was on the phone with Delaney *all night*."

Leighton's eyebrows shot up and she turned back to Wesley. As she kicked his foot to wake him, Dr. Gibson dismissed the class.

"Oh my God. Wesley. You stayed up all night *again*?" Leighton asked.

Wesley dropped his textbook into his bag. "No. I got, like, an hour of sleep. I think."

"Wes. You can't keep doing this every night," Quinn said, standing in front of his desk.

Wesley stood, slipping his arms through the straps of his backpack. "Yeah. I know. I'm going back to the dorm to take a nap before my next class."

"And turn off your phone," Cole chimed in.

Wesley nodded and gave a half-hearted wave, then turned to exit the classroom.

Cole and Leighton packed up their things and stood, their hands meeting like an involuntary habit, and they followed Quinn out to the sidewalk.

"It's weird to be back, isn't it?" Quinn said.

Leighton nodded. "I was just thinking that. It's almost like we experienced a lifetime in those few days away."

Cole chuckled sheepishly. "I'm sorry every-thing was so crazy."

"Oh, no, don't apologize," Quinn said. "I had a blast. I mean, there were some things that weren't the greatest, but…I'm so glad we went. I feel like the four of us are so close now, and I love that. Thanks, Cole, for letting us force you to take us home with you, and for allowing us into your life."

Cole nodded. "I'm glad we all went too, actually." He smiled at Leighton, squeezing her hand tighter.

Quinn's phone chirped in her pocket and she grabbed it quickly. "Oh, crap! I'm late for a study date."

Leighton snickered. "A study date in the morning? With who?"

"Marcus!" Quinn answered over her shoulder as she hurried off.

Laughing, Leighton shook her head. "Oh, goodness. What are we gonna do with that girl?"

Cole smiled. "We'll just let her be Quinn."

COLE

Cole and Leighton had planned to go see a movie, but they'd ended up at the lake, sitting in Cole's car with their seats reclined, the sunroof open, and the music on. LANY was the chosen soundtrack for the evening, playing low in the dark space. The perfect degree of heat blew softly through the dashboard vents, keeping them comfortable against the cold night surrounding them.

Cole breathed a relaxed sigh, reaching his hand out to take Leighton's. "This beats a movie so hard," he said, keeping his head against the headrest, still watching the stars.

Leighton chuckled. "Why's that?"

He tilted his face toward her. "Because I can talk to you...and I can kiss you as much as I want to." He leaned in and pressed his lips against hers, kissing her through an entire chorus of the song.

When the kiss ended, Cole lingered in her space, leaning across the center console with her face cradled in one hand.

"I love you," he said, wrapping his words in certainty and tenderness.

"I love you too," Leighton replied.

Cole settled back into his seat, his hand finding hers again. "I want you to know that I'll never take that for granted. I'm lucky you're even still here, and I don't take that lightly."

Leighton frowned. "Ya know, you're pretty easy to love. I don't deserve so much credit."

"Oh, c'mon," he said, smirking.

"I'm serious, Cole. I love you even more now than I did before."

He looked at her in disbelief. How was her unhindered, intentional affection possible? They didn't arrive on this side of his confession without braving the aftermath of the truth, but it still seemed too easy.

"I don't get it," Cole said quietly.

"What is there to get? That you could be worth loving? You really expected me to walk away, didn't you?" Leighton asked.

His gaze fell away from her and he nodded. "I'm sorry I didn't have more faith in you."

She touched his cheek. "Do you have any idea how incredible it feels to truly know you? To know that I love *you*, and not just some condensed version that you've allowed me to see? I loved what I saw then, and I love what I see now. You need to start believing in that—that you're worthy, and people care about you."

One corner of Cole's mouth turned upward. "Okay. I already quit smoking…one habit at a time, please."

Leighton grinned. "It might take a while, but I'll be right here, helping you through it."

Cole let out another content sigh. "Thank you. I know I need a lot of help."

"That's all I've ever wanted," she said. "To be able to be here for you."

This time, Leighton leaned over to kiss him, and he could hardly believe how good it felt to be alive, to be in love.

Leighton's unconditional love made Cole feel the light again, like sun shining on his skin. It reminded him what joy and compassion were—how they were much bigger, much more powerful than the shadows of his past. He was consumed by a new-found desire to let Leighton's bright world eclipse his own, so he could forgive himself and live on. And he wanted that with his whole heart.

Thirty-four

"Oh, hey, Wes," Cole said, stepping into their dorm room and closing the door behind him.

"Hey," Wesley answered, shoving a small stack of clothing into his backpack. "You're not with Leighton tonight?"

"No. She had plans with Quinn. A girls' night or whatever. I *was* gonna ask you if you wanted to go grab dinner with me, but it looks like you're up to...something."

Wesley sighed, finally looking at Cole. "Okay. If you promise not to make fun of me, I'll tell you."

"I promise."

Wesley sat down on his bed beside his packed bag. "As you know, today is Delaney's birthday. We've been texting all day while she's at work, and when she called me on her lunch break, she was really upset. It's her *birthday* and she's having a horrible day."

"Let me guess," Cole started, sitting down on his own bed across from Wesley's. "You want to drive up there and see her?"

"I want to surprise her. Is that ridiculous?"

Smiling, Cole shook his head. "No. It's really

nice, actually. Delaney would love that."

Wesley sighed with relief. "I figured if I leave now, I should get there around ten-thirty, just thirty minutes before she closes the store. Does that sound good?"

"No," Cole said, blankly.

"What? Why?"

"Because you didn't ask me to go with you."

Wesley snickered. "Oh, geez. Fine. You really want to?"

"Yeah, I do. That's a long trip to drive alone at night. Especially when you're not completely familiar with it. Plus, it'll be fun."

"Okay," Wesley agreed, jumping to his feet. "But I'm driving. Pack your shit, let's go."

Halfway through the drive to Lachlan, Cole's phone rang. He turned down the music to answer it.

"Hey, Leighton."

"Hey. What'cha up to? Are you out with Wes?"

Cole chuckled. "Yup. I *am* out with Wes."

"What's so funny?"

"Well, we're on our way to Lachlan. Wesley wants to surprise Delaney for her birthday. Then I guess we'll crash at my house and be back tomorrow evening."

"Aww," Leighton gushed. "Tell Wesley he's the sweetest guy in the whole world."

Cole glanced at Wesley. "No. I am not gonna do that."

She laughed. "Don't worry. You're sweeter."

"How does that work? If he's the *sweetest*?"

"It just does, okay? Don't question my logic."

"Hey, I'm sorry I didn't tell you I was leaving," Cole said. "It was kind of a last second thing, and I didn't want to bug you when you were out having fun."

"Oh, it's okay. I love that you're road tripping with Wes. That's exactly what I wanted—you two being friends."

"Yeah, I guess he's pretty cool," Cole said.

"Stop talking about me," Wesley complained, glancing away from the road for a quick second.

"All right, well I will let you get back to your navigating skills. I just wanted to say good night," Leighton said.

"Okay. I love you, Leighton."

"I love you too."

"Hey, you know what? I haven't been this far away from you since before we met. I think I miss you already."

Leighton laughed. "You saw me a few hours ago, and you'll see me tomorrow."

"I know, but still...I just really love you. You know that, right?" Cole asked.

"Of course I do. And you know that *I* really love you too, right?"

"Absolutely. It's what I live for." Cole said it like he was joking, but he meant it.

"Okay, I really have to go now. Quinn is making gagging noises."

Cole glanced at Wesley. "Yeah, none of that here. Probably because Wes is in the middle of his own sappy romantic gesture and doesn't have the room to talk."

"You said you wouldn't make fun of me," Wesley said, feigning hurt feelings.

Leighton's laugh was sweet and joyful. "Okay, you were right; I miss you too."

"But I'll see you tomorrow," Cole said warmly. "Good night, Leighton."

"Good night, Cole."

"Oh. Hey, Leighton?"

"Yeah?"

"I love you."

Then he hung up before she could reply.

A few seconds later, he received a text: *I love you too!*

Cole grinned, feeling content for the first time in a very long time.

Wesley pulled his Explorer into the gas station around ten-forty, parking far away from the building so Delaney wouldn't see them coming.

Wesley took a deep breath and let it out. "Oh my God, I'm nervous. Why am I so nervous?"

"Because you like her," Cole said.

"Hey, Cole?"

"Yeah?"

"Thanks for coming with me. I probably would've turned around two hours ago if you weren't here," Wesley said.

"Sure. It was fun." Cole hesitated, averting his eyes toward the windshield. "Ya know...Tucker was the only best friend I've ever had. And I didn't think I could ever find another friend even remotely as awesome as he was…but I think I was wrong. You've been such a great friend to me, Wes. I guess I just want to thank you for that."

Wesley smiled, visibly touched by Cole's honesty. "You don't have to thank me. I've kind of spent my whole life in Quinn's shadow and I didn't realize how much *I* needed a friend. I mean, I've had Leighton, but…"

"A guy needs other guys sometimes," Cole finished for him.

"Exactly," Wesley said. "I'm glad I got to know you. And I'm glad Leighton's with you. It's nice knowing I don't have to worry about her."

"Thanks, man."

"Okay, enough with this bullshit. Let's go inside, shall we?" Wesley said with a cheeky grin.

Cole laughed. "Absolutely."

With Cole trailing behind him, Wesley made his way carefully to the double glass doors, keeping his focus on Delaney at the counter.

"I bet your heart is just *racing*, huh?" Cole asked quietly.

"Shut up," Wesley whispered, holding back a laugh as he grabbed the door handle.

He pulled the door open and stepped inside, Cole following him. Delaney slowly turned her attention toward them, and her expression instantly ignited. She rounded the counter and rushed for Wesley, jumping into his arms. He spun her around twice before setting her back on her feet.

"I cannot believe you're actually here!" She touched Wesley's face, her blue eyes brimming with joyful tears.

"I had to see you," Wesley said, gripping both of her hands. "Happy birthday."

She planted a quick kiss on his lips. "It is now...Oh, hey, Cole."

"Hey. Happy birthday, Delaney." Cole hugged her.

"I can't believe you guys drove all the way here. Just for me," Delaney said. "Fifteen more minutes and I am all yours."

She returned to the register when a customer came in, and Wesley and Cole walked to the back of the store to pick out some drinks.

"Did you see her face?" Wesley asked. "That was worth every mile. Seriously."

Cole nodded. "I'm glad you decided to come here. She really needs this."

And suddenly, everything was wrong.

Like that pivotal moment that defines *before* and *after*. Cole knew it when they heard the angry voice at the front of the store. When they heard Delaney's frightened cry.

Wesley moved first, gliding down the aisle toward a piece of his heart. Cole was close behind, his throat closing around the breath that fought to escape his lungs. When they reached the end of the aisle, across from the counter, neither of them were prepared for the scene that was playing out before them. It wasn't real. It *couldn't* be real.

A man, his face obscured by a black balaclava, pointed a gun straight at Delaney, demanding in a gravelly voice that she move faster. She whimpered as she struggled with shaking hands to empty the money from the register into a plastic bag. Cole heard the clink of coins as she spilled them to the tile floor.

Impatient, the man rounded the counter and stood behind Delaney, holding the gun just inches from her head.

"Back off, she's giving you the money," Wesley said, his tone stern and fearless.

It was as though the robber hadn't noticed their presence until now. His head twisted toward them, his beady eyes glaring through the holes of his mask. With one swift motion, he turned the gun on them, and instinctively, they both put their hands up.

Cole had seen it on television countless times before, but the reality of a gun pointed directly at him, in the unpredictable hands of a criminal, brought a level of anxiety and terror he'd never experienced.

"Mind your fucking business," the man growled.

Cole flinched.

Wesley, on the other hand, stood unshaken. "Well, *she's* my fucking business, so I'm telling you to *back off.*"

"Wesley," Cole whispered in warning.

In a sort of demented retaliation, the man turned the firearm on Delaney, pressing it hard against the side of her skull. She shook as she fought to hold back her sobs. With clenched fists, Wesley took a step forward, but Cole grabbed the back of his shirt to stop him.

"No, wait, *please*. I'm sorry," Wesley said, his bravery depleted. "Please just go. You've got your money."

"Not all of it. Empty your pockets right here." The man tapped the counter with the barrel of the handgun and looked at Cole. "You first, pretty boy."

Cole swallowed. Somehow, his feet carried him forward, closer to the gunman. He kept his eyes fixed on Delaney, trying to pass some silent comfort to her as he slowly reached into the pockets of his jeans.

"If you try pulling *anything*, I will shoot her," the man threatened, closing his forearm around Delaney's neck to keep her still.

With trembling hands, Cole set his cell phone, wallet, and keys on the counter. He felt an odd fear in relinquishing his phone, like he was cutting himself off from the world, submitting himself to the hands of this evil person. Cole mentally berated himself for allowing his anxiety to distract him, for not calling the police when he'd had the chance.

But as he turned away from the counter, he saw that Wesley had the same realization. Wesley held his phone against his thigh, attempting to discreetly dial without getting caught. Cole stopped and glanced back, but the gunman's angry eyes were already on Wesley.

The man immediately shifted the gun to target Wesley.

"No!" Delaney screamed.

Wesley looked up and his phone slipped from his grip, clattering to the floor. Cole could hear the faint voice of the 911 operator on the other end.

The man shoved Delaney away from him. He pulled back the hammer with a definitive click, cutting through the fear that hung so heavily around them. Cole's heart pounded as the man aimed the gun back at Wesley.

Wesley drew in a sharp breath, frozen in place as the man's finger moved over the trigger. But Cole didn't hesitate. Without a second thought, he stepped into the space between Wesley and the gunman. The gun went off like a deafening explosion in eerie silence, followed by the shattering of glass on the back wall behind them.

At first, the only movement was the gunman as he grabbed the bag of money and fled the store.

Then Cole as he collapsed to the floor, blood spilling from the hole in his chest.

Thirty-five

C ole stared at the yellow glow of the fluorescent light, flickering faintly above him, nestled among the stained ceiling tiles.

And he knew he was going to die.

But that was okay. His body had shifted the trajectory of the bullet, just as he'd hoped. He'd saved Wesley's life. And a fragment of his heart felt renewed, redeemed. He'd done for Wesley what he couldn't do for Tucker. Cole embraced this acceptable end as he felt life slipping away from him.

Then Leighton's face flitted across his foggy mind, and instantly, the lethargy he'd submitted to began to dissipate.

He didn't want to die.

Cole knew it with every pulsing vein in his damaged body that he wanted to live. He *had* to live. He knew what loss had done to Delaney—how it had dismantled and ruined her—and he couldn't bear for Leighton to suffer that same fate. He wanted to experience every new day with her. He wasn't willing to give that up. He wasn't ready to say goodbye.

Cole's will came alive like a spark, and all of his senses returned. He could see Wesley's petrified face, he could hear Delaney crying. And he could feel it—beneath the pressure of Wesley's hands, he could feel the hole in his chest, burning and stinging and aching deep within him. He could feel the warm wetness dripping over his shoulder and he lifted his head to assess the damage. All he could see was blood, staining his shirt like an inkblot spreading on paper.

"Wes," Cole choked out, fear gripping him.

A slight glimmer of relief crossed Wesley's tear-stained face. "Cole! Oh, God. Please hang on, man. Help is coming. Just stay with us, *please*."

Then Cole dropped his head back, the agonizing pain and panic too much to bear.

And everything went black.

WESLEY

Wesley was frantic, pressing a towel firmly to Cole's chest in the space just below his left collarbone. This wasn't happening. This had to be a dream. Wesley prayed he'd wake up any second, but he was still here, every square inch of his hands covered in Cole's blood.

There was *so much* blood...

"Delaney! Why isn't he awake? What's happening?"

"I don't know!" Delaney cried, pacing back and forth at Cole's feet. She kept looking to the large windows spanning the front wall of the store, anxious for the paramedics to arrive. "He's still breathing, right?"

"Yes."

"Just keep applying pressure. You *have* to stop the bleeding!"

"That's what I'm doing! It isn't stopping! What if it doesn't stop?" Wesley nearly choked on a sob as it rose in his throat. He was fighting to stay calm, to keep his hands from trembling as they tried to work, but he was teetering on the edge of a complete breakdown. He wasn't sure how much longer he could hold himself together.

Delaney stopped pacing. "Wait. Wouldn't there be a second wound?" she asked, dropping to Cole's other side.

Wesley glanced at the shattered freezer door where the bullet hit. "An exit wound. Oh my God, you're right."

After Wesley gently rolled Cole to his right side toward Delaney, she unbuttoned his shirt and they worked hastily to remove it. Wesley's stomach lurched when he saw what the shredded, bloody fabric had been concealing.

"Oh, shit. Delaney..."

She peered over to see what Wesley was staring at. In the back of Cole's upper shoulder was a gaping wound, much grislier than the one in his chest, exposing a mess of destroyed, bleeding tissue. Wesley and Delaney exchanged mortified glances as they carefully returned Cole to his back.

"Oh, God, why are they taking so long?" Delaney whimpered, grabbing another towel off the stack she'd taken from one of the store's shelves. She stole another glance at the quiet parking lot before she slipped the towel beneath Cole to press it firmly against his shoulder.

"Wait, what's happening?" Wesley tensed up as Cole's breaths became considerably shallow.

Delaney gripped the top of her head as the tears streamed down her face. "What does that mean? Why is he breathing like that?"

Wesley struggled through his panic, forcing his mind to correlate the symptom with the injury. But his fear muddied his vast pool of knowledge and he couldn't quite grasp any logic.

Cole coughed and sputtered, blood spurting from his mouth.

"Oh, shit..." Wesley started hyperventilating. "He's gonna die. We have to do something!"

Delaney put her free hand on Wesley's shoulder to bring him back down. "Listen to me, Wesley. I know you're smart. You know so much about so many things. So *think*. How can we help Cole?"

Wesley took a deep breath and pressed his quivering lips together, attempting again to focus through the panic. He looked at the hole in Cole's chest and thought about the inner workings of his lungs and the physics of breathing. Then something came to him.

"Delaney, do you have any heavy tape?" he asked, reaching his hand into his back pocket for his wallet.

Without questioning him, Delaney jumped up from the floor and rounded the counter to grab a roll of masking tape from beneath the register.

"I don't know if this will work, but we have to try," Wesley said, removing his license from his wallet.

Taking a new towel, Wesley wiped at the injured area on Cole's chest, his throat tightening when the red saturated the white terrycloth much too quickly. He then covered the bullet hole with his license, his own blood-smeared face smiling up at him from the plastic card. Wesley dried his sticky hands on his jeans before swiftly ripping three pieces of tape off the roll. With shaking fingers, he sealed three sides of the license against Cole's skin, praying and pleading inside his pounding head for it to be enough.

"What does that do?" Delaney asked, a hopeful lining to her skepticism.

Wesley wiped at his wet cheeks with the back of his hand. "The bullet probably pierced his lung, so when he breathes, he's sucking air into his chest through the wound. The air compresses the space and collapses the lung. The license acts as a flutter valve, letting air out when Cole exhales, but plugging the hole when he inhales. If it actually works. But he's probably bleeding into his chest too, so...the paramedics need to fucking get here."

A short moment later, Cole's breathing had improved.

Delaney gawked at Wesley. "You are incredible. How in the world did you know to do that?"

"I started thinking like you told me to, and I remembered something I'd read once about two soldiers. One of them got shot in the chest, and he only survived because the other soldier created a valve over the wound just like this."

"That's amazing," Delaney said, still applying pressure to the back of Cole's shoulder. "Thank God you're so smart."

Wesley would've smiled at that, had they been in any other situation. Instead, he pressed another fresh towel to Cole's chest, careful not to interfere with the valve's function.

It was strangely quiet, with only the sounds of Cole's labored breathing and their own fearful sniffles to fill the space.

Delaney bent to kiss Cole's cheek. "Please don't leave me, Cole," she begged in a teary whisper as she stroked his hair. "I can't lose you too."

Wesley held his breath, straining to hear the faint sound in the distance, desperate for it to grow louder or even be there at all. "Do you hear that?" He stared at Delaney as she listened with him.

"I hear it. Sirens," she said, her face twisting with a fresh wave of tears.

Wesley leaned close to Cole's ear. "They're here, buddy. You're gonna be all right. Just please hold on, okay?" As soon as Wesley straightened up, the sobs escaped him. Like a bursting levee, his body released every stifled emotion.

The wail of sirens crescendoed, until it was right on top of them. In seconds, the doors flew open, and paramedics and police officers swarmed in, their sudden loud presence jarring in the melancholy space.

Wesley watched the paramedics work quickly to further stabilize Cole before they carefully secured him to a stretcher. All the while, they questioned Wesley and Delaney about Cole's injury and the treatment they'd given him. Wesley couldn't tear his eyes away from Cole's colorless face as he choked out answers he couldn't believe were reality.

Then, as swiftly as the paramedics had breezed in, they were gone, the sirens screaming once again as they whisked Cole away. And every cell in Wesley's body writhed in panic in the silent aftermath of Cole's departure.

The sudden stillness made Wesley's ears ring with a shrill, constant note. He stared at the pool of dark red blood on the white tile, his stomach twisting tighter and tighter.

So much blood.

He thought he might vomit.

"Excuse me," an officer began as he approached Wesley and Delaney. "Can I ask you a few questions?"

Breaking free from his daze, Wesley forced his eyes away from the blood puddle to look at the officer. "Right now?"

"Well, that would be most helpful...if you wanna catch the guy who shot your friend."

Delaney slipped her hand into Wesley's. "What can we do to help?" she asked. "We're in a hurry to get to the hospital, so we'd like to make it quick, if that's okay."

The officer nodded, keeping it simple, and asked the two for a description of the shooter. He said he'd be in touch and walked off.

"Come on, let's go." Delaney pulled Wesley into motion.

He grabbed Cole's phone, wallet, and keys off the counter on his way out the door. They felt like precious mementos in his hands. And that notion scared the hell out of him.

Wesley stepped outside through the automatic sliding doors of the medical facility. The night was dark, the moon and all the stars smothered by thick clouds that blended with the black sky. He shivered as he made his way to a bench and sat down, holding his phone in his bloodstained hand. He hadn't remembered or cared to wash it off.

Swallowing his dread, he tapped Leighton's name on the screen and raised the phone to his ear. He knew the sound of her voice would undo him, and he was right.

"Leighton..." he stammered.

"Wesley, what? What's wrong?"

"Something...happened." He struggled to compose himself. How could he tell her this? "It's Cole...He was shot." His own words sounded ridiculous and impossible as they spilled out of his mouth.

"*What?*" Her breaths quickened in instant panic.

"There was a robbery at Delaney's store...Leighton, you *need* to get here."

She was crying now. "Wesley...is he....is he dead?" Her question was followed by a deep wail, and Wesley's heart broke all over again just hearing her fall apart.

"No. No, he's alive, Leighton. They brought him to the hospital. Delaney and I are here waiting. We don't know much yet. But I'll text you the address, okay?"

"Where was he shot?" she asked, fear shaking her voice.

"Just grab Quinn and get up here."

"*Wesley...*"

"In the chest," Wesley answered glumly.

Leighton sucked in a sharp breath. "Wes...it's *three* hours away. What if...what if something happens to him before I get there?"

Wesley sniffled, holding back another breakdown. "You can't think like that, okay? I know this is scary, but we have to believe he'll be all right."

"Okay," Leighton choked out. "I love you, Wes."

"I love you too. Drive safe. I'll see you soon."

LEIGHTON

Leighton sat behind the wheel, tears streaming down as her shaky foot on the gas pedal propelled her down the highway. She'd been going a steady eight miles over the speed limit, praying she wouldn't get pulled over. The road was clear at this late hour, but her mind was not.

Quinn was curled up in the passenger seat beside her, sniffling quietly, the hood of her sweatshirt pulled over her head. She'd just gotten off the phone with her brother and hadn't spoken a word since. Quinn's reaction to the news surprised Leighton; she hadn't expected Quinn to take it so hard.

"Cole saved Wes's life," Quinn muttered, finally. "That's what Wes told me."

Leighton's chest tightened as a renewed flood of emotions consumed her. "Really?"

Quinn sat up in the seat and wiped the mascara-tinged streaks from her face. "He said he felt like the guy was aiming straight for his head. He's sure he'd be dead right now if Cole wasn't there." Quinn sputtered, losing control of her composure. "Cole *purposely* stepped in front of the bullet. Did you know that?"

Leighton couldn't speak. She merely shook her head in reply. She'd always known Cole's heart was capable of such compassion.

"I could've lost my brother tonight…How often do I take him for granted?" Quinn asked, hanging her head. "And Cole takes a *bullet* for him. Damn, Leighton. You have found something incredible."

Leighton nodded in agreement. "Let's just pray I get to keep him."

Calling Cole's parents was one of the hardest things Wesley had ever done. Mrs. MacHendrick had answered, her groggy voice already on edge as if she'd imagined a million times before what a horrific late-night call might feel like. She'd cried and pleaded for answers Wesley didn't have.

It had seemed like only minutes had passed before Cole's parents rushed into the waiting room and found Wesley and Delaney. The way Cole's mother clutched Wesley for unfound comfort. The way she sobbed at the sight of her child's blood on his hands and his clothes rattled him from the inside out. And as Wesley stood over the sink in the bathroom, watching the bloodstained water run from his hands, swirling over the white porcelain and down the drain, he broke down once more, his legs fighting to hold up his shaking frame.

And now, Wesley sat. Waiting. Delaney sat beside him. Cole's parents sat in the row of chairs across from them. Wesley kept watching them, his heart breaking over and over at the sight of their pain and their worry and the throb of his own.

"It's cruelly ironic," Cole's mother said, breaking the awful quiet that surrounded them.

"What is?" Cole's father asked, his voice so small, so feeble.

"Our son failed in shooting himself when he *wanted* to die. And now that he doesn't..." A sharp breath cut her off.

Mr. MacHendrick pulled his wife toward him, holding her head to his chest. "It's not fair," he cried. "This feels like how it would've been...if Cole *had* succeeded. If you hadn't stopped him."

She nodded knowingly. "It feels just like I thought it would. But worse, because it's really happening. Oh, God, Michael, we can't lose him. We still haven't even gotten him back yet."

Wesley looked away as Cole's mother buried her face into her husband's chest. This was all too much.

The opening double doors across the waiting room caught Wesley's eye, and he flew up from his chair the second he saw the doctor emerge. Cole's parents stood with terrified faces. Delaney was at Wesley's side, her fingers digging into his arm as the doctor approached them.

"Is he okay?" Wesley questioned, his tired eyes begging for a positive response.

The doctor bit his lip and looked to Cole's parents.

"It's okay," Cole's father said. "You can talk to us in front of them. They're very close friends of our son."

The doctor nodded. "We were finally able to get Cole stabilized enough to assess the extent of his injuries...His condition is still quite critical."

And then the doctor continued—sucking chest wound, hemorrhaging, pleural space, hemothorax, chest tube, contusion, laceration, fractures, clavicle, scapula, wound cavity, blood transfusion—on and on and on, alarming medical jargon weaved between familiar words.

Overwhelmed, Wesley pulled in a deep breath and expelled it slowly. Even as the doctor explained the terms, Wesley was still lost in the terrifying ambiguity of it all. What if they were just sitting here waiting for Cole to die? A fragile strand was all that held them now, suspending them over a pit of impending grief. And it would either snap or it wouldn't.

"So...what does all this mean? Is he *going* to be okay?" Cole's mother asked, blotting her cheeks with a tissue.

The doctor hesitated. "I'm sorry, I don't have an answer for that yet. But we're truly doing everything we can. Cole is currently being prepped for surgery to repair the internal wounds and realign the fractured bones. I will update you as soon as I can."

Cole's parents stared at the doctor, their eyes silently begging for comfort.

The doctor sighed. "Just keep hanging in

there and hope for the best."

They all watched the doctor hurry back to Cole, to either strengthen or snip that strand between life and death.

"If you and Cole weren't there, I would've had to face that all by myself," Delaney said after countless silent moments.

She and Wesley were sitting on the floor, leaning against the wall across the room from Cole's parents, who were completing consent forms. They'd grown restless and couldn't stay in one spot for long. Already, the sterile smell of the cold hospital air was making Wesley feel nauseated.

"I know," he said. "I thought about that too."

"Do you think he would've killed me?" Her voice was a sad squeak as she looked up at him. "He didn't seem to mind firing at you in front of *two* witnesses. Imagine if he had *none*."

"I don't want to imagine that," Wesley said.

"You would be dead right now if Cole wasn't there." Delaney wept softly, resting her head against his shoulder. "He couldn't save Tucker, but he got to save you."

Wesley could hardly breathe. His chest was tight and aching as he thought back to his conversation with Cole when they'd first arrived at the convenience store. At the time, it had just seemed like road trip bonding-induced honesty. But now it felt like a divinely orchestrated goodbye. Wesley swallowed back another urge to vomit.

"I can't lose him," Delaney whispered. "He

can't die. God wouldn't let that happen, right?"

Wesley shrugged, wrapping his arm tightly around her. "I don't really have much of an understanding of the will of God."

"But He made Tucker die. I guess He could make Cole die too."

"I don't think it's like that," Wesley said. "God is omniscient—He knows what will happen before it happens. But I don't think He *makes* them happen. He's not just sitting up there randomly picking us off out of spite."

Delaney squeezed her eyes closed, like she was afraid of her own thoughts. "Sometimes it feels like He does."

"I know. But this is a crazy world we're living in, and some choose, of their own free will, to do evil. No one—good or bad—is exempt from the consequences of those choices, unfortunately."

"So because some asshole decided to rob a shitty convenience store, Cole might die?" She lifted her head to look at Wesley. "That's not fair. And *don't* tell me life isn't fair. If I hear that from one more person, I will lose my mind."

Wesley could see the anger simmering around the edges of her grief. "You're right. It's not fair."

That was the only answer he had.

Thirty-six

Leighton nearly forgot to turn off the engine before she got out of her car. She bolted across the parking lot, leaving Quinn behind, and barely paused for the automatic doors to let her into the waiting room. Heaving, she scanned the room, her eyes finding Wesley first.

Just the sight of him tore her open all over again. The splotches and smears of red on his shirt and his jeans. The disheveled, broken look on his sweet face. It filled Leighton with an urgency to get to him.

He set down his styrofoam cup of coffee as she gravitated swiftly toward him. And then she was collapsing against him, needing him more than she'd ever needed him before. Wesley tightened his arms around her as she shook against him.

"Please don't tell me I'm too late," she whispered, looking up at him.

"You're not. He's still here."

Her heart contorted with something between relief and fear.

"He's *still* in surgery," Wesley added. "As far as we know."

"An update would be nice," Cole's mom chimed in.

Leighton left Wesley to go to her and pulled her in for a hug. Cole's dad wrapped his arms around both of them. When Leighton broke free, she turned to see Quinn embracing her brother. How long had it been since she'd last seen them hug...*really* hug?

"Are you doing okay?" Delaney asked, placing her arm around Leighton.

Only Delaney could ask such a question. Leighton knew exactly what she meant, and she hated that a part of her could now relate to Delaney. This was what it felt like to lose the love of your life. Except Leighton felt like she was losing hers in slow motion, while Delaney lost hers all at once. There existed no appropriate scale to measure which was worse.

"Just keep hoping," Delaney said, fighting to keep herself composed. "I never had that."

Leighton nodded and hugged her, aching for Delaney and for herself. She wasn't thankful for many things at that moment, but she was thankful for Delaney, and the unbreakable bond this night was surely building between all of them.

After giving Quinn strict orders to call her the instant the doctor set foot in the waiting room, Leighton grabbed Wesley's wrist and requested that he accompany her on a short walk down the hall.

"I can't just sit there. I'm gonna lose it," Leighton said, rubbing her temples as she walked beside Wesley.

"Yeah. I was feeling that too."

She wiped her clammy palms against her jeans. "Wes? Can you tell me how it happened?"

He turned his head to glance at her. "Are you sure you want to hear that right now?"

"I have to know."

Leighton held her breath while Wesley told her what happened, fearing that if she exhaled, what was left of her world would crumble around her. She squeezed his arm with all her might, as if she could somehow pass that strength through him to Cole. When Wesley finished, she finally let herself breathe.

"Come here," Wesley said, taking her by the hand and leading her into the chapel.

The small room was lit by a soft, calming light. Two parallel rows of pews sat before them, overlooking an altar with an illuminated crucifix on the wall.

Wesley went to the last row and brought Leighton to sit beside him.

They dwelled in the comfort of each other's silence until Leighton asked, "How bad is it?"

Wesley shifted his eyes toward her, keeping his head still. "How bad is what?"

"Cole's injuries. You haven't really gone into any kind of detail about that part. Is there something you're not telling me?"

Wesley slouched in the pew, pressing his shoulder against her. "No. I'm just afraid to upset you with graphic details."

"I'm already upset, Wes. Just tell me."

"Well, they told Cole's parents that there's

no damage to his heart and there's no spinal injury, so that's really good."

"Wesley. I want specifics."

He sighed. "Okay. Fine. I told you the bullet hit him in the chest. Well, it tore through muscle, fractured a few ribs, went through his lung, and exited up through the back of his upper shoulder. Is that enough yet?"

It was *too* much. But she needed to know all of it. "What did it do to his shoulder?"

"It broke his collarbone and his shoulder blade. He's going to need lots of physical therapy."

"If he survives," she added, her lip quivering.

Wesley straightened in the pew. "Don't say that, Leighton."

"I'm sorry...I'm just so scared."

He drew her into him, resting his cheek on her head. "I am too."

Leighton closed her eyes, letting the tears pour down her face. "What if he's finally getting what he used to want so badly?"

Wesley didn't answer her, but Leighton hadn't expected him to. It was an impossible, horrible question to think, let alone ask. She wished she was stronger, had more faith, less fear. But there was too much at stake, so much to lose, while Cole lay somewhere within these walls, surgeons' hands mending vital, intricate pieces of his delicate framework.

What Leighton wouldn't give to see him, touch him, kiss him again. Her desperation sparked a panic inside her. If Wesley wasn't holding onto her, she was certain she'd run screaming through the halls until she found the face her heart was aching for. Because what if the last time really was the *last* time?

Everything was alight. It wasn't white exactly, just bright. Cole stepped forward, his feet moving effortlessly. He wasn't aware of his own weight or the ground beneath him; he just moved. The sound of his name made him stop. A familiar voice. He spun around.

"Hey, Cole," Tucker said, his grin as gleaming as the space surrounding them.

Cole stared at him with wide eyes. "Tuck?"

"Yeah, Cole, it's me."

Cole took a shaky breath. "I've spent so much time thinking about all the things I wish I could say to you...and now I can't remember a single one of them."

Tucker chuckled. "It's okay, man. You and I—we're good. There's nothing you could tell me that I don't already know. You're my best friend, remember?"

Cole's throat tightened. "Of course I remember. But I just wish I could—"

"Apologize?" Tucker interrupted with a smirk. "Cole. You have nothing to be sorry for. Listen, I made my choice that night. Unfortunately, it wasn't the right one. And *I'm* sorry."

Cole shook his head. "No. I did so many things that hurt you..."

"And *I* should've listened to you and stayed to work it out. I should've called Gavin and had him pick me up. *Anything* but what I did. Cole...you *have* to forgive yourself."

Cole looked away. "It's so hard to do that. I miss you so much."

"I know. I miss you too. But ya know what...if you asked me to come back, I wouldn't. This place is real. It's incredible. I love you and I love Delaney and my family, but...I am truly happy *here*."

"So it's everything they say it is?" Cole asked.

"No. It's better."

"I guess I'll be seeing for myself."

"*Pssh*. Maybe in seventy years."

Cole touched his chest and he felt the pain. His skin was covered in thick bandages beneath his shirt. Tucker laughed his same old laugh that Cole had missed so terribly.

"You're not dead, Cole."

"Then what is this?"

Tucker smiled. "I just wanted to tell you that it's okay. I want you to live your life and I want you to be happy. Do you promise you will?"

"But, Tucker—"

"Please promise me, Cole."

"I promise."

Tucker and the light and the nothing that was everything around him suddenly vanished, and Cole was pulled into a completely different reality. The sounds came first. Beeping. Bustling. Voices. He fought to open his eyes but his eyelids were so heavy.

"Cole?" came an unfamiliar voice hovering over him.

His eyes opened slowly, rolling around grog-
gily as he tried to focus.

Navy scrubs. Stethoscope. Smiling nurse.

Then, horrific pain in all its searing fury.

Cole was *alive*.

Leighton glided down the long, stark hallway of the
progressive care unit as fast as she could without
breaking into a run. It was as though her feet were
trying to keep up with her heart, and her heart
needed to be near him. Her eyes needed to see his,
looking back at her.

Finally, Leighton reached the room and she
stopped outside the door, lingering for just a moment. How would it feel to see him this way? No
worse than the thought of losing him, of course, she
decided, stepping past the doorway.

The room was dim and quiet, save for the
hum of medical equipment, as she made her way to
the bed. When she saw him, she lost all control. A
sob erupted from deep within her, breaking the silence.

Cole stirred, and despite the minimal light,
his glorious silver-blue eyes were brighter and more
vivid than ever, and they found Leighton immediately. It tore her heart right open to see him looking
back at her. It was exactly what she'd prayed for,
what she'd feared she'd never see again.

"Cole," she breathed, bringing herself to the
side of his bed. She wanted so badly to throw her

arms around him, to hold him tightly against her, but she couldn't. Instead, she bent to press a kiss to his forehead, the feel of his skin like a miracle.

Cole raised his free hand toward her face, but winced and lowered it back to his side. His other arm was in a sling, held securely against his broken body. The left side of his bare chest and his entire shoulder were covered in clean white dressings, taped carefully in place to his skin. A tube had been inserted between his lower ribs, draining blood, fluids, and air from his chest. Leads monitoring his heart rate were scattered along his upper torso, and he breathed in oxygen through a nasal cannula. He looked so tired, so beaten, so fragile. But he was still beautiful.

Leighton sat in the chair at his bedside and slipped her fingers beneath his, careful not to disturb the IV in the back of his hand. "I...I'm so..." She struggled to string her thoughts together as she wept.

"It's okay," Cole whispered, his voice scratchy and slurred.

"I'm so afraid," she finally managed. "I'm afraid to believe that I won't lose you."

The shine of his eyes was magnified by his tears. "I'm still here because of you."

"Because of *me*?"

"I didn't want to fight...to live...until I thought of you," he said quietly. "And it was the same way before—I stopped wanting to die when I met you."

"I love you so much, Cole. I didn't know if I would get another chance to tell you that."

He tried to smile. "I love you too."

Leighton laid her cheek against Cole's forearm, spilling her tears onto his skin. All this while, she'd been trying so hard to heal him, to take his pain away. But just by being there and loving him, she already was. She didn't know love could have that kind of power.

"Are you okay?" Cole asked softly.

She lifted her head. "You don't have to worry about me. You just have to keep getting better."

"I will." His eyes shifted away from her, like he went somewhere else.

"Are *you* okay?" Leighton asked.

He nodded slightly. "I think I had a dream about Tucker."

"Yeah? What happened?"

"It's the first time I've dreamed about him since he died. I got to talk to him."

"What did he say?"

"He's happy...and he loves me. And he told me to forgive myself and live my life." Cole's eyes were wet again, and he swallowed, unable to say anything more.

"Do you think it was real?" Leighton asked.

Cole's eyes shot back to her. "How could it be real?"

She shrugged. "I don't know. You hear stories all the time of people getting glimpses of Heaven during surgeries or near-death experiences. Maybe it's really true."

A tear slid down Cole's cheek. "I would love to believe that."

"Then believe it. If it brings you comfort, why not?"

He closed his eyes and sighed. "Okay."

They were silent for a moment, and Leighton savored the sound of Cole's breathing as she stroked his hair.

"Are my parents okay?" Cole asked.

"You just saw them before you saw me. You do remember that, don't you?"

"Of course I remember. I meant...do you think they're okay? They were doing that thing they do, where they're smiling but crying at the same time, trying to be strong for me instead of expressing how they feel. I don't know if I'm making any sense. I'm on *a lot* of drugs."

For the first time in what felt like centuries, Leighton laughed. "Yes, Cole. You're making sense. And I think your parents are going to be okay. But leave it to you to worry about other people when you're the one with a hole through your body."

He chuckled and then gasped. "Holy shit, that hurts."

"Do you need me to get the nurse?" Leighton asked.

"No, I'm okay." He grabbed the small, wired device on the bed beside him and pressed the button to release more pain medication through his IV.

"I should probably go and let you get some rest."

"No." Cole's voice was suddenly strong and adamant. "Please don't leave me."

"Okay, I won't," Leighton said, returning eagerly to her seat beside him.

He smirked. "You have no idea how huge of a fit I had to throw to get them to let you in here. I am not letting you go yet."

She ran her fingertips softly over his cheek. "Then I will gladly stay here with you till they drag me out."

Cole smiled, his sleepy eyes closing. "You'll just find your way back in," he muttered. "No one could ever keep you away."

COLE

Cole didn't know how long he'd slept, but by the transformed light of the room, he knew it was morning. Leighton was still at his bedside, curled up in the chair.

"Hey," his voice croaked, his throat still sore from intubation. "Leighton."

She twisted out of her cramped position, instantly awake. "Is everything okay?"

"Yes. Well, as okay as it can be, I guess. I can't believe you're still here."

"Of course I am. I told you I wasn't going anywhere."

"I know," Cole said. "I'm just surprised they didn't kick you out."

"Oh, they tried. She reached into her pocket for her phone. "Whoops, Wes has texted me like twenty times. He really wants to see you."

"Is he still here?" Cole asked.

Leighton nodded. "Everyone's still here. They've been here all night."

"Really?"

She stood and caressed his face. "You are more loved than you could ever imagine. You need to know that."

Just moments after Leighton left Cole's room, the door opened. Wesley hesitated behind the curtain before stepping into view.

"Hey," Cole said.

Wesley lingered near the foot of the bed, his eyebrows knit together, and his eyes cast to the tile floor. His jaw was clenched tight, like he was trying to hold back everything inside of him.

"You okay?" Cole asked.

Wesley sucked in a deep, shaky breath and finally raised his eyes to meet Cole's. "I'd be dead right now if it wasn't for you. You know that, right?"

Cole's eyes welled up as he nodded.

"Saying thank you isn't nearly enough," Wesley said, his voice trembling. "But it's all I've got."

Until now, Cole had let doubt seep in and distort the reality of what had happened the night before. But Wesley knew—he believed Cole had saved him. And that changed everything. Cole allowed himself to own that like he had in the moments after he'd been shot. He damned his self-hatred, his doubt, his hopelessness, forcing the darkness out and letting the truth—the *real* truth—bring him back to life.

And for the first time since Tucker died, Cole felt whole again.

six months later

Leighton was waiting by the front window when Cole's Jetta pulled into her driveway, parking behind Delaney's car. With a giddy shriek and a smile bigger than the sky, she launched herself off the couch, and ran barefoot out the front door and off the porch. Cole let out a grunt as she threw herself at him, nearly toppling him over. He dropped his bag to the pavement and wrapped both arms around her.

"And to think, it's only been a week since we last saw each other," he said with a grin.

"A week is much too long, though," Leighton said, leaning back with her hands clasped behind his neck. She'd been waiting so impatiently to see that face. That one week had felt like months.

"What's the matter?" Leighton asked, tucking his hair behind his ear.

Cole sunk his teeth into his bottom lip. "Nothing's wrong."

"You're nervous, aren't you?"

He tried to laugh it off but his wandering eyes gave him away.

"Cole. Are you afraid to meet my parents?"

She tried to keep the amused smirk off her face but it just wouldn't go away.

"Okay, maybe."

"Why?"

"It's just…it's been a long time coming. And I really want them to like me."

Leighton's smirk warmed into an adoring smile. "Baby, they already like you."

Cole bent to pick up his bag. His motions were still careful and calculated to protect the left side of his frame, but it was out of habit rather than necessity.

"Well, then they only like me based on what *you've* told them."

"So?"

He touched her cheek. "I think you might be slightly biased, babe."

Leighton shook her head. "Nope. I'm just extremely perceptive. And smart."

She took his hand and led him up the porch steps to the front door, stopping for a moment to kiss him.

"Ready?" she asked.

Cole nodded. "I'm ready."

He followed Leighton inside and to the kitchen.

"Surprise!" Wesley yelled from his spot at the large center island counter beside Delaney.

Cole looked confused and slightly mortified.

"I'm just kidding," Wesley said, hopping off the bar stool and approaching him. "The surprise is that we made cookies." He put his arm around Cole. "By *we*, I mean I helped Delaney. Okay, I'm lying. I only preheated the oven. And I licked the spoon. But I did keep her company."

"Yes, and you stole half my chocolate chips. Don't forget that part," Delaney added.

Wesley returned to his stool at the marble counter, grabbing a cookie from the platter before him. "They're still so good, though. No harm, no foul."

"Where's Quinn?" Cole asked.

"Off on her usual shenanigans with Marcus," Wesley said. "She'll be here a little later."

"Hey, I'll take your bag to your room," Leighton offered, taking it from Cole and exiting the kitchen.

She slung the strap over her shoulder and trotted up the stairs, stopping at her parents' bedroom door. "Hey, Mom? Cole's here."

Leighton's mother dog-eared the corner of the page in the book she was reading and closed it. She set it on the small table beside her and removed her reading glasses before she stood.

"Well, it's about time," she said with a smile, brushing her thumb over Leighton's cheek as she breezed past her.

Leighton dropped off Cole's bag in the guest room down the hall and caught up to her mother on the staircase. Leighton wanted to be there with Cole when he met her.

"Mom, this is Cole," Leighton said, once they'd entered the kitchen and were standing face to face with the other half of her heart.

Cole extended his hand, painting on a

friendly smile. "Hi, Mrs. Tucker. It's so good to finally meet you."

"Oh, you can call me Sarah."

"What? *I* don't get to call you Sarah," Wesley complained, his mouth full of cookie.

Leighton's mother snickered, turning to playfully swat at Wesley, then stopped. "Wesley Alexander, what is *that*?"

She reached toward the image on the inner bicep of Wesley's right arm, easily visible in his heather-gray tank top, but he quickly crossed his arms over his chest to hide it.

"Don't tell my mom?" he pleaded.

"Wes...when did you get a tattoo?" Leighton asked, her eyes wide.

"Oh, you finally did it. Awesome," Cole said.

Leighton turned to Cole. "Wait. You knew about it?"

He shrugged. "Yeah. He told me a few days ago."

"Let me see it," Leighton's mom said. "If you show me, I won't tell your mother."

Wesley sighed and held out his arm, revealing two black and gray roses, slightly overlapping.

"Roses, huh?" she commented.

"It signifies Quinn and me," Wesley said. "We both got it done together."

"Aww, really?" Leighton melted, stepping closer to get a better look. "You are the cutest siblings ever."

Leighton's mom pointed a finger at her. "Don't even start."

"But without an awesome brother or sister,

who's gonna get a tattoo for *me*?" Leighton asked dramatically.

"I would," Cole said without missing a beat. Then he blushed, like it had tumbled from his mouth before he had the chance to reel it in.

"You would?" Leighton's stomach fluttered with butterflies.

Cole looked nervously at Leighton's mom, then back at Leighton. "Yeah. I would."

Wesley crammed another cookie into his mouth. "Good thing Quinn isn't here right now. She would *hate* this."

Delaney dipped her toe into the pool behind Leighton's house as she pulled her blonde hair into a messy knot on top of her head. "Can I just spend the whole summer here with you?"

"I wish you could," Leighton said, lowering herself to sit at the edge of the pool, her legs slipping into the warm water.

"Yeah, too bad I have to work."

"I thought you liked working at the library."

"Oh, I do. I just wish I was free to hang out more this summer...and be with Wesley."

"Yeah, but you'll be with us in the fall!" Leighton softly clapped her hands together.

Delaney grinned. "I know! I'm so excited. Thank God for Mr. Lindsley helping me transfer. I cannot wait to get out of Lachlan after everything that happened."

A silence fell between the two girls as the memories of that horrific night easily flooded back in. But they vanished just as quickly when the French doors opened, and Cole and Wesley stepped out onto the deck.

"Damn," Delaney said. "We got some models up in here."

Wesley hugged himself to shield his body. "Hey. I'm not a piece of meat."

Delaney positioned her thumbs and forefingers to mimic a camera and pretended to snap photos of him. Wesley charged after her and threw his arms around her. She shrieked as he backed her to the edge of the pool, threatening to push her in.

Then he stopped and pulled her close, still holding her tightly against him. "Do you really think I would do that to you?"

"No, but *I* would!"

Delaney jumped out of the way just as Quinn's palms connected with Wesley's back, shoving him forward and into the pool with a big splash.

"Oh, Quinn must be here," Wesley said dryly, pushing his soaked hair out of his face.

"Wes, honey, you're not supposed to submerge your tattoo in water while it's still healing," Quinn said in a motherly tone.

Wesley splashed at her. "Gee, thanks, I wonder how *that* happened." He lifted himself out of the pool and sat on the edge near Leighton.

"What took you so long to get here?" Leighton asked, shielding her eyes from the sun as she looked up at Quinn.

"I had to turn around and go back home 'cause I forgot to feed Shaq," Quinn answered.

Delaney laughed as she sat down beside Wesley.

"You know, he *could* afford to miss a day," Wesley said.

Quinn snickered. "Oh, shut up. You love him."

"I do *not*."

"I thought he was kind of sweet," Delaney chimed in.

"See? He's not evil, Wes. I think it's all in your head."

Wesley groaned. "I don't shred my own limbs just for the sake of blaming your stupid cat. I'm not having this conversation again."

"But we have matching tattoos," Quinn said, sticking out her bottom lip.

Chuckling, Wesley shook his dripping head. "I know; how did you ever talk me into that?"

"I've always wanted to get a tattoo," Leighton said wistfully, lifting her foot from the water. "Something meaningful. On my foot or my ankle."

"Really?" Cole asked, rounding the pool to the deep end. "Like what?"

"I don't know yet." She shot him a facetious grin. "But if you keep me around long enough, you might have something to do with it."

"Isn't that bad luck or something?" Quinn asked.

"I think we've already survived our fair share of bad luck; I'm not afraid of silly superstitions," Leighton said.

Cole smiled. "That's my girl."

With one swift, graceful motion, Cole dove

into the pool and glided beneath the water, traveling to the shallow end where Leighton sat. He emerged from the surface and stood right before her, the water flowing down his body. Leighton couldn't help letting her eyes wander over the evidence of all his hard work. She blushed as he placed his hands on her knees and positioned himself between them.

Suddenly self-conscious, Leighton wrapped her arms over her bare stomach. She'd never been this exposed in front of Cole before. He reached for her wrists and moved her arms away from her midsection.

"You're beautiful," he whispered, his eyes burning into hers.

Grabbing her by the hips, Cole gently lifted her into the pool and drew her close to him, sinking down until the water lapped at their chests. Leighton locked her legs around his waist, resting her hands on his shoulders and her forehead against his.

Leighton could feel the uneven thickness of scar tissue beneath her palm. She ran her fingertips lightly over the purple-pink flesh on his shoulder. She traced along the faint surgical incision. Then she lowered her face to plant a soft kiss on the circular scar in his chest.

"I love you," Leighton said. She combed her fingers through his wet hair, pushing it back from his face.

Cole kissed her deeply in reply, and their surroundings disappeared for a moment.

"Do you guys wanna be alone or what?" Quinn asked, sitting down on the pool steps.

"Sorry," Cole said bashfully.

Leighton didn't care. She didn't want their closeness to end. She laid her cheek against his imperfect shoulder and closed her eyes, feeling him breathing against her.

"So what's the plan for tonight?" Wesley asked.

Leighton didn't lift her head. "My mom said we could order pizza when my dad gets home from work. Or we could do our own thing."

"Pizza and hanging out sounds good to me," Delaney said.

"Hey, Quinn, where's Marcus?" Cole asked, tightening his arms around Leighton.

"Oh, he left for Florida earlier today—family vacation. Otherwise he'd be here. He loves you guys."

Wesley smirked. "Does he?"

"Yes, I promise. He's just more on the reserved side."

"Which is why you two balance each other out so well, right?" Delaney offered.

Quinn smiled proudly. "Of course."

Leighton and Delaney observed their boys for a moment, watching the football spiral back and forth through the air.

"Cole seems like he's doing really well. I'm so happy to see he's able to get out there and play again," Delaney said.

"Oh, he's improved so much. It took a long time, though, for him to start getting back to normal without being in pain. It was rough. Especially dealing with school and physical therapy on top of it."

"I bet...I know I've said this before, but I am so grateful he has you."

Leighton turned to her. "Thanks. I'm grateful we have *him*."

Delaney sighed, returning her gaze to the guys. "I love seeing them together. Watching them now...I can almost forget that it's not Cole and *Tucker* out there. But I love that, because it's like Wesley is picking up where Tucker left off..."

Leighton reached over and rubbed Delaney's arm. "Aww, Delaney..."

Delaney blotted at the tear creeping in the corner of her eye. "Please don't get me wrong. I don't wish Wesley was Tucker, and I'm not trying to use Wesley as a replacement or anything like that. I love Wesley—I'm *in love* with Wesley. I just think having him in our lives helps ease the pain of that Tucker-shaped hole that Cole and I both have. We really needed Wesley."

"He is pretty incredible," Leighton said. "Can I just tell you how much I adore you two together?"

"Yes," Delaney said. "You absolutely can."

Leighton laughed. "Seriously though, you know how important Wes is to me. So I have to thank you, because you're everything I've always wanted for him."

Delaney groaned. "Don't make me cry again."

"I'm sorry, but it's true. I'm feeling sentimental today; you'll just have to bear with me," Leighton said.

"It's okay. I love this, actually. It's been a really long time since I've had a best friend. Then you come in and you're all the things Ava couldn't be for Cole. But you're also all the things she couldn't be for *me*. Ava and I were never close. That was really difficult with her being the girlfriend of my boyfriend's best friend."

Leighton smiled. "And Quinn's an added bonus?"

Delaney laughed, glancing over at Quinn who'd taken her phone call from Marcus across the yard. "Yes! She totally is. That girl is crazy, but I love her."

They were quiet again for a moment, just watching, and Leighton glanced at Delaney to see her pretty face filled with delight.

"What are you thinking about?" Leighton asked.

Delaney blushed. "Honestly? I was just thinking I really can't believe Wesley's mine. I never thought I could ever be this happy again."

Leighton smiled as Cole strolled across the yard toward her, his belted khaki shorts sitting low on his hips and his white T-shirt slung over his shoulder. She could never get enough of him.

Everything about Cole had changed since that pivotal night. The way he spoke. The way he carried himself. It was as if a light surrounded him, chasing away that vacant darkness in his eyes. Every day, he looked more like the boy in the photo on the MacHendrick's refrigerator.

"Hey," Cole said, giving her a sweaty peck on the cheek. "What are you ladies up to?"

Leighton exchanged glances with Delaney who giggled. "Just some girl talk. You know how we do."

"We *pretend* to know," Wesley said. He guzzled the rest of his lemonade as he plopped down into the chair beside his girlfriend.

They all looked up when the door opened, and Leighton's father appeared, a cordial smile on his face. Cole immediately began fumbling with his shirt.

"Hey, Dad." Leighton hopped up and grabbed Cole's hand, dragging him—still half naked—toward her father. "Dad, I want you to meet Cole."

Cole blushed slightly but kept a straight face as they shook hands. "Hello, sir."

"Let me guess, he gets to call you Adam," Wesley said.

Leighton's dad snickered. "Watch it, Wes." He returned his attention to Cole. "You can call me Adam, Mr. Tucker, Leighton's dad, whatever. But you don't have to call me sir. I'm not *that* important."

Cole flashed a nervous smile. "Okay, I'll keep that in mind."

Leighton watched her father's eyes flicker to Cole's scars, exposed like an open book before him. They were the evidence of a hugely intimate piece of Cole's story, carved permanently into his body.

"I'm really glad to have you here with us, Cole," he said.

"Thank you, Mr. Tucker. I'm happy to be here."

Delaney clutched Wesley's hand as he used the flashlight on his cellphone to navigate through the woods behind Leighton's house.

"I don't know, Wesley. This feels like how horror movies start."

He stopped and turned to her, her face barely visible in the darkness. "Do you trust me?"

"Yes."

He slid his arm around her waist, guiding her beside him over the brush. "We're almost there, I promise."

A few moments later, they stepped out of the woods and into a massive clearing. The cloudless navy sky arched above, flecked with the brilliance of the stars. The broad hills rolled beyond them, and the twinkle of fireflies stretched as far as they could see, as if the earth was competing with the sky.

"Where are we?" Delaney breathed, her eyes wide.

Wesley chuckled. "It's just a golf course. But it'll have to do until I can take you to Paris."

He led her across the short, thick grass to the center of the vast space. He lay flat on his back with one arm bent behind his head and he patted the spot beside him. Delaney obliged, slipping her hand into his.

"Wow," she said, gazing up at the starry canvas. "How did you find this place?"

"Playing manhunt at Leighton's sixteenth birthday party. I was hiding in the woods and I kind of got turned around. I ended up here instead of back at Leighton's. Needless to say, I won that round. No one found me. But it kind of became my spot after that."

"Have you ever been here with anyone else?"

Wesley turned his head to look at Delaney. The moon lit up her skin as the stars reflected in her eyes. Fireflies flickered like a halo over her blonde hair that spilled over the grass around her. And Wesley was so in love.

"No," he said. "You're the only one."

A smile crinkled her eyes. "Have you ever seen a shooting star?"

"A few. You?"

Delaney nodded. "Do you believe in wishing on them?"

Wesley pondered for a moment. "No. But I wish on them anyway." He let out a sheepish chuckle.

"What?"

"It's silly to do that in the first place, but to admit it is even worse, isn't it?" he said.

"It's not silly to want something that badly."

Wesley squeezed her hand tighter. "I guess you're right."

"If you saw a shooting star right now, what would you wish for?" Delaney asked.

"Nothing."

"Yeah right. There has to be *something*."

"Fine. I'd wish I could stay with you forever."

"Forever?" She raised her eyebrows. "Are you sure about that?"

"Well, I've wished it every day for the last six months. I'd say I'm pretty sure. What would you wish for?"

Delaney tilted her head against his shoulder. "To stay with you forever."

"Are *you* sure about that?" Wesley asked.

"It's the only thing I *am* sure about."

Leighton still didn't believe in love at first sight, but she knew what had always drawn her to Cole since the moment she first saw him. As he held her attention from across the room, everything else faded away. It wasn't just the fact that he was beautiful, standing tall and sure. It was *Cole,* who he was, that had her captivated. He no longer piqued her curiosity, but he'd unfurled her wounded heart, tearing down her own walls that she hadn't even realized she'd been hiding behind.

Then Leighton's wandering eyes connected directly with Cole's—that shock of silver-blue, bright and loving—and he smiled at her. There was nothing but joy in his gaze as it multiplied her bliss and unleashed the butterflies. And Leighton didn't look away.

Returning his phone to his pocket, Cole crossed the room and settled into the couch beside her.

"Sorry about that. My parents wanted to say good night," he said sheepishly, threading his fingers through hers.

She leaned against him. "That's okay."

"So, what do you wanna do? Are you tired?"

Leighton shook her head. "I just wanna be with you."

Cole grinned. "I can do that."

"I'm so glad you're here," she said.

It was something she said to him often, and each time, it held multiple meanings. This time, she was glad he was here in her home with her, in a place she'd waited so long to share with him. But she was also glad he was here in the most literal sense—being, breathing, heart beating, *living*. Leighton never took that for granted, and she vowed to herself that she never would.

"I'm glad I'm here, too," he said.

Something in the way Cole looked at her let her know he meant it in all the same sacred ways she did.

And Leighton loved that she didn't wonder about him anymore.

beautiful life,

YOU ARE WHOLE.

– BRIGHT BONES

acknowledgments

THANK YOU

My husband, Daniel, for cheering me on every step of the way, always listening, always eager to hear more. You make what I do feel so important. Thank you for letting me pick your nurse-brain when plotlines cross into territories of your expertise. Thank you for all of our beautiful mornings, finding inspiration in our wanderlust adventures downtown. Thank you for putting up with my forever plotting writer brain when I try to solve the *Criminal Minds* episodes before the characters do. I love you, best friend. I could never do this (or anything) without you.

My Jude Wesley, for having patience and under-standing when I needed to spend time on my book. I love you more than you could ever imagine. I hope I can make you as proud of me as I am of you.

My parents for all of your love and encouragement. For all the times you've handed out my info cards and spread the word to your friends (and even strangers!). I know that, no matter what, I'll always have your support and guidance, and I am so grateful for you and all you do! I love you!

My brothers for letting me use your beautiful lyrics to add that extra splash of emotion to this story. I'm so proud to share these pages with you. I cannot wait for the world to hear Bright Bones.

My family and friends who have supported me and shown me so much love over my work. Every word of encouragement is so special to me; you have no idea!

Tanya Gold for being the best line editor I could ever ask for. You became a friend as well as a teacher and I can't wait to work with you again in the future.

Mountaineer, my happy place, for all the caffeine boosts, and for being my favorite spot to sit and edit.

Anah for helping me get back on track and begin to find myself again. My experience with you not only helped me in my own struggles with anxiety, but it also helped me to bring Cole to life in a deeper way.

The ladies at FCS for always making me feel special and loved. You've been extremely supportive of me, and your unfailing eagerness and interest means so much. Thank you for putting up with my white coat syndrome for the last five and a half years. ☺

My online writer friends and bloggers. I've learned so much from you, and it's fun sharing in this journey together.

My readers. I cannot express what it means to me that you've taken the time to not only support me, but to read my words and care about my story. I'm so blessed to be able to share my passion with the world. No matter how big or small my corner is, I am grateful for every single one of you. To thank you a million times would never be enough.

Avery, my sweet girl, for not only making me a mother, but for showing me the power and bitter-sweetness of love that transcends death. Through your life and your loss, I have experienced both the greatest joy and the most profound grief. This story is a small window into what it feels like to ache for you.

about the author

NICOLE FELLER is a perpetual shutterbug with a nostalgic heart and a fondness for classic charm. You can often find her downtown, drooling over old houses and abandoned buildings, or enjoying a cold brew at the coffee shop with her husband, Daniel. When Nicole isn't writing or exploring, she enjoys hoarding succulents, listening to LANY, reading love stories, binge-watching her favorite television shows, and fangirling over Chace Crawford and Matthew Gray Gubler. But her most favorite thing in the world is being Jude's mom. *Paper Walls* is Nicole's second novel.

Nicole and her little family live in the sweltering, autumnless land of west central Florida.

keep in touch!

WEBSITE: www.nicolefeller.com
INSTAGRAM: nicolefeller_
TWITTER: cole_feller
FACEBOOK: www.facebook.com/nicolefeller
E-MAIL: nicole@nicolefeller.com

author's note

Paper Walls addresses the issues of anxiety, depression, self-harm, and suicide. Those of us who have suffered in those realms know that there's nothing fictional about any of it.

When I first started writing this book, I was at my lowest in my struggle with anxiety. I spent four years trying to fight it on my own before it grew so debilitating, the fear was literally ruining my life. Getting treatment was the best thing I ever did for myself. I quickly learned that it's okay to ask for help.

There is *nothing* weak about asking for help—it's the bravest thing you can do.

RESOURCES

To Write Love on Her Arms – www.twloha.com
Anxiety and Depression Association of America – www.adaa.org
Half of Us – www.halfofus.com
National Suicide Prevention Lifeline – www.suicidepreventionlifeline.org | 1.800.273.TALK

ALSO BY NICOLE FELLER

Still the Song

Jonah Weston and Hannah
Morgan were made for each other.
Inseparable from the start, they
fell into their very own epic love
story.
Until Jonah left.

After one final straw, going away to college had
been Jonah's only escape from the hostility of his
father.
But the distance quickly took its toll, and Jonah's
once-perfect relationship with Hannah tragically
turned to ash.

Now, five years later, the death of Jonah's father
forces him to return home and face everything he
left behind.
What he discovers turns his entire world inside out.

READER REVIEWS OF *STILL THE SONG*

"I loved this book! The characters are lovable and they draw you in to root for them. I didn't want the book to end."

"I absolutely loved this book!!! The love story between Jonah and Hannah was so raw and yet so beautiful. I loved watching their story unfold, but at the same time watching Jonah discover himself. I highly recommend this book!!!"

"A very well written story, with surprises! The backstories/memories were a great way to show us what happened in the past. I felt like I really knew the characters by the end."

"Still the Song is one of the best books I've ever read. Nicole has a beautiful way with words. I could not put this book down, yet when the book ended I was completely satisfied! It didn't leave me searching for answers. I cannot wait for Nicole to finish her next book."

"I could hardly put it down from the first page. Amazing, Nicole!"

"What an awesome book! I read it in one sitting. Such an incredible love story!"